D0056140

BITTER
INSTINCT

BITTER INSTINCT

ROBERT W. WALKER

BERKLEY BOOKS, NEW YORK

A Berkley Book
Published by The Berkley Publishing Group
A division of Penguin Putnam Inc.
375 Hudson Street
New York, New York 10014

This is a work of fiction. Names, characters, places, and
incidents are either the product of the author's imagination
or are used fictitiously, and any resemblance to actual
persons, living or dead, business establishments, events, or
locales is entirely coincidental.

First edition: May 2001

The Penguin Putnam Inc. World Wide Web site address is
www.penguinputnam.com

Library of Congress Cataloging-in-Publication Data

Walker, Robert W. (Robert Wayne), 1948–
Bitter instinct / Robert W. Walker
p. cm.
Sequel to: Blind instinct.
ISBN 0-425-17963-X
1. Government investigators—Fiction. 2. Medical examiners (Law)—
Fiction. 3. Philadelphia (Pa.)—Fiction. 4. Women physicians—Fiction.
5. Serial murders—Fiction. I Title.

PS3573.A425385 B56 2001
813'.54—dc21

00-066705

PRINTED IN THE UNITED STATES OF AMERICA

10   9   8   7   6   5   4   3   2   1

This is to acknowledge Stephen R. Walker, who penned all of the truly "killer" poetic lines in this novel. Any bad poetry found within these pages may be attributed to the author, who has long been metrically challenged. So allow me to thank my son, Stephen Walker, for inspiring the premise for *Bitter Instinct* via his poems, which continue to surprise and move his father.

PROLOGUE

SCRAWLED in careful longhand in a reddish ochre color across and down Anton Pierre's thin, bony back, an exquisite living poem ripples with his movement. And the movement speaks. It speaks the poem into existence as it crawls, glides, moving with his lithe body. At first, snakelike, the poem slithers with his groaning. Soon, however, it seems to assume an angelic flight with Anton's lilting gasp for breath.

It is a poem penned with a needle-pointed, flesh-cutting quill. The poem's ink, laced with the toxic concoction, runs into Anton's bloodstream, the poison doing its work. Anton Pierre believes both poem and poet inspired, and, in fact, he'd earlier jokingly called his killer the Lord Poet of Misspent Time. They had toasted to the name, and the poet thought it appropriate, replying, "Yes, Lord Poet *Messenger* of Misspent Time, I would add. That's what I'll call myself." They shared a laugh then and they drank to each other's boldness, Anton's in baring his body, the poet in baring his soul.

Anton had been searching for a sponsoring poet, someone whose work he could respect. He had found his poet, or rather his poet had found him; either way, results had come about, results without regret.

"Perhaps you are what you claim to be, the reincarnated soul of all the great poets." Anton Pierre had said to the poet on reading some lines the other had dashed off as if it were no more difficult to compose poetry than to breathe in the moonlit air. "You have the flare of a classical poet, but your subjects are abjectly modern, dark, and melancholy."

"I'll take that bit of critical analysis as a compliment," the poet had said, toasting again. "Dear boy, you must know that melancholia sells, and it is precisely that which my poetry is meant to evoke."

Now Anton feels a sense of pride fill him at being *chosen*, that he will stand before the coffeehouse masses to bare himself so that others might read him: literally read his living poem from his back side. His Lord Poet of Misspent Time promises this opportunity, saying, "These words and your body, Anton, will reach the minds and souls of everyone tonight—all the world's a stage, right? And the poem inspired by you? It shall be repeated throughout time."

Inside Anton Pierre's head a silver rainshower of uncontrollable and musty images now swirl. A desperate euphoria engulfs him. An overwhelming and hungry sensation of warmth and happiness crawls along the corridors of his mind, curls up catlike, and replaces any sense of pride or feelings of self, for he no longer comprehends the self. The self has been washed away by a peaceful serenity invading his brain. This paradoxically gentle tidal wave ends all limitations and boundaries of self, of time, of place, and of will. The next to choose dies on the vine, replaced by innocent ignorance of his own demise—on this plane. Works like a charm—keeps all thoughts pure and unencumbered. He feels no melancholy, no bitterness, only a sense of loss just out of reach, running ahead . . . shadowlike, just out of his grasp, like a butterfly being.

Perhaps if he had understood the deeper meanings of the poem that he'd allowed to be etched into his back, then perhaps he would know the intent of the Lord Poet Messenger of Misspent Time, as the other had begun to think of himself. Meantime, in Anton's inner ear, whispered words travel the shell-like coils, but these words can't make themselves clear; the auditory sense has been disengaged along with all other senses.

"Aaaaway-ken-to-aware-wareness . . . place of angels," were the last words to solidify in Anton's brain.

Inside the killer's head, a sense of accomplishment rises, dragonfly-like and divine. The mission has been accomplished. No lack of sensation here inside the poet's mind, for it is filled with the words, sights, sounds, and odors of this moment, soothing the angelic Anton into calm acceptance of the death and the rebirth he so deserves; he soothes Anton with assurances, contentment, and serenity, and what the final serenity promises. Now sending forth a gift to the pleading heavens, the poet knows that the archangels must be as elated as he himself is proud.

It has been a long time coming. Anton had required a great deal of courting.

The poet did not always know what brought the ethereal shadows swirling into and through both mind and body, down to the T-cells and pores. They—the ethereal voices—were felt as energy, electrified and stinging, but in a good way, like a good scalp massage, only this massage energized the brain and the will. It amounted to sound but a sound that was as much felt as heard. They—the sweet existence of sounds—made life bearable; knowing of their existence made all the years of inexplicable horror in this life manageable.

They were known throughout history as beings of light and air, and scholars of the occult had determined that there were exactly nineteen *Angelic Calls*—poems written by the angels as instruction to a human host. And now he was that host to whom they called, asking for nineteen of their own to be returned to them.

The poet's soft voice fills the room as he attempts to further lull Anton into the life of that not-so-distant river that parallels this one, saying, "Now I know and you know, Anton. We have learned our lesson well and we know. We know what draws them near: primarily a total immersion in faith, a faith that speaks of their existence."

Along with this immersion in faith, a stick of expensive sandalwood incense helps both the poet and his chosen one, as does relaxing music, a cool evening breeze, dim lighting, an aroma of candles, all carefully arranged before the reading of favored poems for Anton Pierre's delight.

They had talked all evening about this polluted, corrupt, and profane existence, and that *other* world spoken of by poets. They had agreed on the awful, corrupting power and putrid breath of this world, which dances with the devil. They had gotten round to Anton's role in it all, and to the fact that he should have been born into a far different, far more advanced and less noxious world. When asked to elucidate, the poet had said, "A world filled with radiant light and joyful spirit, a world blessed and ethereal with rarefied air and subtle, fragile life-forms who nonetheless prove spiritually powerful, filled as they are with love and a glorified nature."

Anton's eyes sparkled as he pictured it. "Spielberg ought to make a film about such a world," the boy had kidded.

Now the author of Anton Pierre's death takes a deep breath and sips the last of his margarita, from the place where he has been sitting on Anton's veranda, enjoying the sense of closure along with tonight's calming breeze and the "Blue Danube Waltz" played by the Philadelphia Symphony Orchestra. Anton had excellent taste in music. The past pushes in on the poet, making anger rise; why had it taken so long to understand the one true purpose of one's gift?

The poet pushes back from the chair, stands, and salutes the bustling city below with the drink in his outstretched hand; next comes a salute to the stars, a sense of finality and fulfillment washing over him. "Yet so much more remains to be done," the poet says, and downs the final drop of tonight's Chardonnay. "Lovely evening, really," the poet tells the cool night air.

With Anton Pierre in the bedroom behind the poet killer, struggling to catch his last breath of this putrid world, both victim and killer now might rest. "But the term *victim* hardly applies here," the poet tells himself, "and the word *killer* proves a misnomer as well. Both words, more suited to a mystery novel, pointed to wrongheaded thinking and ridiculous conclusions." After all, Pierre was dispatched from his sad existence for one reason only, and it had been done without the least feeling of malice, prejudice, disgust, or anything smacking of the negative. Revenge or profit? Nothing could be further from the essence of the matter. The poet hasn't killed Pierre for his possessions, his position, or his woman; the poet hasn't actually killed Anton Pierre at all. In point of fact, Anton's release comes as a direct consequence of Anton's beloved nature. "Good guys finish first," the poet mutters. "The good die young, innocent."

The poet has merely acted as catalyst, freeing poor young Anton Pierre from his ugly prison, this vile existence wherein one's own body is infested by vermin.

The Lord Poet of Misspent Time, Anton had called him. "I like the sound of it, no matter its meaning. Meaning takes second place to musicality these days anyway, so . . . In any event, the label will be kept, and deservedly so."

A return to the bedroom to stare at the dying boy. Genuine pride in having helped liberate naive, innocent, young Anton from this filth-ridden world fills Anton's benefactor. "I feel great compassion for you, boy." His benefactor kneels over Anton and speaks softly in his ear, taking the boy's naked body in his arms. "Who else fights today for human dignity? I'm engaged in a war here, an all-out, fucking cosmic battle. A war between all darkness and all beings of light, and the stakes are high, Anton, absolute in fact. The whole fucking universe is at stake."

The poet begins to gently rock the dying white form in his arms, tears streaming now. The boy's skin seems as white as an albino's, as unblemished as fine porcelain. The poet's tears stain the boy's forehead here where Anton's body is held close and rocked. "You'll become a warrior for good, Anton. You are needed elsewhere."

A siren wails somewhere out over Philadelphia's nightscape, disturbing the peace of Anton's last moments. "I'm guilty of caring too deeply, too abidingly," the poet says to the near-empty, lethargic shell that had been Anton Pierre, wondering what the boy's real name might have been, and then wondering if it mattered what he called himself. The boy's soul is yet slipping off to become one of the legion to whom the poet answers. "I believe in the actions I take; I believe in the forces driving me, forces that speak through me, act through me, use me and my poetic genius. I am a mere humble pawn in this flawed world of impurities."

A shudder erupts from some final, volcanic center inside Anton Pierre's thin, white body. The poet lifts Anton's head and gazes into his dying eyes, bringing the young man's final pure light to his own eyes, and there shines resigned acceptance in the dimming orbs, and the angels dancing over Anton's irises smile at their messenger poet. The angels are pleased, pleased at finally finding and embracing Anton Pierre. "Go—go on angel's wings, dear, sweet youth," mutters Anton's poet.

Helpless, yet in smiling reverie, his veins circulating the poison that formed the very words of the poem on his back, Pierre groans the groan of the warm and comforted feline, feeling no pain, completely happy in a pure and beneficent embrace now. With the virtuous poet sponsoring him, the virtuous angels welcoming him into their legion, Anton becomes the chaste chosen.

Yes, the poet cares so much and knows much. In fact, the poet has learned a great deal from his otherworldly tutors. Thorough and meticulous, they have filled his mind with all the knowledge of those who have spoken through him since childhood. Through the World Wide Web, they now have come to reveal themselves and to help target the chosen, and the work has been rewarding, for they have assured him a place among them, and they have said what he has done makes him a true man in every sense of the word.

The poet has heard them speak it even as they revealed their identities. Enticing dark friends from beyond are those same entities he converses with in his dream and reverie.

He had assured Anton Pierre that he, Anton, ought to have been born an angel, or at least a saint. So lovely and gorgeous *is*—yes, *is*—he, for he *lives* now and forever . . .

Yes, the poet cares far too damned much. He simply loves too deeply and too well, certainly too passionately, but then no one knows of the true depths of his passions, not really. Certainly no one knows the depth of his involvement with young Anton Pierre, here tonight.

Lovely thought, lonely reality, he thinks, for no one can share in the beatific work, the calling. The poet wonders if Byron, Shelley, Keats, and other inspired poets had not been called to perform such miracles in their day. If so, perhaps Byron alone acted on the choices offered him. Did Byron hear the same voices?

"No one not hearing the voices could possibly understand; no one not hearing and feeling himself directed by the angelic spirits surrounding the poet could know the depth of the connection. They guide the poet's every movement and breath."

Anton lets out a long, languishing burst of air.

"Yes, of course, that is it," the poet mutters, and the dying Anton Pierre, whose eyes glaze over with his slow passing, responds with an angelic smile.

"A final toast," the poet bellows out, "to that other world which you're moving toward, Anton, I promise you."

Anton's angelic, startled reply is telepathic, speaking of stunned and amazed innocence at what he now sees. The poet hears Anton's voice inside his head telepathically sending a message: "And I love you, too, my beautiful poet friend, and you will reap the reward of pure love for freeing me from this, our shared purgatory."

The poet loves Anton Pierre, far more than any of the boy's blood relatives, who detest him for his difference, for being a woman born to a man's body. Even given the brevity of his and Pierre's encounter, which fate has brought to them, the Lord Poet believes he loves the youth far more than any who called Anton friend, certainly more than his current lover, Tom, who has hurt him so deeply and so often. Tom's reward, his punishment, will be to live out a full life in this realm of the putrid, where the spirit is corrupted with the body.

From what the poet has gathered, Pierre had recently been hurt for the umpteenth time by family, by so-called friends, and by Tom. Well, no more . . . no more pain or suffering ever again. Michael, Raphael, and the other angels have seen to that—with a little help from a poet whose soul belongs to them.

He has helped Pierre flee from this world for the most passionate of reasons. He cannot allow the Anton Pierres of this world to suffer.

He sits now with Pierre while the young man's life wanes, the life force now like a flickering wisp of moonglow.

The poet holds on to the young man's hand, so like a glove now, a sheath for the sword of soul.

The body is a simple vessel, a mere repository for spirit.

He weighs time. A light on the horizon from the open window, a cool breeze tickling Pierre's fevered brow at the moment between darkness and dawn, a special moment when the ethereal creatures come to take their own.

The Lord Poet of Misspent Time recalls the lines he has penned on Anton Pierre's back. The poem honors Anton, as it is meant as much for the boy's memory, his sepulchre, as for the masses who will learn from it.

"Or will they?" the poet laments.

With the boy's head in his lap, brushing fingers through his hair, the poet recites aloud the poem to his loving Anton for a final time:

Chance . . . whose desire
is to have a meeting
with stunned innocence . . .
A flickering
with every heartbeat
born is a picture
burned into skin
a little story
wherein ends illusion.
The cut of it
against my back
marks time
in distances wide,
the time it takes
to retell a new breath.

Anton Pierre's eyes roll back in his head, fully dilated, the poison having done its work. It will be a killer difficult to detect, and it creates in the boy a peaceful end, now that the initial convulsions have passed. The poet holds the young man's head in his hands, rolls him facedown, and places him gently on the pillow on the floor. The poet next covers the marked boy with a sheet up to his waist, leaving the poem revealed to those who find the body. He next kisses his cheek and bids farewell.

"Safe crossing, my sweet friend," he softly coos, locating the door and quietly leaving the apartment.

He leaves the building, unseen save for a homeless man who pays him little mind. He steps out onto the wet shimmering bricks of a newly gentrified neighborhood, where cheap pavement meets expensive stone, the renovated warehouse courtyard silent and slick with a summer shower that futilely attempts to wash this world clean.

A mewing cat from the alleyway abandons her search of a garbage heap to follow the Lord Poet of Misspent Time, whose left hand carries a valise, the tools of his trade. It's as if the cat wishes to be his next protégée, begging him to skin her and scrawl a poem across her back and send her over to . . . to some cat heaven.

He ignores the animal. Still, the poet's soft-soled steps from this place are like a cat's, like the fog of Carl Sandburg's poem that "comes on little cat feet," and he thinks of J. Alfred Prufrock, the eponymous hero of poet T. S. Eliot's "The Love Song of J. Alfred Prufrock," and he wonders who knew first, the poet or the creation. And which of the two was more real, Prufrock or Eliot, the poet. Which of the two saw the world for what it is, and which of the two did something about it. *As I have done this night,* he thinks.

ONE

Technology is not going to save us. Our comput-
ers, our tools, our machines are not enough. We
have to rely on our intuition, our true being.

—Joseph Campbell

TWILIGHT had painted the common grounds about the
FBI buildings at Quantico in lavender and purple
shadow beneath the lamps lining the walkways. The
springtime hills around the Virginia compound appeared
cluttered. Blooming dogwood splashed color up and down
the forests. From a distance, it looked like swaths of lin-
gering snow, the flowers snuggling and wiggling and boring in—alive amid greening blades of wild grass, all at
odds with the carefully kept, manicured lawns of Quantico.
The training grounds were empty, classrooms locked up for
the night, most lights turned off, most buildings vacated or
nearly so, but the bright fluorescent lights of the forensics
lab glared out at the night like so many defiant eyes.

Using two pairs of surgical tweezers, FBI medical examiner Dr. Jessica Coran lifted the mask of skin over the
chin with a surgical dexterity that Dr. John Thorpe had
learned to expect. Jessica's long auburn hair had been
wrapped in a bun, held tightly by a single hairpin, the way
her mother wore her hair in treasured family photos. Jessica hadn't known her mother for very long before she had
passed away, but from the warm feelings that welled up inside whenever her father had talked about her, she knew
she had been a loving and gentle person. Jessica resembled

her in many respects, the high cheekbones, the classic up-turned nose, the deep emerald eyes, but her height Jessica inherited from her father, who had also been a medical examiner. When she had graduated from medical school and still had four grueling years ahead in order to specialize, her father had beamed with pride both at her accomplishment and at her decision to continue in forensic medicine.

She knew what he would think today, if he were alive, to see her a full-blown FBI agent as well as a medical examiner. With his military background and the years he spent as a medical examiner in the U.S. Army, she knew he'd be proud beyond anything she could imagine.

Dr. John Thorpe, known to his closest friends simply as JT, now watched as Jessica gently tugged the freed mask of the face up, over, and past the protruding nasal cartilage. She next inched it ever so carefully about the eyes, revealing the red mass of flesh and crisscrossed arteries below the forehead's outer husk, to at last find the victim's cranial bone. JT had seen this operation go horribly wrong before, and had even bungled it himself. Tearing the outer flesh of the victim left unmistakable signs of botched work, causing lacerations no one wanted to see at an open-coffin funeral.

Jessica Coran accepted the rotary diamond-stylus deluxe Windsor bone saw that Thorpe reluctantly extended to her. JT held on to it long enough to plead, "Let me do this part, Jess."

She glanced at her lab partner, released a pent-up breath, nodded, and relinquished the saw. "She's all yours, JT."

Jessica watched JT, his potbelly at odds with his otherwise slim frame. She knew he was closing in on yet another middle-age crisis, but since he had divorced his wife, Rhoda, he had no one to share his crises with. Also since his divorce, the man lived on McDonald's burgers, fries, and fish fillets, when he wasn't defrosting the ultimate in junk cuisine—the oxymoronic gourmet dinner. The curl of his lips gave JT a perpetual half grin, and his dusky brown eyes shone like those of a schoolboy whenever he became excited over a case. Jessica trusted him as a forensic expert, trusted his skills and knowledge, but even more important, she genuinely liked him as a person. He made her laugh, a thing few other men were capable of doing, and their friendship had weathered many storms.

"Tell me again, Jess, why're we exposing the brain?"

"Only way to be certain what caused the woman's coma—the drugs or the beating she took."

"Yes, of course, but—"

"If there're signs of significant—"

"Swelling, I know. But coma is coma, and dead is dead. What difference will it make to her or her family to know if the coma were drug-induced or caused by trauma?"

"You need a vacation, JT."

"What kind of crack is that?"

She had stepped away from the corpse, away from the wet steel slab, where a constant flow of water kept debris moving for the drain in the center of the blindingly white tiled floor. The drain gurgled and burped like an impatient animal awaiting its evening feeding. Overhead, an equally constant jet of air protected her and JT from contamination, a constant fear.

Jessica took a step toward JT, where he stood holding on to the saw. "You know very well what difference it makes."

"All right . . . all right . . . I do, yes."

"Then repeat after me," she shouted over the scream of the saw against bone as JT proceeded. "The truth is *in* there." She ended by pointing at the brain, then snatching her finger out of harm's way just as the cranial cap gave way and into JT's outstretched left hand. He fumbled like a water boy on a football field startled to find himself in possession of the football, but when he dropped it, it fell into the widemouthed basket beneath the head, placed there to prevent anything from making contact with the ceramic tiles at their feet.

Jessica wondered at the magnitude of the horror that had been inflicted on the victim, a young black woman named Adinatella LaMartine, hardly in her twenties. The young woman had been a stellar student at Washington's Howard University, where she had aced all her political science classes. On seeing their daughter's body at the morgue, her parents spoke of her having been chosen as a White House intern for the fall, and now this: abducted from a parking lot during or just after a frat party, raped, savagely beaten, and overdosed on what was looking more and more like some deadly concoction of *arborescens*: azaleas and/or rhododendrons ground up in some sort of honey cake, a poor man's Spanish fly. They had the same poisonous effect as mountain laurel. Toxicity level proved high at six, and in too great a quantity, the drug became as poisonous as arsenic. A fast-acting narcotic, it initially caused drooling, vomiting, and increased tear formation, followed by paralysis, a slowed pulse rate, and lowered blood pressure, leading to coma, depending on the dose. Still, it remained a remote possibility that the beating she had taken had sent her spiraling into a coma long before the drug took effect. Which came first in this case meant a great deal in prosecuting a suspect. If the defendant had taken a comatose young woman into the nearest hospital, he might be spared some jail time, having shown some mercy and some sense. However, if he beat to death a comatose victim, that would add jail time, showing depraved indifference for life. If he beat to death a dead body, that would be regrettable but it would not be murder. In all scenarios, Jessica felt the young man had shown depravity, but only proof of the exact sequence of events would put the killer behind bars.

The "Twinkie defense" and the "Oops! defense" were created for such cases as this.

Date rape to date murder. Whether planned or accidental, the evil results were the same. So Jessica proposed to learn the exact sequence of acts before the end of the business day, and this necessitated a cranial examination. Toxicology alone could not tell them the entire story. Meanwhile, toxicology experts continued to work to determine the exact nature of the poison. Even so, something told Jessica that the killer had not meant to kill in this case. Probably he had slipped the girl something to render her unconscious and helpless, so as to have his way with her, and then, realizing too late that she was not going to come out of it, the fiend began to savagely beat her. His assault was his stupid way of attempting to bring her back to the land of the living.

When JT had asked Jessica how she could possibly know the sequence of events, she merely replied, "The mess her abductor made of her, the mess he left behind. It just looks like bushels of panic." Complete and utter panic, she now thought. "He drove the comatose woman not to the nearest hospital but to her room on campus, depositing her there, leaving all manner of evidence, from bloodstains and bodily fluids to witnesses who saw him going in and out, some of whom thought the girl drunk. Since the killer had her keys, he let himself in and dropped her, unconscious, onto her bed, where she lay until her roommate came in late in the day and began attempting to rouse her."

"Yeah, messy," JT conceded. "Messy and stupid."

"Fits right in with the nature of the crime and the criminal. He hadn't planned her death; he planned on a good time, to get off, drive her home, and never see or hear from her again. He perfectly fits the definition of a disorganized killer."

"Yeah, guess he does."

"Nothing at all like your last major case, JT. The tat-tooed corpse. Where the victim's daughters and sons used rabid dogs as murder weapons."

"What a weird odyssey that turned out to be," he agreed.

"Strangest case of your career, Doctor. You really must write it up for the *Forensic Journal of Medical Inquiry*. They'd eat it up."

"You think so?" She could practically see the wheels turning in his head.

"I know so," she assured him, thinking of the case that had led JT across America in pursuit of, first, a tattoo artist who could identify the mangled body of the victim, and then in pursuit of the killers—the victim's own children, who so despised and feared the father that they had planned his murder for over a year.

As JT put aside the ear-shattering saw, he shouted, "So, what do you hear from Inspector Sharpe of Scotland Yard these days?"

It had been nine months since Jessica returned from a bizarre case that had taken her to London. In that time, she and Richard Sharpe had seen each other on several occa-sions, but, except for phone calls and e-mails, they had not had contact now for two of those nine months, and she missed him terribly. Still, his retirement from Scotland Yard was imminent, which meant they could be together at last. However, Richard's superiors had asked him to post-pone his retirement for a case. Richard had telephoned her about the matter, and while he had, she suspected, already agreed to work the case, he wanted her to tell him it was all right.

Jessica and Richard had worked the Crucifier case to-gether, and somewhere along the way, they had fallen into each other's arms. Jessica's relationship with James Parry by then had become strained, the distance between them finally taking its toll, what with Parry a bureau chief in

Hawaii and her in Quantico, Virginia. JT had caustically joked, "So you traded one ocean for another as an obstacle between yourself and a man who shows some interest in you. Quite interesting."

She had perhaps too readily told Richard Sharpe that he was perfectly correct in continuing his investigation of the case, and so she allowed him to take himself off the proverbial hook, but she wondered if she should not have ranted and railed at him. He'd promised her that they would be together by Christmas. Instead, she had tried to sound as adamant as possible over the phone, shouting, "Solve it and get your sexy self across the Pond. I need you in my life, Richard, and that means close by!"

Still, she wondered why she had not shown more anger over his decision, why she had not pouted and shouted. Why she hadn't let him know he had hurt her in postponing their plans for reunion, plans that had them living together here in Quantico. She second-guessed her reasoning, her motives, her resolve.

"Perhaps people are right about me; maybe I don't want a real relationship, anything smacking of true commitment," she told JT as she placed a magnifying glass on a swivel arm over the victim's exposed brain.

When JT did not answer, she knew why. She could read him like a book. "Perhaps having so much space between Richard and me creates a kind of comfort zone. That's what Dr. Lemonte always said about what James Parry and I had."

"Did you tell her she was full of shit?" asked JT.

"Yeah, not in quite those words, but yeah, I did."

"How do you feel, Jess, deep inside? I mean, about having all that distance between you and Richard."

"I've had separation anxiety since I left England, and I felt the same thing all those years I was separated from James Parry. I did love him. I don't for a moment believe I sabotaged the relationship—either consciously or subconsciously."

"But if you're feeling separation anxiety over Richard, why aren't you astronomically pissed off at him for taking on another case when he could have come to you?"

"Shoe's on the other foot, I guess," she replied. "How often did I do exactly that to Parry? Frankly, I don't know why I didn't throw a fit when Richard told me he was staying on at the Yard."

"Conditioning, I imagine," replied JT, continuing with the cleanup.

"Conditioning?"

"Daddy's little girl, military brat learns to take it on the chin."

"Hmm . . . always with a controlled and professional response? Maybe it's true what they say about our ghosts becoming our teachers," she finally conceded. She'd been raised by a man who demanded that she do the right thing in any given situation, so she did as her father would have expected; did as her wonderful professor and mentor, Dr. Asa Holcraft, expected; did as Otto Boutine, her first FBI mentor, a man who had died saving her, would have expected. All the ghosts were coming back to haunt her.

In London, she had dodged her ghosts, thrown caution to the wind, falling in love with Richard Sharpe while they worked the case of her career, a case the *Forensic Journal of Medical Inquiry* had pleaded for her to write up and forward to them.

While in England, Jessica—ostensibly there to help Scotland Yard uncover the identity of the Crucifier—had fallen into the arms of Richard Sharpe. While a fiend who killed his victims in the manner of Christ on the Cross roamed London's underground, Jessica Coran had experienced wild abandon with a man for whom she felt a great passion—while withholding her love, the ultimate gift.

"Love is not conditional, Jessica!" her psychiatrist friend Donna Lemonte had often scolded.

While a perverted religious lunatic terrorized all of London, Jessica had found a man for whom she dared think pure love a possibility. In fact, she wondered if her soul had been given voice through Richard, telling her that life before him had not truly been a life, and that now a life without Richard would prove to be a living death.

She thought now of the manuscript she had begun writing while lying in Wessex Hospital in London. Jessica had begun tape recording her feelings for a book on the nature of evil, and how evil—like currents through an ocean—worked through mankind, often in a subtle, even banal manner. Certainly since London, Jessica believed she'd never again see the scale of horror she had confronted in Richard's homeland. Then came the worst school massacre in American history in Littleton, Colorado, where evil so disguised itself that no one, not even the shooters' closest friends and relatives, saw it coming, and now this poor young black girl on her autopsy table. Evil lumbered on and lurked in every crevice in the everyday lives of people.

Evil-thinking, evil-plotting, evil-acting malignancy. It pervaded, surrounded, and permeated all corners of life, she now reasoned. Certainly it lay thick and all but palpable inside the human psyche and here in her autopsy room. Here evil grinned back at her like a maniacal foe and a familiar one, perched gargoyle fashion over her autopsy table.

Likely after reading about poisons on the Internet, Lawrence Hampton, the man behind bars, decided to give his date flowers. He now intended to run an insanity defense, and he was giving police nothing. Jessica's line of forensic inquiry might prove him monstrously evil in having beaten a comatose woman to death, or it might prove the accidental overdose killed her. The sequence of events meant everything in this case. Young Hampton had botched his entire ugly plan by ensuring the girl's death from the beginning, because he didn't know what amounted to an unsafe formula or dosage.

Cleaning up, John Thorpe tossed the saw onto a metal table, shattering Jessica's reverie. "You were right, as usual. God, look at the swelling to the brain. Lot of internal injury to the melon. You don't get that kind of reaction from a dead person."

"She took a hell of a beating."

"I agree, she went into coma before she died. Given this evidence, he killed her with his hands. Must've gone into a rage after the drug refused to wear off."

"So we nail his ass in court for the more tortuous death. It'll add fifty years to his sentence by itself. Good work," she agreed. "Now get some photos of this, log it, and we'll try to put Adinatella back together again."

Jessica thought about Adinatella's family, her father and mother, who had brought her into this world, how they must have felt when they left the hospital with their infant daughter wrapped in a blanket; how they must have nurtured her and sent her off to college. All the love and attention showered on Adinatella, and in one moment some stranger snuffs out their child's life, and for what? To fulfill an animal lust.

"Shameful waste of a beautiful young woman," said JT, as if reading Jessica's thoughts.

"It's an awful sorry business we're in, JT."

AFTER another hour of autopsy work, John Thorpe and Jessica Coran walked from the dissecting room, leaving interns to handle the final cleanup and the disposition of the body. Jessica dug her left thumb into her right palm to remove her right surgical glove, and then followed up with the left. The pair of medical examiners stripped their surgical garb as they walked, dumping their green hair nets and aprons into a hamper. Going to their respective locker rooms, Jessica called out, "Question for you, JT."

"Shoot."

"Do you really think I may have . . . might be . . . may've gotten involved with Richard Sharpe because he's . . . you know, at a distance?"

"Good God, Jess, you're not paying any attention to all that bullswallop going around about you, now, are you?"

"Bullswallop? Going around about me?"

"Usual crap out of the usual mouths, about how you like to keep your friends and lovers at safe arm's length. I mean, it's nobody's damn business but your own."

"I hadn't heard anything to that effect," she confessed.

"Oh, sorry. I wouldn't't've repeated it had I known you hadn't . . . I mean, I don't do that silly gossip thing. I mean . . . sorry."

"You think there's any truth to it?"

"Not the least."

"Come on. You do, don't you?"

He hemmed and said, "You just happen to fall for the wrong guys, and they're always out of reach, one way or another." He saw the flame of hurt flash and die along her face. "I mean . . . first Otto Boutine, both married and your superior. I know . . . I know all about his wife's debilitating disease, that he was a romantic figure as a result of the wife's inability to . . . Well, all the same, the man was out of reach, or should've been."

"Otto was different from all the rest. You can't compare—"

"Then that guy Alan Rhychman in New York who stands you up in Hawaii just so he can run for police commissioner. What a hoot."

"Alan saw a chance to make a difference in New York, and he *has,* from what I've heard."

"Still, out of reach. And then came Jim Parry, not only Mr. FBI but Mr. Hawaii as well."

"James and I had a fulfilling, long-lasting relationship that beat the odds for a long time. You've got to admit that."

"Still, out of reach, Jess."

"It isn't like I've had a lot of choice, given my commitments and lifestyle."

Rubbing stiffness from his neck, JT continued: "Love makes fools of fools."

"All of us, I know."

"Nay, nay! Not an ounce of truth to it, my dear friend," he facetiously added. "And so now we are moving on, a healthy thing. Now it's Inspector Richard Sharpe, Scotland Yard. Nay! Pay no heed. Love must remain blind and stumbling. If Cupid should see too clearly, can it be called love at all? If love is measured and controlled, Jessica, it's no fun. So relax, enjoy, and stop worrying about controlling your every step and your every relationship. Remember the centipede who was asked, "How in God's name do you walk with all those feet at once?' The moment he considered the question, he stumbled over himself. So, does that answer your question, just a bit?"

"Donna Lemonte always says that I put up barriers around me."

"Just because you've switched from the Pacific Ocean to the Atlantic? At least Scotland Yard's closer to Virginia than Hawaii—"

"*New* Scotland Yard," she corrected him. "And it's not the Atlantic to us; to us, it's the Pond."

"Whatever you call it, your shrink friend is going to see it as a big barrier. You must always consider the source."

"Thanks for being your usual candid but sensitive self, JT. It's what I love most about you."

"A friend should be candid and sensitive, however much the truth hurts."

"So, when are you going to hang out your shingle and start charging for all this psychoanalysis, Dr. Thorpe?"

"Honestly, I'm only an amateur at love, psychology, and relationships myself, a novice. So any advice I may have for the lovelorn you may want to drop in the hamper along with the dirty linen."

"I'll take that advice, John," she replied dully, dropping her shoulders and turning to the door marked LADIES' LOCKER ROOM.

"G'night," he said, and suddenly feeling the weight of the day and the long autopsy, JT trundled off through the door marked GENTLEMEN'S LOCKER ROOM.

As the door was closing on JT's tired form, she shouted, "I ought to arrange to have *your* brain dissected, JT. No one would believe it! It'd make *The New England Journal of Medicine!*"

"I can see the screaming title: 'Thorpe's Brain Found Befuddled over Relationship Issues!' " He had turned and now held the door open with his right foot.

"Likely a defect in the DNA strand, the relationship gene," she added.

"Not every problem has a genetic excuse, Dr. Coran, or are you now grasping at self-justifying straws?" He allowed the door to close on his half grin.

"Touché," she said to the door, turned, and went to her locker. She desperately wanted to shower and change out of the uniform of the death investigator.

TWO

All things are poisons, for there is nothing without poisonous qualities. It is only the dose which makes a thing poison.

—Paracelsus (1493–1541)

AFTER a shower, Jessica emerged in a powder-blue business suit, and feeling an urge to be alone, she found the elevator and rode it to the building's roof. She often went there after an autopsy, to fill her lungs with fresh air and to clear her head. In the back of her mind, the tune "Up on the Roof" softly played.

The roof remained her secret hideaway, and she stood now looking down over the edge to the very spot where, years before, she'd taken a shot at a man escaping her lab after attempting to kill her. She'd been injured, but her FBI weapons training stood her in good stead. Jessica had sent a bullet down the length of the building. Some saw it as a lucky shot, but she knew better. In either case, the cannibal who'd been known as the Claw died as he deserved—slowly, made a vegetable by her single "lucky" shot.

She looked out over the Quantico, Virginia, compound of the FBI, a collection of Jefferson-style Colonial buildings nestled into the back side of the Virginia hills. Springtime filled the trees with blossoms, and the hills around sported dogwood in bloom, while the grass had turned from brownish ochre to pale green, which would soon become an opulent black green in the shadow of the dense forest surrounding the hills. Birds chased each other amid the trees, their songs reaching up to where Jessica stood, a breeze playing about her hair and cheeks.

One thing appeared certain. She felt a fierce, dry, desertlike void in her life; she missed Richard Sharpe, and she could hardly wait for his retirement from Scotland Yard. He'd promised to join her here in Quantico; they had spoken of making a life together. She daydreamed about their coming reunion, and how they would mold their future. Perhaps this time would be the charm; perhaps this time she had gathered in the golden prize, that of complete and whole companionship of the sort she had sought all her adult life.

She dared not think it true. She feared to hope.

Too many rugs—hell, whole carpets—had been pulled out from under her before; she had had to endure too many disappointments with men. And Sharpe, for all his gallantry, his compassion and goodwill, his promises and kisses, remained a man. She had never before known a man who had not in one way or another disappointed or left her. Why should Richard be any different?

"Ah, there you are, Dr. Coran! Jessica!" shouted her immediate supervisor, Eriq Santiva, a dark-skinned Cuban-American with the lively step of a tango dancer and the infectious smile of a boy. The wind tore at his long-flowing black hair, and it whipped his expensive suit jacket like a cape; had he a sword, she might imagine him a swashbuckler. She could barely hear him over the piercing spring wind and her thoughts.

Closer now, he shouted, "So this is your hideaway?"

Jessica loved Eriq's Cuban accent. "How did you find me?"

"You forget. I'm not just the director of the Behavioral

Science Unit, I'm a detective. Besides, John Thorpe does not stand up well under interrogation."

"So . . . what brings you to my secret office?"

"I know you have your hands full with this date rape/murder case you're on, but we have another and more mysterious case in Friendship City."

"Friendship City? Where the hell's that? Iowa?"

"No, no. The City of Brotherly Love."

"Philadelphia?"

"Bingo, go to the head of the class."

"What've I missed?"

"Nothing. It hasn't been our case, and for good reason, until now." He leaned out over the parapet, his dark eyes taking in the grounds below. "Philly authorities thought they could handle it on their own, but finally they want FBI input, and they requested our best. I told them that would be you."

"Thanks for the buttering-up, Chief, but what sort of case are we talking about?"

"Seems we have a multiple murderer, a guy who leaves no trace, except for some writing, which I've had a chance to examine. Weird kind of poetry, actually."

"Given your expertise with graphology, I have no doubt you've come to some conclusions about the killer. Did you bring the poems with you?" She looked at a manila folder in his hand, which the wind threatened to rip away.

"No, not exactly. This poet doesn't use paper."

"Then what does he use? He writes on the wall over the vic's bed, the mirror in the bathroom, what?"

"Try the body."

She looked squarely at him. "The body? What part of the body? Chest? Abdomen?"

"Back—from neck to buttocks—is how I'm getting it." He lifted the photo from the file, showing her some of the killer's handiwork. "Deep grooves. Victim shows no sign of ligature marks, no evidence whatsoever of being tied down for this. They seem to be . . . well, conned into it."

"What's the method of murder?" she asked, trying to read the writing from the photo of the victim's back at the same time, but finding it impossible to concentrate as the wind continued to tear the photo from her grasp.

"Poison."

"Really? Interesting."

"Poisoners are like terrorists, as far as I'm concerned," he told her firmly. "Less interesting than cowardly."

"Yeah, point taken."

"This case is a regular Agatha Christie whodunit, actually."

"Exactly how is the poison ingested, and what kind of poison are we talking about here, Chief?"

"Something in the ink, the coroner in Philly suggests, since the throat and larynx are clear of any heavy concentrations. Goes directly to the bloodstream via the cuts carved into the back."

"Needle marks?"

"Philly coroner couldn't find a single puncture mark anywhere on the bodies, nothing but the scratches—words cut precisely into the flesh with what appears to be a quill pen."

"Cuts carved into flesh introduce the poison . . ." Jessica tried to imagine the preliminaries of such a murder. She knew that Eriq wanted her to become so fascinated over the particulars that she'd accept the assignment. "Intriguing case. Why don't you take it, since you're the handwriting expert?"

"Too much going on here right now for me to step off the plate. Wish I could, and I intend to write up all my thoughts on this guy and forward them to you in Philly, if you'll take the case."

"Literally a poisoned-pen death. Does sound like an old British kind of whodunit. What a quaint and old-fashioned yet weird way to dispatch someone."

"A strange poem left across the victims' backs," he added, agreeing. "Likely without their suspecting a thing." Santiva's dark Cuban eyes studied her for a fleeting moment, seeming to measure her interest in the case.

"But what kind of fool lets you write a poem across his—or is the victim a her?—back? Can't tell from this view, man or woman?"

"We have victims of both sexes, all young and somewhat frail of build, and as for back writing, it appears to have become a fad of epidemic proportions among the young."

"A fad—really?"

"Bored with the usual tattoo thing, rings and piercings, the coffeehouse rock-club set, especially around Philadelphia, have moved onto this as a new adventure. Some say it's based on one of those urban legends."

"Really? I've not heard that one."

"About a family that committed mass suicide using poison via a pen into the flesh."

"So the local authorities think somebody is acting out this urban legend?"

"Local poets are hiring kids to display their poems, which are scrawled across their bodies, calling it Living Poetry and sometimes Live Art; then these kids disrobe during an open-mike night at a local pub or coffeehouse and their poems are read by the patrons. It has, of course, graduated to frontal view and full frontal nudity in some places, but I'm given to understand from detectives working the case that it began as strictly a rearview thing."

"An excuse to moon the crowd?" she asked.

"In the best tradition of the comedian Jimmy Carrey,

yeah. Nowadays, boobs and genitalia have been introduced so as to . . . to . . ."

"Spice up the poetry? Raise or lower the bar?"

"Depends on the bar you're talking about," he countered.

"And the prevailing tastes?"

"Eye of the beholder, precisely."

"A meeting of pure art and body art. Interesting. What will they think of next? But why haven't I heard about this fad before?"

"Philly PD task-force people say it's relatively new, and if you haven't seen someone with body poetry on his or her back . . . Well, Jess, you have to admit that if it isn't in your lab, you don't always know what's trendy, what's hot, what's not."

"Are you suggesting I'm not with it?"

Smiling, he apologetically raised his hands in classic submitting-to-arrest posture. Then Eriq retrieved the photo and slid it into the file. "A copy is being blown up as we speak, and I'll get it to you. As to your being with it, don't blame yourself for not being able to keep up with the youth of this ever-changing U.S. of A. This thing appears to have originated in certain areas of Philadelphia, spread from there."

"I see, and now it's all balled up with some psychotic murder spree there."

"Some nude club dancers have been 'written up' and they're using it in their acts these days." Santiva pursed his lips and seemed to reflect on some image in his head. "Saw one myself in Miami last time I visited family there."

Jessica feigned shock, her eyes growing wide. *"Realllly?"*

"Really, yes."

"So, are you telling me you're sending me out on a case that does not involve hacking and mutilation?" she chided.

"Lead investigator in Philly is Detective Lieutenant Leanne Sturtevante."

"Ah, a woman. Good. Maybe I won't have so much trouble fitting in. You want me to link up with this Sturtevante person?"

"You can arm yourself with your usual objectivity and scientific method, Jess, but this case is going to require your skill and hard-won knowledge. No one in history—much less in Philly—has seen anything like this before."

"Thanks for the vote of confidence."

"Philly PD have set up a task force."

"All right, task force. Worked with 'em before."

Santiva turned and looked her in the eye. "Glance over what they've accumulated. See if they're on the right track."

"The right track being . . . ?"

"All right, see if they are on *any* track."

She nodded. "Sure, meet with them, act as a liaison."

"Well, a kind of medico-legal, third-string liaison on the case, yes."

"Third-string?"

"First there's Philly PD; second our local field office, which is heavily involved. Then there's you, and Dr. Desinor."

"Kim's assigned to the case, too?" Jessica smiled at the thought of working with her friend and the FBI's resident psychic expert, Kim Faith Desinor.

"That's a go."

"We haven't worked a case directly together since—"

"New Orleans, I know."

"Sounds interesting. Tell me, who's our ASAC in Philly these days? Obviously, we'll be working closely together."

"You may not like this, Jess."

"Whaddaya mean?"

Santiva now stepped away from the ledge and stared off

at the setting sun. From below, a late-evening regiment marched drills as dusk descended and the lights went up. Finally, he spat it out. "It's Parry . . . James Parry."

Jessica looked like she'd been struck in the face. "Jim? Jim's now ASAC-ing in Philadelphia?" She quickly regained her calm. "Wow . . . A stone's throw away compared to Hawaii, and I'm the last to know," she said in a matter-of-fact voice. "Wouldn't you know, that bas—"

"Sorry to be the bearer of bad news, Jess."

"Christ, why didn't you tell me sooner?"

"When sooner?"

"Before now sooner."

"I just got the news."

"When the . . . when did this happen?"

"Few weeks ago, Jess. Didn't know myself until yesterday. You know how slow certain information flows in the Bureau. It was all done hush-hush, really."

She stared hard into Eriq's Latin eyes, which gave nothing away. Still, she believed he shared her pain. "Did he . . . did he request the transfer?" She had pleaded with James Parry for over three years to make just such a transfer so that they might be closer. They had broken up just before her trip to London, but given the distance between them, even the most crucial moments, even their *breakup,* had occurred over the phone. This had left a wide hole in her soul, a feeling that some needful thing was forever gone.

"You know how the Bureau works. He got into serious trouble with the Hawaiian Nationalist Party—something he said about native rights on the islands, and the State Department got involved because it might lead to an embarrassment or some such bullshit. Politics is what got Jim, pure and simple. Chances of there being an international incident over the issue of homeboy rule in Hawaii, *which is as likely as turning over L.A. to the Native American population there,* are nonexistent."

"The State Department?"

"And your friend Parry likes stepping on toes, I think. You know how he loves to piss off Lauren Fennelly at the State Department."

"Yeah, he's complained about Fennelly for years—to no avail."

"Anyhow it all caught up with him. Everybody wanted him out, and so he's . . . well, suffice it to say that leaving a post in Hawaii for Philly wasn't his choice."

"Son of a Bristol whore," she muttered, mimicking what Richard Sharpe might say.

"What's that, Jess?"

"Never mind."

"Well, does this color things too gray and grim for you, having to work alongside Parry?"

"No . . . it's hardly reason enough by itself to turn down an assignment."

"Are you being honest with me, Jess?"

"I'm trying to be, yes."

"And with yourself?"

"Don't you start psychoanalyzing me, Eriq."

"Sorry. You see now why Bureau policy says don't get emotionally involved with fellow agents, Jess?"

"Practice what you preach, Chief. I hear via the grapevine you're seeing someone in the secretarial pool."

"Man, try to keep a secret in this place."

She stepped back to the ledge and stared again at the expanse of the government compound, her eyes falling on the twin towers most people here called home—the Hearth, they'd nicknamed it. She had imagined that once Richard boarded a jet and showed up in Virginia, they would share her apartment for a time and then go house hunting through the pleasant, surrounding valleys. "We won't speak of marriage," she'd told him. "We'll cohabit, as they say. Play it by ear, one day at a time."

It had all sounded wonderful when they'd made plans. Now she wondered what Richard would think of her working in such close proximity to her former flame, James Parry. Would he have a typical lover's response? Richard seldom did the typical thing. She had told him all about her and James's long-term, long-distance, once successful, and now failed relationship; she'd told him she feared the same would happen with them.

Richard had seemed so understanding. "I mean to love you as you are, Jess, with all that has gone into creating Jessica Coran up to this moment. My own prior experiences and experiments have been equally dismal." He had then kissed her tenderly and warned that her only competition for his time would be his children.

Working again with James could seriously endanger her wonderful relationship with Richard. Working a case with Parry—just entertaining the possibility of it seemed dangerous. Still, a side of her felt a surge of anger at anyone who might stand in the way of her doing her job.

"Well, Jess? What do you say? We'll need to give them an answer before long. Mull it over; get back to me as soon as you can."

"I'll certainly give it serious thought, Eriq."

"Look, I can't do a damn thing about Parry, but you've wanted to work with Kim again for a long time. You two made one hell of a team in New Orleans, and her psychic abilities might be of great use in Philadelphia. So . . . please consider all sides and let me know by ten P.M."— he glanced at his watch—"eleven at the latest. Otherwise, John Thorpe can take this one. He did a fine job on the Tattoo Man case; call it typecasting, if you will. In any event, the team we put together has to be in Philly by nine A.M. tomorrow."

"Give me a little time to think this one through."

"Sure . . . sure. I'll line up JT as an alternate, just in case."

She nodded and he rushed off, a thousand and one other duties awaiting his attention. Once Eriq had gone, she stood alone again with her thoughts, but now those thoughts came in a confused scramble. "James Parry in trouble with the Hawaiian Nationalist Party and the State Department again. It figures," she said to the wind. She clearly recalled how he had covered up an illegal search and seizure on an island reservation where the Bureau had no jurisdiction. It had taken some time, but their indiscretion and subsequent cover-up appeared to have come home to roost. She wondered when and if she, like Parry, would face serious reprimands from the Bureau. Or had James been the shining knight and gentleman to the end, taking all the heat for her as well as himself?

Not so admirable to be removed from a job as the Hawaii FBI chief to Philly's chief's job, but quite admirable to defend her honor and position . . . *if* he had . . . It appeared obvious that no one in either the State Department or the Bureau suspected her yet of any wrongdoing in Hawaii. If so, there would be no teaming of her and Parry in Philadelphia. That much seemed certain. Had Parry kept her from harm's way, and had fallout from their actions cost him his position? Why had it taken the State Department so long to find the truth behind the Lopaka Kowona case and its aftermath? Breaking a State Department treaty was no small matter. Had that day and the subsequent lie that she'd shared with Parry come back to haunt her?

It had been the first and only time she had ever hidden the truth on an autopsy protocol, but it had been the only choice left her and Parry, and under the circumstances, the island politicians having trumped them, it had kept peace between the races. At the time, a race war felt as imminent as the next island storm. She and Parry stood on the front line, on the storm's edge. Now it appeared as if Parry had been engulfed by the persistent political problems in the islands, and perhaps someone who knew his darkest secret had leaked information to the State Department.

Then again, knowing Jim's penchant for rushing in where angels feared to tread, perhaps he had brought down some new shower of complaints over himself. Perhaps his transfer had nothing whatever to do with her. Only one person could tell her the specifics of Jim's problem with the Bureau's high-muck-a-mucks in Hawaii . . .

Either way, hardly reason to go to Philadelphia to work alongside Jim Parry, a man who found it impossible to play by Bureau rules. She had done her own share of rule breaking over the years, but in bringing down the Trade Winds Killer together, they had broken every rule in the book. The only saving grace? They had gotten results.

Yes, she concluded, she wanted nothing to do with Jim, and by extension, nothing to do with the Philly case. End of story.

Eriq Santiva could just send someone else. John Thorpe would do just fine. Philadelphia would have to survive without Jessica Coran's profiling expertise and skill with a scalpel.

Besides, she didn't like the sound of being a third-string liaison for anyone, much less James Parry. She had gotten every one of her scars the hard way. This was no time to play second banana to the likes of James Parry.

JESSICA lay stretched out on her beige leather sofa, listening to Bach on her CD player, toying with the telephone, sipping at a glass of freshly uncorked Merlot, and wondering if she should call Richard Sharpe. The wine had mellowed her out, and she knew she could not dismiss a case simply on the basis of a whim. Still, before deciding to work again with James Parry, she wanted to discuss the awkward circumstances with Richard. But she hadn't told Richard about how she and Parry falsified records to put an end to the unrest in Hawaii. How much of the unsavory affair could she—should she—confide in him? What would he think of her falsifying an autopsy protocol, even if it were for the best of reasons? *The road to hell is paved with good intentions:* she toasted to the old saying, draining her glass, then wondered aloud, "Is a lie a lie if it is told to keep . . . to keep what? The peace?" She had not even confided this secret to John Thorpe. She stood and paced the room, phone in hand.

If Parry had been professionally "flogged" because these facts had come to light, then she, too, might soon be facing the Bureau's wrath, which would affect not only her but also Richard Sharpe, John Thorpe, Kim Desinor, and other close friends as well.

The sounds of Bach's "Well-Tempered Clavier" wafted through the apartment, and she stepped out onto her balcony, still holding the phone. Perhaps I'm making too much of the whole damned thing, she told herself.

Still, she owed Richard the truth. After all, he had granted her the courtesy of a phone call when he decided to continue with a case in London. Sure, he had already decided before making the call, but at least he had been man enough to lay his cards on the table.

She had to call him, one part of her brain sternly admonished her. "Or I might simply refuse the case," she said aloud to the night sky. She paced back into the living room, relief washing over her at having decided to remain in

Quantico. Someone had to nail Lawrence Hampton's coffin shut for what he had done to Adinatella. Sure, Hampton was the murderer, but his guilt remained to be proven beyond a doubt. Besides, what was so damnably important about Philadelphia's problem? Screw it. She'd tell Santiva—in a nice way—where he could stick it. "That's certainly an option," she announced to the empty room.

Jessica felt greatly relieved at having come to a decision on her own, without Richard. After all, he certainly did not call her every time he made a decision about a case in London.

She didn't know when she had fallen asleep on her plush couch rather than in bed. Still, her sleep was disturbed by a recurrent dream she'd had since childhood. In the dream, Jessica saw herself lying in a strange, garishly futuristic room; alongside her lay a little boy—or was it a girl? The child was wailing. This place felt cold and damp, and Jessica felt the depth of the child's fear. Together, they found themselves huddling within an impossible maze, a labyrinth from which no escape seemed possible, no matter the direction taken. They found every avenue blocked by a force which, while invisible and outwardly benign, was impossible to overcome.

Then something new insinuated itself into the familiar dream of frustrated efforts. Jessica's back began to burn, as if she'd been branded. As if her back had been set afire. Part of her psyche chalked it up to the photos Santiva had shared with her. Still, the nightmare had a singular reality and urgency about it as the maze widened to reveal itself as Philadelphia.

In her dream, someone was writing out her life in poetic lines across her back. This shadow figure had a gentle touch and an airy presence, as if the child she'd hoped to free from the maze had metamorphosed into a killer. The childlike being gleefully used an ancient pen that dug deep into flesh. Jessica could not make out the poetry etched into her flesh, but remorse and old regrets she thought long ago put to rest became wormlike letters that dug and burrowed into her now.

THREE

The world is a perpetual caricature of itself; at every moment it is the mockery and the contradiction of what it is pretending to be.

—Charles Dickens

JESSICA had had such dreams since earliest childhood, and a stint with Dr. Donna Lemonte had helped her to deal with the dreaded feelings of entrapment, near escape, and failure represented in the dreams. While the setting changed from dream to dream, the goal and the outcome always remained the same: *escape attempt fails.* Once the maze proved to be a concentration camp; another time it was a children's camp by a lake; another it was an opulent mansion yet a prison nonetheless, in which a trapped little boy/girl ran in circles, attempting to escape. Jessica would then appear from out of nowhere, like a guardian angel, assuring the little one that s/he had nothing to fear, that there *was* a way out, and that the adult knew how to find it. All the child needed was to take her hand and follow her lead; the entire time Jessica told the child repeatedly that she knew the way, that she had just come *back* that way, and that it was within their combined grasp, just around the next confusing turn.

Yet it always eluded the child and Jessica, leaving her with an overwhelming sense of futility, not fear, just a quicksand of hopelessness.

The dream, always lavish with color and extravagant with emotion, filled Jessica with both a sense of awe and a sharing of the child's enormous belief in the uselessness of their attempt to find freedom and happiness.

The worst part of the dream was the elaborate nature of the construct in which the boy/girl always found him/herself a prisoner, and the notion that the adult could unlock its secrets. Even as she promised her charge escape, the escape routes she knew so well always *changed* from moment to moment, inevitably leading back into the prison. Mazes within living mazes, undulating like the living poems on the backs of the victims in Philadelphia. The mazes came to life, reconstructing themselves like snakes in a pit, even as she led the freedom-starved child toward an exit.

The little boy/girl always grew impatient and horribly afraid that the maze master would find out about the escape attempt, and worse, that s/he had been betrayed by Jessica, that s/he could not trust her after all. The dream followed this cycle, turning back on itself, tripling in intensity, never reaching resolution.

Jessica had thought the dreams at an end; Dr. Lemonte had skillfully led her to realize that the fearful child in the dreams was none other than her own inner child, her inner self and soul. Donna—shrink to the FBI women, the shrink others had encouraged her to see—had explained, "In our dreams we often change sexes, especially when dealing with small children. You are, in effect, in the dream, subconsciously attempting to free yourself, and you are failing to do so. You are no hero to your inner child if you can't free him/her from what you've become."

Jessica's only chance at healing, according to the psychologist, was to deal with her inner child, talk to her true self, nurture a healthy and trusting relationship between Dr. Jessica Coran and the child she had buried within her so many years before, at a mazelike military base, be it in the Philippine islands, in Germany, or in Washington, D.C.

Giving time to be the child she had imprisoned in stone within herself must take precedence in her life now, she had been told.

All the various prisons came to represent that dark little place called a military base, the squares and rectangles of an artificial village, all neatly set off, each with its own four-by-four garden, all the blurred places where she, as a military brat, had grown up. And it all made sense, and all the child faces she saw, all pleading with her for escape, all came to represent her. It had all made perfect sense, like the pieces of a puzzle finally located and fitted together.

So why had the dream returned here and now, after so long? And why had it thrust upon her a sense of desolation, fear even, that she had in all this time accomplished nothing for her inner child and the relationship between her adult self and her child? Was it the same dream or a new one? Did it represent something real or imagined? Had it to do with the Philadelphia case, the one she had so cavalierly tossed aside? What of the dead or the soon-to-be dead—the next victim engulfed by the enticing words of the Poet Killer? Why did she feel so absolutely, emotionally cold?

She snatched at invisible covers and gave in to the fears of the child residing deep within. She allowed his/her fears full vent, as she had on so many other occasions, having promised her former child *self* that she would never desert it again. Giving herself over to her child, experiencing the childhood dread, was supposed to work. But she felt powerless against the overpowering sense of dread and futility. How could she help the child she was supposed to have been, the one she had hidden from the world, if she could not free herself from fear today, in the here and now?

The fear proved too great. Nothing Dr. Lemonte had told her was working.

An FBI forensic specialist in need of a shrink. Even Jessica found it laughable. What would others think of it?

Suddenly the phone came alive with its purring noise. She lifted the receiver, wondering if Richard had somehow read her thoughts from an ocean away.

"Jessica?" came the female voice at the other end. "It's me, Kim."

Kim Faith Desinor was the FBI's psychic specialist and a psychiatrist with the Behavioral Science Unit, the same unit Jessica worked for. A scientist of the paranormal, Kim was usually used by the Bureau as a last resort in a high-profile case. Kim had most recently helped local police on a case that involved child torture and murder. Using her psychic detection ability, Kim Desinor solved the Child Snatcher case in Houston, working with the infamous Texas Cherokee Detective Lucas Stonecoat and a police psychiatrist named Meredyth Sanger. Kim had confided to Jessica that working with Stonecoat had been like riding with John Wayne or Clint Eastwood in a nitroglycerin-carrying covered wagon with bad shocks.

Jessica had worked with Kim to solve the case of the Heartthrob Killer in New Orleans four years before.

"Kim, how're you doing?"

"More to the point, how're you doing, kiddo?"

"So you've heard?"

"Regardless of the popular image, the FBI is actually a fairly close-knit community, sweetheart. Some of us care about your welfare."

"So, everybody now knows about Jim and me possibly working a case together again?"

"Including Jim, yes."

"Like old times, and I'm the last to know . . ."

"Not quite like old times. There is the matter of your new love, Richard Sharpe."

"You think I shouldn't do it?" Jessica sipped at her wine between words.

"Talk to Donna Lemonte."

Lemonte had gone from being Jessica's shrink to one of her most trusted friends. "God, lately that's everybody's answer to everything I say."

"Why not see what Donna has to say about it?" pressed Kim.

"I want *your* opinion. Woman to woman, friend to friend."

"Okay, do it."

No hesitation in this woman. "Why? Why should I take on this kind of . . . crap?"

"Closure, that's why."

"Closure?"

"Every relationship that ends really ought to have closure, especially one that ends badly, say, like . . . over the phone!" Kim's last words hit home.

"Exactly what I would say to a friend in my situation. Still . . . shit, I don't need this, Kim."

"I know you better than that," Kim persisted. "A relationship without closure is as lousy as . . . as a mystery novel missing the last page. Nothing gets settled, emotions are in turmoil, and it lingers on endlessly without your knowing the final *why*."

As usual her friend made sense. Still Jessica said nothing, thinking of the dream she'd been yanked from.

"Go with me to Philadelphia, Jess. I'll help you any way I can."

Jessica knew Kim meant that she would help her with any personal turmoil involving Parry as well as the case. "Thanks," she muttered.

"Meantime, we have a unique case in Quaker City."

Jessica felt a bit foolish. She hadn't given the case half the thought she'd given to James Parry. No doubt psychiatrist Donna Lemonte would have made great gobs of critical gravy over her failure to scrutinize the case with her usual fervor, all due to James Parry. Jessica hadn't been seeing Donna professionally for years. Although she was now more of a friend than a doctor, perhaps a talk with Donna was in order.

Kim asked, "Do you know that the killer in Philadelphia is leaving poems at each crime scene? Etched into the victims' backs?"

"I know. Do you recall the Night Crawler in Miami?"

"Sure . . . who forgets the creepiest of the creeps?"

"He did the same—left poetic lines like crumbs wherever he went. His poems were filled with venomous hatred toward women. It's not unusual. We learned a great deal about the bastard from his handwriting."

"Miami was a bitch. Sure, I saw the clues left by the killer there. He used lines from that poet who never capitalized, the British counterpart of e.e. cummings."

"Yeah, e.j. hellering's poems. Killer used them to get his point across, but hellering's stuff wasn't what I'd call memorable by any stretch."

"This guy's poetry is not maniacal, and it's not filled with anger or hatred, Jess. The crime scenes are bloodless, pristine in fact, and it's all in terrible contradiction to the idea of a rampage, yet the word keeps insinuating itself on me. Strange. As to the poetry I've seen thus far, it's . . . it is rather mesmerizing, haunting on some strange level I can't quite comprehend."

"Really? It's that good?"

"To my mind it recalls some of the English-lit. classes I endured in college, but the subject matter is modern."

"Coleridge, Keats, Wadsworth?"

"Don't you mean Wordsworth, dear?"

"English literature was never my best subject," Jessica replied, "and I found a lot of the old poetry to be a wad of it, so I'll stick with *Wads*worth."

Kim laughed.

Jessica now asked, "So if not Wordsworth, then who? Shelley, Keats?"

"Try Gerald Manley Hopkins, or better yet Lord Byron. Again not in style or even form, but something melancholy and haunting about the quality of the mind behind it. Brooding . . . like Byron."

Jessica paused before saying, "Really? Byron. Haven't thought of Byron since I was in college."

"I don't mean to say that the poetry is equal to Byron's, or even that it's similar. And as I said, it's certainly not written in the same style. But something about it reminds me of Byron."

"Such as?"

"The Byronic hero—man against the herd, man against establishment—but in this case life itself, being born into this existence is the fiend, the reviled establishment, if you will. And I think, or rather feel, that the Poet Killer is himself or herself a flawed character in the *scene* the killer is creating, perhaps wantonly so."

"Somewhat melodramatic, isn't it?"

"Scatch the surface of Byron and what're you left with but melodrama? I'm telling you this poisoner thinks of himself as the lone man standing against the machine of society, the establishment, the human condition, you name it."

"That is remarkable. You've gotten all that from the victim photos?"

"Copies actually, but yes. Eriq faxed 'em to me. But I really need to see the originals, lay my hands on the real deal. Parry's told me that can be arranged."

Over the phone line, Jessica heard Kim's hands thumbing through papers. "Let me read you what we have so far from the killer. It's known that this fellow left behind flowers and wine along with the poems. Some task-force members think these may be offerings, keepsakes for the deceased to take to the other side with them."

Jessica took a moment to listen intently to the poetic lines, nodding as she did so. When Kim had finished, she said, "You may be onto something here, Kim."

"Aside from the classic feel of the poems, the killer's . . . I don't know . . . writing to the gods, the fates, the angels, as well as to the victims he dispatches, but he's not directing a word to anyone in authority, anyone, say, like you or me . . ."

Jessica asked, "What're you saying?"

"He's not at all interested in us. His poems are an homage to the victims, what you'd call . . ."

"Eulogies?"

"Exactly."

"That *is* a new wrinkle. A guy kills you and then writes your eulogy."

"Loves to write your epitaph on your corpus delecti," Kim quipped. "Really would like to get my hands on the originals."

Jessica knew what she meant. Kim was a *psychometrist:* she "read" information from the objects a victim or a killer handled. She had received vivid images both in the New Orleans case and in the Houston case merely by handling objects belonging to the victims.

"Want to feel the originals, don't you? But that means laying your hands on the bodies in Philadelphia."

"Hands-on, right. One reason I need to go there. I want you to hear another of the poems. Listen to this one, Jess."

Kim read the lines the killer had penned, the lines that had killed one of his victims:

> *Chance . . . whose desire*
> *is to have a meeting*
> *with stunned innocence . . .*

and to tell it again;
luminescent green
is the color
of the script,
and ice-blue hues
embrace the images.
They make skin
crawl with miniature
electric devotions,
huddled and yearning,
hushed whispers waiting
on the shadow
of a flickering light.

"Whew . . . pretty heavy shit," Jessica remarked, unsure what to say.

"The Philly detectives think the killer is working out of some sense of pity for his victims. Maybe he sees his murders as an act of mercy."

"Yeah, I got that much from Eriq. But this sounds like a type of mercy killer we haven't seen before."

"Mercy killer, maybe . . . that is, we only know that Philly PD has characterized him as such. Seems the fellow kills his victims after sharing wine, cheese, and a laying-on of a deadly pen."

"Wine and cheese I get, but what kind of pen is he using?"

"Something around the turn of the century or a couple, few years before. Definitely dips the thing, as he's left drops of poisonous inkstains on bedclothes and floor. From the depth of the cuts, it's been surmised that the delivery system is sharp."

" 'Cutting edge' long before high tech adopted the word?" suggested Jessica, wincing. "Sounds painful."

"Not if you're knocked out on booze. Bread and wine,

wine and cheese, sometimes pizza; point is, they spend a long and pleasant evening together, killer and victim, ending with a bit of poison—a poison, by the way, that continues to defy analysis. No one seems to be able to agree on its properties or give it a name. And as a final touch, his victims appear to sit for the poetic writing, er . . . killing, willingly."

"Persuasive guy, this Shakespeare. What kind of profile do they have on him?"

"Mixed bag. Not even sure he's a he; could just as well be a female killer, given the choice of weapons. As to the victims, two women, one man, all young, all into New Age thinking and beliefs, all living in an area that's gone apeshit for this new craze of 'living poetry,' and curiously enough no other tattoos or nose rings or tongue piercings found on the vics."

"Conservative about how they used their bodies, but all talked into doing the body-writing thing," Jessica mused.

"Save for that, their ages, the fact that they appear to have been easily beguiled, and their close geographical proximity to one another and to the clubs, they have little in common."

"Sounds like an unusual victim type."

"Well, this guy in Philly—or woman—his or her poetics are different."

"Do you get a sense that maybe it's a woman, Kim? And what exactly do you mean by different, huh? How so?"

"I don't know for sure, but one thing's certain: it's a gentle person, feminine, I suspect, in many ways. At the same time I'm getting this singularly masculine word insinuating itself on any reading I do."

"What word is that?"

"It's paradoxical, just the opposite of femininity."

"What's the word, Kim?"

"Rampage."

"Rampage? As in *kill spree* rampage?"

"All I know is the word keeps coming through loud and clear."

"Hardly a gentle, feminine word."

"Precisely . . . so . . . how am I to be sure of the gender of the poet?"

"Maybe it's coming through from somewhere else? The victims, maybe?"

"I don't know . . . yet. But *rampage* keeps forcing itself into my readings."

"Maybe it has some symbolic meaning, then?"

"Maybe it's a quiet rampage, like a personal quest."

"Rampage . . . quest . . ." Jessica muttered. "You think?"

"The word *quirk* or *quark* is also coming through, along with a number."

"What number?"

"Nineteen . . . means nothing in and of itself, but I get it strong and clear."

Jessica bit her lip. "Let's hope that's not a preset number of victims he's planning to sacrifice."

"I can't say one way or the other, not really."

"What do you think of the poetry itself?" asked Jessica.

"I believe the poetry is original. Nothing else like it in my experience, and the killer is definitely sending a message of some sort."

Jessica thought of her parting words with Eriq Santiva earlier. He had left the ball in her court, saying she must decide by eleven P.M. and *that* hour had come and gone. Now Kim sat perched on the phone with her, doing all she could to persuade her to take on the case. Had Santiva sicced Kim onto her? Kim's words even sounded like Santiva's, as she ended with, "So, Jess, are you in or out? Do you want to have a look into this or not? I leave the decision up to you."

Yes, Kim sounded as if she were reading lines from Santiva's script. "Eriq put you up to this phone call, didn't he?" Jessica wanted her to admit it. If she did, then perhaps there was no cause for alarm; if she denied it, then there must surely be.

"What, I can't call a dear friend and beg her help?"

Both women knew that if Jessica took on the case, it would be for two reasons: her unquenchable curiosity as a forensic scientist, and the need for closure on a long-term relationship.

"Well, all right, Jess. Eriq and I discussed it from top to bottom, and we both feel that you're the best person for the task, and frankly, I'm not sure I'm going without you."

"I'll see you at the airstrip at six A.M. tomorrow, Kim."

"Good . . . good. Would you like me to inform Eriq?"

"That's your call."

"*My* call?"

"Thanks, yes." Decision made, Jessica hung up, still wondering when and how she would tell Richard of her new case and its connection with James Parry.

THE Poet Lord liked the apartment dimly lit, and so the thickly embroidered, burgundy-and-gray tapestry that covered the larger windows pleased his eye on waking. Music of another period poured from the CD set on continual play. The poet had slept to the music of an Italian opera. Incense filled the room with a delicate sandalwood scent, and the tapered candles had burned down to stubs, creating tentacled stalagmites of the cooling wax over the arms of the candelabra at his bedside.

The poet clawed toward wakefulness, somehow touching foot to floor and staggering through the apartment, clicking on the coffeepot and showering for the day.

The apartment walls stared back at the poet. All the eyes watched from all the paintings, prints he'd gathered as cheaply as possible, framed and placed at increasingly smaller intervals around the rooms. In fact, the wall could hardly be made out for the prints. Maxfield Parrish, Edward Burne-Jones, Waterhouse and his disciples, Hieronymus Bosch's visions of heaven, an assortment of enchanted visions of paradise, some depicting it as another realm entirely, others depicting it—or its closest approximation—as a place here on earth. All the poet's paintings spoke of lost times and lost souls. Each of his victims had seen this shrine, and all had shared his taste in art, music, and literature. None of them had the least interest in Beanie Babies, makeup kits, inflation, or current events. None had watched a TV sitcom in years, and none of the one's he'd helped to pass over even knew firsthand what a skin blemish was. Prerequisite to having the poet sponsor someone as a living poem.

With coffee in hand, The Lord Poet Messenger of Misspent Time did what every Philadelphian did on a Monday morning: he struggled to consciousness. He staggered about his small castlelike place with its black-sky ceiling overhead, its earth tones all around, and its stone-tiled floor selected specifically for its old-world appearance.

The staggering was a dance performed each morning, but it was particularly acute after pulling an all-nighter with someone special, someone not of this world, someone chosen to be sent over.

After a pot of coffee and a roll, he located the remote and scanned the news channels for any mention of the body's having been discovered. Nothing, nada, zip, not a word. He imagined that the body would be found before long. The poet would keep an eye out and an ear open. While it mattered little to him what authorities thought of his work, he wished to stay informed and to remain above suspicion so that he might carry on with the necessary labor. After all, he had a universe to save. A crusade had been taken up, and this crusade to stomp out ignorance, eradicate fear, and end the poverty of impoverished souls—this had become the true calling of the poet.

But for now, it was off to work, a taxing, energy-draining job, the nine-to-whenever grind.

Still, the poet paused to think of each of his lovers, the ones he had chosen for the ultimate journey. He pictured his first victim, Micellina Petryna. She had been so beautiful in her purity and naïveté. There was an angelic quality even in her self-deprecation. The most worthy never know their worth, he thought now. She had attracted the poet the moment she stepped into view, and when she received the first love sonnet the poet had written to her, she had not been frightened off, but rather touched.

They met for coffee on several occasions, talking mostly—of poetry and literature, the classics and the modern classics. Each flattered the other on their choices of the best lines ever penned by man- or womankind. She was hungry for the attention he lavished on her, and easily led as a result, and the very qualities that made her angelic also made her vulnerable to the lies, lies necessary to carry out the mission.

He recalled how, on that last night they'd spent together, he'd told her how much he both admired her and helplessly loved her in that special spiritual way reserved only for the most intimate of souls, those souls who miraculously did what most could not. "And what is that?" she'd asked, staring into the poet's flaming eyes.

"To both locate and then hold on to the gift of a soul mate."

They had closed down the little coffeehouse where they'd met. She'd so opened up, revealing every detail of herself and the horrors of her everyday existence. She'd been molested as a child by a stepmother, and she had sought therapy for the emotional scars. Now she promised,

"I'm working on relating to other women more and more, but I gotta tell you, it's not easy. You . . . you're so understanding, so gentle and caring. I've never met anyone quite like you. There's a fire in your eyes when you're listening to me talk, and that's so cool, so attractive."

She was right about the poet; he was the most gentle being she would ever encounter in this world. His eyes blazed with the light of attentiveness whenever someone bared his or her soul, as Micellina, Caterina, and Anton had all done before leaving this world.

True enough, a fire burned behind the poet's eyes, the fire of a crusader, a person on a quest for the holiest of spirits on this plane. The Holy Grail was not a thing, not a chalice, not an object, but a soul, a rare soul indeed. It mattered not a whit that some sordid and polluted moment existed in their pasts on this plane, or even if they were presently sleeping with someone, for they remained innocent of their own true natures, innocent of the power they wielded, the power of their souls when taken by the angels. And while none of the chosen had been old enough to have committed any great sins against God or man—none had been cheats, liars, whores, none had practiced prostitution or promiscuity of either the worldly kind or the ethereal kind that characterized so many so-called experts on art and creativity. Certainly, no one in this life remained pure. People didn't long endure on this plane without smut attracting to them. Only the children of the angels, chosen by the poet to go over, remained pure of heart and being.

This had certainly been the case with Caterina Mercedes, the poet thought, groggily getting up and searching for something to wear to work this morning. While Micellina had been easy to lead, Caterina had been a holdout. It had taken a great deal more persuasion to convince her that it was in her best interest to have a private moment with the poet. When she finally acquiesced, it proved almost as hard to get her to meet with him a second time. She had serious reservations about seeing him privately, and she had serious doubts as to his intentions, almost up to the end. But the poet's dexterity with words, both spoken and written, finally won her over. In the end, Caterina, like Micellina, felt a joyous and heartfelt obligation to carry out the poet's plan—to write her into eternity. They had both, in the end, willingly gone over, first believing they would achieve a kind of immortality among their peers for displaying the poems on their backs, but in the end knowing that he had a greater immortality in store for them.

Then came Anton Pierre, a beautiful young man, not unlike the two women who had preceded him in physical beauty and mental purity.

The poet stepped from the modest apartment, located the elevator, and with his valise in hand soon stood on the avenue fronting his building. A penniless man with a squirt bottle in hand asked if he could hail a cab for the poet. He nodded, indicating that yes, he would like the beggar to help him, but to remain at a safe distance. As he waited for the cab, he felt a wave of revulsion wash over him at the sight of the derelict. When a cab pulled over, he threw a five-dollar bill at the homeless man and rushed to enter the cab, glad to be speeding off.

It wasn't every day he took a cab to work, but it looked like rain again, and he'd left his umbrella in the stand, the one with the Victorian hounds that stared out at the poet, hounds whose eyes burned with a fire to match the poet's own.

FOUR

We must not make a scarecrow of the law,
Setting it up to fear the birds of prey.

—William Shakespeare

Dr. Jessica Coran stepped from the soupy Virginia fog that enveloped Quantico Naval Air Station to greet Dr. Kim Desinor. Taking her by the hand, Jessica said, "The boys at the hangar have a new toy to play with, a Soviet-built MiG tactical helicopter. It's not exactly new to us, nothing like a big mystery, but they're incredible machines. I think I've convinced them to transport us to Philadelphia in it instead of in that boring departmental Cessna Citation."

"That boring Cessna is just fine with me, Jess."

"But you want to know you're flying, don't you?"

"Flying's one thing, hovering Peter Pan fashion in something like a spinning top is quite another."

"No, it's more like a magic carpet ride or a floating platform. Come on, you'll love it. I think they've got clearance."

"Why do we have a Soviet helicopter?" Kim asked.

"Part of the struggle to fight boredom, the struggle to stomp out ignorance, all of it. We swapped ours for theirs. Happens all the time. They have our technology, we have theirs, everyone's happy, and no need for the spy business."

"With the Russians? We do this with the Russians?"

"KGB, Russian military, sure. Look at this machine, will you?"

Kim glared at the thing like an angry cat.

Jessica, ignoring this, said, "I've only had the privilege of flying in her once before. She's decked out with lounge seats and a Bureau VIP bar—at a cost government watchdogs must never know about."

"So, I see you've already met the pilot and crew, as usual. Are you staking a claim?" Kim knew of Jessica's love for flying, one of her many passions. In fact, Jessica had earned her pilot's license some years back.

"Staking a claim? I'm spoken for, remember? Richard Sharpe. You're not still sore about New Orleans, are you?" Jessica recalled how on first meeting Kim, she had behaved badly. Not in the best frame of mind, knowing she was being stalked by an escaped convicted bloodsucking killer who had fixated on her, her nerves shot, Jessica had drunk too much on the flight, and she had flirted with the pilot. She recalled how wrong that first meeting with Kim had gone, and how patient Kim had been with her, showing her great understanding and giving her the benefit of the doubt several times.

"All I know is that every time you fly off someplace, you cozy up to the pilot or you wind up at the controls of the plane."

"Come on. I wasn't at the controls for more than ten minutes."

"Or you land yourself a new bureau-chief boyfriend, or a boyfriend who happens to be Scotland Yard. I'm so impressed!" She did a mock curtsy right there on the airstrip.

"You make me sound like a loose woman on the prowl!"

Kim laughed. "Not at all. Liberated, a role model for others all over the globe who have succumbed to the stereotype of barefoot and pregnant and in the kitchen."

"Please, give it a rest, Kim. What about your love life?

You still seeing Alex Sincebaugh, or has he uprooted himself and returned to New Orleans?"

"He's holding on in Baltimore, but he hates his situation. I'm not sure how long he's going to fight it."

"You can take the boy outta the bayou, but you can't—"

"I see him most weekends and holidays. Some truth in that old saying 'Absence makes the heart grow fonder.' "

"That's crap and you know it; only works for a while before the charm of the distance between you wears off. I know from experience."

"The alternative, cohabiting, is just as impossible, if not more so."

"What's a girl to do?"

Boarding the wide-bodied helicopter, Jessica patted her inside suit pocket to be certain she hadn't forgotten her special scalpel; her father had given it to her the day she'd told him she meant to go to medical school. Nowadays, she never left home without it. In fact, she felt downright superstitious about having it near at hand.

Jessica and Kim looked at each other in the modified, VIP interior of the monster chopper. While they worked together at profiling sessions in the same building and in the same unit, each saw surprisingly little of the other.

"Pity the bar's not open," Kim lamented.

"And what would you do with an open bar this ungodly time of morning?"

"Not the bar, the bartender, dear. You like pilots, I have a weakness for bartenders."

Jessica laughed. It felt good after the tension of the day before. "Here, have some coffee." Rolls and coffee lay on the table between them. "Eriq's so thoughtful."

After they sat down, Jessica watched Kim gulp back stomach bile instead of the rich coffee as the churning blades suddenly roared to life. An attendant young enough to be Jessica's daughter quickly secured the coffeepot and soon they felt themselves slowly rise above the airstrip. With a sudden, violent jerk, the helicopter veered to the left and sped diagonally upward.

"What the hell's that pilot doing?" Kim shouted over the thrum of the MiG.

"His job!" Jessica smirked.

Next the chopper pilot poured on the speed, plastering them to their seats. "Like a carnival ride," Jessica shouted.

Kim felt every cell in her body tug outward. "I feel like a piece of cargo being tossed around in the hold!" This despite the seat belt she wore. "What did you tell the pilot, Jess? You didn't tell him that you wanted a wild ride, did you? You did, didn't you! Tell me you didn't!"

Jessica's smiled and her eyes lit up. "Doncha love it?"

In a moment the helicopter leveled out. The noise of the rotors took on a new pitch, the sound a whisper by comparison. Next the helicopter took on a new feel—that of a bird in flight, smooth and controlled.

At this point, Jessica unfastened her seat belt and said, "Maybe I'll just have a word with the pilot."

"It's a little too late to tell him to take it easy on his joystick, wouldn't you say?"

"I won't be but a minute."

"You're incorrigible, you know that?" Kim protested as Jessica made her way to the nose of the helicopter. "Why don't you tip him?" she shouted, knowing the sound of her racing heart and the rotor blades only drowned her out.

Kim opened a briefcase she'd carried on board and drew out a manila folder. She was opening it just as Jessica returned with the coffeepot. Jessica again saw the three victim photos that Eriq Santiva had shown her earlier, but included in this group were blown-up shots of the backs, the rust-colored, near-red lettering left behind by the killer. "Damn but this looks like something out of an Edgar Allan Poe story."

"And the narrator of the tale, this Killer Poet, has to be as mad as one of Poe's narrators," Kim agreed.

"It's likely a selective madness, one he controls when in the company of others. He's got to be some kind of sadist beneath it all, a true sociopath."

"Maybe not, Jess."

"What do you mean?"

"Read the poems. They're hardly sadistic or evil in intent; our boy or girl is—at least inside his or her mind—doing good, perhaps doing God's own work."

Jessica recognized the one poem as the eulogy that Kim had already read to her over the phone. The other two began with the same three lines about chance meeting innocence.

"Read 'em through," said Kim. "Familiarize yourself with the style, the voice, whatever you want to call it. After a while the poems get a little scary and . . . and something else, but I'll let you decide."

"Scary?"

"I don't know . . . disturbing, like they have a life of their own. This murdering poet writes some truly engaging stuff; it catches you up so much that you actually forget that it was used as a murder weapon."

"I'll have another look." Jessica read the two poems she hadn't yet seen or heard. The first read:

> *Chance . . . whose desire*
> *is to have a meeting*
> *with stunned innocence . . .*
> *is a humming that wells up*

in silver moonbeams appearing
to the eyes like twin specters
softly caressing the drapes,
trembling, yet unafraid,
languorous and expectant
of a touch in return.
Beneath it all: a bed
of fibrous dictation.
I am drawn forth, found out,
brushed with the feather
of your glance.
Speaking to a mirror
sparkling with never-
before phrases,
all against the marble
life flickering.

"Strangely sonorous stuff," offered Jessica, nodding. "I see how you might get caught up in it, but not enough to allow someone to Etch A Sketch on your back."

"The poetry is so . . . melodic and obtuse at once, so that while I'm not always sure what's intended, I don't much care so long as I can hear the music."

"You mean it's kind of like reading Carl Sagan on the universe?"

"Maybe." Kim laughed. "I mean that while he's difficult at times to follow . . . what a way this guy has of lullabying you into thinking sound makes sense, huh? And I'd hardly call it pathological or the words of a lunatic."

"Maybe it all makes sense to the killer, Kim. How many times have we seen a killer create rationalizations for actions that led to murder? Whether it looks like the ravings of a madman or not, he may well be channeling voices in his head that ultimately tell him to kill."

Jessica next studied the blown-up shot of the second

deadly poem. Again, the torn flesh looked like blood-orange script on a clay tablet, but this was poisoned ink written into human flesh.

She read the second poem:

> *Chance . . . whose desire*
> *is to have a meeting*
> *with stunned innocence . . .*
> *is drawn up and perched*
> *to fall into the mirror pool,*
> *through meshes of metaphor*
> *to disentangle and leave behind*
> *unbound fingers of touch.*
> *Sensing sounds in choruses*
> *of falling water crashing*
> *on nearby rock,*
> *I hear harmony touching*
> *my hand where gazes*
> *fall into place.*
> *The breath that exhales*
> *across the candle fails,*
> *and so it remains, flickering.*

"And so, and further thoughts?" Kim asked.

Jessica breathed in as much air as she could and slowly exhaled. "It's definitely the work of the same person. Along with the one I read before, and the one you read me, it feels almost as if . . ."

"Yes?"

"As if these weren't three separate poems at all, but—"

"Go on, but what?"

"But one long ongoing . . ."

"Dirge, yes. I agree."

"Like a lament."

"A death march," agreed Kim.

Nodding, Jessica added, "Over in London they'd refer to it as a threnody."

"Yes, a hymn, a requiem, all one piece. I just wanted someone else to tell me I wasn't crazy."

"You think they follow in a sequence?"

"I'm not sure. I mean I've transcribed them and put them in the order of the killings, but there seems to be something . . . I don't know . . . missing, as if the killer doesn't know all the pieces yet himself. Or perhaps it wasn't meant to be written in order, because—"

"Because the missing parts haven't as yet been completed."

"Which likely means more bodies."

"Exactly."

The chopper began its descent. Jessica strapped in once again. Kim had never loosened her belt.

JESSICA stared out the window. She knew Philadelphia well, having lived there for a time with her military family. She now pointed out the banks of the Delaware and, in the distance, Burlington, New Jersey. Then she pointed to another river. "That's the Schuylkill River."

"School-kill? Is that anything like roadkill? What a strange name for a river, but it seems to fit with the chaos of the modern age," replied Kim.

"It's pronounced 'school-kill,' but it's an Indian word. Oh, look." Jessica pointed again. "Scullers on the river."

Both women watched the machinelike rhythm of flashing oars in the hands of competing crews. The oars looked like blades, and their smooth, deft movement through the water was perfectly synchronized, giving boat and crew an appearance not unlike that of a gliding animal in its natural haunt.

Jessica and Kim made out the roofline of Colonial country houses and villas, and next the looming dome of Memorial Hall, a remnant of the Centennial Exposition. Soon they were over Boathouse Row, the Fairmount Waterworks, and the best view of the skyline of modern Philadelphia and the promenade leading up to the Museum of Art, the stairway made famous by the movie *Rocky*. The streets here, lined with parkways and universities and museums, reminded Jessica of Washington, D.C.'s Pennsylvania Avenue.

The city was famous for both its Quaker roots—hospitality and brotherly love—and for the ease with which people could get around, thanks to William Penn's surveyor general, Thomas Holme. Holme had laid out the city streets in 1682 on a grid quite visible from the air. The resulting rectangle, two miles long and one mile wide, enclosed approximately 1,280 acres between the Delaware and the picturesque Schuylkill River.

"East-to-west streets are named for trees," Jessica told Kim. "North-to-south are numbered."

"How . . . efficient."

"Quaint, too, but there's a catch."

"Naturally."

"Early settlers counted back from both rivers, requiring each street to be additionally identified as Schuylkill Second or Delaware Third, and so on."

"You're putting me on."

"Actually, city fathers put things right around the turn of the century. The numbering now begins on the Delaware River side and moves westward to the city limits. Makes cab hopping a lot easier."

"I should think."

"If you'd like, Dr. Coran," came the helicopter pilot's voice over the PA system, "I'll take you over the city first. We can pass the air station field for a helipad at Police

Precinct One downtown. This'll cut out the need for a cab, and you'll have a nice view of the downtown area."

Jessica put on a headset resting on her chair and spoke. "Thanks, Pete! That would save us a lot of hassle."

Center Square with its massive Colonial-style city hall then came into view. When it had been erected in 1901, Philadelphia's city hall stood as the tallest and largest public building in the United States. "This area is the true heart of the city," commented Jessica. "Philly is a walker's city."

"A walker's city?"

"Down here it's impossible to get lost, given the layout, and in any direction you're going to run into an oasis with a park bench."

Kim and Jessica saw the greenery of George Washington Park, David Rittenhouse Park, Benjamin Franklin Park, and James Logan Park, each flanked on all sides by traffic.

"Rush hour looks like hell," commented Kim, pointing out a long snake of snarled metal on the street below.

"It is. Streets look quaint and narrow from up here, don't they?"

"Yes."

"Fact is, the streets *are* quaint and narrow."

"A quaint pain in the ass for those poor devils stuck in gridlock," muttered Kim, breaking into a laugh. "While we blithely fly above it all."

"Yeah, like winged goddesses."

"Goddesses; really, Jessica," Kim replied in mock amazement.

A moment of static gave way to the pilot's voice over the PA again. "Doctors, welcome to Philly. Home of the Flyers, the 76ers, the Eagles, cheesesteak sandwiches, Mummers, funky South Street, gateway to the Jersey Shore, the Liberty Bell, and don't forget soft pretzels."

The chopper pilot worked his magic, aligning the machine with what looked to Kim Desinor like a postage stamp—the helipad atop the building. Jessica smiled at how calmly Pete brought the huge Soviet-made monster into the center of the *X* on the helipad marker. But her smile waned on seeing the people awaiting them at Philadelphia's police headquarters. Pete had called ahead, alerting officials of their arrival.

An uncharacteristic quiver could be seen in Jessica's jaw as she made out Area Special Agent in Charge James Parry, his broad-shouldered form standing beside what appeared to be the chief of police and most likely the detective in charge of the Philly task force, a towering dark-haired Sigourney Weaver look-alike.

Jessica saw that behind his resolute stance, Parry's nerves must be somewhat frazzled, the quiver in her jaw being matched by the clenched fists. He appeared as anxious about the prospect of working with her as she was with him.

"He knows you're coming, Jess," said Kim, as if reading her mind. "He likely wants closure on this relationship as much as you, so just go easy."

Jessica sat silent, unable to respond, her thoughts racing. She flashed on all the extremely happy moments she'd spent in James's presence, all the trips they'd shared, all the passion, and all the heartache.

"You okay, Jess?" Kim had reached out a hand to lay over her friend's. She had not missed Jessica's narrowing eyes and gritted teeth on seeing Parry.

"It's been a hell of a ride getting here," Jessica replied, "but it's going to be even more hell seeing this through, I fear."

Kim said into Jessica's ear, "But nothing you can't handle."

"Thanks for the vote of confidence. I'm not so sure."

"You've faced far worse foes. This will be a cakewalk for Jessica Coran."

"I'm not at all sure."

"Hang tough, girl."

"You sound like my father."

"I'll take that as a compliment."

"Absolutely."

The helicopter touched down and the blades began to slow. To Jessica, the big Soviet chopper's last groan felt like her insides, and it sounded like the final breath of a dinosaur. She steeled herself to get up, step out, and meet anew her former lover, James Parry, special agent in charge of the Poet Killer case.

"God, I feel like I'm going to stumble or say something stupid," she confided in Kim.

"If you stumble, just be sure not to fall into his arms."

"You'll catch me, then?"

"Count on it."

"Thanks, Kim." Jessica clamped onto her friends hand and squeezed.

"Don't mention it. What're friends for?"

WHEN she looked directly into James Parry's eyes, Jessica felt her knees weaken with the memories—vivid, precise, and unbidden—that flooded her mind, memories of the most intimate, most delightful moments on holidays they had spent traveling around the globe. James's sandy-brown hair now had a liberal dusting of gray, making it appear lighter, but otherwise he looked the same. A tall, handsome man with broad shoulders and a winning smile, he stood as straight as an oak. She wondered how she would ever completely free herself of him, but then she wondered if it was worth the energy even to try. The sadness and pain of her memory of James would be a part of her forever.

After all this time, after all she and Richard Sharpe now meant to each other, one part of her mind fought to hold on to her and Jim's love, or at least to the spirit of that love. At the same time, another part of her fought to pry it from memory. She felt like a wounded wolf wanting to chew its paw off to free itself from a trap.

Focus, she heard her father's admonition from the grave, *focus on the job at hand, Jess.*

During introductions, there was just enough awkwardness between Jessica and Parry to alert even the dullest mind in the group. Afterward, something inside Jessica told her to relax. She owed the investigation her full attention and support, and she owed Parry nothing other than her thanks for a long and wonderful relationship, and her thanks, after all, for his having once saved her life. Instead of focusing on James—who failed the "cool" test, first by stammering that he'd already had the pleasure, then by offering his hand to shake only to retract it immediately— Jessica turned her attention to the other man, a solidly built fullback type with a limp, who appeared to rock his way along rather than walk.

The police chief introduced himself as Aaron Roth and added, "I am putting all my faith in this team, ladies and gentlemen, and I fully expect to see results soon. Is that clear, everyone?"

He then introduced the tall, stick-thin woman beside him as Lieutenant Leanne Sturtevante, whose firm handshake, take-charge air, and strong voice made it clear that, as she said, "I am heading up and coordinating the Philadelphia Police Department's task force on the Poet Predator, as the press has dubbed the murderer." Jessica recognized Sturtevante's need to take immediate control of the situation—not unlike herself—and she knew they would have difficulty working together unless they tried extra hard to be sensitive to each other's rough edges.

Sturtevante next said, "If you'll follow me, I'll show you our ready room and introduce you to Dr. Shockley, who has had the bodies protocoled." The detective started away as she talked, setting a brisk pace for Jessica, Kim, and the men.

"How much does the press know about his MO?" Jessica asked.

"They know the killer's leaving poems for us to ponder, but they don't know he's cutting the poems into his victims' backs," replied Sturtevante. "They know his weapon of choice is poison, but they don't know the poison is in the ink. Still . . . it's only a matter of time before it all comes out."

"We're trying to keep a lid on the details for as long as possible," added Parry, "but the newshounds smell something, and it's impossible to get them off the scent. Everyone in Philadelphia knows we're withholding information at this point."

They entered the building's rooftop service elevator. As the door closed, Roth pushed one button, Sturtevante another. "We'll want to see more than the protocols from Dr. Shockley," Jessica said. "We'll want to see the bodies."

"Both of you?" asked Sturtevante.

"Both of us," replied Kim.

"That can be arranged, right, Leanne?" said Roth.

"Absolutely."

Chief Aaron Roth sucked in his gut and nodded to them with a perfunctory smile. "I'm afraid I must rush away to a charity fund-raiser." Gritting his teeth, he added, "Commissioner expects me to play a part. Keep me apprised every step of the way, Leanne."

Jessica saw beads of perspiration forming on Chief Roth's forehead even in the relative cool of the elevator. His breathing sounded like the thrum of a poorly working refrigerator. She also smelled the acrid odor of tobacco that clung to every pore and hair of his body. A heart attack waiting to happen, she thought when the elevator doors opened on Roth's floor. He stepped off and waved an automatic good-bye.

"It was nice to've met you, Doctors. Happy hunting, as they say." He then coughed and turned away, puffing down the corridor, dabbing at perspiration on his brow with a soggy handkerchief.

The others remained in the elevator car and descended deeper into the building as Sturtevante began her briefing.

"We don't have much of a ready-room display, just some photographs and the poems, of course, which you're all familiar with; nothing unusual or out of place at any of the scenes. Fact is, the crime scenes this guy leaves behind are remarkably"—she searched for an appropriate word—"tidy. Tidy as your grandma's parlor."

Parry added, "Not so much as a candy wrapper on the floor. Wine bottles, flowers, candy boxes may have been handled by the killer. We've dusted for prints, but we've come up with zip."

"The guy is thorough about cleaning up after himself, and you know how useless a smudged print can be." Sturtevante raised a hand to her neck and rubbed furiously, apparently at some pain there.

Parry stared across at Jessica. "Whoever this guy is, he's at the opposite spectrum from Lopaka Kowona."

Jessica recalled how horrid the Kowona crime scenes had been, victims hacked to pieces and brutally mutilated. "The guy kept parts of his victims in his refrigerator," she told Kim.

Sturtevante turned to Parry. "I'd love to hear about your infamous Hawaiian case at some future time, Jim."

"I mean, unlike Kowona, our poet uses no knives, doesn't have a love affair with blood, and he's thorough about tidying up; like you say, Leanne, tidy as Grandma's parlor." James looked directly at Jessica as he spoke, as if they were the only two in the elevator.

The bell rang and the door opened on the lower-level floor where a sign pointed the direction to the morgue. They all stepped out into a bare, stark hallway painted an institutional green.

"Do you have anything on the killer's choice of weapon?" Jessica asked Sturtevante as they made their way toward a sign over a door that read PPD MEDICAL EX-AMINER'S OFFICE. "What've you so far on the poison he's using?" She wondered if Sturtevante sensed her need to ignore James's eyes for the moment.

"It hasn't yet been fully identified, and as for the killer, we know about as much as the proverbial schoolroom dunce."

"Not fully identified?" Jessica shot back.

"It's base is black India ink, possibly purchased at a specialty shop in the vicinity of the murders."

"Specialty shop?" asked Kim.

"Nestled amid our target area, along Second Street, there's a bookstore called Darkest Expectations that sells it, as well as a stationery store named Ink, Line & Sinker. Upscale, hip shops. Only blocks from where we found the last victim."

"No hemlock, no arsenic, no strychnine traces?" asked Jessica.

Sturtevante shook her head. "Whatever he's using, it isn't your run-of-the-mill poison."

"I'll want to talk to your toxicology guys. What about you, Jim? Have you got a team of toxicologists working on identifying the poison?"

"We do, but it's the same with our lab. They don't know what they're looking for. It's been one hell of a problem."

"If we can ID the poison, it might say something about the poisoner," said Kim. "Behaviorally speaking, that is."

"It might well be a hybrid poison, some sort of designer drug," Jessica suggested.

"Chief Parry holds the same belief. Meantime, our people are thinking it's something new, like you say, possibly a hybrid."

"Have they ruled out coldfire, then?" Jessica thought of her young victim in a morgue drawer back in Quantico.

"Trypto-otilin? Yes, we've had our share of cases involving coldfire, and yes, they have ruled it out," replied Sturtevante.

"Spanish fly? Azaleas? Rhododendrons? Other plants and flowers? I mean, doesn't this guy come with flowers and candy in hand?" Jessica asked.

"They have looked at all the usual suspects. You know how many poisons exist in the world?" Sturtevante asked in a strained voice.

Jessica realized only now that the detective had been offended by her tone. The two stood in the glow of light filtering through a glass door on which was lettered DR. LEONARD W. SHOCKLEY, ME. The two women sized each other up, their eyes locked.

Jessica said evenly, "I have a dictionary-sized book on the subject of poisons."

"That you've no doubt read, so you have *some* idea what our lab people are faced with . . . and how do you test for what you don't suspect? There's no way to test for everything, and everything on earth, if—"

"If used in excess, kills, I know," finished Jessica.

Kim, sensing the hostility between the other two women, jumped in. "It would appear no one's seen the like of it before, whatever this poisoned ink is. They're sure to have tested for mercury, right?"

"Right," Sturtevante echoed.

"Let's have a look at the victims," Jessica suggested.

"Step inside." Sturtevante opened the door. "You're expected; all has been arranged."

"We aim to please," added Parry. "I knew you'd want to take a hands-on approach, both of you. And it's as good a place to start as any."

His deep-set blue eyes reminded Jessica of the Hawaiian nights they'd spent together, and a sudden weakness in her knees made her wonder if she could handle this. She wondered as well if she could work alongside this man as if nothing had ever happened between them. His eyes seemed to mutely ask her the same question. Jessica wanted both to be alone at this moment and to be alone with him; they had so much to say to each other, so much clearing of the air to do.

Jessica again heard her father's voice from deep within telling her to be strong as she unconsciously clutched at the heavy steel scalpel in her breast pocket. Somehow her father's gift gave her the strength and resolve she needed.

On entering the morgue's outer corridor, she saw a white-haired Dr. Leonard Walter Shockley through what seemed a series of prisms—glass office windows, rows of them. He looked to be conducting some test on a gas chromotographer no doubt, attempting to separate out various chemical substances in order to make some scientific determination about some evidence. He looked like a ghost, a very busy and preoccupied ghost. As they came toward him, he didn't show the least interest in them and didn't even look up from his work.

Jessica wondered how Shockley might react to her and how she should treat him—professional to professional or as the daughter of an old friend. Shockley had known and worked with her father many years before, and had in fact attended Jessica's graduation from medical school. Jessica rarely saw him anymore, since the death of her father. She already felt surrounded by people she must prove something to, and now she feared another was about to be added to the list.

FIVE

As Jessica stared at her surroundings—the Philadelphia PD's Crime Lab Unit and adjacent medical examiner's office—a feeling of déjà vu swept over her, and for a moment, she thought she might be returned to a time when she was chief medical examiner for the District of Columbia. The place could not be more identical. Perhaps designed by the same architect in the mid-fifties? Like hundreds of other such places, Philadelphia's crime lab appeared as busy as any in the nation, and just as understaffed.

As they entered the main lab, Lieutenant Sturtevante said to the coroner for the city of Philadelphia, "Shocky, it's time for the show."

A stoop-shouldered gnome of a man with a greenish tinge to his skin turned from the cadaver he was scrutinizing with forceps, probe, overhanging magnifying glass, and the intensity of a medieval alchemist or some aged wizard in a fairy tale. Dr. Shockley stood, feet planted, rubber-gloved hands on hips, staring as if he were stumped by a complex mathematical problem, his eyes wide behind bottle-bottom glasses. Suddenly allowing a smile to spread across his wizened features, he said in a delighted tone, "Well, if it isn't the last of the female studs, Stud-e-vant! Have you caught yourself a man yet? Can't catch a man,

how're you supposed to catch a murderer?" He laughed at
his own jokes, and it was clear that the two were following
a familiar routine.

"I've got *you,* Shocky. All the man I can handle at one
time."

"If there was ever a woman I couldn't satisfy, I suspect
it'd be you, dear."

"That's enough of that, Shocky. Let me introduce—"

He waved Sturtevante off, going directly to Jessica,
peeling away his rubber gloves, fluids and pieces of tissue
flying as he grasped her hands in his, eyes twinkling as he
heartily pumped her arm as if hoping for water to spout
from her mouth. His grip felt like steel, stronger than she
had imagined, as he nearly shouted, "So, Sturtevante, our
two famous detectives have arrived, Dr. Coran and Dr.
Desinor. Been so looking forward to it, ladies. Around
here, the more the merrier. As for you, Jessica, I feel a hug
coming on."

"Really? And it's wonderful to see you, too, Uncle
Leonard."

"Uncle?" asked Sturtevante.

"Not by blood but by affection," said Jessica. "One of
my father's best friends."

"One of? I was your father's best friend, sweetheart," he
countered.

"Sorry, Doctor. I meant—"

"Never you mind. It's just wonderful to have you here
and on the case with me."

"Do you really mean that, or are you just being polite?"
she challenged the old man.

"Unlike many of my associates here in Philly, I'm not
afraid to say it. I need all the help I can get!" He took
Kim's hand next and shook it as heartily as he had Jessica's.

Shocky, as Sturtevante had called the ME, had gotten

their names and faces right, explaining, "I recognize you, Dr. Desinor, from your pictures, and you, little Jessica, how you've grown."

"Dr. Shockley and my father worked in the military together for a time," Jessica told the others.

"Well, this is like old home week for you, then, isn't it, Dr. Coran?" asked Sturtevante, letting on that she knew about Jessica and Parry's past involvement. No doubt Jim had told her, but why? Did he have some burning need to confide in another woman, someone safe? Or did he feel he owed it to Leanne Sturtevante to give her this deep background knowledge, for the good of her case?

Shockley continued, oblivious to these undercurrents. "I remember seeing you in L.A., too, at the convention, but then you disappeared. I learned only later that you'd gone off after yet another maniacal killer."

"Yes, a sociopath whose murder weapon was a blowtorch," said Kim.

"Not near so subtle in his MO as this fiend you're dealing with here," Jessica told Shockley.

"Yes, we have one hell of a subtle monster roaming our streets, Jessica. A most perspicacious SOB, to say the least, one too swift for local authorities to net. The newsies are having a field day with Sturtevante's supposedly inept handling of the case. Right, Leanne?"

"Go to hell, Shockley," replied Sturtevante.

"All right, then let's talk about Las Vegas, dear Jessica, shall we?"

"Vegas?"

Shockley guided her away from the others. "It was so very disappointing to learn that your session at the conference on rebuilding the crime from a single desiccated forearm—as you managed to do in Hawaii—had been turned over to Cyril Hanley."

"I heard that Hanley did a first-rate job," Jessica protested.

"Hanley's a good forensics man, yes, but he lacks something . . . hasn't the fire you have, Jessica, not even a spark of it. Besides, you're a good deal easier on the eye than Cyril, even in his best plaid shirt and bow tie." He finished with a hearty laugh, his impish face inviting them all to laugh with him, but no one did.

"Cyril has had problems with the fashion police before. Thank you, Dr. Shockley. I'm sorry you were disappointed at missing me in Vegas."

"Never you mind. There will be other conferences. Besides, who else could have put an end to that madman you trailed all across the west?" He turned to Sturtevante, adding, "The vile maniac turned perfectly good people into toast, using a torch! Yes, we are most certainly fortunate to have Dr. Coran and Dr. Desinor here, on this far more beguiling case."

Sturtevante remained impassive, simply saying, "Yes, we are indeed fortunate, and in the meantime—"

"In the meantime," Shockley repeated with a leering smile. "Yes, yes, yes . . . in the meantime, we have our own peculiar murder to deal with. One wonders if the killer does it tongue in cheek."

"Really? I sense no humor in the poems he leaves behind," countered Kim.

"I refer to his method! Such flare is usually reserved for the magicians of story—mystery writers. Imagine it."

Jessica did so; she imagined the panache, the flamboyance, the staging and the theater that went into the murders. She imagined the care with which the killer must procure his victims, while Shockley's words mirrored her thoughts. Shockley finished with, "Yes, he's a showman, this fellow, and he likely thinks long and hard about his deeds, rationalizing them away. Still, I suspect he spends at least as much time with his chemistry set, mixing his poisonous concoction, which we're still in the dark about."

Kim, hands behind her back, said, "I understand that the poison was taken in at the cuts created by the pen on their backs."

"What could be simpler?" Shockley asked with a grin. "Come, come this way. You'll find our first victim in good repair, all the autopsy protocol in shape as well. You two suit up. You'll find everything you need through there." He pointed to a door marked LADIES.

After quickly donning blue medical garb, masks, booties, and surgical gloves, Jessica and Kim returned. They then followed Leonard Shockley toward a second autopsy room where the body lay.

Shockley spoke as they walked. "I suppose you're curious about the victim type?"

"I do have some concerns along those lines," said Jessica.

"The detectives have surmised that the victims willingly submitted to the killer's pen, but it's unlikely they knew what they were in for. What's unusual is the absolute care the killer took with each victim to preserve their environment and their bodies."

Jessica nodded. "No hacking, no mutilation, no disarray of the rooms, I've heard."

"Exactly. Rather the opposite. He is meticulous with his victims."

"*Lovingly* meticulous, I understand."

"For God's sake, Jessica, the bastard provides a pillow, a blanket, a careful placement of the arms and legs. Comfort is key. The body is not only given a gentle send-off, but the condition of the body is near perfect."

"Perfect health, you mean?"

"No sign of anything whatsoever to check out, no."

"So, although he's giving them this peaceful kind send-off—"

"He has certain standards."

She squinted at the old ME. "Standards?"

"None of the victims were in pain or suffering or ill health, no."

"What about mental state, depression?"

"Every kid this side of the Mississippi is depressed."

"Any history of depression in the victims?" she persisted.

"None that I know of, but it may be a viable line of inquiry," agreed Shockley, opening the door to the room where the cadaver awaited her inspection. He stopped her before the sheet-covered corpse. "But, Jess, I'm talking about the killer's victim type—someone in perfect physical and I suspect mental condition. Perfectly healthy and young. That's what our killer wants."

Jessica stared down at the prone figure below the sheet. She then tore the shroud away for a complete view, the fabric spiraling away like a fleeing specter.

Below her gaze lay the body of a thin, shapeless woman, not a blemish of any kind save the stitching done by Shockley and his team. Even the woman's nipples, the areola, appeared white and an extension of her breast skin. Her breasts formed two perfect and symmetrical buttons, so small as to make her appear genderless. A gaze into the woman's face, and Jessica felt she must be the most pure-skinned white woman she had ever encountered, dead or alive. Even given the purplish hue from the postmortem pooling of blood as tissues had broken down, even with the bruises caused most likely by the rough handling of the body by so-called professionals, this corpse appeared nearly flawless. "Not so much as a single freckle," she whispered.

"How were the bodies discovered?" Jessica asked

Sturtevante, who, along with James Parry and Kim Desinor, had joined them in the autopsy room. Everyone wore blue surgical masks.

"In every case, the body has been discovered by a friend who'd come looking for the deceased."

"No, I'm asking in what *posture* were the bodies found? Facedown, faceup?"

"Facedown, on their stomachs, resting comfortably. Placed in bed or on pillows. Whoever the killer is, he wants the poems seen immediately, so in walks the hapless friend to discover first the poem, then their dead friend—or at least the two simultaneously."

"She looks like a beautiful young boy," Kim said matter-of-factly.

"I hadn't noticed," jested the old coroner at Jessica's side. "Of course! Fact struck me immediately, a thunder-bolt in the ass. I mean, how often do you see the human body without a single blemish?" Shockley darted a glance at Sturtevante. "Tried to tell our lieutenant in charge of the case, but she didn't think it important."

"I doubt there's a person within an eight-mile radius whose body is without some sort of blemish," replied Jessica, thinking of her own physical imperfections.

"No such thing as true alabaster skin, they say, and yet here it is," added James Parry. "Wouldn't you say, Jess—uh, Dr. Coran?"

Other than the brief acknowledgment at their meeting and businesslike exchange in the elevator, these were James's only words to Jessica. Kim Desinor looked like she was about to answer, but she hesitated, allowing Jessica a moment to gather her thoughts.

"As pure as pure gets, it would appear. Not so much as a mole or a birthmark anywhere," Jessica replied. "Tell me, Jim, is this true of the other two victims as well?"

"As a matter of fact, yes."

Sturtevante stepped closer to the body. "We haven't
been getting a whole lot of sun here lately. Fact is, I can't
recall what the sun feels like. Either way, we have plenty
of pale-skinned people running about." She stopped talking to watch Kim Desinor. Kim placed her hands over the
body and seemed to scan it with her fingertips, ever so
lightly, her eyes closed. Jessica placed a finger to her lips
to indicate that the others must remain quiet while Kim
worked.

Kim's body began a near-imperceptible shiver, and she
began to take on a slightly blue tinge like that of the long-
frozen corpse. "Blue frost," she muttered. "Blue frost . . .
cold to the bone."

Kim came out of the trance she had put herself into, the
blue tinge disappearing from her features. "Please, can we
turn her over? I'd like to have a go at the back."

"Can we roll her, Dr. Shockley?" asked Jessica.

"Let me call in a couple of my attendants. Strong young
fellows who won't break her neck in the process."

This done, they all stared at the strange, eerie lettering
on the back of the victim. It was one thing to view such an
unusual desecration of a body in photos, quite another to
look on the real thing. Here it stared back at you as if the
words were alive, the color of the ink vivid, the color of the
bruising around the cuts gruesome. Hues no photograph
could reproduce. Here lay the poem about chance and innocence that ended with flickering life.

"Strange or not, each of the victims had assumed a stage
name or at least a changed name," Sturtevante told them.

Kim wasted no time in fingering the pen markings, trying desperately to learn something from her reading of the
body.

Nothing happened until they all realized that the blue
cast that had left Kim's skin had returned, the color far
deeper this time.

"What the hell is—" began Shockley.

"Shhhh," Jessica cautioned him.

Jessica watched Kim with great intensity; she saw the tears begin to form in her eyes, tears that instantly turned into frozen little pearls. "She's freezing cold. Get her out of here, away from the body. Now!" Jessica ordered.

James and Jessica guided a weakened Kim Desinor from the autopsy room to Shockley's office, Lieutenant Sturtevante opened doors along the way. There Shockley pointed to a leather couch, saying, "Lay her down here."

The others gathered round Kim to watch the blue tint disappear and the tears turn again to liquid.

"She loved him," Kim said aloud.

"Loved him?" asked Sturtevante.

"Who loved whom?" asked Parry.

Talking over the other two, Jessica asked, "For whom did she die, Kim?"

Kim's reply came like the whisper of a child. "She loved him, he loved her . . . her killer. The number nineteen . . . keeps coming at me, insistent, along with some letters which . . . which I haven't been able to understand just yet. I think I'll have to arrange them. They're some sort of call letters or insignia."

"Nineteen? Nineteen what?" asked Parry.

"She loved him?" Sturtevante repeated. "Then that ought to make our search easy. We go after the boyfriend with more fervor."

"Boy*friends,* you mean," corrected Parry. "She had a lot of male friends, as well as female friends, all of whom tell us the same story, that she was a lovely, open, caring person who got dumped on a lot because she was a good listener. And all of her so-called boyfriends claim to have had a platonic relationship with her—no sexual involvement—but if you believe that one, I have a bridge in Brooklyn I'd like to sell you."

"But she did not sleep around," Sturtevante added to correct any false impression Jim may have left. "All the friends say the same: they know no one who would have wanted to harm her."

"You don't understand," complained Kim, still lying prone. "Their love was transcendent . . . transcendental. Not your normal boy-girl relationship, not based on sex."

"Transcendental? I always took that to mean finding a way to get out of your dental bills, or that it was an insurance company—Occidental Transcendental, something like that," quipped Parry.

The others, glad for something to laugh at, laughed at Parry's lame joke, except for Kim, who remained stonily silent, and Jessica, clearly remaining aloof from any joke Parry had to make about anything.

What then?" asked Parry. "Did they cut into one another with this poison pen in a pact of some sort? Did they read poetry together, only he chickened out and bailed? That doesn't explain the other two deaths."

"No, it's not a suicide pact, since the killer obviously isn't willing to include himself in it," countered Sturtevante, vigorously shaking her head.

"But it might explain how he gets them to this point," suggested Jessica. "Conning them into a pact, then bailing."

"Perhaps the victims went first, and were under the impression he would follow, but once the poison is introduced, our man steps off," added Shockley. "Not a bad theory."

Kim shook her head. "He loved her, too."

"Loved her, yeah, enough to kill her," Sturtevante commented. "I've seen it before. Love kills."

"Got that right," Parry agreed.

"No, no. He loved her too much, too much to allow her a moment's suffering," insisted Kim. "At least in his head."

"What suffering?" asked Parry. "She was in perfect health, according to Shockley. Right, Doctor?"

Shockley nodded repeatedly, saying, "Perfect health, yes."

Kim remained adamant about the feelings she'd received from the corpse. "All I know is that he . . . he killed her, poisoned her, out of love, and the suffering she felt was of the soul, not the body."

"Loved her right into her grave? Is that what you're saying?" asked Sturtevante.

Parry gritted his teeth. "Do you really expect us to believe that?"

Jessica wanted to tell him a thing or two about love, but she held back. Kim clawed her way to a sitting position and replied, "Believe what you will, but I have to follow what my intuition tells me."

"He killed her because he loved her? You psychics are all alike; you deal in double-talk."

Kim shot back, "These are my honest impressions, *Chief* Parry. Not double talk." Kim made it clear Parry's position as Philly's top-ranking FBI field operative didn't intimidate her.

"Lieutenant Sturtevante," began Parry, "you buying any of this? You think this guy killed three people because he loved them?"

"That he so loved them that he killed them for it?" She mulled over the idea for a moment. "My team has looked into the boyfriend and the ex-boyfriend, and both of 'em have come up clean with solid alibis."

"What about other acquaintances?" asked Jessica.

"Of course we're looking into every acquaintance we learn about, but getting information out of people takes time. So far, nothing has shaken out."

"I want to see the other bodies," Jessica replied. "See what, if anything, they have to tell us. Kim, you can rest here, regain your energies."

"Got a little cold inside her. Strange . . . I again kept getting the single word *rampage,* as in the other reading."

"Rampage," Jessica repeated. "I wonder what it is, this rampage . . ."

"Micellina," said Shockley.

"What's that?" asked Kim.

"Her name . . . Micellina Petryna."

"Even her name is beautiful," Jessica said.

"As was—is—her soul," Kim added.

"She was striking," Jessica agreed, "in her near perfection."

Parry stared longer at the body.

"If you like that body type," Sturtevante said to Jessica.

Jessica nodded. "Apparently our killer does . . . like that long, lean look."

"Whoever's doing this, he writes to each victim, creates a new poem for each," said Sturtevante, "and an expert in poetry I'm working with says the poems are excellent examples of what's going on among the young nowadays, that typically adolescent interest in the dark side, in death and the beyond, and a search for absolute perfection and peace, and maybe the meaning of life."

"But the result is death," Jessica countered. "Who is this expert you're working with?"

"A friend at the University of Philadelphia who teaches poetry and writes it as well, a Dr. Donatella Leare. In fact, she has given me many insights into the killer. I'll leave her notes with you."

"That would be helpful. Thanks."

"Shall we visit the next victim?" asked Kim, standing now on wobbly feet.

"Not you. You've had enough."

"I've only just begun. Out of my way, Coran." Kim pushed past her friend and colleague, asking Shockley, "Will you please lead the way, Doctor?"

One step, however, and Kim nearly fainted; the session had taken more of a toll on her strength than she cared to admit. Jessica helped her back down to a sitting position. "Get her some water, a Coke, something."

Parry rushed out to do her bidding to a chorus of "Sorry, sorry," coming from Kim.

JESSICA now sat hunched over a desk, staring at Dr. Leonard Shockley's protocols on each of the victims. The others had all disappeared, each, in a sense, off to follow his or her own nose, his or her own separate leads. Jessica's instincts told her that more could be learned through the patterns left behind by the killer, and any similarities she could find or infer among his victims. These could only be ascertained by studying the reams of paper. Research was mining for small nuggets of information that led to a shock of recognition, nuggets of details and specifics that, taken altogether, might point in a direction. *The first step in any journey is the hardest, but it may also be the step most filled with discovery.* She recalled how her father had put it. Her mentor in forensics, Dr. Asa Holcraft, had put it more succinctly: "Baby steps. Go lightly. Crawl if you have to."

Neither Leanne Sturtevante nor James Parry needed to remain at the crime lab morgue, and Kim had been physically and emotionally drained by her earlier experience with the deceased. She had a time-out coming, but she refused to leave the building, remaining on Shockley's ottoman. There she now rested with the intention of finding out what she could from the second victim before leaving altogether. Jessica had begun studying the paperwork in anticipation of Kim's return.

Jessica was secretly glad that Kim had not revealed that they believed the poem on each victim somehow connected, as if they were part of one long dirge that had been divided into discrete sections. After everyone had gone, Jessica suggested to Kim that they keep this theory between themselves for the time being. She had also told Kim that perhaps the number nineteen, which kept insinuating itself into her visions, might be the number of victims or sections of the poem, or both. Kim agreed that this could indeed be a possibility.

Going over the bodies and the protocols Dr. Shockley had created, Jessica again drew a bead on the absolutely healthy condition of the victims, each a sad loss—of the sort doctors hated to see—for none of them, male or female, had so much as a gallstone to worry their insides, and not so much as a mole to worry their outsides. Excellently proportioned, artistically so, their lithe, sculptured bodies reminded her of marble statues in a museum.

"They'd have no need of me or any doctor," she said to the silent room, "except for the fact that they are all murdered."

Shockley so quietly appeared in the doorway that his voice, breaking the utter silence, startled her. "You're here to discover and proclaim the deeper cause of death, beyond the weapon—poison—the thinking of the poisoner, which may or may not lead us in a direction that could put an end to his sociopathic behavior. Isn't that the essence of a criminal profile?"

"In a nutshell, yes, but, Doctor, I'm not sure our killer is a sociopath, not in the strictest sense."

"Really, now? That's rather novel, isn't it? I have heard it said the word *sociopath* is interchangeable with *serial killer,* and our man is a serial killer."

"Not all sociopaths kill," she countered.

"They're just more prone to murder than the rest of us?"

"Not all serial killers are sociopaths. In fact, the serial

mercy killer is working out of the deepest of human emotions, which makes him or her the antithesis of the sociopath."

Shockley smiled and nodded like a shaggy dog. "Sociopaths can't empathize or sympathize with the pain and suffering of others, I know that much."

"Fact is they only live for the brief duration of self-gratification they find in controlling others, bringing others to tears, to a state of demoralization, to bloodletting and torture. This alone in all the universe fulfills their perverse needs; for many, what is abnormal is the norm."

"Chancy word indeed, *normal*. But tell me, do you think our killer of these young people with his poison and his flowers and music and poetry, do you think he gets any less of an erection than your run-of-the-mill lust murderer, who can only ejaculate if he tortures and mutilates?"

"Are you asking me if I think our poisoner is working out of something other than a sense of mercy?" She considered this idea, knowing the old man was using his best Aristotelian technique on her. *He poses a series of questions so that she might unearth a truth that might eventually determine the depth of his own conclusions.*

"Can you be sure of the Poet's motives yet?"

"I can't be sure of his or her motives just yet, but it would appear the killer took great pains to select a method of murder that is not the choice of your usual sociopathic chainsaw murderer," she insisted. "I don't think we're dealing with a heartless, unfeeling person here, but quite possibly the opposite."

"The opposite? What is the opposite of such a person, Dr. Coran?"

"Someone who is subconsciously acting on some . . . some delusion of grandeur, that he is some sort of . . . saint, and that what he does is indeed an act of mercy on the one hand . . ."

"But, on the other hand . . . ?"

"A thrill, a conquest, a victory. Dr. Desinor has said that she felt the killer was on some sort of crusade."

"Precisely the definition of a sociopath of the sort we find in religious zealots, my dear, wouldn't you say?"

"Someone whose aims are glorified to a pathological intensity, working out of a sense of mission or a sense of a destiny ordained by God. That would make our killer a complicated nutcase, whose vision and fantasy are religious in nature, like Jim Jones in Guyana and David Koresh in Waco, Texas."

"Yes, well, if you believe so." Dr. Shockley lifted his brow, a shrewd look on his face. "Isn't such a man always more frightening than all the chainsaw killers combined?"

"Yes, of course, especially if he is preaching such distortions as I heard in the case of the Crucifier in London."

"Read all about it in the journals. You really should write that case up for the benefit of the rest of us, Jessica." And then he abruptly added, "So, where have all the others gone off to?"

"No need for them to baby-sit here. They'll do just as well to follow leads independently of us."

Shockley nodded, looking to her like the actor who played Santa Claus in the original *Miracle on Thirty-fourth Street*. He plopped wearily into the chair across from her, the desk she'd been given between them. "I heartily agree. That man Parry looked quite anxious to end his stay in my little death chamber. Behind my back, the PPD personnel, all of them, call this place 'Shock Theater,' where the 'Shock Doc'—that'd be me—operates like some ghoulish Dr. Frankenstein." He laughed at the image, his white hair falling over one eye, and for a moment, Jessica thought he might drop off to sleep where he sat.

"I'm 'Shocky' to my friends," he told her, "and I would be pleased to count you, my dear, among them. You needn't call me uncle. You're hardly the child I knew when your father was alive."

Hearing footsteps, Dr. Shockley turned, and Kim Desinor showed up in the doorway, asking, "Which way to the second autopsy room and victim number two?"

"Are you sure you can handle that now, Kim?" asked Jessica.

"I am. Let's have at it."

Jessica stood. Shockley, taking more time to get to his feet, joined the women, both of whom were already halfway down the corridor, en route to the waiting body.

JESSICA had already begun to relax in her new surroundings, but she felt a great deal more at ease without James Parry in the room. A momentary and fleeting thought, like a scuttling bug, reminded her she had yet to contact Richard Sharpe in England to tell him of the case, and that she'd "run into" James Parry as a result. She wondered if he'd believe such a sequence of events, or if she simply ought to tell him the truth. But what *was* the truth? she now asked herself.

Standing over the second victim, banishing such concerns from her mind for the moment, she concentrated instead on the corpse. She and Kim both immediately saw the surface similarities: although the two women looked quite different, each had flawless skin and trailing, curling black hair, flowing freely, a dark ribbon of it, the effect pure and beautiful. In fact, each looked like the stereotype of the Pre-Raphaelite woman, the woman of poetry and song made famous by the poet Dante Gabriel Rossetti.

Kim then waved her wandlike hands over the prone body.

"Her name was Caterina Mercedes," Shockley said softly.

Both beautiful names, Jessica thought. Beautiful women, beautiful and flawless skin; hair like winding vines; pouting, large but soft lips; high cheekbones; statuesque; perfectly proportioned; yet their most striking feature other than the smooth and flawless skin had to be their slim, even boyish physiques. Something about the eyes in this one, too, reminded Jessica of the other victim; aside from the crystal blue green of the orbs, there seemed a hint of the piercing life hiding deep within the corneas, like seeds, somehow reflecting light even in their dormancy. How incredible those eyes must have been in life, she surmised.

As much to shake herself from the unreasonable feelings welling up in her as to learn anything, Jessica broke the stillness, asking Kim, "Are you getting any feeling from this one?"

"Anger . . . pure and unadulterated anger. She hates him passionately."

"As passionately as the other loves—loved him?"

"Even more so. Nothing so transcendent as hatred. She feels used, conned. Not at the time, not while he was in the act of poisoning her, but now she feels the hatred so strongly that she hasn't completely left this plane of existence."

"That's pretty scary. Anything else?" Jessica coaxed.

"Only that this one's not cold; this one's on fire."

Jessica only now realized that the blue aura surrounding Kim had turned to a red glow, and that Kim found herself afire. She was again faint, and Jessica grabbed her where she stood beside Dr. Shockley, who flinched at the heat coming off the psychic. "Please, help me to sit," Kim begged, nodding toward a nearby stool.

With Kim recuperating, Jessica asked Shockley, "How do you see these killings, Doctor? Did your protocol first link the killings?"

"The killer did that for us."

"The poems, you mean. His MO."

"Fairly obvious about himself, wouldn't you say?"

Poems, left on each victim like tablet writings, of course, not that he was kind enough to leave a signature in the literal sense, but this was, in police parlance, quite a John Hancock after all. Still, he did leave another signature of a sort: the poison in their systems. If only they could decipher the message. . . .

Shockley got on the intercom, called for his attendants, and saw to the careful return of the body to its freezer compartment. Jessica stepped nearer to the old man and asked, "Had to've been a potent poison to work as it did in the slight wounds he opened with . . . with a pen."

"What we've managed to determine is that the killer used a quill pen, the old-fashioned sort you dip into an inkwell. It certainly cuts more deeply than your typical fountain pen."

"Clever of you to come up with the type of pen he used," she complimented.

He shrugged it off. "Wasn't hard for me to detect this fact alone, although I've been stumped by the exact nature of his poison. It has contradictory elements."

"Contradictory elements?"

"It may act as both a stimulant and a downer. A real downer in the end, of course. At first exciting the victim, then leaving her to languish."

"What makes you think so?"

"Wouldn't you have to be high to allow someone to cut your flesh to this extent? He may even tell them the anesthetic is in the ink, for all we know, and they being young and trusting souls . . . who knows."

"I see. But why has it been so bloody difficult to isolate the exact nature of the poison?"

"Trace amounts of this and that, from boric acid to

retinol. None in a lethal enough dosage in and of itself to kill has been isolated out, but the base poison continues to elude detection."

"You isolated boric acid and retinol in the system?"

"Well, not I. And not surprising, actually. Boric acid is used in baths, and retinol—vitamin A skin conditioning—has become a common enough over-the-counter wrinkle cream. Our toxicologist, Dr. DeAngelos, did the work on that, but as it turns out, Mercedes's doctor had prescribed retinol for a recurrent problem she thought she was having with bags under her eyes. Of course, it was a pure figment, as there are and have never been any flaws beneath her eyes, but her doctor prescribed it, he says, as a way to calm her down."

Jessica took a deep breath, sighed heavily, and released her pent-up frustration all in what seemed a single, flowing movement. "The choice of American women everywhere these days, yes."

SIX

. . . the blood of the moon steeps
through me, but you cannot find me,
as I have disappeared into your darkness,
while seeking out your flesh, only to find
instead your deepest secret.

—Stephen Walker

JESSICA encouraged Kim to rise to her feet. Together they sized up each other's tolerance level, and without words, each decided she would go on from here to autopsy room number three. "Something in me needs to get this done tonight," Kim insisted.

"All in one fell swoop? Kim, suppose it puts you out of commission for the duration of the case?"

"I can't tell you what it is; all I can tell you is that I have to . . . I must see all three victims in quick succession. That is what my intuition is telling me."

Autopsy room number three housed the third victim, as Shockley had told them. The doctor stood waiting at the door, a grim look on his face, a single wave of the hand inviting them in; the stance and manner of his invitation called to mind a maniacal ringmaster in a circus, but Shockley's little circus had death in all three rings.

The seasoned old ME had prattled on about the increase in crime and the necessity for still more autopsy rooms and MEs to do the work. He moaned over the circumstances, the fact that hospital pathologists knew less today than they had known when butchers and barbers were the local coroners. Then, apropos apparently of murder-minded barbers, he started telling them how he had recently seen a revival of the musical *Sweeney Todd* at the local opera house. Finally, he muttered to Jessica, "Don't suppose you'd care to come to work for me, heh?" His wrinkles danced with his laughter, the gray-framed eyes twinkling.

The third victim, although male, possessed a soft and beautiful countenance like the deceased women: a pouting mouth, high cheekbones, and skin every bit as flawless as the other two victims. "Beginning to see a pattern here," Jessica said to the others.

As if wanting to get it over with, Kim had instantly put her gloved hands on the body. From her deep trance, she struggled to say, "This one, like Micellina, thought the killer loved him."

"How long had he known him?" asked Jessica, fishing for more detail.

"Forever and never, but perhaps only since nineteen."

Jessica was beginning to feel some of the angst Parry felt around Kim. She always spoke in riddles, because she saw in images, symbols as opposed to facts. Jessica knew it was useless to ask if she meant nineteen days, weeks, years, or since the young man's nineteenth birthday. Instead she asked, "What does he look like?"

"An angel, like Michael, the Messenger . . . angel on a rampage. The letters arranged spell *quark*."

Jessica moaned, but managed to ask, "Quark? As in physics?"

"Astrophysics," Shockley corrected.

"Like the way *rampage* came to me; in Ouija-board fashion; now the word *quark* has arranged itself."

Jessica felt this line of questioning useless. So she changed her tactics, asking, "Hair color?"

"Like light."

"Light? Light gray, light brown?"

"Light . . . . like white jewels, like goldenness open to the sky."

Giving up on hair, Jessica asked, "Eyes?"

"Lime green, radiant, radiating light. A green reflecting pool."

"Sounds gorgeous, or maybe not . . . Maybe the SOB wears contacts?"

Jessica knew from experience with Kim that no image could be taken at face value; lime-green eyes might simply mean that the killer saw life through a green lens. Lime suggested bitterness, so perhaps the killer saw the world as green bile, slime even, the opposite of green lawns and green as the color of hope, new life, and growth. She knew that the moment one locked down on the meaning of a psychic image, it was hard to shift the idea. Like interpreting dream images, there was more art to it than science. Certainly, psychic symbols and representations could not be taken on face value.

"How tall is our man?"

"A giant in his eyes."

"How is he in bed?"

Dr. Shockley gasped, then laughed at this.

"No way to know. He did not sleep with the women; he sees the women as virginal, pure, angelic."

"Virginal? Are you sure? They're both over twenty."

"It's how he, the killer, perceived them."

"And the young man?"

"Virginal as well."

"A virgin? Are you sure?"

Shockley, shaking his head, put in, "The boy's twenty-three years of age. He's hardly likely to be a virgin at his age, unless of course he was raised a Mormon!"

Kim countered, saying, "It appears . . . that is, it feels so."

"Feels so to the killer, you mean?" asked Jessica.

Kim shook her head. "No, feels so to me, here and now."

"I didn't bother to look with the women," Shockley confessed, "whether or not . . . the question of their virginity . . ." His shoulders rose as if attached to puppet strings as he stared across the cadaver at Jessica. "It isn't something one goes looking for, not since the late seventies anyway. Once I established that there was no sexual assault, I saw no need to . . . to search any further, you see."

"Do it now, for the first victim, the Petryna woman, and I'll check the Mercedes woman," suggested Jessica.

"But the police told me that each had multiple boyfriends, including our young Mr. Barona Gaitano, here."

Kim erupted, saying, "Barona? His name was Barona?"

"Changed his name to it, yes. Was Luis. Quite a leap, wouldn't you say? Gaitano's his real name, though."

"Barona Gaitano . . . has a showbiz sound to it, doesn't it?" asked Kim.

Ignoring this, Jessica said, "Check on victim one's virginity, Dr. Shockley. See if there is any evidence of sexual activity or assault. I'll do the same for the other woman."

"Will do."

Returning to where victim numbers one and two had been stored, Dr. Shockley at their side, Jessica said, "If they could be proven to be virgins, and if we can determine that the young man was saving himself for a true love, it will tell us something about the sort of people the killer targets, and it will hand us one more piece to add to our jigsaw puzzle."

Kim agreed. "Yes, this could all figure into the killer's game plan. If he selects virgins as his victims, flawless in every way, it tells us something about him."

The white-haired Shockley nodded all the way down the corridor, muttering, "Virgin sacrifices? Is that what we're dealing with here? It'd be a first for me! Unfortunately, there is no way to prove it."

They soon had their answer when Shockley examined the first body and Jessica examined the second. The attendant was annoyed to remove the cadaver from its freezer compartment for a second time and wheel it into the room where Shockley worked. Beside him, Jessica quickly examined victim number two for any signs of sexual activity. Kim anxiously looked on, pacing behind her.

"False alarm," announced Jessica, who felt no surprise in learning that Caterina Mercedes was no virgin. Shockley had come to the same conclusion with respect to Micellina Petryna.

Kim, looking on, said, "I felt it so strongly."

"No more virgins out there to sacrifice, I'm afraid," the old coroner said.

"As for the male," Kim began, "only his friends—"

"Could possibly know," finished Jessica.

Shockley added, "And they might not tell. Something else Sturtevante needs to run down."

After some silence, Jessica heaved her shoulders and sighed. "Nothing else to accomplish here. I can listen to Shockley's protocols on tape at my leisure, back at the hotel."

But a revolving red light went on in Shockley's lab, a sure signal that another corpse was on its way, and a moment later, the doors to the crime lab burst open and an attendant wheeled a corpse through.

"Dear God," muttered Shockley through grinding false teeth. "We've got another one." He ought to have been apprised of the body's earlier discovery so he could have sent out an evidence tech unit to sweep the crime scene.

"Dammit," Jessica muttered. "Does this mean what I think it means?"

"We've screwed up is what it means," Shockley replied

as he rushed for a look at the body and to speak with the attendant.

"I left messages, Doctor. Didn't anyone find you?" the attendant was asking when Jessica and Kim joined the ME.

"Not a word. We've been in and out of the autopsy rooms and the freezers," Shockley replied.

Then a second young attendant rushed in shouting, "Dr. Shockley, Tim Brothers somehow stupidly turned off the red-light special, and what with the panic button off, none of us knew. I mean, we just now learned. It's another male victim of that poison-pen guy."

This was obvious, as the victim lay facedown in the gurney, the glaring, ugly poetry on his back dried with blood, red and rusty. "Damn it all, man, tell me something I don't know. All right, let's have a look at this latest victim, shall we?"

With the three of them in surgical garb, they moved toward the Poet Killer's fourth suspected victim.

"Looks all too familiar." Kim's remark came with the tones of fatigue and frustration.

Again they found themselves in autopsy room number one, where Jessica read aloud the toe tag, ANTON PIERRE, even as she stripped away the sheet to reveal the male corpse. Anton's eyes, wide open and sea blue to emerald green, displayed the usual marblelike stare, stony and without life, but the color, like those of the other victims, mesmerized and made one believe some life danced just behind the stillness. Jessica wanted to reach for the stethoscope to make certain this beautiful, untouched victim—untouched but for the now familiar poetic scars on his back—lay just beyond in the realm of sleep, not death.

He hadn't been deep-frozen and thawed out, she silently told herself. Not like the others. He hardly looked dead; it hardly seemed possible that the healthy-looking person on the slab could be a corpse.

"Perfection," muttered Kim.

"Once again," Jessica agreed. "Now it's even; two women, two men, for a total of four victims."

Shockley added, "Another perfectly proportioned man at that. Look at those pecs."

"Forget the pecs. Look at the rest of him," said Kim, with a slight shake of the head.

Jessica added, "And his skin."

"More darkly tanned than the others."

"Hardly what you'd call a sun worshiper, however."

"Not a freckle or a mole on him."

"It's as if it's a prerequisite—a flawless complexion—to die in this manner," finished Jessica.

Although the victim's skin in this case was several shades darker than the women and the other man, the body itself, displayed as it was, showed not a single blemish, save for the normal discoloration to the frontal areas, face, chest, and legs, where the blood had settled. Obviously, once again the victim had been left facedown to display the handiwork of the Poet Killer to authorities. Thus gravity had caused the blood to pool in areas of the front, creating large purplish splotches on the skin.

Jessica stared across the cadaver and into Kim's eyes. "Is it only coincidence that Anton Pierre, Barona Gaitano, Micellina Petryna, and Caterina Mercedes all have such extraordinary features? It must fit into the killer's fantasy, whatever that fantasy might be."

"Agreed," Kim replied, staring at Anton Pierre's perfectly proportioned body and beautiful face. "Some people would kill for a body that looks like these."

"And obviously someone has," Shockley put in.

"Think you want to try a 'deep read' on Pierre?"

Kim bit her lip, sighed heavily, and nodded. "I'll do what I can."

Jessica stared across the cadaver at her colleague and

friend, Kim Desinor, whose complexion rivaled those of the two dead women for purity. Kim had shoulder-length hair these days, the natural flip framing her large, energy-filled eyes and accentuating her high cheekbones. "Fearful you'll use up all your magic our first day?" asked Shockley, who remained skeptical of Kim's psychic abilities.

Kim didn't answer, her gloved hands now moving like two markers over a Ouija board as she gritted her teeth in concentration. Jessica again thought how perfectly beautiful she was.

"It is rather a radical, even alien idea nowadays, but regardless of their sexual proclivities, our killer may well have *seen* these four as virginal in some context only he fully understands. We may rule it out as a fact, but we shouldn't rule it out as a fantasy, part of the killer's fantasy," Kim suggested.

"Yeah, he may have so strongly wanted it that way that he saw them as such, regardless of facts," agreed Jessica. "It's the kind of designation or imprinting a madman might stamp on his victims."

"I recently had a case of murder after months of stalking," said Shockley, "and the shooter did just that. He saw his victim as pure, put her on a pedestal, and when she inevitably fell off it, he killed her."

Jessica had learned to put aside the horror of such moments, that so much human potential and life itself had been snuffed out as one might crush a caterpillar underfoot. So much waste. All the victims were young, with so much lying ahead of them, each barely out of the teen years. Wasted . . . the single word said it all, a waste of human promise and potential. No one could imagine what might have burgeoned from these beginnings.

Jessica realized that the image of the virginal soul, or the state of actual virginity, might not fit here, but the appearance of it—that is, the physical appearance of purity displayed by each body—might have a great deal to do with the killer's choice of victims. That it might well play into his selection process. "Perhaps the Poet wanted a perfectly unblemished 'slate' to write on. It might be that the killer, while not strictly interested in virgins in the literal sense of the word, did find people who gave the appearance of purity in one form or another."

"While not virgins, they may have easily given that impression of innocence and naïveté that proved, in the end, the most alluring trait of the virginal or celibate life," agreed Kim. "Virginal behavior, virginal by nature, virginal appearing, or a combination of all three."

Jessica silenced herself as Kim's psychic persona took center stage once again.

Kim's energies, however, had been drained like a used-up battery from the earlier readings. She received little from Anton Pierre, save the overwhelming sense of confusion, mixed with a bit of awe. She concluded in a few flat words: "He never knew what hit him. Didn't see it coming. Innocence sums him up, innocence and perplexed ignorance of how he came to be dead."

"And as for being, as Madonna says, 'like a virgin'?"

"The overwhelming trait I get coming through is confused innocence, like a child who has been lied to. Again the number nineteen and the words *rampage* and *quark* returned during my reading. Something insistent there."

"You think the killer is nineteen and on a rampage, his mind 'quarked'?"

"Such a direct interpretation would only lead us in a wrong direction. No, the nineteen is a symbol for something greater than age. And as for the word *rampage* . . . again it may hold some other meaning we are not aware of or do not normally associate with the word. The same will likely be true of *quark*. We need to pursue these words and the symbolic meanings ascribed to the number nineteen. I'll set myself that task."

"That sounds reasonable."

"Our killer's MO is certainly not one of a man on a rampage, so I must assume it stands for something other than our normal interpretations would allow."

Jessica's eyes lit up with a notion. "Perhaps its opposite, then, rampage equals peace, serenity, perhaps what serenity betokens? Absolute peace?"

"Possibly, but I'm not at all certain at this point."

While Jessica and Kim were talking, Dr. Shockley had been on his cell phone, taking heat for having not responded to the call at the murder scene. Jessica imagined that a nearby hospital pathologist or someone on Parry's team had had to be called in to walk the grid and to pronounce the victim dead before authorities ordered it shipped off to Shockley.

Dr. Shockley now said, "Couldn't tell you for a certainty, but I'm suspicious that my superiors are pissed off. Meantime, I am tired and I am retiring—for the night at least. Jessica and Kim, good night. Carl will be nearby to help you out and to lock up."

The sound of the closing door reverberated throughout the lab when the old man disappeared. Jessica said, "I agree. Let's save our sanity and get out of here for now. Come at it fresh in the A.M."

"Agreed. Bed is waiting."

The women made their way out of the semidarkened crime lab, secure in the belief that they had done all that was possible for the night, and that Carl would put Anton Pierre's body on ice; they found the elevator and took it to ground floor.

"If we extrapolate from one body to the next, all that appears before us is a series of fine, hairless, flawless young specimens." You are your father's daughter, Jessica, she heard herself say to this. Reducing a life to the word *specimen* had been an ongoing argument between them when he was alive. He maintained that an ME must be as objective and emotionally controlled as his scalpel. She maintained that the more the ME knew about the personality of the victim, the more he or she could tell with a scalpel.

"You were right, Jessica, to suggest that our victims have, if not the actual and physical status of virgins, then the mental state of virgins. Petryna's soul was virginal on exiting this life in the sense that she and the others never harmed a living thing, ever. They were the kind of people who, as they say, couldn't harm a fly. I get that much from my readings."

"Are you sure they all had this sort of nature?"

"I'm quite sure of that much."

"Meaning the killer may have liked them that way?"

"Perhaps . . ." Kim muttered. "I couldn't say for a certainty."

"A big maybe." In the cramped car of the elevator, Jessica bit her lower lip as she went over what she had seen so far. Her thoughts felt at odds, a bewildered one combating with a chaotic one, the clash creating only larger confusion. She threw in a healthy dose of anger and frustration at having missed out on Anton Pierre's crime scene. She imagined how angry James and Sturtevante must be at the forensics team at this moment—missing in action during a key crime-scene investigation. She excused her absence on the grounds of complete exhaustion as the elevator doors opened at ground level, and she and Kim made their way to the hotel on foot, taking in the night air.

Once they reached the brightly lit hotel, they staggered to the lobby elevator and rode it up to their rooms. They said their good-nights when Jessica, her room on a lower level, stepped off the elevator. Jessica imagined that Kim, like herself, would fall directly into bed and into a deep silence and weariness called sleep.

The following day at Shockley's morgue

"SAD to see such healthy people die so uselessly," Dr. Shockley muttered. "When I think how useless my old bones have gotten . . . Sad to see these bodies go to the crematorium or the grave. Waste of excellent cadavers, which we could use around here for instructing the med students."

"You're not into the body-snatching business now, are you?" Jessica asked, knowing what a great demand existed for such excellent specimens as the three corpses now in Shockley's care.

"If I thought I could talk the next of kin into it, I'd split the proceeds," he said, and cackled again.

"Well, you routinely hand them the papers to sign for permission to harvest body parts, so why not pursue it with the families?"

"One in a million can walk away from the remains of a loved one. Forget about it. Still, just look at this Adonis. Hardly looks dead, does he? Am I right? What a specimen of *Homo sapiens*."

"Fact is he looks like that statue of David," Jessica observed.

"Michelangelo's *David*?" Kim asked. "I don't see the resem—"

"No, no, not Michaelangelo. The infamous one that looks like the boy David most likely looked like, the one by the sculptor Donatello."

"Oh, yes, I know the piece you mean. A portrayal of David at the time of his slaying of Goliath, presented as the pubescent child he had to have been at the time rather than a muscular Hercules."

"Donatello, living in the mid-fifteenth century, defied conventional wisdom. He believed in being true to nature and history. I've always admired his perfectly horrifying rendition of the street prostitute Mary Magdalen as well."

They had come back fresh to examine Anton Pierre's body, and Jessica, staring hard at the handsome face through a high-intensity magnifying glass, noticed an unusual pattern. "I see a blemish or the faint remains of a rash, I believe, on his forehead."

They had found small areas of patchy redness on all the victims caused, Jessica believed, by the toxin.

"Just another rust-colored rash?" asked Shockley, coming closer to have a look.

"No, no discoloration. Rather a faint shadow under the scope. Take a look."

"Teardrops," said Shockley.

"Teardrops? No way. Teardrops form a line as they drop down the face. These are polka-dot fashion. Besides, they're *above* the eyes."

"Let me put some infrared light on the subject," Shockley suggested. "Hit the light switch on the wall beside you, Dr. Desinor."

Kim did so, and except for the red glow of the infrared light Shockley held over the dead man's striking features, pitch darkness surrounded them. Their white lab coats turned a Day-Glo purple.

Studying the supposed rash more closely now, Jessica could clearly see a pattern of small circles with rivulets running away from each, all under the red glow, all about the young man's forehead.

"Teardrops," Shockley again said.

"But the splatter pattern is . . . all wrong, as if . . ."

"Yes, I agree. Jessica, dear, we finally have something the killer left behind."

"Then the tears are his; the killer's left his secretions on the victim?" asked Kim.

"We'll have to lift his DNA with great care. I have just the fixative and gel for the job," Shockley assured her.

"Are you sure? We damage it, it's gone. Are you sure we shouldn't simply do an electron bombardment photo?"

"And destroy the only evidence we have?"

"We'd have the photos."

"Photos will tell us nothing. We can't test the photos for human DNA properties. These teardrops, if we can lift and fix them, can tell us if our killer is male or female, his approximate age, skin color, what kind of secretor he is, possible blood type. Of course, this will take some time."

"The green," said Kim, taking Jessica's arm. "It was green tears that I saw. The green reflecting pool. He cries in the color green."

"Green tears?" asked Jessica, her voice giving way to confusion.

"I didn't recognize it before, but the green pool I saw— he cries in green for all the lost hopes, dreams, intentions of this world that have never come to fruition. He cries for the loss of angelic aspirations."

An attendant in blue surgical garb stuck her short-cropped head through the door and said, "Pardon, Dr. Shockley, but the red light is spinning again, and there's a call for Dr. Coran and Dr. Desinor. The caller says it's urgent."

"I'll take it," said Jessica.

Kim followed Jessica back toward her temporary office to take the call, but Kim said she had to find some caffeine and sugar quickly or she would keel over, so they parted near the elevators. Jessica took the call alone.

Detective Sturtevante's voice rang out. "Sorry to disturb you there, but this is about the case . . ."

Jessica thought she detected a tinge of sarcasm. "Go ahead."

"Then you haven't heard? I thought Parry and you were tight."

"Heard what? I haven't seen or heard from Parry since you left together, yesterday."

"Unfortunately, we think we may have victim number five already. If it's true, this guy's really stepped up his timetable in a big way."

"Can you send a squad car for Dr. Desinor and me?"

"It's waiting for you outside the lab, east exit of the building."

"Thanks. See you when we arrive and we're all sorry about the confusion of the other—"

"And Dr. Coran . . ."

"Yes?"

"Good to have you on the case. Don't think I had the opportunity to say so before."

" 'Preciate it, Lieutenant."

"I know we need all the support we can muster on this one."

Leave it to Sturtevante to call me support staff, Jessica thought. "Right. Male or female?" she asked.

"Come again?"

"The victim, male or female?"

"Male, but he pretends otherwise."

"Come again?"

"Likes dressing up in women's clothes. He's something of a . . . let's say an androgynous sort."

"I see."

"Might have something to do with all this, you think? This look of the victims? To me, they all appear to be rather difficult to pinpoint as to sex. The men are as pretty as the women."

"Perhaps, could be. We've been remarking on the same

thing here. I mean to say that their lifestyles, all of the victims, were . . ." She hesitated. "In one fashion or another, they were atypical, sexually speaking."

"Agreed. And they dressed the part, playing down which sex they belonged to, playing down their sexual characteristics. Add to that the thin, lithe bodies, none of them dating in the normal sense, all looking for some spiritual answer to the sexual dilemma."

"You've given this some thought."

"I have, yes."

"I did notice the asexual nature of the bodies, both the two females and the feminine males. Long, slender, no telling them apart from the back, even difficult from the front, such small breasts on the women."

"Yes, the killer's body type of choice."

"Could have a great deal to do with what's going on inside his head."

"We'll never know if he decides one of these days to take his own medicine."

"You think he may be suicidal?"

"His poetry leads me to think so, yes."

"We've duplicated the poems and have had them forwarded to every teacher and professor in the area and beyond, to see if anyone recognizes the handiwork," Jessica told her.

"Good thinking. As you know, I'd already started down that road with the local professors at the university. Listen, I must rush off. I'm glad we've had this chat." The detective abruptly cut the connection, and Jessica wondered for a moment if the androgynous nature of all the victims had spoken more to Lieutenant Leanne Sturtevante than to others working the case. She wondered momentarily about Sturtevante's sexual orientation. Then she admonished herself for the thought.

"Kim!" she called out to Desinor as her friend passed by

the office, a cup of steaming coffee in one hand, a half-eaten Snickers bar in the other.

Kim poked her head inside, asking between chews, "What was the call about? Who was it, Parry?"

Jessica stepped around the desk and walked over to Kim, taking the coffee and sipping from it. "Thanks, I needed that."

"Hey, go get your own." Kim retrieved the cup.

"There's been another killing, Kim."

"Oh, Jesus. Our boy has gotten busy since our arrival, hasn't he?"

"Yeah, I'm afraid he's been bad again—"

"Damn him—or her," Kim corrected herself. "Damn."

"In any case, the killer has struck again, and we're up to bat."

"What about Shockley?"

"This one's our house call. I think Shockley knows it. They already have a car waiting on us at the east exit of the building. Let's go." Jessica grabbed her medical bag and a lab coat.

"Right behind you."

Shockley saluted them as they passed by his office and found the elevator. Jessica got the distinct impression Dr. Leonard Shockley looked upon all the care and political tiptoeing being done around him as so much silly cloak-and-dagger.

"Have a good time at the show," he called out to the two ladies standing before the elevator.

Jessica and Kim smiled. The elevator arrived and they stepped aboard.

"What do you think of old Dr. Shockley?" Kim asked.

As the elevator descended, Jessica replied, "I think he's good for my ego."

"That goes without saying."

"But he's also shrewd, and I believe at some point he'll declare himself."

"Declare himself?"

"Show his true colors, make his professional move. He has great acumen. That much he proved with the tear find."

"True enough, but you've got to believe that some of us co-inhabitants on the planet are genuine, Jess."

"Some few, sure." Jessica placed a hand on Kim's shoulder, reassuring her. "You know I'd trust you with my life, as I have in the past."

"Same here."

SEVEN

Instinct is the express train—no stops, no detours, no layovers nor delays . . . Instinct is knowing without knowing why.

—from the casebooks of Dr. Jessica Coran, ME

L IKE everyone else entering the murder scene at 1102 South Street, Suite 3-35, Jessica felt an eerie sensation of disbelief that anyone here lay dead, much less murdered. The music and odors coming from the room were pleasing to ear and nose. A Loreena McKennitt CD had been set on continual play—presumably set in motion by the deceased or his killer—and one haunting melody after another softly caressed the ear. As sandalwood incense burned, McKennitt's dulcet voice and heartfelt lyrics sounded like the wail of the dead man's spirit, the sad Celtic strings and flute filtering through the window and onto the street below.

This strange feeling came from what was missing at the scene of the murder of Maurice Deneau. The place proved to be chillingly pleasant, normal and calm; nothing appeared out of the ordinary, nothing the least disturbed in the apartment, and the body lay posed, facedown so that anyone discovering Maurice would first be struck by the etched poem on his back. The body, thus posed, appeared in deep, comfortable slumber. Beside the dead man, on his nightstand, lay a book of poetry, a gilded marker inserted three-quarters of the way through Lord Byron's *Childe Harold,* Canto II, and the book was dog-eared at the opening of his famous long poem, *Don Juan*. Other books on a nearby shelf showed Maurice to be a lover of Wordsworth, Coleridge, Keats, Shelley, as well as Pope, Swift, Voltaire, Milton, and two of Jessica's favorite poets, Gerald Manley Hopkins and Robert Browning. Two modern poets graced the bookshelf as well, one named Lucian Burke Locke and the other named Donatella Leare, the poet and professor at the university, Jessica recalled, that Leanne Sturtevante was using as an expert and consultant.

Jessica was taken by the dark, layered cover art on both Leare's and Locke's books, a gut-wrenching Hieronymus Bosch landscape of hell on Leare's cover, the dark and sinister wasteland of a bleak cityscape on Locke's.

The walls were lavishly hung with large prints by the famous Edward Burne-Jones, G. W. Waterhouse, and other Pre-Raphaelite artists.

In the hallway, a tearful male friend, Thomas Ainsworth, who had discovered Maurice's body when he had let himself in with a key, kept up a constant, heart-wrenching wailing, like an ancient requiem, over the death of "Mayonnaise"—as he called the victim. When pressed to explain why he called Maurice Mayonnaise, he said the term was his on-line moniker. From all appearances, Thomas loved Maurice and would not harm him for the world, and he knew no one who had any reason whatsoever to harm Maurice.

"We'll confiscate the computer and any disks," declared Parry, guiding a pair of FBI agents to the machine. "Have them checked for anything that might help determine when, why, and how Maurice came to this end."

"Why Mayo as a moniker?" Jessica wondered in a near whisper to Parry.

"I dunno. Maybe he 'spread' for everybody?"

"Not if he's anything like the other victims," replied Sturtevante, who had left Ainsworth for now, joining them in the death room. "All the victims kept tight rein on who they slept with, according to all and everyone who knew them. Ainsworth is saying the same about Maurice here."

Ainsworth's wailing rose to a frightening level. "I'd better stay with the friend," Sturtevante said.

"Question him further for any word the victim might have had about a rendezvous with a sponsoring poet," suggested Parry. "He's got to have told someone of his great achievement."

Kim and Jessica turned their attention to the clean and perfectly healthy-looking dead man on the bed, his beautiful hair and skin at odds with his condition. Looking about the room, Jessica's trained eye saw nothing untoward, nothing out of place, knocked over, or shattered. This tidiness was reflected in the bureau mirror across from the bed, along with the image of Maurice's cadaver.

"How oddly strange and peaceful it all feels," she found herself whispering to Kim, who nodded, agreeing.

"And green," Kim pointed out. Drapery and floor rug were lime green. "It's a significant hit. The green pool I saw in my last vision."

"Yeah, it's almost creepier than walls and windows splattered with blood."

None of the usual elements found at a murder scene were in evidence: no blood-drenched sheets or carpets, no walls stained with sputum or brain matter, no overturned furniture, no drawers turned out, and a victim without ugly, gaping gunshot wounds, without the usual missing face or limbs. The crime scene didn't present a mutilated body or deep slash wounds. Why are we here? and what's going on here? were the first reactions of the investigators.

Sandalwood incense had struck Jessica's nostrils when she'd first entered the crime scene, and she saw fat, squat candelabras hunkered like strange pronged little beasts from a Tolkien novel on each bedside table. In fact, the home was filled with candles—large, small, thin, wide, and of every color. According to the first uniformed officer on the scene, some of the candles in the bedroom had been burning when he arrived, while some had been extinguished, presumably by the breeze at the open window. This meant that the discovery of the body had come on the heels of death.

Jessica hardly knew what to do with so pristine a crime scene. She had become used to horror, terror played out on a victim, hours of torture and mutilation. This . . . this felt more like a wake. Peace, serenity, acceptance seemed to be the rule here, as opposed to battle, chaos, or disharmony of any sort.

The open window allowed the hum and rhythmic noises of the city to enter along with the night breeze, a kind of beautiful noise of life that wafted through. Large paintings done by Maxfield Parrish, depicting serene and dreamlike worlds, and other paintings depicting medieval knights on horseback, beautiful and ornately dressed maidens, with flowing hair trellising down through tangled briar against a backdrop of raw nature, decorated the bedroom walls. Wild rushing streams, filled with spirits and banked by wildflowers and forests, played with the eye. Mere wall decoration or declaration? Jessica wondered.

Jessica's eye fell next on the gilded and grand frames that set off the many paintings that made Maurice's home a shrine to the past, or rather a fantasy past. The frames were themselves baroque artworks, which looked as if they might fetch a handsome price at any antique store. The bedroom furniture—as was true of all the furniture in the home—looked out of time, ancient, large and ponderous, yet there remained a certain charm to it. A strangely alluring style Maurice had chosen to surround himself with—something a Spanish lord might have owned in a previous century. In one corner stood a full six-foot-tall suit of armor, and from the ceilings chains hung, twisting and spiraling snake fashion to hold innumerable cast-iron-like lanterns. In another corner, Jessica felt a wave of shock come over her, surprised to see a replica of what looked like an iron maiden.

"Some icebreaker, huh?" asked Kim.

Sturtevante, who'd rejoined them now, seeing Jessica fix on the ancient weapon of torture, whispered in her ear, "Already checked it out. It's a fake, like the armor, cheaply made in Mexico, only a hundred bucks."

Jessica nodded and continued her overview of the place, her attempt to sum up the man by his surroundings. On the ceiling black sheets had been hung to simulate the night sky, and on the sheets blinked the stars and the heavens. An enormous, even breathtaking blue moon, shrouded in misty cloud—thanks to a covering of gauze—also stared back at Jessica. The entire effect beckoned any and all to lie back and contemplate the depths of the heavens.

"Where do you suppose he got all this unusual stuff?" Jessica wondered aloud when James Parry stepped in from another room.

"Looks positively foreboding. Remember how Lopaka Kowona filled his home with cratelike furniture? This kinda reminded me of that, in a twisted sort of way," he told her.

"No way, Jim. This stuff may be strange, but much of it is expensive, antique strange. Maurice paid a bundle for most of his things. Believe me." The sofa and chairs were hardwood and done in the style of pirate furniture aboard a galleon at sea.

"Maybe he got a discount. According to his friend Ainsworth, he worked for Moulin Rouge," said Lieutenant Sturtevante. "Says he was their order specialist, their interior designer, computer wizard, and he did all the floor and window displays. I called his boss, who says he was really an artist. 'Shame to lose him,' the man said."

Aside from the curious and interesting surroundings, Jessica's eyes finally focused on the sheaf of feathery paper, like ancient parchment, that lay on the bed beside the deceased. On it someone had roughly scrawled the lines of a poem in black ink, written in the hand of Maurice's killer—or was it Maurice's handwriting on the yellowed parchment? The paper looked antique, like so much else in Maurice's domain, a sort of anachronism in reverse. Jessica wondered if there was a name for such relentlessly perverse taste. Pathological antiquarianism?

"I suspect he got the yellowed parchment through the store."

"Moulin Rouge?"

"Either that or Ink, Line & Sinker, a stationery store, or Darkest Expectations, a bookstore a few doors down on Second Street," said Sturtevante, seeing Jessica study the paper. "I've seen reams of the stuff in the shops around here."

"We need to get a sample of Maurice's handwriting. Locate a handwritten note, a laundry list, anything usable. We'll check it against the lines on the parchment, rule him in or out."

Parry began a search for the needed sample. Jessica lifted the parchment with tweezers and asked Kim to have a look at it. "Tell you anything?" she asked the psychic.

Kim came around Jessica, her eyes also focused on the parchment with the tightly controlled lettering. She caused a hush in the room as she lifted the poem and read it aloud:

> *Black empty*
> *Soliloquy of soul,*
> *Come for all*
> *Who know*

Of ill-spent hours
Before the Lord Poet
Of Misspent Time
And Careless Youth,
To claim forsooth,
Dominion over the us
And the ours,
Of selfish lives that rot
On the vine
Such as yours,
Such as mine . . .

"Doesn't have quite the resonance or verve of the earlier poems," Kim declared.

"Now you're a critic?" Jessica laughed. "All right, you're right. It stinks. Something certainly missing in this poem that makes it feel unlike the killer's voice. Feels—"

"Unfinished," said Kim, stepping to the window and peering out on a light drizzle that had made the streets slick, the sheen reflecting the city lights. "I think it's Maurice's; maybe it's his attempt to impress his killer."

"To impress his lover, who killed him?"

"That'd be my guess."

Jessica and Kim now studied the lines etched into the victim's back. "Poem and victim posed for our benefit perhaps? To shock authorities, to shock society, to send a message, or all of the above?" she asked.

"Or none of the above?" Kim returned. "Like I said earlier, I believe the killer sees both his poetry and the resulting death of his 'host' body as being quite a private matter between killer and victim."

The poem, longer than previous ones left by the killer, snaked from the base of the neck down Maurice's back like a series of tattoos.

Stating the obvious, Jessica said, "Now, this is the work of our killer poet. This guy writes fluidly and well."

"Now *you're* the critic?"

"Hey, this poem's got bite, at least as deadly a bite as any cobra."

Jessica then began to read the poem aloud.

> *Chance . . . whose desire*
> *is to have a meeting*
> *with stunned innocence . . .*
> *waiting on pools of sensation*
> *that swirl in brilliant orange*
> *to swallow and overflow*
> *in the center where*
> *toucher becomes touched,*
> *texture vibrating chords*
> *of the unconfined delicate.*
> *Deliberate and graceful,*
> *the moods eddy and flow*
> *over my hands, your closed eyes*
> *undulating within a seashell sigh,*
> *entwining in airy depths,*
> *waning in flickering light.*

"Whaddaya make of it?" asked Parry, who'd returned on hearing Jessica's voice bring the poem to life.

"What do I make of it?" asked Jessica. "I make it out surreal that we're all standing here reading a poem off the back of some kid who's been murdered." Her frustration mirrored the feelings rising in the investigators.

All the detectives stared now at the poem tattooed on Maurice's back.

Kim startled the others by going to her knees at the bedside of the deceased. Her eyes had closed as she heard the final words of the poem, as if to enfold the lines into her psyche, and now her hands, one on the body, the other clutching the yellowed parchment paper, trembled. Jessica watched her for any change in expression, any look of anguish that might signal a need for her to be brought out of her trance. At the same time, she made mental note to get a good handwriting analysis of the paper script and the body script.

Kim's hands began to relax now, and a peaceful calm came over her. She revealed nothing audibly or otherwise to those around her, until suddenly her countenance took on the look of a person in the throes of great and abiding pleasure, ecstasy even. In the next moment, she collapsed, her body now draped over the deathbed. The others, astonished, reacted in knee-jerk fashion. Sturtevante gasped and said, "Help her up!"

At the same instant, Jim rushed to Kim's aid in a gentlemanly attempt to do exactly what Sturtevante suggested. However, Jessica sternly whispered, "No!" and put her body between Parry and Kim. "Allow her to finish her reading."

"I thought she had."

"Look at her."

Jim and Sturtevante stared at Kim's prostrate form. One of her hands remained on the poisonous poem while the other had let go of the parchment poem.

Jessica cautioned in a raspy whisper, "She's clearly in a trance state. You don't jerk a person back from where *she* is; it could cause serious problems."

"But she's contaminating the crime scene," muttered Parry.

"I'm responsible for the integrity of the crime scene, and I say let her fucking be."

Approximately five minutes passed, during which they watched Kim's face and body for indications that she was going deeper and deeper into repose. Kim's body language clearly said that she was shutting down, simulating the state of the victim beside her. Jessica feared that if Kim simulated death too closely, she could fall into a comatose state from which she might never return.

Parry must have felt the same fear, as he whispered into Jessica's ear, "Maybe we ought now to carefully bring her around?"

Jessica agreed. "Yes, perhaps we should revive her."

Jessica drew nearer to the bed. Placing a hand over Kim, she was preparing to calmly urge her friend back into consciousness when she noticed the dizzyingly fast movement of the eyes beneath Kim's eyelids. What had appeared peaceful slumber was in fact filled with agitation. Her sleep proved fitful beneath the outward calm, as if disturbed by nightmare images. None of the others could guess the nature of Kim's journey into the mind of the victim, and none could know what clues she might carry back from her psychic journey.

Even though she was a scientist, Jessica believed in Kim Desinor's psychic powers because she had seen the miraculous work Kim had done in the past; she had learned from Kim that there truly were more things between heaven and hell than were dreamed up in scientific circles.

"Is she . . . is she okay?" asked Sturtevante.

"I've never seen her work before, but I've read of cases she's solved by tapping into the consciousness of living victims," said Parry. "Like the one in Houston a few years ago. But this . . . tapping into the mind of a dead man; this looks damned dangerous."

"Rest assured, she's the best," Jessica replied.

Suddenly Kim's body began an epileptic-seizure-like paroxysm that first set her teeth gnashing and then chattering with the extreme cold she felt. Jessica felt the cold as well when Kim gripped her wrist, and her own body trembled in response. Jessica hugged her friend, providing the warmth that Kim's nonverbal gestures screamed out for.

"Are you . . . all right . . . Kim?" she asked between gasps, feeling the tip-of-the-iceberg effect, and at the same moment wondering how much cold Kim could withstand.

Kim could not for the moment reply.

"Get some blankets, hot coffee!" Jessica shouted. "And close that window!"

Sturtevante and Parry rummaged through the place for these items, Sturtevante making the coffee. Meanwhile, Jessica, still trembling, struggled to get Kim on her feet. Once she was standing, Jessica walked her in circles to get her circulation going, saying, "Keep moving, dear; walk with me." The longer she held on to Kim, the colder she herself became, until her own teeth began to chatter.

In another few minutes, Kim and Jessica, wrapped in blankets, moved into the other room, far from the body. Here they drank steaming-hot coffee out of hefty mugs that once belonged to Maurice Deneau. The others stood by, their eyes telling Jessica how anxious they were for any tidbits of information that Kim might reveal, but Parry remained silent, hesitant about asking. Seeing is believing, and they had seen the psychic suffer during her time spent in trance.

Kim now appeared confused and disoriented. Unsure of her surroundings, she asked Jessica, "Wh-where are we?"

Jessica informed her.

The others watched as a strange, rust-colored rash that had shown up on Kim's cheeks and arms began to dissipate, these "stigmatalike" signs disappearing as quickly as they appeared.

Kim looked about the kitchen area where they sat, nodded, and then complained, "Have a nasty, strange, rustlike taste in my mouth."

"That's Sturtevante's coffee," said Parry, making light of it.

"No, this isn't coffee. It's something Maurice tasted before he died. It's metallic, like . . . like sulfur, only worse, coppery sulfuric taste." She began nervously switching the coffee cup from one hand to the other, back and forth. "My stomach . . . doesn't feel so good. Tingling sensation in all my extremities, particularly these," she said, holding her fingers up to the light as if they were on fire. She placed the coffee cup aside. "I fear I'll drop it. My fingers feel so numb."

"Where you've been, I don't wonder," said Jessica, sipping at her coffee.

"Exactly where is that?" asked Parry, one of Maurice's books in his hand. "Where precisely *were* you just then, Dr. Desinor. I mean when you were, forgive the phrase, 'in bed' with the . . . the victim."

"Go ahead, say it," Kim replied, "in bed with the dead."

"All this morbid poetry, it's rubbing off on you, Kim," Jessica joked.

"Judging from his diary entries," Parry commented, "Maurice fancied himself a poet. He's written a lot of verse in his private journal. It's pretty maudlin stuff, about how he is too much put upon by the forces of this world, but I'll wade through it. Who knows . . . maybe it'll reveal something about him or his killer."

Sturtevante insisted, "You going to tell us what you saw when you were in trance, Dr. Desinor?"

"Didn't see a thing, sorry."

"Nothing? Not a thing?" the detective repeated.

"*Felt* a great deal, but no, my mental eyes were closed. I saw no images, no faces, no visual revelations. Too overwhelmed, I suspect, by the feelings of the moment—which I suspect is how Maurice felt."

"Then what did you feel?" pressed Sturtevante.

"Feel . . . what did I feel? Felt a gnawing, ratlike pain in my abdomen; felt surprise, amazement, if you will."

"Go on."

"I felt dry-throated, my—or Maurice's—entire body went cold—cold as a parched desert in winter; felt my throat go arid as sand, like . . . like I was choking on dust, but this dust was laden with sulfur, or some such chemical. Next, I felt nausea and numbing and tingling all at once, especially in the hands and feet—fingers and toes, actually."

"Anything else?" urged Sturtevante, clearly taking mental notes.

"Toward the end, I felt an overwhelming sense of calm replace the painful cold; the calm flooded over me, replacing any sensations of pain or discomfort. I was left with no sensations any longer. The ultimate sensation—peace and unfeeling."

"Who said, 'Only the dead are at peace'?" asked Parry.

"The quote is 'Only the dead *know* peace.' Old Mexican saying, I think," replied Jessica. "Else it came from an old John Wayne western."

Jessica saw Jim smile at this. His boyish grin brought on flashes of memory for her—memories of times when each of them noticed every small detail about the other, from the way her hair fell across her cheek to the way he traced her lifeline on her palm. She recalled how, at one time, they could not get enough of each other, how the wine of endorphins fed their love—"the true nectar of the gods," she had once told him. She wondered how they might begin to relax around each other after so much had happened between them. She wondered if it was possible to work a case alongside Jim, or if the two of them were foolish to try.

Sturtevante continued to interrogate Kim. "Then you're telling us that you saw nothing about the murder?" The detective's voice carried an edge like a knife blade. "You can't even tell us who wrote the poem left beside the body, or the poem on the body? If the two were or were not written by the same person?"

"I didn't say that."

"What can you tell us, then, about the poetry on the parchment?"

"It's the work of the victim; his parchment, his pen, his words. I got those words again, pressing in on me—*rampage* and *quark*—and another word insinuated itself on my mind as well."

"What word?" asked Jessica.

"Preflight."

"Like a preflight check you do on an airplane?"

"I can't say, only that it's somehow important."

"You're sure the poem on the paper is Maurice's?" repeated Sturtevante.

"Yes, I'm sure."

"Good guess, I should think," the detective muttered.

"Maurice's poem was written to his killer. It was written in praise of his killer. An attempt to honor his own killer."

"Then they had a suicide pact?" Jessica perked up at this.

"I believe so."

"You believe so, or you'd decided as much before you ever arrived here?" Sturtevante demanded.

"Compare the handwriting, Jessica, with Maurice's lines from his diary," Kim calmly replied, unruffled by the detective's skepticism. "The lines on the death poem will, no doubt, render this a moot point."

Jessica silently compared the two poems. "I have to agree with Kim's assessment of the difference here in literary quality; one is professional, the other amateurish."

"Maurice's poetry is stilted, somewhat clichéd, and filled with awkward, passive constructions," continued Kim. "No fresh images, nothing to recommend it beyond its mediocrity."

Jessica added, "The poet who saw Maurice to his grave does not deal in mediocrity."

Kim immediately added, "Or awkward language, clichéd diction, or stilted imagery! This guy, whoever he is, writes more haunting, evocative poetry—in my opinion—than anything I've read in years. Take it for what it's worth, Lieutenant."

"Then the killer's a professional poet, someone capable in every respect where language is concerned?" asked Parry.

"Precise and calculated," Kim replied, "with every word."

"Then he doesn't just write this off the top of his head in the throes of murder? He premeditates the entire act, writing draft after draft."

"I think it's time we shared a suspicion we hold about the Poet Killer with you two," Jessica said to Parry and Sturtevante.

"And what is that?" Sturtevante looked shaken by the direction the discussion had taken, but Jessica could not be certain of her expression.

"We've compared the poems he's left behind thus far, and aside from the opening repetition or chorus of three lines, they all have the theme of flickering life—that is, that the soul is never quite extinguished by death but merely takes on a new form."

"We believe the killer is involved in a fantasy that has to do with some sort of migration of souls," added Kim.

Jessica continued. "And that he's in the business of helping that migration along."

"Speculation," muttered Leanne Sturtevante, staring now at the firmament ceiling motif, which had been carried out even here in the kitchenette.

"We believe all the poems are linked," said Kim. "In fact, that each is a part of a whole, a kind of epic poem he's going for."

"My God," said Parry. "Then that means he's premeditating more slates to write on, more murders."

"Kim keeps coming up with the number nineteen."

"That may mean the killer will require nineteen bodies to complete his or her performance art," added Kim, who sipped again at the steaming coffee in her now-warmed hands.

The room fell silent as this notion floated like a spectral presence among them.

"I'VE compared the handwriting in the diary to that of the poem on the yellowed, fake-but-fun parchment, which Sturtevante suspected had come from the stationery store Ink, Line & Sinker," Jessica began.

"What's your take on the handwriting, Jess?" asked Parry, standing over her at the table where she sat examining the two documents.

"With my admittedly limited experience in handwriting analysis, I'd say these two, parchment and diary, are by the same hand."

"I see."

"Of course, we'll know for sure when our specialists in handwriting have a look-see." Jessica looked up to Sturtevante and set her jaw firmly. "I think Dr. Desinor has scored a major *hit* here." She then put a hand on Kim's arm and asked, "How're you feeling?"

"Better . . . much . . ."

"Did you get a sense of the killer at all from touching the victim's back, from placing yourself in his . . . his place?" pursued Sturtevante.

"Nothing beyond a vague sense of his belief in himself and his actions."

"Can you elaborate, Dr. Desinor?"

"No, I was . . . fell into the victim's mind-set, not the killer's."

"She's tired, Lieutenant. Give it a rest," Jessica said, her voice clear and final. "Allow Dr. Desinor to regain her strength now, please."

"Sure, sure." Sturtevante raised her hands in the universal gesture of truce, but her eyes registered a sad defeat. Like everyone else in the room, she had wanted answers to questions plaguing the investigation, answers that eluded them all.

Seeing this and Jim's dejection as well, Jessica pulled out a large magnifying glass and said to the other two, "Come with me. I have something additional to share with you."

They left Kim at the kitchen table and returned to the bedroom and the body. Jessica asked Parry to help her to gently turn the body faceup. This done, she held a high-intensity flashlight in her teeth, the magnifying glass in one hand, and supported herself over the body with the other. "Bingo!" she declared.

"What? What is it?" asked Sturtevante.

"Teardrops on his forehead, just as we discovered on the Anton Pierre corpse."

"What does this mean, Jess?" asked Parry, perplexed.

"It's his DNA, the killer's DNA. Unless there's evidence that Anton and Maurice stood on their heads while crying, or were strung up by their heels, they're not going to have tears on their foreheads. No, these near-invisible tracks were left by the killer."

"Excellent . . . excellent find," muttered Sturtevante. "Now we can find out some characteristics of the killer—race, sex even."

"Exactly, and it'll be a direct match once we make an arrest."

"Terrific find, Jess," Parry complimented.

"Can't take all the credit for this one. Dr. Shockley identified the marks after I pointed them out on Pierre's forehead."

"And as for the other bodies?"

"Too degenerated to tell, but two in a row now, that tells us something."

"Imagine, the guy kills them and then sheds tears over them."

"Not altogether unusual," countered Jessica. "Signifies a certain amount of remorse in most cases."

"Not here, not this time," said Kim, standing now in the doorway, looking at the others. "These tears are green tears . . . green with hope and love and rekindling life, green with life and regeneration, don't you see?"

Sturtevante again appeared shaken by Kim's words, as if the psychic had somehow unmasked her, digging into her mind. She showed her agitation by pacing the room and then rushing out.

"What's with her?" asked Parry.

Jessica shrugged. "Isn't this case enough to get to anyone?"

"I suspect that she thinks she may know someone who might fall victim to the Poet Killer," replied Kim. "At least, I think she fears as much."

"Thanks for sharing the good news of the teardrop find," Parry said to Jessica. "How long before it can be processed?"

"DNA testing takes time, but Shockley has it on the front burner. Still, it will take at least ten days, maybe more."

"He'll kill again before then."

"I don't know how to speed up the process any more than we have, but at least we're confident the tearstain pattern points to the perpetrator and not the victim. In time, we will have a DNA profile of the killer."

Parry instantly snapped, "Finally! A break. Maybe the one that will nail this bastard."

EIGHT

You can go for a walk with them, see a movie with them, go swimming, eat dinner, even ride in a car with them while they are driving, but the sociopathic among us are quite literally different in every respect. They merely look like us. It is the ultimate disguise, making them an alien race within our own, and they know how to play us all for fools.

—from the casebooks of Dr. Jessica Coran, ME

MAURICE Deneau had bought into the killer's con, hook, line, and sinker. The party of detectives sat in silence for some time, contemplating the nature of the beast they pursued. Taken to its logical conclusion, they realized, he must be a creature pleasing to the eye and ear, to all the senses, in fact; he must be an evil so cloaked in goodness that no one, not even his victims, know of his evil. Either that or they worship him for his darkness or his twisted ideas and perverted faith.

Jessica could not help but draw correlations between this sociopath and a killer priest she had encountered in London the year before. That psychotic's vision of the Second Coming had gotten a series of people killed, but his victims had also been willing participants in their own crucifixions. And now here she sat in a second-story apartment in Philadelphia, the heart of early America, ostensibly fighting the same fight, racing the same race, and wondering at the familiarity of this evil.

If Kim Desinor's psychic impressions could be relied upon, only one of the victims thus far had recognized the evil this killer presented. That had been Caterina Mercedes, but even then it took death to waken her to the evil she had allowed to close in around her and finally envelop her.

Maurice Deneau's friend, Thomas Ainsworth, wanted to stay the night at the crime scene, so Sturtevante had to deal with him, asking him if he had someplace else to crash. Ainsworth was a frail, thin, and pale young man, perhaps anemic, perhaps HIV positive. Otherwise, he looked a great deal like the victim in size, weight, and build, and he proved that the idealistic innocence of youth still existed in modern-day America.

"Can I pack a few of my things? I was staying with Maurice, you see, and . . . God, if I'd only been here, maybe . . . maybe I could've done something. We had a fight, you know. No big deal, but I was making him pay . . . and now this."

"Sorry, nothing goes in or out until we release the place. Could be a couple of days," Sturtevante told the young man, whose eyes were fire red from crying. His reaction was to pace the hallway like a nervous cat. "Do you have anywhere to stay tonight?" she repeated.

"Guess I can call my parents."

"Might be a good idea, son. Maybe go stay with them for a while."

"Yeah . . . yeah . . . ain't safe around here anymore, is it?"

"That's quite the understatement, Thomas."

Kim had regained enough strength now to stand and walk, and together, she and Jessica headed for the door, while Parry went to officially call in the paramedics to remove the body. With this decision made, they could never go back to the crime scene as they'd found it, so this moment always felt crucial in a stone-cold murder of this sort.

As the team vacated the crime scene, leaving the body to the paramedics for transport to the police morgue, Jessica asked Kim, "Did you get any sensation from Maurice that he knew in the end that he was being murdered?"

"None whatsoever, no."

"This monster we're dealing with, then, is smooth."

"Caterina Mercedes's body was a seething cauldron of hatred for what the killer had done to her. At some point, she realized what was happening to her and why. It felt like. . . it was a horrid betrayal. But the others never knew he'd poisoned them. *And they still don't.*"

"You said Caterina Mercedes felt betrayed. Would you say she felt she had been conned into dying?" asked Jessica, feeling the night air wafting up the stairwell from an open door at ground level—as if to beckon them outside.

"Yes, but Maurice Deneau didn't. He never picked up on the con or realized that he was ever in any danger. Whatever poison our man is using, it effectively shuts down rational thought, lulling the victims into a calm acquiescence, but something in Caterina fought back."

"What made her different?" asked Parry, who'd hurried down the steps, catching up as they stepped out into the predawn darkness. "Any suggestions, Dr. Coran? Any medical reason one person would be more immune than another to whatever poison this creep is using?"

They continued on toward the patrol cars that had brought them to this section of town, the famous Second Street off downtown Philadelphia, where the killer moved efficiently and safely among the upwardly mobile, artistic community. "Any suggestions, Dr. Coran?" pressed Parry.

"It would help to know the exact nature of the poison. We need to send it out for analysis to the FBI Crime Lab in Washington. The local guys are coming up zip on it."

Kim suggested, "Perhaps Caterina had a stronger tolerance for the drug."

"Possibly, but more likely our killer made a mistake. More like the dose was too low or too high, in which case she would have a far different reaction than that of calm acquiescence—what the killer apparently needs in order to leave his deadly poetry for us to read," Jessica answered, rubbing the soreness from her neck, taking in the crisp yet damp evening air. It smelled of a coppery rain that had turned into a mist, and it touched her cheek with the feel of a sodden cloth.

"Or she was lucid enough to suggest that she do the same to the killer's back, using his inkwell, the same as he had used on her," suggested Sturtevante. "In a con, that's when things go wrong, when the mark doesn't cooperate as you predict. I worked for the fraud division for several years. We handled con artists, flimflam men, hucksters, and hoaxsters," she informed the others. "I know how these creeps work to relieve the old and the innocent of their life's savings. I've just never known a con artist who set the stakes at life itself."

"He doesn't see himself as pulling a hoax, I don't think," said Jessica, "not from all that we've surmised."

Kim immediately agreed, bolstering Jessica's notion. "He doesn't see it as a game or a flimflam; he doesn't enjoy killing for the sake of killing. It's a means to an end. To the transmigration of the soul into what he believes is a higher form, I suspect. It is the only way he can get his victims to quickly and efficiently cross over. His endgame, if you will, is to return them to some otherworldly force, or forces, that he sees or hears in his head. That would be my guess."

"Apparently his victims don't see him as any kind of threat whatsoever," Jessica agreed.

"Fact is, they likely gravitate to him as *heroic.*"

"Heroic?" asked Parry, perplexed.

"He's a grim, dark figure who seems to incarnate all they aspire to and surround themselves with. Look closely at Maurice's surroundings, his choice of habitat, the very things on his walls," Kim explained.

"And look as closely at what he has to say in his diary," added Jessica. "Somewhere in it he may tell you what he most loves in life, and I suspect it is the belief that one day he will die."

"A death wish?"

"More closely aligned with the notion that there's a better world beyond. Possibly a parallel universe far better and into which he ought to have been born," said Kim. "It's less a death wish per se than a desire to transcend life as we mortals know it."

Jessica added, "So his savior, even if temporary, is the man who can both see and understand the desperately melancholy youth, and so becomes the young person's hero."

She saw Parry's eyes bore into her, questioning.

"I noticed a book of Byron's works on the nightstand, the pages marked," Jessica said.

"Got it right here," said Parry. "I'll look it over, see if it uncovers anything, along with the diary entries. Got some confidential stuff here that might prove helpful down the road. Listen to this."

Parry began to read from the diary. " 'I chose the name Mayonnaise because I like licking it off my sexual partner. Learned early in life that the only way to keep people close is through sex. I've always had a hard time making friends, but even a harder time sustaining friendships. I know people tire of me, that I whine too much, but I also know that I'm worthy of someone's unconditional love, if only I could find it.' "

"Doesn't exactly sound as if he's into abstinence," Sturtevante quipped.

"Sounds like the usual teen angst stuff," said Jessica.

Jim Parry continued to scan the diary, resting it on the volume of Byron. Jessica filled her lungs and stared at the crowd that had gathered about the crime scene. Uniformed policemen held people in check at a temporary barricade.

As she was about to slide into the patrol car, James said, "Listen to this part."

As much as she wanted to object to his reading aloud the victim's private words here on the street at this moment, Jessica said nothing. Jim read, " 'I am lousy at maintaining and cultivating a friend, or at least a worthwhile one. What's the point of trying? In the end, it only causes pain and suffering. They all die off like neglected weeds. I have allowed the weeds to infest my garden. It's all my own fault. I am a poor gardener in the field of friendships.' "

"Like I said, the usual teen angst, heartache, and suffering."

"But listen to this," he insisted.

"Hey, that's private, personal stuff there!" shouted someone who'd bolted from the crowd, having gotten past the police tape and uniformed cops. "Give me that!"

They looked up to find a pretty young woman of perhaps twenty glaring at them. "That's mine!" She snatched at the diary, but Parry held it overhead, too high for her to grasp.

"Sorry, no, young lady. This belonged to the victim, and as such, it is evidence in a crime."

"*Goddammitalltohell,* I knew Maurice would wind up like this one day!"

"Like what?" asked Sturtevante, trying to calm her.

"Cops pouring over his life, his apartment, and his stuff! Damn fool, Maurice."

Lieutenant Sturtevante introduced herself. "I'm the one who left a message on your answering machine to get over here. Got your number out of Maurice's Rolodex. I'm a homicide detective with the PPD." But the words *homicide detective* did not appear to register with the young blond woman, who remained distraught. "Tell me, miss, exactly what kind of relationship did you have with Maurice?"

"He was my brother, dammit. My fucking, wide-eyed, idiot brother. He liked to pretend otherwise, that he was my sister, and he liked to believe that the fucking world was filled with goodness and light—that is, when he wasn't so depressed he couldn't drag himself out of bed. But he thought the best of everyone and everything. Opened his door to anything off the street. 'Helping out,' he called it."

"I see."

Jessica thought it quite likely a different view of Maurice than that held by the person who had killed him.

The sister shouted now, "Where is he? Have you sent him to the hospital? How badly is he hurt? One of those creeps he let stay with him hurt him, didn't they?"

She thought he'd been beaten but was still alive. No one had informed her of her brother's death.

"Where can I catch up to him? What hospital did you send him to?"

"He's . . . I'm afraid you can't," said Sturtevante.

The young woman stared at them as if they were all mad aliens. Her head began a slight shaking, her lip quivering. She eyed the window of Maurice's bedroom, where what looked like an innocent game of shadow play was going on. The attendants wrapping the body for transport. The sister rushed for the stairs leading up to the apartment. She hadn't gotten far when a uniformed cop restrained her and she saw Thomas Ainsworth coming slowly out of the building, dejected and trembling. She tore loose from the officer holding her and rushed toward the boy, tearing into him with her nails and screaming, "You did it! You got

Maurice into big-time trouble this time! Didn't you? Didn't you?"

The sister ranted until she was pulled off, and then she suddenly froze, petrified at the entryway, seeing the prone body on the gurney. "Where the fuck are the medics? Why aren't you resuscitating him? Why're you all standing around doing nothing, reading his private papers?"

Jessica went to her, put an arm over her shoulder, and simply pronounced her brother dead.

"No, nooooooo!" the girl cried, and tore at the cold, black, and unyielding polyethylene body bag. "Open it! Open it! I don't believe it," she wailed. "Not unless I see it, I won't believe it."

"Open it," Jessica ordered the ambulance attendants. One of them, biting his lower lip, zipped the bag open, and the sister screamed, her wail penetrating the night sky. She fell prostrate across her brother's form, clutching him.

As Jessica pulled her away, the distraught sister nearly pulled Maurice's entire head from the bag, as if attempting to drag him back into life from his eternal sleep.

"I loved him so much," she cried out.

Jessica guided her up the stairs, and snatching away yellow crime-scene tape from the door, she found the only privacy that might be had. The others followed. Jessica pulled up a chair and sat Maurice's sister at the table where they had all sat earlier. She poured the young woman a cup of leftover, lukewarm coffee and offered it to her, but the sobbing, heaving girl refused it. Her eyes had become black concentric circles, her black hair a tangle of thin noodle-shaped snakes.

Jessica asked, "Do you know of anyone, anyone at all, who may have wanted your brother dead?" Even as she asked the stock question, she knew it hardly began to cover the circumstances here. Perhaps none of the conventional questions applied, and she feared that perhaps she might never know the right questions to ask.

"No, no one. But it had to be one of his strays. I warned him. So many times I warned him."

"You warned him?"

"And he'd just call me mommy in that sassy tone of his, and I just went on warning him." Her entire frame shook, racked with grief. "He didn't damn deserve this!"

"Did he speak of anyone staying with him here, recently or otherwise?"

"No, no one but Ainsworth. *Worthless* is what I call him."

"Maurice mentioned no one else that he may have recently become infatuated with?" she pressed.

"No, but he stopped talking to me about anything to do with his personal life. He couldn't take the least criticism, crumbled under it the way a butterfly might. He so . . . so liked being needed, and he had such a need to be loved."

"So you think your brother Maurice may have brought this on himself?" asked Jessica, now seeing the resemblance in brother and sister. "What precisely did you mean by that?"

"It was his way of doing good for his 'karma,' he thought. But it was really self-indulgent in a peculiar way."

"How so?"

"He was a fool, taking pity on every stray animal, and taking in runaways, street people, all that, and I told him how dangerous it was, like playing Russian roulette, but it made him feel, I don't know, angelic and above all the rest of us. Some such shit. A shrink could've had a field day with Maurice, could've made him into one of those whachamacallits, a case study."

"So, he brought home stray humans?" Jessica asked of the sobbing teenager.

"Human strays, yeah . . . God damn it all."

"We're going to need to ask you some questions, Miss Deneau," said Sturtevante.

"Deneau was Mayo-Maurice's name, not mine. I'm Harris, Linda Sue Harris." She said this with a proud defiance.

"Big surprise, a fake name?" asked Parry, standing in the doorway now.

"No, not fake," Linda Sue countered. "He had changed his name to Deneau legally."

"Man, this kid sounds confused. First he has his name legally changed to this highfalutin moniker, and then he puts it out he wants to be called Mayonnaise?"

"He *was* confused! Unclear what he wanted, what he wanted to be, all of it. He was forever preoccupied with the questions the rest of us eventually let go of. You know how it is. Still believed fairy tales and myths were true. He never fucking grew up."

"What kind of questions?" asked Jessica.

"You know, the usual claptrap about who am I, what am I, where did I originate from, where am I going to after this life, all of it. Went from one belief system to the next, trying to tie it all together, but nothing ever really satisfied him."

"What did the family think of the name change?" asked Parry.

"Not much, but then they didn't give Maurice much thought anyway. They didn't approve of his lifestyle."

"Then his family name was—"

"Harris. Maurice's real name was Patrick William Harris—Pattie, I grew up calling him—but that was too . . . too standard issue for him."

"For his soul, you mean?" Kim interjected.

"That's right, for his friggin' too sensitive soul! I loved him for it, his sensitivity, but I also hated him for it—for the depth of it, for the obsessiveness of it, and now for this."

"For getting himself killed over it?" asked Jessica.

"For doing this, for hurting me and our parents. I know it has to do with his personality. He was a victim waiting to happen."

Jessica offered her a shoulder to cry on. She took it, and after some long moments of sobbing, the young woman sat back again, wiping her eyes with a handkerchief Parry had provided earlier. "I hate him for what he's done."

"Did he think he was born at the wrong time and place?" Kim asked. "I mean, judging from his paintings and furnishings . . ."

"Try wrong dimension," she countered. "Maurice was a misfit in this life; always had been."

"Can you explain that further?" pressed Jessica.

Linda Sue looked into Jessica's eyes. "Pattie, he once told me he thought he'd been born with the heart and soul of a butterfly, that he'd somehow gotten his wires crossed and ought to be in life as a butterfly, said his life as a human would be as short as a butterfly's life as a result. Said he was born in the wrong time and place and with the wrong name, so he dreamed up Maurice Deneau. Been going by it since he turned old enough to vote."

"And how old is . . . was Maurice?"

"All of twenty-four going on thirteen. Never wanted to grow up. Damn you, Pattie," she finished with a fist to the sky, as if cursing his spirit.

Parry knelt beside her now and said, "Tell me, was Maurice . . . Pat . . . was he—"

"Gay! Spit it out, and what's that got to do with anything? Damn people, damn people for condemning my brother. Yes, his sexual orientation was gay, but he wasn't loose. He didn't sleep around, and I doubt he'd give you a second look, mister."

Jessica stifled a laugh at this.

The girl continued: "He remained true to anyone who was man enough to remain faithful to him. That was Maurice, and for the time being that jerk Tom Ainsworth was it, but they were having problems, you can bet, but Maurice and Tom've been together for the past three years, you know?"

"Sounds like your brother was a caring person," offered Jessica.

"Caring as we humans get, but what did it get him but killed? He took people in, people who were in need. Tom got tired of it. Maurice lent them money and gave them things, and as a result he had people coming and going through his life all the time, and secretly, I think he liked it that way, regardless of what he told himself in that diary, or what he told me." She dropped her head, sobbed further. "The Good Samaritan, that was Maurice, and Jesus but he liked the role he played."

Jessica gently urged Linda Sue to go on.

"He believed in a pure and saving-grace kinda love that he had been searching for since his birth, but Ainsworth wasn't it, and he looked for it in all the wrong places. Said he'd recognize it when . . . whenever it came along. He was a fucking romantic; absolutely addicted to it."

"Why do you think Thomas Ainsworth got him killed?"

"That idiot kept hurting Pattie. Ainsworth slept around. He . . . Pattie knew that Ainsworth had just been using him these past months. It sent Pattie into a grave . . . grave depression. Sent him out nights looking."

She wrung her hands and dabbed at her eyes. " 'Course, it wasn't all Tom's fault that it ended in failure. Nobody could measure up to Maurice's standards. The perfect partner would have to be from another era, like one of those freaks in the paintings all over his place. Crazy bastard." She burst into tears once more.

Sturtevante now held up the parchment with the poem they suspected to have been written by Maurice, and she asked point-blank, "Ever see anything like this before around your brother's place?"

The girl stared. "The Poet Killer. I saw it on the news. My brother was killed by the Poet?" Newspeople had not been told that the killer left his poems emblazoned on the backs of his victims.

"Do you know this handwriting? Ever see it before?"

"Never."

"Then it's not your brother's?"

"No . . . no . . . well, I mean, isn't it the killer's handwriting?"

Jessica took Linda Sue's hands in her own. "We need you to be clear on this, Linda. We have reason to believe that this particular poem may have been written by your brother."

"He didn't, you know, kill himself, did he?" she asked.

Jessica shook her head emphatically. "No, of that much we are certain."

The sister stared at the poem, reading its every line. "Sounds like Pattie's prattle. Yeah, looks like his handwriting."

Sturtevante said, "I'd like you to come back to the station house with me, Miss Harris."

"What for?"

"Routine questions. Get a fix on your brother's acquaintances, his routine, that sort of thing. Any bit of information, you know, could lead to something else, which in turn could uncover something new in the case, you see."

"Until the trail leads to his killer, you mean? You have no idea the times I told him the road to hell is paved with good intentions." She sniffed back sobs. "I won't let you all treat this as a typical death, do you understand me?"

Sturtevante put a hand on her shoulder and said, "Of course."

Jessica reassured her. "There's nothing typical about what's happened here."

"No, dear," added Kim, "there's nothing typical at all about this case. You're not to worry on that score."

NINE

You shall see them on a beautiful quarto page,
where a neat rivulet of text shall meander
through a meadow of margin.

—Richard Brinsley Sheridan (1751–1816)

Philadelphia Police Department, three days later

IT had been two days since Jessica's skilled hands and scalpel autopsied the remains of Maurice Deneau, but the procedure on the young man netted them nothing new save for the added DNA sample taken from the tearstains believed to have come from his killer. Thomas Ainsworth agreed to having a sample of his DNA taken so as to be ruled out as a suspect; he'd claimed not to have touched the body beyond attempting to shake Maurice awake. He claimed that when he found this impossible, he immediately called the police, and at no time did he shed tears directly over the body. In fact, he found touching the body repulsive.

All internal organs proved absolutely healthy and disease-free. They had simply ceased to function, along with the brain and the heart. Jessica could simply find no cause of death beyond the unknown toxins in the poisoned ink. Still, they knew the delivery system must be the ink, as they saw no internal destruction to lips, gums, throat, or stomach lining, and there were no exterior marks on the body save the poem. Some poison delivered through pen and ink, but what?

Maurice's autopsy had shown only what they suspected: a young man in good health who had suffered a sudden trauma to his system, primarily his brain. A death by narcosis in which vital organs simply shut down domino fashion after the brain had ceased to send signals. They ran tests for any traces of the usual suspects: arsenic, strychnine, household chemicals. But the usual routes to certainty were leading nowhere, and Jessica's attempt at getting results from toxicology had totally failed.

She called a meeting with Sturtevante's boss, Chief Aaron Roth, to air her complaints about the PPD's toxicology lab. When she entered the room, she wasn't surprised to see the old coroner, Shockley, and his toxicologist, Frank DeAngelos, allied against her.

Chief Roth, clearly a man of few words, said, "Let's hear it, Dr. Coran."

She decided it would not do to mince words with these men. "Toxicology on all previous victims has netted us nothing substantial, and so we remain in the dark as—"

Dr. DeAngelos, PPD's top toxicologist, immediately shot to his feet to defend himself and his department. "It always proves difficult to test for a mystery substance." The thin man's black mustache twitched mouselike over his lip as he spoke. "Not knowing what to test for, and unable to test for all the myriad possibilities—almost any substance can be turned into a poison—we don't know where to begin."

Jessica calmly sat down here in the operations room, where the photos of all the victims had been pinned on every wall, their dead eyes now looking down on the living in what looked like accusation. Earlier in the day, this room had been filled with the men and women on the citywide task force that was working to crack the case.

Jessica said evenly, "May I suggest—"

"No, you may not suggest how to run my department," said DeAngelos.

"Frank, let's hear Dr. Coran out, please," scolded the chief.

"May I suggest, Dr. DeAngelos, that your people begin with anything that works like an anesthetic. I'll go out on a limb here and suggest that our killer might be an anesthesiologist. He knows how to quickly and efficiently put people to sleep for a long time."

"We've tested for the usual barbiturates, such as Brevitol," said DeAngelos.

"Then what about the unusual; what was used commonly before Brevitol?"

Jessica had been after DeAngelos since Maurice's body had been brought in, desperately trying to get some fix on the toxins found in the victims. She had also attempted to understand DeAngelos's perspective, and to remain open to any educated conjecture about the type of poison or drug the killer used. In fact, she had all but camped on his doorstep and badgered his people for results, for all the good it had done her.

Disappointed now with the lack of progress, her blood pressure rising, Jessica was angry and upset. She put DeAngelos on the defensive, confronting him. "I just learned that your people have still not forwarded samples of the ink poison to D.C. Is that true?"

"My people are busy, Dr. Coran, and we are all doing our damnedest to solve this mess."

You're only testing for household chemicals and over-the-counter drugs."

"We've tested for PCP, heroin, cocaine, all the usual street crap."

"Dammit, Doctor, test for *everything*. Every known substance, if you must."

"Do you know what you're asking?" he grumbled back.

"I can't approve that kind of overtime for my people. We have to work within a strict budget, Dr. Coran. Postmortem investigation doesn't come cheap. This isn't the goddamned FBI; here in Philadelphia, we don't collect taxes the way the feds do. We aren't funded to—"

It was maddening. "Dr. DeAngelos, we are stymied in this case until we can identify the drug or poison the killer uses."

"I am quite aware of that."

"The poison must be exotic, colorless perhaps, certainly odorless, with the possibility of a metallic taste or aftertaste. We have told you that we suspect it produces a reddish-colored rash, which dissipates after time."

DeAngelos defended himself before Police Chief Aaron Roth and Dr. Shockley. "Whatever it is, our mystery poison isn't the standard text, and as for these symptoms, all of them you learned from Dr. Desinor's suppositions about the nature of the poison. A woman who holds no credentials in toxicology—or even pharmacology, as far as I know."

"She enumerated the suspected symptoms while under trance, and once again I can tell you—"

Dr. DeAngelos demanded, "How can she possibly describe symptoms of a poison we have not as yet identified? This is sheer madness, Chief. Talk about putting the cart before the horse."

Finally, Jessica blurted out, "Dr. Desinor's psychic abilities are well documented, sir."

"Ah, and we're all to jump to the orders of your pet sorceress, I suppose?"

"She has at least given us some intriguing clues to pursue, Dr. DeAngelos."

"I do not deal in the intriguing. And I tell you, we are doing everything in our power at this time. In addition, we've tested for iodine, lead, and mercury—all of which leave a metallic taste in the mouth, and all of which tests, thus far, have come back negative."

She tried to calm both herself and him. "All right, but have you tested for Flagyl?"

"Flagyl?"

"Metronidazole, the antibacterial used to treat vaginal infections," said Shockley, coming alive at this suggestion, curious at to what Jessica was getting at.

"Vaginal suppositories. My God, Doctor, at what point do we draw the line? Do you think we can test for every substance in the universe?"

"Flagyl leaves a metallic taste in the mouth," Jessica stated flatly.

"All right. I'll have Heyward test for it. Meantime—"

"Please, sir, come to some result, some conclusion, and quickly," Jessica warned, "or else I'll be forced to personally scrape together samples for the FBI lab in Washington for processing."

DeAngelos busied himself now with stripping off his lab coat, saying he had a luncheon appointment with Sturtevante and Parry. Putting on his regular coat, he said, "As for our little chat, Dr. Coran, do whatever you like. I am, as I have said, constrained by a budget that has seen no increase for over six extremely difficult years. You may want to discuss that with our chief here."

"Well, then, why in God's name are you hesitant to pack off a sample of everything to the FBI lab? I should think you'd be pleased to get it off your hands. Can you arrange the transport or not?" Nerves frayed, fatigue overcoming her, Jessica no longer played at politics or pleasantries with DeAngelos. In the back of her head, she wondered why Sturtevante and Parry were having lunch with him, and why she had not been invited. Apparently, lunch meant the case.

"I'll put my best man, Dr. Heyward, on it, as soon as I get back."

"Hold lunch and do it now," she demanded.

DeAngelos gritted his teeth, stared at his boss and the chief, read the signals, and with his thin mustache quivering, considered his options while Jessica thought about how uncooperative he'd been since the day they'd met, even going so far as to get her name wrong, calling her Dr. Cohen. He appeared to be one of that breed of men who find it difficult, even painful, to take orders from a woman.

"All right, then, go see Heyward yourself," he said, storming out.

"Good. I'll deal from here on out with Dr. Heyward," Jessica shouted after the man, then turned and stared at Shockley and Roth, both of whom returned a shrug and a frown.

Dr. Shockley said, "I've never seen DeAngelos forced so handily into a corner, Dr. Coran. Bravo!"

As the chief quietly concurred, Jessica bid them good day and went in search of Dr. Heyward.

JESSICA knew Dr. Arnold Heyward only as the even thinner, slightly built shadow of DeAngelos. The man was virtually joined to the other doctor's hip, ready at a moment's notice to do his bidding, a kind of Igor to his Frankenstein. The relationship, while not unusual in a laboratory situation where democratic principles did not apply, seemed to her worse than usual. It reminded her of a nobleman with a serf.

Having bid the chief and Dr. Shockley good-bye, she was about to step on an elevator to locate Heyward when DeAngelos, apparently having undergone a change of heart, caught her in the hallway outside the ops room. "Look here, I'm sorry for the defensiveness. It's just that this case has us all unnerved. I'll get word to Heyward for you this minute, before I go to lunch."

Taken aback by his sudden reasonableness, Jessica held her tongue while he dialed the toxicology lab from a nearby office. "Heyward!" DeAngelos barked into the phone. "I want you to catalog and box up all items we have on those poison-pen killings for the mail and—"

"No, no!" Jessica interrupted.

"You'll find Heyward quite capable of cataloging and boxing up items for the mail." He then said into the phone, "Talking to our FBI expert, Coran, here, Heyward. Seems she thinks her people in D.C. can do a better job than we can, so off we ship everything we have. Got that?"

"Not the U.S. mail," protested Jessica.

He finally slowed to hear her objection.

Jessica had flushed red by this time. "Don't waste time with the mail. Send it to the Bureau office here in Philly, to James Parry's attention. They'll helicopter it to the FBI lab direct."

"There you have it," he said. "Did you hear that, Heyward?"

Jessica heard the disembodied phone voice snap back with, "Yes, sir!"

"So now, Dr. Coran, you see it comes down to the almighty dollar."

"Pardon?"

"You have a bottomless budget to work with; we do not. My apologies for the municipal legislators and the state legislators, all of whom routinely find it more fashionable and politically useful to spend dollars on AIDS fund-raisers, cancer research, tourism, baseball, football, and yet another new sports facility—anything other than the field of death investigation, Doctor."

"I quite understand, Dr. DeAngelos."

"Do you really?" He sneered as if there was no way on God's green earth that she could understand.

She calmly replied, "Yes, matter of fact, I understand completely."

"In your rarefied air of governmental budgeting, I'm not so sure you do."

"I wasn't always with the government, sir. At one time, I was chief medical examiner for the city of Washington, D.C."

"Really? I congratulate you. Then you do understand my circumstances after all, don't you?"

He had her cornered. As much as she disliked the toxicologist's attitude, she knew he was right. The last area for which local government granted funds was death inquiry. It had been so twelve years ago when she worked the trenches of D.C. as pathologist for Washington Memorial Hospital, and it remained so today.

"Not unlike the attitude toward nursing-home laws and improvements in care for the aged," she agreed, and for the first time, they seemed to fall into mutual civility.

DeAngelos apologized. "I'm sorry for my jaded appearance; one has to develop a thick skin to survive around here. But inside, I am as appalled by these killings, and as upset about them, as anyone on the task force."

"I'm quite sure of it," she managed to say, not at all believing him. DeAngelos seemed far more concerned about his department, its political standing, and its financial woes than he was about the victims in the case.

"Although it is hard for me to muster complete sympathy for people who are foolish enough to unwittingly court their own end. People who live the lives of victims, victims to the end. Perfect victims."

Jessica thought of all the cynical medical professionals she had seen over the years; their number rivaled that of the police professionals she'd known, men and women who, having seen so much of human wickedness, having worked over the bodies of countless victims of trauma and murder, had become apathetic and spent. Dr. Frank DeAngelos needed a long vacation and possibly a career move. Perhaps Philadelphia would do well to promote him to a job where he could do less harm.

Still, in some deep recess of her own being, Jessica, too, hated people who set themselves up for murder, and it certainly appeared that the poisoned Philadelphia children had this in common.

"You have to agree," he softly said.

"Still, I wonder if such thoughts get in the way of our professional judgment, Doctor."

Dr. DeAngelos said a curt good-bye and rushed off to the elevator. He moved like a man who feared being late for a rendezvous with a lover.

By five in the afternoon, Jessica had logged in more time in the autopsy area and adjacent labs than was necessary, but it felt good—productive. After the verbal struggle with DeAngelos, the more time she spent with the most recent victims the calmer she became, and the more certain she felt of her ground.

As always in her experience, being in the forensics lab had a calming effect on her; solutions, even minuscule ones, had a way of restoring her. She was doing everything in her power to learn as much as possible about the killer.

After Jessica completed her final protocol on Maurice Deneau and had filled out the last piece of paperwork, she sat down and listed all the similarities she had noticed among the victims. They certainly seemed all of a type. Something in their appearance or manner, perhaps their diffidence, aroused the killer's interest, of this she had no doubt. She knew this to be common among serial killers. Generally speaking, she had found the serial killer to be a creature of habit. This had been so with other monsters she had tracked over the years, and it appeared true here. This need to repeat an experience, to prey on a given type, was often a killer's undoing, and in cases where the killer chose random victims, victims without a scintilla of commonality, authorities had far greater difficulty reaching any definitive conclusion. Often they did not at first see the resemblances among victims, but once these were pinpointed, the information spoke volumes, especially to anyone trained in forensic psychology.

She knew she must send her findings to such an expert once she had something concrete. Another trained person, someone other than Kim Desinor, who had up to this point, agreed with Jessica's speculations—someone removed from the case, without emotional involvement, might help Jessica hone in on the killer's thinking and motivation. This could have a great impact on the task force's success in identifying and locating the Poet Killer.

This murderer preyed upon men and women of a distinct body type and look. If the investigators learned the killer's habits, they could begin to follow the right path to a logical conclusion. There was no scientific certainty in such procedures, but years of experience had taught Jessica truths that others either did not see or ignored.

She entered her findings on a computer, saved them to disk, and was wondering exactly who to send them to when the phone rang beside her. Lifting the receiver, she heard Chief Santiva say, "You're working late."

"Yeah, well, I think it's called for. The Poet has been busy."

"Anything give in the case so far?"

"Aside from my nerves?"

"Anything we can hang our hats on?"

"Who wants to know, Eriq?"

"We all have people we have to answer to, Jess."

"They don't really expect anything this soon, do they?"

"I told them we have our best working on it, so they have high expectations. Tell me what you've got. I'll take it from there."

"Watch for a packet of photos I put in overnight for your attention, boss. I want you to tell me what you can extrapolate from the handwriting."

"Photos of the latest poems?"

"Straight off the backs of the vics, yes."

"I'll give them my fullest attention and get back to you. Meanwhile, do you or Desinor have any general impressions I should know about?"

Jessica's assessment of the killer thus far initially left Eriq silent. Then he asked, "Are you both getting the notion that this guy kills people so as to save them from living 'trashed lives'?"

She looked down at the list she'd composed of the victims' characteristics. "Not sure. At least one of the vics was homosexual, they were all Caucasian, no crossbreeds but one cross-dresser. No people of foreign origin, no drug users, no addicts, no drug dealers, pimps, prostitutes, deviants with records, nothing unsavory so far as I can see."

"You don't make a cross-dresser out a deviant?"

"Just a confused kid looking to establish a sense of his own identity. They—all the victims—had that in common, I'm beginning to believe. They were into playing musical chairs with their names, for instance."

"What about musical body art? Were they into that scene?"

"Sturtevante tells us they frequented the clubs that catered to the body poetry fad going on here, yeah, but previous to their deaths, so far as autopsy shows, none of them were into tattoos or body piercing; no tongue or nose piercings—"

"But they all would have known of the urban legend, the

roots of the fad, and they all would have consented to the one tattoo that killed them?"

"Our guy has to be quite persuasive. To be blunt, any corpse candidate not deemed 'proper' or 'worthy' by his standard wouldn't get his backside poetry."

"Anything else strike you?"

Jessica told him of her growing belief that the killer preyed on people who, for whatever reason, looked the part and played the part of willing victims. "The dead are men and women who fell under the spell of a kind of old-world charm and beauty of spirit—all romantics who saw the world through ideal-clouded eyes—even here, in a place that supposedly enshrines the opposite of such notions."

"Interesting. Our killer is into charm and beauty, then?"

"Actually, the vics are perfectly androgynous. The males could pass for female, and vice versa. I think that's the physical look that attracts our guy, while the mind-set is that of mystical romanticism."

Eriq sounded like a big brother when he asked, "Are you alone there in the lab? Where's everyone else?"

"Yeah, pretty much for the moment."

"Go get some dinner and rest. That's an order."

"One I happily accept."

"Everything go okay between you and Parry?"

"Sure, why wouldn't it? You hear anything to the contrary?"

"No, no . . . just asking. I'll check in later, Doctor. Good night."

" 'Night, Chief."

"Damn," she cursed herself after hanging up. Why had she made such a to-do over his question about Parry? She looked around the lab and other offices. "This place is like a morgue," she gently joked, wanting to hear herself speak. Everyone on the day shift was long gone, leaving the lab area as abandoned as the proverbial country cemetery, and the lights in areas not in use had been dimmed. Jessica felt a sense of aloneness begin to creep into her skin, and again she wondered why she had seen and heard so little from James Parry.

"We're not making much of a team," she lamented aloud.

Kim, too, had confided that she had seen little of Parry in the days since their visit to Maurice Deneau's flat.

It didn't help matters to learn that Parry and Sturtevante were independently scheduling meetings with the toxicologist DeAngelos.

She toyed with the idea of calling Jim, forcing things. She lifted the phone, put it back, lifted it again, finally returned it. She paced the room, thinking, angry that Parry had excluded her from his lunch meeting with DeAngelos; then she wondered if DeAngelos had called the meeting to "report" on her?

Jessica looked at the clock, seeing the hour hand inch toward six P.M. She again wondered why she was still in the lab. She knew why. Something nagged at her, something about the deaths and the manner of the killer's writing, something trying to get out, something trying to talk clearly to her, but she couldn't read the garbled signs. She felt so damnably handicapped, as if some vital fact floated just out of reach. All the parts were here, before her, yet they refused to coalesce into a larger configuration, like a puzzle with all of its hundreds of pieces present, but each an ill fit.

"What am I missing?" she asked herself over and over. Frustration weighed heavy on Jessica's shoulders, while anxiety watched in the background, whispering, "The Poet Killer's going to strike again and soon . . . very soon, but when, where, how, and why? Why indeed does he kill, and why in such a manner as this?"

TEN

Like a fiend in a cloud,
With howling woe,
After night I do crowd,
And with night will go . . .

—William Blake (1757–1827)

J ESSICA lifted the phone on her desk in the makeshift office that had been provided by the Philly ME's office and asked the operator to put her in touch with Dr. Arnold Heyward. When he came on the line, she said, "Dr. Heyward, this is Dr. Coran. I fear I won't sleep tonight without some assurances that—"

"Thought I was the only one left in the building," he said, cutting her off. "I mean other than the maintenance crew."

"Had some loose ends to tie up," she replied dryly. "Did you get it all out to Parry's people?" She needn't explain what *it* was to Heyward, not since DeAngelos had given the order.

"It's done, Dr. Coran, and might I say that I think your decision to forward samples to D.C. appropriate, under the circumstances."

It sounded pretty lame and perfunctory, and well rehearsed to boot, but Jessica simply said, "Thank you, Dr. Heyward. I only hope it nets us some results. I've asked an associate in D.C. to place it on a front burner as soon as it arrives. We've done the same with the DNA samples taken by Shockley. I hope your department isn't taking this personally."

"You understand, Doctor, that these things take time. I'm only sorry we could not find any concentrated poison to have been of use."

"Yes, well, thanks. Did you test the wineglasses?"

"We did, of course, and found nothing other than . . . wine, a Pinot Noir, actually."

"Appellation and year?"

"We're not *that* good."

"Was it the same at every crime scene?"

"I think our guy brings it with him; certainly it's his preference."

"Our FBI lab has a high-tech device that separates out every chemical. Those glasses will be tested for everything conceivable. They're bound to hit on something."

"Yes, I've read about the Super-Separator, as they call it, but sorry to say we could hardly afford it at a two-mil price tag."

Once again, the economics of death investigation, she thought. She'd heard it in hamlets small and large, and Philly by any standard was a large, complex city, filled with as much crime as any major city in America. "Yeah, I know, Dr. Heyward. People give lip service to fighting crime, but they don't want to spend any money on it."

"You got that right."

They said their good-nights and Jessica saw that it had grown late, nearing seven P.M., almost four days since the discovery of Maurice Deneau's body. Why had James Parry not involved her more in the day-to-day investigation? What had he gotten from the young man's diary and annotations in his books? The idea the chief special agent on the case was avoiding her grew to enormous proportions in her mind. Troubling, if it were true. She told herself that he must be extremely busy, but that sounded like excuse making for him. Still, if he weren't extremely busy, then what? Busy as hell or else . . . It was the *or else* that worried her the most.

She imagined he might be in turmoil over their having to work together, that their being thrown into this situation was more crippling for him than for her. Perhaps Parry felt as much frustration with the case and the failure of the toxicology lab to isolate the poison in the ink as she had felt; in fact, this was likely. Perhaps he had called a luncheon meeting with DeAngelos to take a crack at the self-important ass himself, wanting Sturtevante in his corner instead of Jessica.

Perhaps this was reason enough to telephone Jim, tell him she had gotten DeAngelos's department off their asses—and get Jim's reaction. Reason enough, she told herself. Perhaps if she made the first move, this awkward game of hide-and-seek between them might end; in the long run, their not dealing with each other on a professional level was not good for the case. She guessed that he was thinking the same thing.

Tired and frustrated, she dialed Parry's office, only to learn that he had left for the day, and that she had missed him by some fifteen or twenty minutes, this according to another agent who sounded tired of hearing his ringing phone. "Any messages, Dr. Coran?"

"No, none. I'll try again tomorrow."

When she looked up, Jim Parry stood in the doorway, leaning against the jamb. "Looking for me?" he asked, his boyish grin reminding her of why she had first gotten involved with him some four years ago.

"Matter of fact, yes. Wanted your take on this cheerful fellow who goes around cutting iambic pentameter into the backs of his victims and leaving them dead by poison. And what's up with DeAngelos?"

"DeAngelos? Had lunch with him today. He's not exactly president of your fan club either."

"Why do you say that? What'd he have to say?"

"Says you're pushy."

"Oh, is that how he put it?"

"Close enough."

"You mean with your sensitivity to offensive language, you can't repeat such words?"

"It wasn't that bad." Parry managed a smile.

"So have you and Leanne cracked the case yet?" she asked. "It would appear the two of you are working it alone."

"That's not fair, Jess, but yeah, sure, with zip to go on we've cracked the case wide open." He let out a long, exasperated sigh and stepped closer to her desk. "This is beginning to remind me of a case we worked in Hawaii in '90, before I met you. Forensics on the case had nothing."

"Are you telling me that your meeting with DeAngelos today went badly?" She leaned over the desk, a half smile on her face. "Now he's a cheerful fellow."

"So, you've been tracking my movements?"

"Damn straight I have. It appears the only way I can know what's going on around here. You haven't exactly been forthcoming, Jim."

"Sturtevante's idea to jump on DeAngelos and shake something loose from him. Identifying the poison is key to the case."

"I should have been asked to the table, Jim."

He dropped his steady gaze, nodding. "Yeah, I know, Jess, and I'm sorry. Some mix-up in communications."

"A big one, I'd say, since Kim wasn't invited either."

"It was a big waste of time. You two would have heard nothing. Trust me."

"What precisely did you discuss?"

"Filled his ear with a lot of questions, but got very little out of him. That is, until he started talking about how you're in his face all the time, how he can't make any headway with the FBI looking over his shoulder. Said the two of you mutually agreed to have all the test samples forwarded to my office for routing to Washington."

"Mutually agreed, huh? He said that?"

"Yeah, is that how it came about?"

"Result's the same; no matter. And according to his assistant, Heyward, the samples're in your hands now."

He breathed deeply, and pushing to a full standing position, said, "Fact is, they're on their way to D.C. as we speak. Your best toxicology team's making it priority one."

"Good . . . good."

"Happy?" he asked.

"Relatively, yes. Very happy, actually."

"I mean about the samples getting off in so timely a fashion."

"Yes, that's what I'm talking about."

"Oh, yeah, of course . . ."

"Maybe this idea of us trying to work together, Jim . . . maybe it's foolhardy to think we can if . . ."

"Come on, Jess. What're you getting at?"

". . . if we don't even hear the simplest of words the same way? If every little thing has to be scrutinized and analyzed for double entendre, innuendo."

"Hey, I only said what I said. No hidden agenda."

"Tell that to your subconscious, and I suppose mine. You can't deny, Jim, that a lot of business has gone unfinished between us. And that right now there are at least eight people in the room."

"Eight in the room? I don't recall that many in bed with us," he replied, smiling.

"There's the me I think I am, the me I want to be, the me you want to be, the me I really am, as well as the you you think you are, the you you want to be, the you that I want you to be, and the you you really are."

He repeated her words. "Eight people between us. How'd it get so complicated? Why?"

She shook her head, still sitting safely behind the desk, glad it stood between them. "I don't know."

He near whispered, "I'm sorry it ended so badly, Jess. Really I am."

"So am I."

"You deserved more than a telephone good-bye."

Her eyes widened. "Well, thank you, Mr. Parry, for that acknowledgment."

"But as usual, distance was the demon."

"Oh, sure, Jim. Place blame on some something other than yourself, some intangible, that poor James Parry could do nothing about, like distance."

"Hey, hold on, Jess."

"You might've come to London when I asked; we might've ended things better there."

"You really think so?" He came closer, a hand outstretched. "You think London would have changed anything?"

"Maybe, but then we'll never know, since you chose to ignore me there."

"Ignore you. I can just see me in a hotel room waiting for you to finish another of your endless autopsies, and you making eyes at this Scotland Yard guy the whole time."

"So, you've learned about Richard, have you?"

"There're no secrets in the FBI community. We leave that for the CIA, remember?"

"After our last conversation, you relinquished all right to any say-so in my life on any subject, Chief. I owe you my best as a member of the profiling and forensic investigation team on a case we happen to be working together *today*. But I'll thank you to keep your opinions on my private life to yourself for the duration of this case, unless you see fit to relieve me."

"Is that what you want?"

"I didn't say that."

"Imagine the repercussions of that one." He paced now, staring at the ceiling, waving an arm and shaking his head. "Imagine it. I replace the famous Dr. Jessica Coran on the case, headline news from here to China."

She raised her shoulders. "What repercussions? I wouldn't make a single wave over it."

He laughed derisively, and when he spoke, his tone was angry. "And with whom do I replace you, Jessica? I didn't ask for you on this case, you know. I don't know whose bright idea it was, but it wasn't mine. I thought you came as a . . . a package deal with the psychic."

She rose to her feet and came around the desk, fists balled, jaw set. "Where did you hear that nonsense?"

"It appeared to be the case. At any rate, you tell me, with whom do I replace the most famous forensic investigator the FBI's ever known, and—"

"John Thorpe," she interjected.

"—and the media and the people of Philly will have my ass by morning."

"You're making far too much of it, Jim."

"Making too much of *your* reputation? Me? Oh, yeah, sure . . . What can the Bureau do to me that they haven't already done?"

"I'm sorry about your losing your post in Hawaii, Jim," she said. "But I've got to know, did it have anything to do with the Lopaka Kowona case? Our final report on the way he died?"

He brushed this off with a wave of his hand and an unconvincing shake of the head. "No, not so's anyone would notice. Fact is, people have long forgotten what I did for the islands back then. If you recall, dear, you garnered all the accolades for putting an end to the Trade Winds Killer. No, our little secret on exactly how Kowona died is intact."

"We were both there when the cameras rolled, Jim."

"Yeah, but you won in the end, and I'm here now in Philly, put in my place due to some nasty bit of political *palua* so convoluted I didn't see it before I was blindsided and pushed out. Nothing to do with our mutual friend Kowona or anything we might want to keep buried. Trust me."

She breathed deeply at this. "That much is . . . is good."

He advanced on her, and now they stood staring into each other's eyes, a pencil's width apart, each smelling the other's tension. His cologne reminded her of their parting in Rome a year ago, a parting she had not known would be their last, a parting that ended their four-year-long love affair. It had been the longest relationship with a man she'd ever had—or ever *managed,* as her shrink would likely put it.

He reached out and pulled her to him, roughly kissing her, his tongue searching her mouth with a fire she had not felt since their last time together.

She allowed the kiss to last a moment too long, but then pushed him away, hard, and nearly shouting, "Damn you, Jim! Damn you, get away from me. Get out. This isn't happening."

"Sweetheart, Jess—"

"No, no! I'm not your *anything,* Jim!" She pulled from his grasp again. "I said get out!"

"We could have what we both wanted before; we could have it now, Jess. Now that I'm in Philadelphia . . . we're close enough now so that we can try for a *real* relationship."

"There's no *we* any longer. I put you out of my head, out of my heart. I love Richard now."

He stepped back, his face going hard and cold, as if her words had frozen him. Looking crushed, he fell into a leather chair, his head in his hands. "I've tried fighting it, Jess; didn't want to grovel at your feet, anything like what just happened. Kept away for that reason. Same time, I've . . . I gave it a lot of thought."

"Please, James."

"How we both wanted the same things, a family some-day, a stable life, and how neither of us could give the other anything resembling stability, and now—"

"It's over, James, truly over now."

"—that I'm looking at making my home so close to Quantico, and you're so near now, that . . . well . . ."

Ironies all around, she thought but did not say. She re-turned to stand behind the desk. Safe distance, safe barrier, yet long ago, when he walked out on her long-distance fashion, she had built up in her mind an impenetrable bar-rier against James Kenneth Parry. She had had enough therapy to know herself, to acknowledge that she didn't "do" forgiveness, not well and not genuinely.

"Forgive me for saying so, Jim, but you were the one who ended our relationship. You had your chance, but now it's over. Long over. I'm in love with Richard Sharpe."

"Sure . . . sure. Lot easier to love a guy who's an ocean away. You found that out with me, and now with him. Makes sense for a woman like you, Jessica."

She glowered at him. "An ocean away and content that way, James Parry. Now, I told you before, and I'll tell you again, get out!"

"You can't say there's nothing left between us, Jess. I won't accept that."

She gnashed her teeth, unable to respond to this, and re-peated, "Nothing. Nothing whatever. I'm finally free of you altogether, James. I guess your coming here tonight made me realize that; for that favor, I thank you."

He continued as if not hearing her. "Now that I'm here, now that we finally have a real chance to commit, you have another man in your life. Timing is impeccable. A little to impec—"

"Please, Jim, just go . . . please."

He pushed himself up from the chair as if his body fought to hold him back. Standing now, looking beaten, he made his way to the door. "Think maybe it was a mistake to attempt to work this case together, but now we're in it, we've got to make the best of it, Jess. Think we can do it?"

"I can if you can, Jim, but no more talk of us."

"That can be arranged, I'm sure."

"Jim, there is no *us* in that sense any longer. I've grieved a long time for what we had, and that grief and despair gave way to a new hope, one that doesn't include you."

His lip quivering, he nodded. "So much has happened since we first met. Hard to let go of it all, Jess, especially now, after seeing you again."

She said no more, allowing him a silent, dignified exit.

WHEN Jessica heard the elevator door mechanically open and close, she began to sob. She cried for her pain, and she felt it was a good cry, the cry of someone who has finally let go of the past.

After ten minutes alone, she heard footsteps coming down the darkened corridor, and she feared that Parry had returned, or that it was Dr. Shockley, Dr. DeAngelos, or possibly Heyward. At any rate, she didn't want any of them to know she was sitting here in the dark crying. She wiped at her tears, and hearing someone just outside the open door, she looked up to find Kim Desinor poking her head around the jamb.

"Kim, it's you." Jessica sniffled and tried to hold back tears. If she could cry over this ending with anyone, it would be Kim.

"Told you you had to face him, get it out. You've gotta be feeling better." Kim leaned into the doorjamb at the exact spot where James Parry had stood.

How did she know about Jim's visit? Jessica wondered,

suspecting her tears had given her away. Had Parry lingered in the building? Had Kim run into him on his way out? But Jessica simply responded, "Like a goddamn Ford truck's been lifted off my back, yeah. Maybe now I can focus on the case."

"I hope you can forgive me."

Jessica looked across at her friend. "Forgive *you*?"

"For a couple of things, yes."

"What's there to forgive, Kim?" Jessica recalled her initial reaction to Kim and Eriq Santiva's railroading her onto this particular case at this particular time.

"Well, first because I told Parry where he could find you tonight."

"Tonight? You did that . . . for me?"

"More than that, I confronted him in his office, told him you had a right to face your accuser, in this case *him,* and put old hurts to rest."

"Had it out with him, did you? Straightened him out, huh? Sent him over here just so I could kick him in the teeth, huh?"

"Yeah, I stuck up for you." Kim halfheartedly lifted a victory fist.

Jessica nodded. "I see. Told him off good, did you?"

"Damned straight; damned right."

"So he came straight over here to *hit* on me, and talk about rekindling our passion. I have you to thank for—"

Kim gasped. "He did *that*? The bastard."

"So what else do I have to forgive you for, Kim?"

"Wait a minute, you haven't offered your forgiveness for this part yet."

"All right, forgiven. What else?"

"When Santiva came to me about the case, he told me I'd be working with James Parry. I immediately told him I wouldn't do it without your help, so . . ."

Jessica took in a deep breath, filling her lungs with air

and her mind with information, and tried to calmly negoti-
ate the minefield of emotions it aroused. "All for my own
good, no doubt?"

"Eriq was at first completely against it, but I convinced
him otherwise, that you needed to have it out with Parry, else
you'd never be totally free of him. Eriq took some convincing. Don't go blaming him, okay? It was totally my doing."

"I see."

Kim held firm to an amulet around her neck as she
stepped into the room. "You needed to see him, Jess. Don't
try to deny it."

Her fists again clenched, her jaw set, Jessica replied,
"You concocted this whole charade to get us together?"

"I hoped it would be . . . would go more . . . pleasantly.
I only wanted you to heal and get on with things."

"The best of intentions, and Eriq agreed?"

"Like I said, I made him see the light."

"I *knew* you two were cooking up some kind of nonsense together."

"How are you feeling now, Jessica—about Parry and the
whole mess, I mean?"

Jessica stood up and came around the desk. She then
looked herself over in exaggerated fashion, working her
hands along her arms, as if seeing what part of her had been
hurt in the fray with James Parry. Finally, she looked slowly
up at Kim, who leaned into the desk.

"Well?" Kim pressed.

Jessica's whiskey voice filled the room. "I feel . . . wonderful; I feel a great weight has been lifted off. You were
absolutely right; I needed to tell the SOB what I thought of
him, and to put a few hurting screws to his hide."

"Mission accomplished!" Kim cheered. "That's the
spirit! Full steam ahead with your hunk from New Scotland Yard, then?"

"Let's get out of here."

"Right-o!"

Turning out the light, Kim offered her friend a handkerchief and a final word of advice. "Time you took what you want from life, Jess. Don't hold back."

"Starting tonight. Where's the elevator out of here?"

EXITING the building, they passed Dr. Frank DeAngelos as he entered. Only a few words of salutation passed among them.

"Quite the sourpuss that one," said Kim. "If what they say about the evil eye is true, dear, you just got it with both barrels."

"Watch my back, will you, Kim?"

"Goes without saying."

"That prick's the very last person on earth I wanted to see tonight."

"Forget about him. How do you feel now about being free—completely free—of James Parry?"

"I am glad I cleansed my spleen of James. You know, I think he is exactly what he accuses me of being, not a bone of commitment found anywhere in his morally bankrupt body."

"I want to hear all about it, every detail, over drinks, once you loosen up. Save it up. Meantime, tell me this. Anything new on the case come of your digging away these many long hours?"

"No, nothing at all, but I managed to get the toxicology out of DeAngelos's hands and into Jay Masterson's lab in D.C."

"Well now! That's a victory. No wonder he hates your guts."

"Hopefully I've done the right thing, but what if—"

"Hold that self-doubt and second-guessing. Save it for someone who wants to hear it. Let's go have a beer. I hear Philly's got some nightlife."

"I'm game."

"You want to stop off at the hotel first, freshen up? Your mascara's running. You look like Marilyn Manson on a drunk."

"I wasn't crying over Jim Parry," Jessica firmly said.

"Good! Then what were you crying over?"

"End of a relationship, release of stress, I dunno, but it wasn't tears of regret, I can tell you that."

"Bravo! Then it's on to the hotel and drinks?"

"Let's make a night of it."

"In a celebrating mood, are we?"

"We are."

"Going to call Richard tonight?"

"No, just have fun. You and me."

"That's my girl. A night without a single thought wasted on a man."

Jessica thanked Kim for her earlier advice, for urging her to see this thing through with James, and they hugged and laughed.

"He seems to believe I prefer long-distance relationships, that I find them a helluva lot safer than the real thing, you know," Jessica confided as they passed the colorfully lit city hall, strolling around Philadelphia's clean, well-lit downtown, trying to ignore the pronounced police presence. The bricked sidewalks were slick from earlier rain showers, the black asphalt mirroring the city lights in crazy and wavy images. A cool breeze and some scavenging black crows played about the two women.

"Beautiful birds," said Kim. "I just love crows and ravens, don't you? Unusual to see them in a flock looking for food at night, though."

"With these city lights, how do they know whether it's night or day?"

"They're disoriented, you think? Or just hungry? Not unlike our victims."

"Maybe he's right."

"What? Maybe who's right?"

"Jim Parry. Maybe he's right about me. Maybe his assessment is right on."

"So fucking what? If it works for you, go for it. Life's too short, Jess. If Parry couldn't figure out how to keep you, then you're better off without him. One door closes and—"

"I know, I know . . . another opens."

They had come to stand below the lights of the hotel where they were staying. Inside, they rode the elevator up, Jessica losing herself in thought until Kim jabbed her in the ribs, saying, "I think God and life and fate owe you a few, Jessica Coran."

"Really? And by what measure are you reckoning fate?"

"By whatever measure makes you happy. Find it, do it, live it, and screw anyone who comes between you and what you love."

"Is that how it is with you and Alex?"

"Alex and I are just great, just now really discovering the depth of our love and commitment to one another."

"God . . . wish . . . hope I find that with Richard."

"You can! Give it time. When he gets here, after you've spent some time together, you still have to be patient with yourself and with him. Time is all it takes when love is real."

Jessica teased, "Maybe you shoulda oughta been a poet yourself, Kim!"

Kim laughed at this. "Sure, ruinous poetry for people to puke by. That's the only kind of lines I might pen. No, I'm no poet. I just know that what Alex Sincebaugh and I have found I wish for every living soul."

They separated, going to their rooms to change for the evening, each promising to call the other when ready to party.

ELEVEN

Rare is the expert who combines an informed opinion with a healthy respect for his own intuition and curiosity.

—Gavin De Becker

AN evening on the town with Kim Desinor proved precisely what the doctor ordered; Jessica completely forgot about James Parry and her confrontation with him, forgot about her worries over the case, taking time off— even in her head—to finally relax. She felt a great weight lifted from her mind as a result.

As she and Kim drank another Philly margarita, a specialty of the house, in a place aptly or ineptly called Recycled Cowboys, they talked about their impressions of the city. They sat at a table in a darkened corner, the western decor betraying signs of the place having been an Irish pub not too long ago. Jessica imagined it the hardest thing in the world to make a go of a new bar or restaurant. The atmosphere notwithstanding, the place remained a brick-walled bar with a karaoke machine and an open mike, and after a few old western balladeers finished replacing the old Irish lullabies, and a few more drinks, the ladies felt no pain.

From here, they located another, more trendy coffeehouse-style bar and grill called Hobgoblins & Gnomes PA, and here the motif was a weird and wonderful fantasyland, a "Middle Earth" kind of place where gnomes and hobgoblins of all sizes and shapes and mis-shapes, wart-covered or otherwise, resided. The tables were toadstools and tree stumps, decorated lavishly with the carved faces of gnomes and other strange creatures, as were the walls. The ceiling was plastered with the stars and the planets, and vines hung everywhere from this mini-firmament. The place was dark and the music loud. Jessica and Kim found themselves surrounded by the faces of the youth of present-day Second Street. Many of them called to mind the victims the FBI women had spent so much time with at the morgue. All around them the laughing, smiling, whooping faces of teens, male and female, many of the same sex making public their absolute affection for one another.

Jessica said over the pounding of the music meant to warm up the crowd, "Do you realize that you and I are the only two people in here who have any idea what an LP record album looks like?"

"Only albums they know about are photo albums. Face it, they're too young to have a notion about the meaning of the term *broken record*," Kim agreed.

"They've never played Pac-Man, and have never heard of Pong."

"They're too young to remember the space shuttle explosion or Tienemen Square."

"*The Day After* is a pill to them, not a movie, and if you asked the average teen today what polio is, he'd say a designer shirt for old farts. As for Cold War fears, forget it."

"On the other hand, they've grown up with the specter of AIDS," countered Kim.

"Most of the people here were likely born in 1980 or '81."

Their mood had significantly soured; they continued to drink. But everything changed after midnight when suddenly the stage mike was taken over by a series of "living poems" who showed off their bodies and the poetry that had been written on them. Jessica watched in awe and sadness as the poems' authors just offstage read the lyrical lines from the gyrating bodies. One of the dangers had style—possibly a moonlighting stripper, Jessica thought. While some patrons appeared genuinely interested in this peculiar brand of art, the art-for-art's-sake crowd, others jeered. Still, applause and laughter won out at the end of each performance, but for Jessica and Kim, the event only dampened their spirits.

As they watched the show, eyes wide, Jessica told Kim, "This is so bizarre, so unusual. I'd never heard of this weird fad, or the urban legend that spawned it before arriving here."

Another round of walking, undulating "poems" took the stage. While some in the audience howled and commented on the body parts of the naked men and women parading by, others tapped with spoons and forks against glasses to show their appreciation. Still others took photographs.

Jessica took note of one poem in particular, whispering into Kim's ear how it reminded her of their killer's handiwork. She listened to the lines with fascination, knowing she must collar the kid with these words on her back before she disappeared, to learn who had created them, and fearing the young woman might well be next in line for the Poet Killer.

She relayed her fears to Kim, who said, "I agree, although her body size and appearance are at odds with the androgynousness of the other victims, and with as many drinks as we've had—"

"No, this is close, real close," Jessica disagreed.

They had listened intently as the poem was read, and the performer continued to dance long after, giving Jessica the opportunity to study the lines further. The poem read:

> *Your feathered wings enclose*
> *me by day,*
> *just as the velvet leather*

of my embracing
finds you at midnight—
where the divine heels
disturb waves of fallen leaves.
Look at me . . .
I am the helpless lover,
drowned in the sanguine lotion
of your touch, directly before,
a moment during, and even
after my death. Now I am
the crystal air, still, perpetual—
melting into wind so that
I may touch you forever.

Jessica stood and approached the young woman, who stood putting her top back on at the foot of the stage. Jessica didn't flash her badge or announce herself, but rather simply asked, "May I know the poet's name?"

"It's Dontella Leare. She's a great poet. I took a class with her. She's simply inspiring." The young ash-blond woman beamed. "You liked the performance?"

"It was the best of the evening."

"So far, you mean," she replied. "There's more."

Another young person, a male this time, had already claimed the stage. "This poet Leare, she teaches at the University of Philadelphia?"

"That's right. If you can't afford to take her class or don't have the time, the bookstore's got all her work. She's a successful poet, an amazing feat in a society that devalues poetry."

"Aren't you afraid of, you know, becoming one of the victims of the Poet Killer, the poisoner?"

"No, not so long as I stick with Donatella; it's kind of like sticking with one lover if you're afraid of AIDS. . . kinda."

"Yeah, I get it." Jessica asked the young woman her name and where she might contact her.

"Is this a pickup?" the girl asked.

"No, no . . . sorry, I failed to introduce myself fully. I'm Dr. Jessica Coran, FBI medical examiner, and I'm part of the task force looking into the Second Street poisonings."

"You're a cop?" the girl almost shouted.

"A doctor, actually."

"Well, you're looking in the wrong place. No one here could do such a thing as what happened to those kids, certainly not Donatella Leare."

"I'll keep that in mind. Thank you, and do be careful."

"Like I told you, one poet only touches my backside." The sexual innuendo in the remark was clearly meant to leave Jessica in no doubt as to the relationship between poet and "poem."

Kim had watched the conversation with mounting interest, doing her best to read their lips. When Jessica returned to the table, she told Kim all the details.

"Hard to believe, isn't it?"

"What?"

"This whole scene, this whole new thing kids have come up with, and now some maniac using it as a weapon to kill them."

"Body art, piercings, now writing on the body. In a way, it's like a natural next step, an evolution of the tattoo, going from image to language, whole communications, even artistic ones. Unfortunately, there's a lot of chaff in the wheat."

"Like trying to find a truly good horror novel amid the crap?" Jessica asked.

"Yeah, like that."

"It still boggles my mind that anyone would endure so much pain for some idea about art."

"People who can't create great art have always opted to

be the doormat for those who can," replied Kim, slurring her words a bit. "Look at Picasso's women."

"So why does all this body stuff come as such a surprise to me?"

"You can't be expected to keep up with all the fads," Kim said. "I saw a feature on it on MTV not too long ago."

Jessica blinked. "You watch MTV?"

"On occasion, sure."

"You're full of surprises."

"The big surprise is that someone would take a fad and turn it into serial murders," Kim countered.

"Let's get out of here," Jessica suggested. "The noise is getting to me."

"Headache?"

"Getting there, yes."

Walking back to the hotel, Jessica thought of how proud she should feel, having faced James Parry and made her position clear. Neither she nor Kim had spoken a word about the dismal state of the case. Tonight, the subject had almost been taboo, but in the face of the performances they'd witnessed at Hobgoblins & Gnomes PA, discussion was inevitable. Still, they had managed to stay off the subject of men, despite having to fend off advances, some from young men half their age, all evening long. When men approached them, they declined each offer of a drink, causing more than one of the barroom Casanovas to believe that the two beautiful women were gay. Jessica and Kim could have cared less. This was a girls' night out.

Now, walking back toward the hotel, they spoke of when they had last had fun, real fun, and both agreed that they had to go back to childhood and innocence to remember a time when either enjoyed an outburst of pure joyous laughter.

"Tonight, we will attempt the miraculous, Jessica," Kim announced.

"And what would that be?"

"To recapture some of those feelings of childhood, and while not absolutely successful, we might come pretty damned close for a pair of adults with fixed patterns of thinking and behavior."

"You think so?" asked Jessica. "And how do we do that?"

"Follow me!" Kim suddenly leaped into a water fountain and was immediately drenched and laughing, calling for Jessica to join her.

"What're you doing?"

"Having fun! Making it rain! I'm a rainmaker now!"

Kim's childish abandon infected Jessica, who, checking for any signs of onlookers, suddenly leaped into the fountain alongside her friend. Together they hugged and laughed beneath the shower.

A police patrol car's whining complaint brought them around, and in a moment, they were explaining their behavior to a uniformed officer who gave them a warning and asked if they needed a lift to their destination.

"It's only a half block to our hotel."

"Better do any additional showering in the privacy of your room, then," offered the policeman, a wide grin on his face.

The women waved the police cruiser off, their sodden clothes and shoes and purses dripping as they went.

"This is so unlike me," said Jessica.

"Good!"

"You are a bad influence."

"Bad or good?"

Jessica sighed. "Good, I'm sure."

"Are you quite sure of that?"

"Quite."

As the hotel came into view, Jessica blurted out, "I'm so afraid of screwing things up with Richard."

"He's got to be quite a man to accept your being here, getting the closure you need on your relationship with Parry."

"I *have* no relationship with Parry."

"Then working out your anger with Parry. Either way, your Richard's a rare chap, I'd say."

"But all he knows is that I'm on a case in Philadelphia. He doesn't know Jim's working the case with me."

"Ah, I see."

They fell silent, each preoccupied with her own thoughts as they entered the hotel, bellhops, security guards, and other guests staring at them, one asking, "Oh, my, do I need an umbrella? When did it start raining?"

They rushed to the elevator and rode up to the twenty-ninth floor, making the cab a puddle and laughing at their foolishness. Jessica still felt a pleasant buzz from her drinking, and the release of all her pent-up feelings tonight had made her feel much better.

The elevator door opened on Jessica's floor.

"You haven't told him?" asked Kim. "All this time has gone by and you haven't told Richard?"

"I've been too . . . too busy."

Kim held the door. "Bullshit. You must be a fool. He hears about it through any other source, and what's he going to think?"

"I'll call him tonight, tomorrow." Jessica wiped at her eyes as water flowed from her still-wet head.

"You do that! Don't put it off another moment. By the way, you look like a drowned rat."

"And you look like a drowned Chihuahua!" The elevator doors closed on Kim, who rode up the two floors to her room. Jessica turned to walk down the corridor, thinking she ought to have made the call to Richard Sharpe days before. Fatigue and booze clouding her thoughts, she fumbled at her door with the electronic key card. Finally, she found herself alone in her room when someone knocked. Through the peephole, she saw that it was Kim. For a moment, she feared her friend had had too much to drink and had somehow come to the conclusion that they were roommates.

"How did you get back here so fast?" she asked as she opened the door.

"Took the stairs. Listen, Jessica, whatever you do, tell Richard and tell him soon, and believe me, it will be a defining moment in your relationship, so watch closely— or rather listen closely—for his reaction. If you get an immediate reaction that is favorable, you know he's worth your time and effort; if you get the opposite, you know he's not. That's all I will say on the subject, so again, g'night."

Kim marched off for the stairwell, leaving Jessica to ponder her words.

Jᴇssɪᴄᴀ had gotten back to her room after one in the morning, and fairly fell into bed. She set her clock to awake at 3 A.M., and until then she slept soundly; in fact, for the first time in days, she had no thought of the case, either consciously or subconsciously. When the alarm clock roused her, she stared at it, estimated the time in London, dialed, and caught Richard Sharpe before he had left for work at Scotland Yard.

"Jess! It's you!"

He sounded so exuberantly happy to hear from her. "I just wanted to hear your voice, Richard."

"It's so wonderful of you to call. It will make my day go by so pleasantly."

"How soon before you come to me, Richard?"

"Soon, I promise."

"I . . . I can hardly wait."

He laughed. "That's my line, love."

"Richard, tell me . . ."

"Yes? What is it, dear?" He immediately heard the sadness in her voice, had somehow honed in on it.

"You don't think . . . Do you think that I like it this way?"

"Like it? This way? What way, Jess—what do you mean?"

"Our relationship. Long-distance."

"Oh, I see . . . Well, honestly, Jessica, I could swear the last time we were together, you very much preferred the real thing to telephoning it in."

She nodded. "Yeah, I did, didn't I?"

"I certainly thought so. I wasn't kidding myself, now, was I?" he teased.

"You know you're constantly on my mind, Richard."

"Good show."

"Yes, it is." She managed a laugh.

"What's this all about, sweetness? What's brought on this . . . melancholy?"

She steeled herself to tell him what she'd been going through, that she was here in Philadelphia, working a case in close proximity to her former lover, James Parry; at the same time, she thought how wonderfully perceptive Richard was to intuit her distress from such a distance. James would never have been so sensitive.

"You haven't been having second thoughts about us, have you?" he asked.

"No, no!" she assured him. "Just that . . . well, I had it brought to my attention recently that I seem to . . . seem to enjoy a good distance between myself and anyone who . . . anyone who gets too close."

"Ah, I see, and that would be me. Talking to that shrink of yours again?"

She wanted to tell him the truth, but she worried he would not understand. "I don't know. Maybe I do only allow myself to get involved with men who, in one way or another, remain inaccessible. I have a long history of doing exactly that." She could hear Kim's voice in her ear, shouting, "Tell him. Out with it."

"Sounds like you're just second-guessing yourself, darling. We all do that. Don't let the nebbishes of the world, or those inside your head, sweetness, get you down."

"There's something I have to tell you, something . . . important."

"Go right ahead, love."

Jessica had called him earlier, but missing him, she'd left a message saying she was presently working a case in Philadelphia. She hadn't wanted to tell him about Parry's involvement in the case via an answering machine, so she had given no more details. She outlined the case and left it at that. She repeated herself somewhat now but ended with the news that she'd been teamed with James Parry.

The night before, Kim had pretty much said, "How your Richard handles the news will be a defining moment in your relationship." Jessica believed her friend's words and she held her breath while she waited for Richard's reaction.

"I see . . ."

He didn't see, she told herself.

"But I thought this fellow Parry was Bureau Chief in Honolulu?"

She explained the situation and circumstances leading to the teaming.

"I see . . ."

He didn't see, not a thing did he see, she silently muttered to herself.

Richard then added, "Are you saying you had no say-so in whether or not you two were to work together? I'm not quite clear on that."

Two questions, level and calm. His reaction was to pose a question, perhaps to give him time to mull over his feelings. It had to come as a shock to him, but he characteristically absorbed the shock.

"I was given the choice. I did not decline."

"I see."

"You see?" She was beginning to hate those two words. What did *I see* mean to him?

"Really, Jessica. You don't have to be . . . so tentative with me. Remember, we, you and me together, we made a formidable team against the Crucifier, and I should think we can overcome this."

"I've been afraid to tell you."

"Afraid? Never be afraid to speak to me about anything, dear."

He was handling the news, and the fact that she'd withheld it from him this long, "swimmingly"—as he might say—well.

"I trust you implicitly, Jessie, I do. I know you, perhaps better than you realize. I really must run, however. Are you all right?"

"Much more than before I spoke to you, yes."

"I know the pain of closing out an old relationship; it's not something done overnight. All my love, dear."

"And mine to you," she replied before hearing the connection go dead.

Richard was right, she now told herself. Silly of her to be so filled with self-recriminations. Still, she had failed to completely inform him of the situation, that Parry still had strong feelings for her. However, she had informed him of the overall picture. She felt a sense of relief come over her, followed by a flood of happiness. Kim had been right. It was a defining moment in their relationship, and he had handled it so well.

Jessica returned to sleep, trying to ease her concerns, replaying Richard's strong, melodious voice in her head. As slumber came, she heard his voice change into that of a stranger without face or body. A stranger who kept repeat-ing the refrain of the poems left by the killer in the melodic voice of a Richard Burton or a Sir Laurence Olivier. She played his deadly words over in her mind again just before consciousness waned.

> *Chance . . . whose desire*
> *Is to have a meeting*
> *With stunned innocence . . .*

Subconsciously, she asked, What does it mean? What does the killer poet intend? So peculiar, she felt that someone ca-pable of combining words so beautifully . . . someone so cre-ative, could destroy lives. We need a cryptologist to decode this so-called poetry, she decided. How can he be both artist and destroyer? What kind of man am I dealing with? her un-conscious asked, and again played over the killer's words:

> *Chance . . . whose desire*
> *Is to have a meeting*
> *With stunned innocence . . .*

Is *he* Chance? Seeking meetings with victims who may, in the end, be stunned by their own innocent acceptance of him and what he plans for them?

Stunned innocence . . . stunned because they suddenly discover they are his victims? Or stunned to discover something else, something about themselves, something he teaches them? Something to do with flickering life?

These questions played in her head, over and over again, as she slept.

THE Poet Lord sleeps the sleep of the innocent, in a spar-tanly furnished apartment; some say the poet lives the life of a recluse, like a monk, a person with little interest in material possessions or things of this earth. But such as these know him only from this apartment; it's hardly the whole person. The Poet Lord's interests are always in the spiritual possessions of the next life, and the condition of the spirit in this life, but at times material possessions have surrounded him. Perhaps in another life he'd been a priest, but not so in this one. He maintains three separate but equal habitats; this is but one of them. It overlooks the teeming life of Second Street.

In dreams, power is turned over to him in the form of a torch. Dreams are like overflowing cups, and lately the poet's dreams run rampant with reward. Few will ever understand—this he knows—and fewer still will have glimpsed the other side, but he knows that he will be embraced by the light, the love, and the ultimate compassion and wisdom of the angels and their Maker. He has had a recent reading of the tarot cards of his choice, the Enochian tarot cards created by the gnostic and occultist Aleister Crowley, a man who saw the images of the cards in a series of visions brought him by the angels who spoke to Enoch, the only man known to have walked in conversation with God.

As always, his reading was done by Madame Lesia Tahach, the Hungarian woman who knows how to read the cards, the stars, the tea leaves—whatever a client wants—and Tahach had told him that he'd soon be on the journey of his life. He trusts this journey will in fact be the journey toward final reward, final closure, and the new life of the Four Quarters—the angelic forces of Air, Water, Earth, and Fire.

The original message of the angels had concerned knowledge of the known universe in order to overthrow existing governments, to usher in the Apocalypse, but now, like their Creator, the angels had no more use for humankind or Earth the planet; instead, they simply wished to recall their kindred spirits. These spirits, at one time numbering ninety-one, now roamed the land, a mere nineteen remaining.

"Can the wings of the winds understand the voices of wonder?" he had once asked Madame Tahach. She only gave him a grim look, as if he were co-opting one of her lines.

While the Poet has a vague sense that his identity might one day be revealed, at present this concerns him little. He has been assured a seat in the ranks of the angels in another place, another time, far more important than this reality, this era.

His last Chosen One, Maurice, despite the outward happiness he displayed to the world, despite his constant smile and immature wittiness, lived in constant pain and sadness. Maurice had opened himself up, revealed the raw edges, the seething melancholy of his existence, the worm at the center of his being. Maurice had been born a woman in a man's body; his entire being screamed this fact to the world he had inhabited before his departure to a place that embraced his soul, not his body. Because he'd been born a man, he had spent a lifetime—several lifetimes, in a sense—fending off this world. How awful the invisible scars that poor Maurice suffered. In a world where many influential religious leaders called Maurice's lifestyle a growing malignancy, the poor boy had few authority figures to turn to.

Maurice was in fact an angel-in-waiting. A Christ-like child of innocence, who knew enough to believe he was special after all.

It was the same as asking Christ to live in a world filled with ugliness and an ingrained ignorance that only bred falsities, contempt, hatred, and prejudice.

The Lord Poet's answer came in his actions. He convinced Maurice to allow him to write a poem in his honor, to pen it across his back, to be displayed in the clubs and pubs and wherever he wished, to declare himself a living, breathing piece of art, a truly special being created by the touch of angels—inspired, as it were, to combat hate crimes and hate thinking.

"I'll create of your living, breathing, moving skin the most beautiful, enigmatic poem the world has ever seen," he had promised Maurice.

"Sounds fantastic!" Maurice had been excited, his hands waving, his eyes suddenly the size of saucers. He had not shown such exuberance all evening long. He loved the idea, and he loved his new friend for suggesting it to him. "When? When do we get started? How long will it take? When can I show it off?"

"Now, immediately."

"You can do that? Don't you need to, you know, do a rough draft, process it for days and nights, talk to ravens and shit, invoke the muse, all that?"

"I already have. I've been giving thought to your poem for years, long before we ever met—on this plane. I know what to write, word for word. It's all in here." He pointed to his heart.

As the Poet Lord had written across Maurice's back, the troubled youth talked about his childhood, his upbringing, school, the sister he loved, and how much pain and harassment he'd endured over being different.

Well, no more . . . No more pain and anguish, no more tauntings, no more regrets, no more harassment. Never again a thought of pain, never again to feel a moment's remorse for what God had wrought of flesh and bone and soul. Maurice was meant to be here, both to learn and to teach, but it had been revealed that he had suffered long enough and deeply enough, and that it was time for his eternal *release*.

When and if the authorities came for the Poet Lord, this is what he would tell them. This is his mission. Daily, it comes clear that part of his purpose has always been to enlighten and inform. He thinks of all the Chosen Ones he has sent over. They constitute his spirit family now; he is never alone. He can never be alone as he has been in his own biological family, in this life.

He knows next with whom he must converse; he has found his next Chosen One. She does not live too far from his apartment. She will come to him, as the others have done; she will make the first overtures. Subconsciously, she wants to be among his pantheon of devotees. One never knows. He recalls how surprised he had been when young Maurice approached him at the Capuchin Coffeehouse the night he'd sent Maurice over. It had taken special eyes to see that Maurice was angelic, that a wand had been waved over him at birth. The Poet had seen it clearly enough.

Now his eye is set on another angel, barely Maurice's age but just as lovely and genuine in her own way. Her name plays over in his mind like the sound of marbles pleasantly knocking together: Selena Sonjata. Lovely name, lovely creature in need of setting free.

He has exactly the words for her. He has them memorized and with a blink summons them to his ear. Words like angels have a life of their own for him, and the words speak to him now.

> *Chance . . . whose desire*
> *is to have a meeting*
> *with stunned innocence . . .*
> *is eminent like wind,*
> *earth, fire, water,*
> *or the cool fall breath*
> *when it comes even,*

unrushed, surrendered
like an ink mark to a page;
one dot is all that is said.
Flickering light haunts
a chamber formed
of delirium left to feel
out the evening, while
an opera of soft words
etch across a mile of skin

TWELVE

*On a dark theme I trace verses full of light,
touching all the muses' charm.*

—Lucretius (99–55 B.C.)

Two days later

ERIQ Santiva forwarded a detailed analysis of the killer's handwriting to Jessica, along with a note to see a Professor Stuart Wahlbore at the University of Philadelphia's linguistics department. Apparently, a search of experts in the FBI files had settled on Wahlbore because he had a computer program that analyzed handwriting.

Jessica reread the most important portions of Santiva's report even as she and Kim made their way to the university to meet with Wahlbore. For Kim's benefit, Jessica read aloud the document, which Santiva had written out in longhand.

> *. . . killer is obsessive-compulsive; he will be neat to a fault. If he works at a desk, everything on it will be organized and aligned; if he works on a construction site, there will be no trash outside the Dumpster. In short, he's a neat freak. Upright anal-retentive are your watchwords. He plans ahead and he colors rigorously within the lines, never varying. This is evident in the control he wields with the poison pen—he writes on skin as if he were writing on ruled paper. No letter leans forward, none back. He's methodical and supremely organized. He pre-*

meditates his every step. In his handwriting, the lack
of high points above the median line, and of low
points and loops below said line, make it safe to as-
sume this fellow has the sex life of a eunuch.

"So we're in search of a tight-assed eunuch possibly suffering a big identity crisis," Kim said as they pulled onto
the university campus's tree-lined, weaving paths. In a moment, they pulled to within inches of a sign that proclaimed a little house as the linguistics department.
Professor Wahlbore stood on the steps, awaiting their arrival, an ear-to-ear grin making him look like Ichabod
Crane in thick glasses, complete with bobbing Adam's
apple.

"Welcome, welcome you are." He spoke like the *Star Wars*
character Yoda, Jessica thought, or was it merely because he
was Hungarian and his English was imperfect? She took his
outstretched hand in hers, and they shook, introductions all
around. Seeing that Jessica was staring at him, he informed
her, "Each summer takes me to archaeological dig, a wonderful site in Arizona on a Navajo reservation." He wore a typical
western-style shirt, a string tie fastened by a Navajo turquoise
brooch. He also wore western-style boots and vest, all at odds
with his scholarly appearance and Middle European accent.

"Coffee I have inside with biscuits my Grete makes.
Come, talk we must. I took liberty to run Rocky against
samples forwarded by FBI."

"Rocky?"

"Name of my computer program; suggests like bull
strong, yes? Sylvester Stallone, yes? But actual fact, it is
flying-squirrel cartoon person I name him for."

Jessica followed, making eye contact with Kim, each
telegraphing her skepticism. Kim's shoulders and eye-
brows lifted with her frown.

Soon they were seated before Professor Wahlbore's

computer, and he demonstrated his alleged mathematically accurate handwriting analysis program. "I've used it to conclusively prove that Shakespeare was in fact Christopher Marlowe."

"Really?" Jessica asked. "Have you conclusive proof of that?"

"No one wants to believe it, of course, especially others with ax to grind, in particular descendants of the Earl of Sussex, and the Sir Francis Bacon believers, but writings of Marlowe's and those of the Bard are identical on twenty-nine comparison points. I can show you, if you like."

"Perhaps some other time. For now, what does Rocky say about the Killer Poet?"

"Rocky has no one to compare him to, of course, but I have continuously running program searching for comparison points, you see, so in time—"

"How much time?"

"Could be a day, a week, a month. Certain I can't be, no, as it is a tedious process, not unlike fingerprint-match search like I'm sure you use at FBI all the time. Saw it once in a Clint Eastwood movie, *In the Line of Fire.*"

"Does the program make any pronouncements on the killer's handwriting sample?" asked Kim.

"Yes, of course, but it does not know if subject has murdered anyone. Still, it senses a confused person, he is, under great stress with a disintegration of the self, an identity neurosis. This I suspect."

"You got neurosis from a look at his handwriting?"

"Not me; Rocky. Programmed Rocky I did with every known variable in handwriting analysis—graphology if you like."

Kim asked, "Are you saying, sir, that it—the program—can make assessments far more accurately than a handwriting expert?"

"Yes, because all the expert perspectives are seen at

once by Rocky; weighs them all up and makes his—its pronouncements, you see."

"Perhaps the FBI ought to have a look at your program, Dr. Wahlbore."

"One of my greatest fantasies, that your FBI will scrutinize my program and how effective it is they will learn in due course. Had it been used in the JonBenet Ramsey case, for instance—"

"What's this icon?" Kim pointed to the screen, where a stylized winged female free-floated, carrying a huge cross and an olive branch.

"Religion or religious icons your killer is interested in particular. Icons, particularly art depicting divine beings. Narrowing that"—he stroked the keys and added—"angels come up. Angels and the angelic, it holds a peculiar, perhaps perverse interest for him."

"How can your program get that from his handwriting?" Jessica asked.

"Analyzes content as well as the handwriting. Each of poems speaks of flickering life, and many of symbols and images used are to do with life in another dimension. Recognized and pinpointed the symbolic language as pertaining to magic and angels."

"Michael, Raphael, Gabrielle," said Kim, remembering her Catholic upbringing in an orphanage in New Orleans. "None of the archangels are mentioned in the poems. How can your program say they are alluded to?"

"A fixation it appears for him, your killer, according to Rocky. In images speaks Rocky. Images of the transmigration of souls, the ones your killer takes."

"Anything else?" asked Jessica.

"Without someone's poetry to compare and contrast it to, no. 'Fraid not."

Jessica studied the program's analysis of the killer's handwriting. It gave them a list of characteristics of the writing from the size of letters to the degree of coherence and legibility. The program also told them some of the character traits they might look for, but nothing proved conclusive. Without a suspect to match the writing to, it was impossible to summon up much excitement for Dr. Wahlbore's findings. Still, Jessica was more impressed than she'd imagined possible. Should they narrow the field and come up with a suspect, this information might be used in an interrogation. If shown that a machine had outwitted him, an intellectually arrogant person, as the killer seemed to be, might conceivably break down and confess. Such an approach had been used in many an investigation, using far less sophisticated machines, from lie detectors to Xerox copiers to fool suspects into confessions.

"The analysis does point to a highly educated, intelligent killer," said Kim.

"We have that task-force meeting to get back to, Dr. Desinor," Jessica reminded her. "We'll certainly keep your suggestions in mind and pass them along, Dr. Wahlbore." She stood to leave, again shaking the linguistics professor's hand.

"Correct Dr. Desinor is, as my Rocky is accurate, that killer is a highly polished individual, well educated, gifted in fact with words. He is, and he will be, cunning, and as for themes and patterns, recurrent in the work, there are a number of these: reflecting pools, mirrors, flickering light, which Rocky takes as metaphor for fragility of life, you see. Here, look at the lines Rocky has culled as repetition, the same nails being hammered by the author."

He showed them a printout of the lines the program had selected as revealing "high-level figurative language," "symbolic resonance and depth," and "complex associative clustering."

<u>From poem #1</u>
. . . The cut of it

against my back
marks time
. . . the time it takes
to retell a new breath.

From #2
. . . luminescent green
. . . color of script,
. . . ice-blue hues
embrace . . . images.
They make skin
crawl with miniature
electric devotions . . .

From #3
Beneath it all: a bed
a fibrous dictation.
I am drawn forth, found out . . .
Speaking to a mirror
sparkling with never-
before phrases,
all against the marble
life flickering.

From #4
. . . to fall into the mirror pool,
through meshes of metaphor . . .
The breath that exhales
across the candle fails,
and so it remains, flickering.

From #5
. . . Pools of sensation
. . . swirl . . . orange to
swallow and overflow

in the center where
toucher becomes touched,
texture vibrating chords
of the unconfined delicate.
. . . closed eyes
undulating within a seashell sigh,
entwining in airy depths,
waning in flickering light.

From #6
. . . surrendered
like an ink mark to a page;
one dot is all that is said.
Flickering light haunts
a chamber formed
of delirium left to feel
out the evening, while
an opera of soft words
etch across a mile of skin . . .

Jessica could readily see the mystical-romantic themes and patterns that emerged, particularly the combination of cutting into flesh to rend a swirling eddy of delirium, and the idea of a flickering soul, whose light, even in death, could not be wholly extinguished, as its fairy light transmigrated to another form. Mirrors held up to mirrors, time endless and boundless. The green luminescence and icy-blue hues paralleled Kim Desinor's psychic hits.

"What do you suppose the Poet means by *unconfined delicate*?" Kim asked of Jessica. "Private parts unfettered?"

"Actually sounds to my ear more an oblique reference to his victims, that they, while always delicate, were now released—no longer constrained by this life and dimension."

"They are freed through their death."

"That's be my guess."

Dr. Wahlbore began to obsess over a single line, going over it repeatedly as if to choke some useful information from it. "*Opera of soft words* is like his *meshes of metaphor;* he thinks a great deal about how language has a powerful connection to all that we consider psychic phenomena."

Jessica tried to imagine being a student in this man's "Language Is Thought" class, listening to his foreign syntax and trying to translate while taking notes. "I would like to take a copy of all your results, Dr. Wahlbore," she said. "They may well prove useful for our investigation." She was not simply humoring the older man. What if the linguistics professor and his strange program were right on? she found herself wondering.

As they found their way to the door, Dr. Wahlbore asked, "About Rocky, my program, what?"

"What 'what'? I don't understand." Jessica looked at him in bewilderment.

"What about my program? Will FBI be interested only if it cracks case wide open?"

"I'll report your findings and how you arrived at them to my superiors, sir," she assured him as she lifted a handkerchief and sneezed into it. The little office of the professor was mildew-ridden and dust-laden. Jessica decided the environment must be hell on the man's computer, if not his sinuses. "We must be off to a task-force meeting, Doctor."

Outside, Kim asked, "What task-force meeting?"

"I just had to get out of there."

"Then you don't believe his findings?"

"I'm not sure, but it was so stuffy and dusty in there, I felt an allergy attack coming on. Can you imagine being a student in that man's linguistics class?"

"Yeah, and I'd cut my throat," Kim replied.

"A case like this, all the kooks come out of the woodwork."

"Still, I see what he means by the poetry's imagery; it speaks of life passing into another form, and it speaks of angels. A close look at the poems will reveal that that little Rocket J. Squirrel computer program may well be right."

"You think so?"

"I think so. I'll go back over the lines, try to look at it from the program's perspective. Hopefully see what I didn't see the first time around," Kim said.

"I think we need an outside opinion from a forensic psychologist."

"What am I, chopped liver?"

"Someone totally removed from the case, Kim."

"There's a guy in the Philly police department named Vladoc, Dr. Vladoc."

"I'll send a request that he analyze the poems for meaning and hidden meaning. See if he comes up with anything more substantially helpful than did the squirrel."

"Good move."

They saw that Wahlbore stood again on the steps of the little house that was headquarters for the linguistics department; he waved them off as they drove from the campus back into the real world.

WHEN they returned to PPD headquarters, Jessica iearned that there was indeed a task-force meeting scheduled for later in the day. She and Kim showed up for it after lunch along with everyone involved in the case. Sturtevante directed the meeting, telling everyone that those closest to the investigation feared the killer would strike again. "Within the week," she emphasized. "The killer's quiet attacks on people via poisoning typically happen over weekends. So we expect to see another victim, likely in the proximity of the others, in the low-rent student district surrounding Second Street."

Jessica had learned that Second was a two-mile-long strip of renovated shops that ranged from specialty boutiques to funky furniture stores, all upscale and hip; the neighborhood had become a showplace for the outrageous and bizarre along with a safe haven for gays and lesbians. While the area could not be called posh, it certainly was the in place for the chronologically young and the inveterately youthful, catering to their interests along with those of the artistic crowd. While the rents still weren't high, all the renovations going on made it a safe bet that they soon would be. Coffeehouses with browsing libraries, renovated neighborhood bars and nightclubs abounded in the area.

Sturtevante told the task force that this geographical area, which Parry now blocked out with red marker on an enlarged map, had been home base for all the victims. Their faces were familiar to many of the shopkeepers in this relatively small community just off Philadelphia's downtown business district. All the victims had been consumers and renters here. The circumstances reminded Jessica of the case she and Kim had solved in New Orleans, where the killer had targeted transvestites living in and around the French Quarter.

Sturtevante finished with, "Somewhere in this same area, the killer prowls, possibly lives."

Next, James Parry took the floor, and he described in meticulous and tedious detail the similarities in each crime scene—information they had already gone over again and again, and it left Jessica feeling drained. Something was still missing, something important, perhaps the linchpin that held all the killings together, but what was it?

Jessica was asked to comment after Jim Parry. She described the condition of each body in relation to both the crime scene and the corpses that had preceded. "We obviously have a serial killer on our hands, ladies and gentlemen, but we believe now that he thinks of himself as a benign being, helping these poor souls to exit this life in as gentle a fashion as possible. At least, that's how it appears to be shaping up. As for the handwriting, allow me to read what our resident expert on graphology in Quantico has to say." Here Jessica read Eriq Santiva's faxed report.

The room had fallen silent and it remained so. Jessica did not share anything she and Kim had learned from Professor Wahlbore, not wishing at this point to cloud the issue with angel talk and what she felt to be a great deal of supposition. Eriq's interpretation of the handwriting was supposition enough for one meeting.

Besides, she wanted to hold in reserve the information that Wahlbore had shared with Kim and her. She certainly didn't want it getting out of house and into the press. She'd decided also to keep the information pertaining to the killer's tears, and any subsequent DNA obtained from the tears, between her and anyone else she considered to be on a need-to-know basis in the case. It was the kind of evidence that broke suspects in interrogation, and it was the kind of evidence that locked men away for life. But if it became widely known, it could prove useless, a burden instead of a boon, as every nutcase in the city and state would come in claiming the tearstains belonged to him. No investigation proceeded without attracting its array of sad souls who would step forward to claim responsibiiity for crimes they did not commit. To publicize such information as the tearstains only fed into this fact, and only through withholding such information from the general public might it become useful as a tool in nailing a real suspect— once one had been found.

"So, let me remind you, ladies and gentlemen," Sturtevante began when Jessica sat down. "We strongly suspect our killer prowls Second Street for his victims, and we also suspect he may live within the area or extremely close to it. Keep these facts in mind while on your stakeouts of the various locations assigned."

Parry added, "We believe the killer frequents the same nightclubs as his prey, blending in so well as to go unnoticed."

"To blend in on Second Street you'd have to stand out pretty far," said one of the detectives, causing the others to laugh.

A woman detective named Brubaker added, "You could walk down Second in your birthday suit, painted green, and no one would think you stuck out."

"Unless you were Brubaker!" shouted a third, bringing on greater laughter.

The female detective threw a wadded-up piece of paper at the other detective. One look at her breasts and Jessica understood what was meant. Brubaker stood out like Dolly Parton.

"Most creative people are not prone to violence of this magnitude," Jessica told the group now. "This killer, if he turns out to be the author of the poems left behind, will be a strange bird, indeed. There's some feeling that the poems may not be original."

"If the SOB is plagiarizing the lines, we'll soon know it, since we have sent copies to all our university sources in both America and England," added Parry.

"If he is stealing the lines, he will indeed fit the profile of the failed artist unable to create anything lasting of his own. Such a person often, out of some internal pressure and anxiety, projects his hatred outward."

"Is this just a theory?" asked one of the women on the task force.

Jessica replied, "My personal take, yes. The failed artist, the man who sets himself up to be a success in some artistic endeavor but fails miserably, a man who has little or no talent and feels unfairly maligned by the system that rejects him, is not an altogether unfamiliar bird."

"Is that true, Sturtevante?" asked one of the detectives.

"One likely scenario here."

Jessica added, "A tracking of much of violent behavior, from Hitler and Charles Manson to the boys who killed eleven fellow students and destroyed the innocence of thousands at Columbine High School in Littleton, Colorado, all demonstrate this fact. Hitler was a failure at all he touched before rising to political prominence by means of the hatred and promises he preached."

Parry added, "Charles Manson had been spurned by America's recording industry."

"And Eric Harris—who from all accounts thought of warfare as his kind of art—had been turned down by the U.S. military."

Sturtevante brought on more laughs when she joked, "Perhaps our killer is a poet who's found one too many rejection letters in his mailbox."

"Laugh if you will, but it makes far more sense than looking for a successful poet," countered Jessica. "Unless I'm missing something."

Jessica was bombarded with arguments over her analysis of the situation, particularly from Leanne Sturtevante. Parry ended the heated discussion with, "I think Dr. Coran has a point, but it's stretching a point to say that we have anything conclusive on this . . . theory."

"You could say that, yes," Jessica agreed, "but this is a brainstorming session, and as such, the theory, like any other, deserves fair attention."

"It's Friday, people," Sturtevante announced. "Everyone has been assigned a location along Second Street. We will canvass the locations, on foot, on the street, and in shops and coffeehouses, and we'll arrest anyone displaying unusual behavior."

"On Second Street? You don't have enough cells!" called out a man who sat against the far wall.

"Then anyone who looks like a threat," she countered.

The meeting broke up on this note of qualification, everyone anxiously awaiting the events of the weekend, and the killer's plans for spending it.

THIRTEEN

Instinct and study; love and hate;
Audacity—reverence. These must mate,
And fuse with Jacob's mystic heart,
To wrestle with the angel—Art.

—Herman Melville

L EADS were pursued and the usual suspects were arrested, held, and interrogated, but all of it netted authorities nothing. One reason local police went through this charade was to demonstrate to press and public that all that could be done was being done, but to insiders it meant a shakedown of the street lowlifes, the bottom feeders, as Sturtevante called them. It, in fact, involved such people in the search for the killer, enjoining them to keep their eyes and ears open. Everyone who maintained a street snitch put the informant on notice. Every cop in the city wanted to know anything remotely to do with the Poet Killer. However, this time around, the efforts appeared futile, or as one indelicate detective kept saying, "It didn't bear a single fruit"—pregnant pause—"cake." No one knew anything about the Poet. Word on the street was stone silent. No one's snitch had a single useful tip. The few leads that did come out only enticed the investigators down the well-trod primrose path. And with each new wasted effort, Jessica and the others became increasingly disappointed, irritable, and frustrated.

But no one felt disappointed that the killer appeared to have taken a holiday, as the weekend passed without incident.

Meanwhile the FBI had enlisted professors of English across the country to study the poems left on the backs of the victims for any clue, any sign of a possible suspect. But no one recognized the work, although some called it Ginsberg-like or a pastiche of Burroughs. It appeared that the killer fit no known profile, either as a killer or as a poet. One old professor saw the poems as existentialist in impulse, while another saw them as an example of New Age philosophy with a Jungian twist. Another saw them as descendants of Edgar Allan Poe's lunatic-narrated dramatic monologues and tales. Everyone thought the poet astute, clever, highly intelligent, well read, and learned—even if he was insane. Not unlike a narrator in a Poe story, after all.

Despite their frustrations, Jessica and the others working the case did learn a great deal about Second Street and what went on there over the weekend. The coffeehouses and pubs, filled to capacity, routinely featured poets who read their work, and many places Jessica and Kim visited were into body art and display. At one such place, the Brick Teacup, the evening began with a tattoo competition and it ended on a somewhat higher-brow note with a poetry competition—poetry written on the backs and chests of young people, both male and female, who didn't feel shy about exposing their bodies along with the words.

Someone acting as master of ceremonies for the night read aloud the words as the "poems" kept moving across stage. A panel of judges made their decision on both the body and the poem, and the artistic merging of the two.

Kim and Jessica felt as if they stood out in the crowd, but looking around, they found any number of touristy-looking people and older men out for a good time. Still, Jessica guessed the average age in the place hovered around twenty-one or two.

After taking in the scene, she began asking questions

of the bartender, who doled out far more coffee and latte than he did hard liquor. The bartender waved her off, saying loudly, "We don't know anything about those killings."

"You can talk to me here or downtown, Steve," she told him, reading his badge. "What's your preference?"

"The boss doesn't like us spending too much time with any one customer."

"I'm not your average customer. Now tell me, you have anyone you have had trouble with lately, any little oddball disturbances at all?"

"The whole damned place is one long oddball disturbance."

"Anything out of the ordinary insanity, then?"

"Bounced a guy out of here last night."

"Really? What was his name?"

"Hell if I know. I didn't stop to *get* his name. Just kicked his ass through the door."

"Why'd he need bouncing?"

"He grabbed one of the poets."

"Which one?"

"One with the big tits . . . so, I'd say he's pretty normal as guys go."

"You notice anything unusual in his behavior prior to his grabbing the girl?"

"Naaah, came out of the blue. He'd had too many bourbons."

"Isn't that unusual in a place like this, a bourbon drinker?"

"He was an older dude. Didn't fit with the usual crowd, no more'n you and your partner do."

"There you go. Then there *was* something out of the ordinary about this fellow. Anything else?"

"Well, I couldn't say, but the girl he grabbed, I think she kinda knew him."

"You think?"

"She called him by some name. Can't remember what."

"What was the girl's name?"

"Dali, I think she calls herself, Dali Esque. Stage name. Don't know her real name."

"Dolly Esk?"

"Not *Dolly* as in Dolly Parton, *Dali* as in the artist Dali, the painter. Dali Esque."

"I see. Do all these kids take on stage names?"

"It's a way of stepping out of yourself, your usual inhibitions, you see."

"What're you, a psych major?"

"How'd you guess?"

"The girl, Dali, does she come in often?"

"Saturday nights, sometimes Fridays, to catch the scene. First time I ever saw her take her blouse off and display, though. She was fine. Hell, I wanted to touch her myself—"

"Do all the girls have to display in order to have their poems read?"

"No, no, it's not required, but if you want to win the door prize, it's, you know, advisable. You get a load of the judges? Two guys and a dyke."

She finished by slipping him her card and writing the PPD's number on it, telling him, "If you think of anything else out of the ordinary, anything at all happens that you think is strange, give me a call."

"Sure"—he stared at the card—"sure, Doctor."

Grasping at straws, she turned back to the bartender, who'd begun to mix a drink for another patron, and asked, "When's the last time you saw Dali?"

"Earlier tonight. She left with some guy; draped all over him, in fact."

"Not the same guy, I hope."

"No, some guy she came in with. Guy looked twice her age. Great tipper, but short as a Shetland pony."

Jessica informed Kim she'd gotten next to nothing out of the bartender. Kim merely replied, "Look at this place. It's a far cry from the raunchy topless bars in New York or across-town Philly, I'm sure, but there's something just under the surface that exudes sexual energy."

"Not exactly the sort of place where naked women wrestle in ten-gallon pools of coleslaw," said Jessica, recalling a story about Daytona Beach, Florida.

"Not even a wet-T contest here," agreed Kim. "But the ages and the look of these young people going onstage and baring themselves, that's got to be a real turn-on for your local perverts. Notch over to the impotent poet in search of a winged angel and maybe you might see the appeal."

"You catch the guy with the camera?" asked Jessica, pointing.

"He's not a pervert. He says he's just doing a job for the owners of the club."

"Really?"

"His name is George Gordonn. He's making a film for this Web site. Says people traveling in from all over the world can get a taste of what happens at the Teacup and decide if they're poetry lovers or not."

"Gotcha." Jessica studied the filmmaker. The fellow was young, somewhat heavyset, noticeably unimaginative in his dress and demeanor. Yet he magically blended in here, like part of the decor, and captured all the video he wanted. "What's to keep him from making copies for himself?" she wondered aloud.

"Fact is, that's how he's paid, or so he told me."

Jessica stared at the young man again, wondering if he was a nutcase or a connoisseur of this newfound art form.

Jessica studied the young women and teen girls who placed themselves on display here. They were young, nubile, innocent-eyed, hardly aware of the power they wielded over the men who ogled them.

"Where to next?" Kim asked.

"We're going coffeehouse crawling, it would appear."

"Why do we do this, Jessica?"

"Do what?"

"Make a living this way, on the trail of maniacs and murderers? What possible reason can we have to justify this life we lead?"

"Who else is going to do it? And if we don't?"

Kim didn't answer.

They went to the next coffeehouse, the local Starbucks, which was situated on a corner. No poetry nights here, they learned, just cash and carry latte and cappuccino. When Jessica asked what was the hottest place to hear good poetry read in the area, the kid behind the counter shrugged and said, "Merlin's most likely."

"Then we're off to Merlin's. Which way?"

"Straight up two blocks thataway," the young man said, pointing. Can't miss it. Exterior's done up like a castle—you know, Camelot, round table, knights, damsels in distress, all that shit."

They spent the rest of the evening watching and listening to poetry written on the backs of young people at Merlin's Café. Here, exposing breasts appeared taboo, and this fact, along with the stone-tiled floor and castle-like decor, lent an air of respectability that somehow spilled over into the caliber of the poetry, or so it seemed to Jessica.

Again, no one working in the place had any useful information. The evening was beginning to feel like a bust when a stunted little man with short stubby legs waddled in like a penguin, his slight stature and strange appearance—he was impeccably dressed in a three-piece suit—calling attention to him. Everyone in the place waved to him and called his name—Vladoc. He seemed to enjoy his notoriety.

"I was told I might find you two here," said the small, dark-featured man, walking up to Jessica and Kim and joining them in their booth. "I am Peter Flavius Vladoc, Philly police department shrink. Please, don't be alarmed to see me. Leanne Sturtevante put me onto you. In fact, she has had you put under surveillance so that I could find you. She knew you'd be in the vicinity, called me up. I maintain a flat here, sometimes working late hours, especially around holidays, and sometimes it's just absolutely necessary that I have privacy, and it's far closer to the campus where I teach than my house in the 'burbs."

Kim raised the glass of dark Guinness she'd been nursing and muttered, "I think, sir, you have some catching up to do." The two psychiatrists appeared already to have sized each other up, and apparently liked what they saw; Jessica guessed that Kim had done her homework on Vladoc.

"We're only human," she said, smiling. "Something to bolster our courage for the ordeal ahead of us." She then toasted and drank as well.

Vladoc nodded, gestured to a waiter and ordered, then said to the ladies, "The poetry, the wine, the camaraderie followed by murder—this is indeed a strange case. I confess, I am envious of your work. Weird fellow this Poet Killer. I wonder if he might not be an academic intellectual type."

"I'm not yet convinced his motive is mercy, Dr. Vladoc, but it sounds as if you have familiarized yourself with the details of the case." Although such details had been kept from public and press, Vladoc, as a police psychiatrist, would have no trouble gaining access to them.

"Word spreads here like spilled wine on a white tablecloth, believe me," the psychiatrist said. "The people here in this establishment know more about the details you think you're keeping secret than you can imagine."

Kim yawned and stretched out her legs, kicking off her shoes.

"Not getting enough sleep, I see," Vladoc said to her.

Jessica added, "Don't get too comfy. I don't want to have to carry you home."

"Caseload back in Quantico is up to the rafters, and Serena Lansforth, my best and brightest up-and-coming talent, has decided she wants no part of this line of work ever again, not since the Milwaukee Mauler," Kim lamented.

The little man laughed lightly—a throaty, big man's laugh. "And weighing in at 289 pounds. . . the Millllwaukeeee Mauler! Sounds like a Wrestle Mania guy to me."

"God, that man was into mutilation." Kim shook her head, remembering. "Just the opposite of our boy in the City of Brotherly Love."

"Serena having nightmares?" asked Jessica.

"Daymares, nightmares, all of it, yes. Sent her to your friend Lemonte to talk it out. She's stopped listening to me."

"Have Philly authorities allowed you some private time with the physical evidence and items that belonged to the victims?" Vladoc asked Kim. "I should say I'm terribly curious about what you two have come up with thus far, and if it is to your liking, I would be extremely glad to go over any and all of my findings with you—put in my two cents, as it were."

"They have precious little evidence," Kim confided in the man, "and they're being stingy with what little they do have. But I've had assurances from Roth that that'll change tomorrow."

"You think the killer might be close in age to the victims, who were all barely out of their teens?" asked Vladoc.

Jessica found herself at ease with the odd-looking psychiatrist, who reminded her of the mayor of Munchkinland in *The Wizard of Oz*. She told Vladoc, "I gave that some thought, yes . . . kind of an acting out of teen angst, or should I say—dare I say—Generation-X angst or goth angst?"

"You into labeling now, Jessica?" Kim scoffed. "At least get with the times. X is out, traveled on down the time line, and we're well into the Double Ought Generation now, the Y2Kbies."

"All right, whatever you want to call the current generation."

"Well, actually," Vladoc said, as if beginning a lecture, "many generations now have grown up with the gothic symbols of dark beauty that have been in existence since before Dante wrote *The Divine Comedy*."

"Part of which is Dante's *Inferno*," Jessica put in. "Otherwise known as hell."

"Yes, as well I know; at any rate, these 'darkside' symbols have been around forever—cabalists, necromancers, alchemists, you name it—but in modern America, where the normal rituals of *Homo erectus* have vanished, we now embrace the ancient rites and rituals, no matter their erotic and pagan beginnings, and we do it with a passion beyond all reason, and so these symbols and rituals and various occult businesses are thriving, especially among the young and on the Internet."

"The ancient religions and beliefs have taken on new power for the young," agreed Kim. "For some, this is good, a faith in something being, for most of us, far better than nothing. For others, however, such beliefs can be a kind of slow poison, if you will."

"Precisely," said Vladoc, his teacher's voice easy to hear over the reggae band that was now onstage. "Nowa-

days we have whole mall unit stores devoted to the romantic idea that being chained to a wall in an *oubliette* beneath a castle is . . . well, you know, cool . . ."

Taking a page out of Kim's book, Jessica kicked her
shoes off and lifted her feet onto the cushions of the bench
opposite her. "I see, I think."

"And this generation, whatever you wish to call them,
has a love affair with dark and gothic symbols, instruments
of torture, pagan beliefs, mystic places, practices, and
magic," continued Peter Vladoc. "In fact, they would return to the Middle or even Dark Ages if they could, just on
the off chance that their romanticized notions about such
times are true."

"You've seen some of the trappings the victims surrounded themselves with?"

"Leanne walked me through the last crime scene, yes.
We talked long on what the task force has thus far
learned . . . and failed to learn."

"Of course, going to the crapper in the Middle Ages
couldn't have been much fun," Jessica interjected, somewhat off the point and clearly beginning to feel no pain.

"Yes, well," Vladoc said in his mellowest voice, "with
indoor plumbing centuries away, and the almost knighted
Thomas Crapper having not yet been born, you can assume
all toilet facilities were outdoor affairs, the original Public
Domain, and if not, the private affair amounted to a slop
bucket in a cell."

"Imagine a visit to the local dentist or doctor," Kim
added.

Jessica yawned. "Hey, maybe I'm out of touch with the
young, but what exactly are their romanticized notions?"

Vladoc shrugged. "The usual."

"What? That dragons walk the earth and that men in
armor, like Sir Lancelot and Sir Galahad, slew them to save
virgins nailed to crosses in fog-laden glens? Come on."

"Yes, all that, but perhaps more accurately that fairies, and fairy godmothers and godfathers, and angels are real, and that they are interested in the lives of those humans who are 'clued' into them."

"Dungeons and Dragons, fairies and elves, huh? The little people with gleeful hearts."

"This is the mythology to which they owe a great deal of their romantic notions, along with pop-culture vulgarizations of the Knights of the Round Table. Romantic notions abound in art, literature, poetry."

"Romantic or fantastic?" asked Jessica.

"The romantic *is* the fantastic," Kim countered. "Hey, I know from experience."

Jessica nodded as the miniature helicopter inside her head began a slow buzz, and she knew she'd had enough to drink for one night. She began a slow descent, alerting Kim that she was no longer drinking. Kim agreed to do the same, while Vladoc downed his Miller draft and called for another.

"You know, if you ask my opinion about this killer and his victims, I would have to say that a young and impressionable person—childlike in his thinking—can derive security only from the conviction that he understands nature and reality and truth, and that he feels safe in his convictions, and if this killer can make him feel so, well then, the con man and the manipulator is well on his way."

It all sounded to Jessica like vague generalities, and she was tiring of Vladoc's pontificating. It reminded her of a philosophy class she'd once struggled through in college. Still Vladoc droned on, saying, "That same young person, given so-called scientific fact to refute his belief in a fantasticized reality, will only be faced with more and greater uncertainties, but then isn't that true of us all?"

"We're exhausted, Dr. Vladoc, and we're going home now, aren't we, Kim?" was Jessica's only answer.

"Sounds like a plan," replied Kim.

"More than magic thinking . . . magic *itself* exists, if you believe in angels and hobgoblins, little people and aliens," continued Vladoc, undaunted by the indifference of his audience. "And I believe your victims held such beliefs. They're all *relatives* in this sense, members of a same-thinking group."

"Are you suggesting the victims were members of a cult?"

"No, not really, but rather members of society that finds it comforting to believe in what you and I would call fairies or angels."

Nodding, Jessica added, "Elves of old have become the aliens of today? Nothing a few lines of a chant or an old-fashioned curse couldn't accomplish, so, too, a TV show like *The X-Files*. What was it Carl Sagan said—something about as mankind's campfire grows larger, so, too, do the imaginings of what's out there in the darkness beyond the flames?"

"Wish I knew a chant now to dispel this dizziness in my head," Kim interjected.

Jessica teased, "I should think that being psychic, you'd know beforehand when you'd had your last drink."

"That's funny. You know it doesn't work that way."

"Oh, excuse me, ladies, I see someone I must speak to across the room," said Vladoc, attempting to make a graceful exit. "It's been interesting chatting with you, Doctors, and good luck on the case. Do send me everything you find pertinent, and I will assist in any way I can." He even bowed before leaving, and they watched him join a group of young women at another table, all college-aged kids, all appearing to know him.

Jessica and Kim located their shoes, got to their feet, and made their way out of the pub.

Outside, as the cool night breeze played through Jessica's hair, she said, "So we have a whole generation that believes in an invisible world surrounding us, an entire world in which magic thinking exists, in all its strange and bizarre permutations, while that strange little Peter Flavious Vladoc looks for a new conquest among the young?"

"I predict he will come to a bad end, especially if he is popping Viagra."

"Do you think he's one of those men who will do anything, go anywhere, to sire a child, preferably a male child? And if so, has it to do with his being so short?"

"I think he could well be our killer, Jessica, but then you know that."

"I *do*?"

"He's here, isn't he? Scouting a late-adolescent prize? He may write poetry very close in style and content to that of the Killer Poet, and he appears to have a fascination with the case, all facts in evidence."

"It's his job."

"What's his job?"

"To follow the close casely—I mean case closely, isn't he? Getting all his information from one source, Leanne Sturtevante, can't be good. He needs to see it from all sides, right?"

"Ah," joked Kim, "so . . . do you think that something's up between those two?"

"Haven't a clue."

"Shocking, isn't it?"

"No, not in and of itself, but Sturtevante's on thin ice with the pillow talk she's cooing to Dr. Vladoc."

They walked on toward the hotel. "You know it," Jessica muttered. "She could sabotage our case against a suspect if too many of the details are made public."

"Agreed."

"So, can you predict how my and Richard's relationship will end?"

"I wouldn't presume to go there, Jess. And you know it."

"You mean I have to go to dial-a-psychic for that?"

"Sure, give me a year or so and I'll give you a 1-800 number I trust."

"Hey, I've seen those ads. Everyone on them swears up and down that dial-a-psychic works."

"Yeah, like my one-eyed, one-legged cat works."

AT PPD headquarters crime lab the next morning, Jessica found Parry on her doorstep, this time with news of a possible break in the case. A half grin played across his face as he said, "A call came to my office this morning from a distraught university dean. The woman believes she has a matchup with the poetry. She's a dean of arts and sciences at the university here."

"The University of Philadelphia?"

"Right."

"And she got our FBI packet, studied the killer's poetry, and—"

"Bingo, a match."

"Then I guess we need to talk to her."

"She suspects a guy working under her at the university, and a check reveals that several of the victims were, at one time or another, in the guy's classes."

"Sounds close enough for a look-see to me. Let's get over there."

"I want you and Desinor to interview her, see what you can get."

"What will you be doing in the meantime?"

"Sturtevante has set up the surveillance of a guy she's gotten some leads on from the street, a kind of Weird Al Yankovic character that a lot of fingers keep pointing at. Sturtevante thinks she's onto something, and I need to review her findings. They're trying to get a warrant to search his apartment now."

"So while you and Leanne are storming in to search and seize this Quasimodo's apartment and belongings, we're going to canvass the upper-crust possibilities, is that it?"

"Just trying to cover all the bases. We don't know jack-shit about the Poet at this point. We have to follow up on citizen tips and anything that smacks of reliable."

"Sure, got it."

"You don't like Sturtevante, do you, Jess?"

"She's a contradictory person; she wants a team effort, she heads a task force, but she's not a team player herself. I find her lack of interest in our autopsy findings curious and strange. She confides only in Shockley, and I find her reluctance to share information directly . . . well, a pain in the ass."

"Can't argue with you there. She's somehow, for some reason, developed a similar set of feelings for you, and somehow I find myself in the middle, a kind of referee."

"Don't put yourself out on my account."

"She's been a street cop for a long time, Jessica. This idea of working closely with the FBI, it's new to her, and her superiors forced us on her. You know how that goes."

"Meanwhile, she tells me she's so glad to have us aboard, so anxious to work with us, so full of shit."

"Get over it; you've seen it before. Now, how about getting over to the university, interview this Dr. Harriet Plummer."

"Yes, sir." She gave him a mock salute. "I suspect our killer is far more likely to spring from that rarefied air than from some sleazy bar where street punks hustle babes."

"See if you can learn three things from Plummer. One, are the poems found on the bodies original or plagiarized? Two, stolen or not, does she recognize the poetry? Three, does she truly recognize the hand at work as this colleague of hers—who, by the way, is named Garrison Burrwith. Take her measurements, and be certain that she is acting out of something other than hurt, anger, or confusion. Meanwhile, I'm doing a background check on Burrwith."

Jessica's eyes met Parry's, and for a moment the look lingered. Then, to cover her sudden embarrassment, she asked, "Anything come of your reading of Maurice's diary?"

"Nothing usable, no. Filled with a lot of whining."

"Whining? About what?"

"Life."

"Life?" she asked. "What about life?"

"You know, the usual soul-search stuff, and then the complaints, asking why can't life be kinder, gentler, all the usual claptrap from a person who can't handle life on its own terms. Guy needed a reality check big time. Reminds me of my college reading of Kafka's *Metamorphosis*. Who cares after a point to read on when the initial whine fest never ends?"

"Perhaps Kim ought to do a reading on the boy's diary." Jessica thought Kim might well be more sensitive than Parry to Maurice's plight.

"Yeah, I'm sure she could get a lot more out of it than I did."

"You mean we actually agree?" she asked, her eyes telling him she was only half kidding.

Jessica immediately lifted the phone and called Kim from her office upstairs, a large closet of a place off the task-force operations room. She'd wanted to be close to all the paraphernalia of the crime scenes that Sturtevante's team had gathered. Getting Kim on the line, Jessica explained what Parry had brought them.

"That sounds a lot more reasonable than rounding up street lowlifes like Sturtevante's people are doing," Kim said, echoing Jessica's thoughts. "Most of whom appear too illiterate to write a letter home much less a poem."

"We'll leave that line of inquiry for Sturtevante and

company. You never know what will drop out in a shake-down of this magnitude," Jessica replied, not knowing why she felt compelled to defend Sturtevante's approach.

"Are we any closer to determining any connections among the victims?" Kim asked. "Did you turn anything over to that house shrink, Vladoc?"

"Fact is, I have. Sent him all the poetry we have, our suspicions, minus what Mr. Rocket J. Squirrel had to say, and he said he'd get back to me ASAP."

"What's he really like, Jess? I mean in the clear—and sober—light of day."

"Don't know. Didn't meet face-to-face this time; spoke to his secretary. She handled everything."

"You never saw him?"

"No. He never came out of his office."

"Strange he wouldn't come out to meet you."

"Burrowed in. Had a patient in with him, a local cop, rookie who had to bring someone down with deadly force, I hear."

The entire way back out to the University of Philadelphia campus, Jessica and Kim discussed the victim profile. "Other than the geography, all living in and around Second Street," Jessica said as she drove the PPD loaner, "and the fact that all were of the same approximate age and body type, they didn't appear to have known each other."

"Although they certainly frequented some of the same shops and possibly the same coffeehouses," Kim noted.

"They may well have been passing acquaintances."

"Many took courses at the local colleges and universities."

Jessica turned the vehicle off the main street and onto the lanes of the campus. "We know at least two of them used Ink, Line & Sinker for paper, pens, and art supplies, and several used Darkest Expectations for books, and Moulin Rouge for wall decorations and furnishings."

"We need to question the people that work there."

"Being done, I'm told, by Sturtevante's people. Nothing anyone remembers out of the ordinary about any of the victims. Actually, on Second Street, you and me, *we* are the strange ones. Everyone else down there sees straight people wearing matching blouses and suit pants, and they know we don't belong."

"Agreed."

"Maurice was taking classes at one of the colleges in town," said Kim. "His diary makes mention of it." She had skimmed the diary after Parry left it with her. "We need to find out who his instructors were, question them about Maurice. See what they knew about him, and see if they know anything about the poetic style of the killer. Might take less time and do more good to investigate the local boys than to ask for a national search on a student or other person whose writing style might ring a bell."

"Here we are, another foray into academia."

"Can't be any scarier than dealing with a Hungarian cowboy," Kim replied.

"I don't know about that. I had a chat with the woman we're about to meet. Called for an appointment, thinking it best."

"And?"

"Dr. Harriet Plummer. She's convinced she knows who the Poet Killer is."

"Really?"

"Works under her in the English department here."

"University of Philadelphia, where Maurice was enrolled."

"Really? Do we suspect he knew his killer?" asked Jessica.

"We do, but it remains only a suspicion."

"Then perhaps someone here at the university who knew Maurice killed him?"

"It's possible they could have bumped into one another."

"We'll see what feathers we can ruffle on campus."

"Maybe we can get everyone in English, professors and students alike, to submit a writing sample for Wahlbore, and let him feed them to Rocky. See what the flying squirrel spits out."

"Sure, just try to get everyone to cooperate. You know how quick these academic types are to scream human rights violation?"

Kim replied to this, "And you think the accused should have no rights?"

"The known rapists and the known murderers ought to be stripped of anything resembling civil and human rights, just as they did to their victims."

"Careful of such views. "Upper-level types don't care for them," Kim cautioned. "I know from experience, and look what's happened to your friend Parry."

"Thanks for the warning." Jessica looked up to see the tall, imposing building that housed the English department, a three-story Disney-like turreted castle with six to ten times more space than the linguistics department's small cottage.

"Feudal system still at work on college campuses," she muttered.

Kim laughed as Jessica stared out at Dean and Professor Harriet Plummer, who was at that very moment coming toward the car as if chased by a demon. The scene recalled to Jessica the phone conversation she'd had with the distraught dean of arts and sciences.

When Plummer had come on the line and Jessica introduced herself, she had declared, "It's about time. I've been expecting you." A faint trace of desperation, perhaps repressed fear, had laced the woman's businesslike tone.

"Oh, and why is that, Dr. Plummer?" Jessica had wondered if perhaps they might not be closer to some solutions to this case than she'd previously thought.

"I received a packet of information on this Poet Killer fiend a few days ago. I put it aside. Busy here, you know, extremely. I had no idea the killer's poems were being cut into the backs of his victims until I read the material from you people."

It'll be all over the evening news tonight, Jessica had thought. "I see," she said.

"I believe I know who your killer is. I believe he . . . he works under me here at the university."

"Do you have any evidence of this?"

"The poems, the style, and the way they were left, yes. Now, will you come to speak to me, or do I have to come to you?" the dean had asked.

"A colleague and I will be right over, Dr. Plummer."

"I'll change my schedule, put aside all else until we talk."

Now, as the dean pounded on the car window, Kim's eyes were alight with the same curiosity about her as Jessica had felt during their phone conversation.

"He's here; in his office. Just so you know, just so in case he sees you and me together, well . . . I may need protection."

Dr. Harriet Plummer had already considered the possibility that something strange might be going on at the U. of Philadelphia. She had pulled the files on three of the victims, all of whom had taken basic-level courses there. The other victims, while not students at the university, the dean had found, were students at other colleges and universities in the area, and furthermore, they were all taking poetry- and fiction-writing courses, some with Dr. Garrison Burrwith, the man she suspected of being the Poet Killer.

This they learned all in the time it took to climb the considerable number of steps to the miniature castle entryway of the English department. Atop the tallest turret of the castle, a clock tolled four P.M.

Once they were inside the safe confines of Dr. Plummer's office, she confided, "He is a professor here at the university—our current writer-in-residence."

"Writer-in-residence? Really?" Kim looked impressed.

"His specialty being poetic expression," Professor Plummer informed them.

"How did you know we would be coming?" asked Jessica. "On the phone you said you were expecting us."

"I got my packet from the FBI several days ago, asking if I recognized the poetry of this awful poisoner."

"Yes, of course. And you suspect this Dr. Burr . . . ?"

"Dr. Garrison Burrwith, yes, but it's awful; you see, he is a member of a prominent Philadelphia family, well known for philanthropy and public service. Dr. Burrwith is something of a prodigy. He's an accomplished violinist, fills in as needed at the Philadelphia Symphony Orchestra—he's that good. At only twenty-six years of age, he's an acknowledged scholar of the Romantic poets, in particular Shelley, Keats, Byron, and Wordsworth."

"And, as you say, you suspect he may be this killer of young people?"

"The poetry is so . . . so like his. He's an accomplished poet with a great ability to capture the essence of the romanticism of the Byronic era, and I feel much of this murderer's poetry does the same. Here, have a look at some of Garrison's work. Compare it with the murderer's work yourself."

Jessica reached across to take the volume of poems that Dr. Plummer offered. The book was gilded and exquisitely bound; it must have cost a fortune to produce.

On the cover she read *Oration of the Gifts of Those An-*

gels of the Four Quarters. Beneath this, *Poems to Still the Forest Soul and Various Jottings by Garrison Burrwith III.*

"Old family name, huh?"

"One of the oldest in Philadelphia. Father is on every board in the city having to do with the arts."

Enough to scar any child, Jessica thought but did not say. "Did you find the poems left on the bodies unique, original, Dr. Plummer?" she asked instead.

"Yes, quite."

"Then we may assume they are from the killer's mind and hand, and not something he picked up somewhere?"

The professor stared back, confused.

"Lifted, plagiarized," Kim clarified.

"As I said, they reminded me of the work of Garrison Burrwith."

"So something in Burrwith's style alerts you to call us?"

"Style and subject matter. Read the page I have marked."

Jessica scanned it and then read it aloud for Kim:

SCORN'S MISTRESS

Opportunity happens by
on soft-soled
and soft-souled shoe;
traipsing merrily
until one stumble
sends Her
falling away
from fortune's prize,
only to be seized by the middle,
lifted overhead,
and flattened
against all earth,
scrunched then
into the dark

of a rabbit warren.
No prize
at the
end
of
rain
bows
lost
in
tombs
of
time . . .

Kim suggested, "Perhaps we should have a talk with Dr. Burrwith."

"You'll find him in his office, down the hall in Room 21-B. Name's on the door. I always thought him an odd duck, but I would never in a million years have taken him for a killer."

"Well, Dr. Plummer, we've got a long way to go before we can conclusively prove him to be the Poet Killer."

"No, you have only a few yards to go to his office; that is all that separates him from me, and for that I have been living in fear since I received your information regarding the killings." The frail, middle-aged woman's eyes bulged. "I had not heard that the bodies had been . . . written on, the poems cut into the flesh. Garrison asked me once if I would sit for such a thing, you see."

"He did? He asked you to allow him to write a poem into your skin, on your back?"

"Along my arm, actually. We . . . we were seeing each other at the time. He wanted to brand me, I suppose."

"I see."

She looked faint. Kim asked if she'd like her to fetch some water, but the woman ignored this and went on:

"Moreover, I had no idea of the caliber of the poetry involved until, as I said, I received the FBI's information. I've been living in fear since then."

"I'm afraid we will have to reserve judgment, Dr. Plummer," Jessica calmly replied.

"Reserve judgment until someone else dies? Another poor unfortunate young person?"

As they left the office, Kim and Jessica heard the dean mutter, "Always knew Burrwith was strange."

FOURTEEN

Darkling I listen; and, for many a time
I have been half in love with easeful death,
Called him soft names in many a mused rhyme
To take into the air my quiet breath . . .

—Keats

DR. Garrison Burrwith's hand, when shaken, felt like a
dead mackerel, but his forthright voice and his penetrating eyes gave both Jessica and Kim the impression of a
man who had nothing whatever to hide. It gave Jessica
pause to think that the woman in the office a few doors
down feared for her life because of this man, and that the
dean had come to this conclusion based solely on the
man's poetry. Burrwith struck Jessica as a charming man,
all pleasantness and helpfulness, handsome and thin, with
perfect posture and perfect skin. When told why they were
in his office, Burrwith's crystal blue eyes registered complete shock. He swore, "I know nothing of the murders
save what I've overheard about the halls."

"We're not here to accuse you, sir," began Jessica.

"No, I mean I absolutely *know* nothing of these murders.
I'd heard not the least word on them until only this morning. Some colleagues of mine were discussing them in the
hallway. The dean broke it up when I came along, but not
before Peter Werner told me the news. Dreadful, altogether
a dreadful thing, indeed."

"Yes, we think so, too, but living in Philadelphia, how
could you not have heard something of the news?"

"You see, I take little notice these days of goings-on out in the world beyond academia," he said, adding, "no TV, no interest in news anymore. 'Fraid I've botched it so far as my colleagues are concerned. They all come up with such interesting tidbits at the faculty meetings and the occasional party, but I have little to say. Puts people off, I know, but I have this dread of dealing with people in social settings, save for the classroom, you see, where I can confine myself to topics I know something about—poetry and literature and how to unlock the secrets of the masters. I know all their brushstrokes and techniques, you see. All quite cozy, you see. For me, that is; makes my students sweat, I fear."

Jessica could see that Kim had been silently sizing up the man. He appeared to Jessica as harmless as a caterpillar, the one in *Alice in Wonderland*. No threat in the least, but rather a being completely engrossed in his little corner of the academic world, complete with glasses and bow tie. He looked like a man out of time, a man who had wandered in from the eighteenth century. Even his khaki clothing and vest appeared somehow turn-of-the-previous-century.

"I know I write some rather depressing and somber poetry, but I'm hardly an Edgar Allan Poe," he told them. "But even then, Edgar was never accused of murder, only writing about the act."

"Repeatedly and in novel ways," replied Jessica, "and he had a fascination with death."

Kim added, " 'The Pit and the Pendulum,' 'Masque of the Red Death.' "

" 'The Premature Burial,' " added a grinning Burrwith, his eyes alight now behind the thick lenses.

" 'Telltale Heart,' " Jessica said. "Poe, like your poetic voice, seems fixated on death at a young age, premature death, burials in vaults and walls—being buried alive."

"There is no writer worth his weight who has not explored death as a theme in his or her work, including the ostensibly staid recluse Emily Dickinson. Kafka's work is all about death or a living death. Would you have him or Miss Emily drawn and quartered for their work?"

"Of course not. We can't confuse the author with his characters, can we?" said Kim.

"Perhaps, most assuredly in fact, Poe lived with a death wish, born of a broken heart; he was, after all, a man born into a world he loathed, and it took from him the one ray of love and life he asked for, his little cousin whom he worshiped. It's a cruel world to any who are sensitive, and for Poe, this realm proved a world he could not embrace or long abide, and one which did not embrace or abide him— at least not in his own time. Although he's been all the rage for well over a century now, in his own lifetime he was regarded as a lunatic. Tragic fellow all around, I'm afraid, a kind of dark angel himself."

Kim asked, "What are you saying, Dr. Burrwith? That . . . Edgar Allan Poe ought to've been put out of his misery by someone?"

"Do you have any idea of how literary America rejected the man? Perhaps suicide was in order, as apparently no one would do it for him. So he turned to alcohol for the answer."

"I know he courted death, given his lifestyle," countered Kim, but Burrwith cut her off immediately.

"The man was clinically depressed and was likely a manic-depressive, all ailments that his time had no cure for, save the poppy-seed sensation and alcohol. Regardless of his dark tales and poems, he was a hopeless romantic. And neither you nor I can begin to conceive the torture he must have endured."

Jessica leaped in, asking, "What about our killer? Do you think he may have a Poe complex?"

"I would have to study the poems, which I understand he left somehow on the bodies?"

"You've not seen them?"

"No, sorry, but I have not. I've heard a rumor that the dean has copies of them, but she hasn't seen fit to share."

"I see."

"The dean and I have not been on the best of terms, ever. She might share them with someone else in the department but certainly not with me."

"What does she have against you?"

"Oh, I can't say, but it has always felt like professional jealousy of a sort. I routinely publish, while she can't seem to find a place for her own poetry. And I once made the mistake of becoming emotionally involved with her. Foolish move for me, really."

"Does every professor and administrator here write poetry?" Jessica asked.

"Not all, but many are *wannabe* writers, yes."

"Here's some of the killer's work, sir," said Kim, pulling forth copies of the poems she had first seen in Quantico. "Would you read them, appraise them, tell us what your sense as a professional poet and scholar tells you about the author?"

Burrwith bit his lower lip, frowned, and considered this for a moment. "Before I answer that, would you two care for a cup of tea? I have jasmine, mint, and green tea here."

It seemed a peace offering. The two detectives took it, and soon the trio were sitting in the semidark of Burrwith's office sipping at tea, steam curling from each cup. Having read the poems with interest, Burrwith finally cleared his throat, began to pace, and said, "Certainly brooding, but the poems you've shown me, the poems are . . . well, remarkable in their depth and passion."

"Remarkable in depth and passion. Can you be more specific?" asked Jessica.

"Why, they're beautiful, evocative jewels, in my opinion."

Jessica thought the thin, pale, and sensitive man before them sincere; he appeared more ordinary and appealing than the misguided Byronic hero of these writings, who, she believed thought himself to be releasing his victims from the suffering and agonies of this life. That being the killer's motive, the man before them simply could not be the author of this work. Burrwith, for all his brooding poetry, came off as a man who was on the side of life, not death.

"Despite my scribblings," he began, pointing to the book Jessica had borrowed from Dean Plummer, "the idea that I could conceive of such murders and carry them out—it's laughable."

"No one has said—"

"I suspect that Dean Blowhard Harriet Plummer put you onto me; I suspect she thinks I could be this horrid killer." He laughed a hollow laugh, then apologized. "Look, as an expert in romantic poetry, I, too, received a copy of the FBI packet Dr. Plummer has in her possession, but I have simply been too busy, you see, to look into it. Had I done so, perhaps I could have headed Harriet off at the pass, knowing how flighty and downright susceptible she is to suggestion."

"And exactly what did you do with our serious request for help, sir? Our tax dollars at work," said Jessica, frowning.

"I wish for the life of me that I hadn't put the packet aside. It's just as well. In any case, I know it has led to your coming directly to me, and I also know the mailing from the FBI was enormous. For Plummer to assume I was *not* on the FBI's list of experts tells me a good deal about my future here, or lack of one."

"Dr. Plummer thought you might be of help to us."

"Nice try. For Plummer or anyone to think me the killer, well, it's preposterous, but ludicrous or not, it makes me uneasy all the same. I must wonder what she's told the rest of the faculty."

"Makes you uneasy because of the gossip it no doubt will cause?" asked Kim.

"Oh, and why is that?" he asked. "Many an innocent man has been sent to prison or the gas chamber on preposterous evidence." A timid knock at the door interrupted them. "Look, ladies—do I call you ladies or officers, agents or doctors? Look, I have a student conference scheduled. My young man is likely in the hallway now, waiting. Allow me a moment to reschedule, please." He then stepped outside, leaving the two FBI agents alone.

Kim began investigating the items on the professor's shelves, from books to knickknacks, a stuffed armadillo to a puppet raven, a dartboard to a calendar of Waterhouse prints. "Remind you of anyone?" she asked, pointing to the calendar.

"Maurice's place was decorated with Waterhouse prints, but they're in vogue nowadays among the young and the romantic."

"Perceptive fellow; knows the dean's out to get him."

"You think she just hates him so much she'd sic us on him for no other reason?"

Kim whispered, "He hardly seems a madman. Maybe *she's* the sick one?"

"But the power of the sociopath is to blend in, and he certainly blends in here."

"And at the pubs and coffeehouses frequented by the various victims?"

"Reminds me of a mad priest I once put away, a man who had been civilized and charming to a fault." As criminal profilers, both Kim and Jessica knew that the greatest skill of the sociopath was his gift for disguise and guile.

"The charming mad priest put me under his spell, even as he put people to excruciating deaths. Strange, isn't it, how Burrwith looks and acts the very antithesis of the self he created in his artistic work." Again Jessica wondered about the dean's dark suspicions of the man. "Setting aside what he looks and sounds like, to your psychic sense, what does he feel like to you, Kim?"

"*Feels* as harmless as he looks to me." Still, she shook her head. "But then, perhaps his dark side, the Poe within, is channeled into his art, his poetry, and so he shows only his light side to the universe."

"According to him, he's not even a part of the universe outside these hallowed walls. Are you suggesting that he has it in him to murder people, that he's perhaps a dual personality?"

"I don't believe our killer sees his acts as murder," said Kim, brushing hair from her eyes. "And neither do you. This guy we're after kills allegedly for the sake of the victim, you see—any means to the end. Murder, no; assisting them to reach another world, assisting them over—"

"Like poetic euthanasia?"

Kim frowned. "Perhaps, but I didn't get a whiff of it on 'reading' him when I shook his hand."

"Yeah, some handshake, huh?"

"If you can call it that."

"Dead fish . . ."

Burrwith returned, all obviously insincere apologies. A tone of contempt and annoyance filtered through each word he spoke now, as if he were angry that he'd had to send a student off merely to bother with the two FBI detectives. "All right, now that I'm free, I can give you the rest of the day. Fire away with your questions. Would you like me to go downtown with you? Take a lie-detector exam, what?"

"No need for a lie detector, Dr. Burrwith," said Kim. "I'm a walking, talking lie detector."

Burrwith stared into Kim's beautiful Creole features, his face scrunched in confusion as he asked, "What do you mean by that?"

"I'm a psychic, Dr. Burrwith, a psychometrist to be exact. When you and I shook hands, I got a reading on you."

"Really . . . really?"

"A sure reading . . ."

Kim's face remained impassive while Burrwith squirmed in the seat into which he had fallen, the air escaping the cushioned seat as if to mock his own loss of breath. "So, have I passed your litmus test? How presumptuous of you—both of you—to come in here and . . . and attempt to . . . what would a lawyer call it? Entrap me? I think our interview is over. It's really too bad. I may have been able to help you, but not so long as I'm being treated as a suspect."

"You're hardly being treated as a suspect, sir," Jessica assured him.

"No matter what sort of spin you put on it, I am being treated shabbily. Now good day."

He had done a sudden about-face since speaking to the student outside, and Jessica thought perhaps he was something of a manic-depressive himself. "Yes, well, I think we're done here, Dr. Burrwith. Thank you for your time." With that, she guided Kim out the door.

"What was that all about?" she asked when they had gotten out of earshot of the man. "Do you think telling him you're a psychic at this stage was a smart thing to do?"

"I wanted to see his response, see if it elicited a reaction."

"That kind of information always elicits a reaction."

"Yeah, I know, and I wanted to see his. See if I could get some sense of him from it. I think he may be hiding something, that he's very practiced at being duplicitous."

"Wanted him to sweat it out, huh?"

"Whoever our killer is, I suspect he believes quite strongly in psychic powers, is heavily into the afterlife and New Age thinking, and if he knows we have a psychic on his tail, he might give something away. But I fear it didn't work with Burrwith. I got nothing beyond the feeling that he's hiding something. I just don't know what that *thing* might be."

"Believe me, I've had the same reaction to some of the sociopaths I've run across. Do you have antennae strong enough to pick up the unfeeling, unemotional psychos among us?"

"I know when a soul is ugly, and I don't get that off Burrwith."

"But then perhaps our killer's soul is not ugly. We're not dealing with the usual maniac here."

"Touché. You're right, of course."

As they exited the dark vaulted-ceilinged corridors of the neo-Gothic building, Dean Harriet Plummer again located them, a young woman in tow. She said, "You might wish to talk to Johnnie."

"Johnnie?"

"My student assistant here. She knew your last victim."

"Please allow me to buy you coffee at the commissary," said the dean, pointing to a café-front window across the way. "Sit down with Johnnie. Hear what she has to say about Burrwith and this business."

Taking a deep breath, Jessica said, "All right."

Young Johnnie Haley told them that a lot of students around the campus thought Dr. Burrwith might possibly be the pen-wielding poisoner.

"Why is that, Johnnie?" asked Kim, seated across from her.

"He's just weird. All the poems and stories we study in class are about gruesome stuff, child abuse, molestation, incest, death, disease, horror . . . you name it. Lotsa kids call him Dr. Death."

"Tell us what you know about his habits. Ever see him at nightclubs or bars or the coffeehouses down on Second Street, or anywhere else for that matter?"

"Only once, the time he had a fight with Dean Plummer."

Plummer had left them alone with the student. "The dean was at a local nightclub?"

"The Brick Teacup, checking out the action with Dr. Locke—"

"Locke?"

"Another professor. He's won awards for his poetry and stuff, I hear. Anyway, the three of them got into some sorta shouting match, but no one could make it out since the place is so—"

"Loud, we know," said Kim.

"Tell us what you knew about Maurice Deneau," asked Jessica.

"Not much, really. Just saw him around, you know. He was just a kid, you know, a big kid. They were just kids, like me. Kids nowadays, we just wanna have fun, you know. Nothing about any of this makes any sense to me."

Despite more digging, they got very little else from Johnnie; clearly, using the girl to incriminate Burrwith was a desperate measure on Plummer's part. They learned that she had once slept over at Maurice Deneau's house, and that she knew Thomas Ainsworth, Deneau's friend. "Both the boys were nice, sensitive young men," she told them, tears welling up now. "Just sweet, sensitive guys, you know. Could use more of their type in the world, you know?"

The coffee left a bitter taste in Jessica's mouth, as did

Plummer's overly helpful coaching of the girl to point the finger at Burrwith. After fifteen minutes of listening to basically useless and superficial information, they sent the student on her way.

As they were about to leave the English department building, where they had walked with Johnnie, once again the chairman of the English department clung to them as if she were afraid to be left so close to Burrwith. "You should speak to a Dr. Donatella Leare, also an expert in literature here."

"But let me guess, she's also had some run-ins with Burrwith?" Jessica said.

"She has, but she's never confided the details. She has excellent insight into poetic expression, far more than anyone on my staff. I have given over the information I received from the FBI to her, and she has shown a great deal of interest in the case. You may find her at home late tonight or early tomorrow. Here is her card." She had escorted them to the parking lot now.

"Thank you, Dr. Plummer. You have been a great help," replied Jessica, tiring of the woman's overbearing manner.

"We wish to cooperate as much as possible. This is a horrible blot on our community, these awful killings."

Jessica's police instincts made her suspect Dr. Plummer herself, perhaps not of the murders per se but of some connection to them. She was too eager to be of help, going out of her way, so far as to dig up a student who'd done little more than sit in a classroom with one of the victims, and who'd been in Burrwith's class. She also showed them registration forms indicating that another of the victims had taken Burrwith's class. This overzealousness was a sure sign that she was hiding *something*. Jessica wondered if the dean's secrets had anything whatever to do with the case; much more likely they had to do with the angry scene the student had referred to, the argument involving

Plummer, Burrwith, and the third English professor, Locke, at the Brick Teapot.

"Dr. Donatella Leare may be able to give you some additional insights, as I said." Plummer continued talking as they made their way to the car. "Meanwhile, I can continue to delve into such things as student records."

"Thank you, Dr. Plummer." Jessica attempted a smile. "You've been most helpful, indeed."

"And perhaps you should talk to Dr. Locke, Lucian Locke. We call him Lucky."

"Lucky?" asked Kim. "How is he lucky?"

"In the vernacular of some of our students, 'He de man,' " replied Plummer, standing now under a brilliant blue sky and a blinding, fiery setting sun from which she guarded her eyes. "Sir Lucky. Just won the well-funded if less than history-making R. J. Reynolds teaching fellowship. 'Lucky' Strikes, you see."

"A fellowship to teach, but isn't he teaching now?"

"This will afford him the opportunity to teach and write in Japan."

"I see."

"That makes him number one on this campus. Reflects well on the entire university, you see. Makes my department shine. It's called professional development. We don't like our faculty to stagnate, you see."

"Publish or perish?" asked Kim.

Jessica replied, "In the case of our killer, it's publish *and* perish."

"Guess I'll be packing my bags soon, hey, Dr. Plummer?" It was Dr. Burrwith. He'd exited the building from a basement door, a door that led out to the parking lot; as he stood at the top of the flight of stairs, his body was silhouetted against the light. He'd come up from behind them, but none of them had noticed, so quiet was his footfall.

"There's no need to deride your *own* work here, Dr.

Burrwith. No one knows the classics like you. We all know that."

"Lucky Lucian, ladies," said Burrwith, unmistakable anguish in his voice. "L-U-C-K-Y with a capital dollar sign. The tobacco industry's latest weapon in their public relations war—fund literature and literacy so they can point to their investment in people's ability to read the surgeon general's warning label on their products. Thereby further excusing themselves for selling addiction and genocide."

"Let's not minimize the fact that our colleague has just won one of the biggest fellowships in all of academia, Dr. Burrwith," Plummer soothed. "Queerly enough, everyone in the department has taken Locke's victory personally, as if it means a professional blow to others. Why is that, Detectives? You know human nature better than most. Why does one man's or woman's success have to be viewed as another's failure?"

"I'm sure I can't say," replied Jessica, surprised by the question. She now sensed there was far more rancor in the relationship between the dean and her colleague than she at first realized.

"Insecurity on the part of the second party," said Kim Desinor. "Textbook psychiatry, chapter one."

"Usually Dr. Lucky is in by now, but he hasn't bothered showing up for his office hours since the big windfall," said Burrwith. "Fortunately for him, the dean here is, in his case, lenient about such matters." The implication that Dr. Lucian Locke was either figuratively or literally in bed with Dean Plummer was far from subtle. "His office is next to mine. It's the one office from which I haven't yet been displaced."

Jessica wondered momentarily if such professional jealousy and bickering could spill over into murder and an attempt to frame someone.

Burrwith swung out with his briefcase and strode off,

his head held high. If he had at one time been infatuated with Plummer, he appeared well over it now.

"Pay him no mind," said Plummer. "The students have all flocked to Dr. Leare and Dr. Locke, you see, and Garrison has been left with lecture classes the size of tutorials. I fear Dr. Burrwith has lost his touch with the young. His communication skills, while always questionable, are now definitely on the wane."

"The other instructors are more in tune with the students?"

"The students persist in calling them a team, Locke and Leare, they say. If you've had Locke and Leare, you know you've covered the territory."

"Then Locke . . . he's a good teacher as well as an award-winning poet?"

"Good? Good? He brings literature to startling life, and the man's forgotten more about the classics than I ever learned. Good man, fantastic teacher, really, and I think he, like myself, enjoys the work tremendously, and the rewards cannot be weighed. He loves his students."

"As do you?"

"To keep my hand in, I continue to teach one course per semester, and yes, I do—love my students, that is. That's what makes this sordid business all the more shocking, to learn that two—no, three—of the victims were enrolled here. I found it rather astonishing, absolutely astonishing"—Jessica thought, Yeah, public-relations-wise—"to learn of the connection, while that smug Garrison Burrwith pretends he never had the least inkling this kind of thing was going on, which made me suspicious of him, you see. How can someone claim to know not the slightest about these horrible incidents? It's a bold-faced lie."

"There has to be more reason for your suspicions of Burrwith. What are they *really*, Dr. Plummer?" pressed Kim.

"He . . . he and I once had a thing, a romantic thing, you see, and well, as I mentioned before, he liked using a pen on me."

"Using a pen on you?"

"To excite me; he would use a pen . . . down there . . . pretend to write in the area of my thighs, the lip of—well, you get the picture. At first it struck me as odd, but so is Burrwith. After we broke it off, he withdrew into himself, and when I learned how these young people, some our students, had died, he just naturally leaped into my mind. You will keep this private, won't you?"

"As much as possible, yes, of course," said Jessica.

Kim bit her lip, saying nothing.

"You *will* be discreet, won't you?" pressed the dean.

"Of course."

"You never know around here if your job is secure, and should my superiors learn of . . . Well, they wouldn't be, how shall I put it, liberal in their thinking."

"We may have to speak with you again, Dr. Plummer. You don't have any plans for leaving the city, do you?"

"Oh, gracious no. Are you suggesting, I mean, does this mean that I am . . . a suspect?"

"No, not really."

But she wasn't listening. "How unusual. Wonder how one adds being a suspect in a murder investigation to one's curriculum vitae?" She half smiled at her own little joke and added, "Imagine, questioned in relation to a homicide investigation. What will the trustees think?"

"We'll keep this as businesslike and as discreet as possible, I assure you, Dr. Plummer."

"Thank you. Truth be known, Locke and I, we've visited some of the coffeehouses on Second Street, to 'plug in,' as he says."

"To plug in?"

"To the youth thinking—the 'scene,' as they call it. We

may well have been seated next to the victims, and then one night Garrison showed up. It's horrible to think of."

"Did you ever notice anyone there who struck you as out of the ordinary, unusual in any way?"

"Only him—Burrwith. He made a scene one night at the Brick Teacup. Confronted me before Locke. It was most unpleasant."

"Did he in any way threaten you?"

"He stalked me for several weeks after our breakup. That was threat enough. That night, I made it clear that in no uncertain terms . . . that whatever we had at one time was dead, absolutely and completely dead and over with. He got the message, believe me."

"He felt replaced by Dr. Lucian Locke?" asked Jessica.

"To say the least, yes."

"And you think him capable of poisoning young people in order to . . . to get back at you and the university for feelings of having been wronged?" asked Kim.

"Poison would be just like him, don't you see? You saw how he sneaks up on you. Beneath that calm exterior lies a volcano waiting to erupt."

"We'll keep an eye on him for you."

"Thank you . . . thank you. And I wanted to tell you out of Dr. Burrwith's hearing that both Locke and Leare are out of town at the moment—an academic conference in Houston."

"When do you expect them back?" Jessica asked.

"Tomorrow, for their classes. They'll likely return some-time late today or tonight."

Jessica took down the addresses of the two professors. The three women shook hands and Dr. Plummer made her way back up the stairs and into the airless castle where she worked, a fortress no architect would construct outside a university campus. She was not a beautiful woman in any sense of the word; her legs looked like stuffed sausages, her waist had lost the battle to differentiate itself from her hips, and her hair was from another generation, down to the bangs and flip. She dominated these men through her power in the department, Jessica imagined, but now, with Locke's having won a lucrative if not prestigious award, he likely no longer needed her or the university.

"Whole lotta shakin' goin' on here, wouldn't you say?" Kim asked, picking up on Jessica's mood. She had also picked up on the same vibes about Plummer. "That woman appears to rule here."

"Soon, I imagine, she will be repaid in kind by the men she uses."

"Some piece of work she is," Kim agreed, the sun reflecting a glint in her eye just before it sank below the horizon.

"Yeah, let's get out of here before she comes back with another bogus eyewitness."

"What about Leare and Locke? Do you think we should talk to them sometime soon?"

"Academics are scary, aren't they?"

"Yeah, you got that right."

"Imagine, this woman has concocted this fantastic modus operandi and motive for the killer, and it all revolves around her love life, her scorned lover. She believes herself the center of the universe?"

"Yeah, it all revolves around me, me, me."

"How're we going to write up this report?"

"Get in the car, and let's get out of here, shall we? We'll worry about the particulars later."

FIFTEEN

Indolence is heaven's ally here,
And energy the child of hell;
The Good Man pouring from his pitcher clear,
But brims the poisoned well.

—Herman Melville

J ESSICA and the team, man for man, woman for woman, felt
stymied. Forensics had revealed little of the killer, and
the poison he used continued to evade toxicologists at
Quantico, Virginia, just as it had evaded DeAngelos's
team. Another night had fallen on the case, and no one
stood a step closer to ending the career of the strange Poet
Killer.

Jessica looked up from her notes and the killer profile
that she, Kim, and James Parry had prepared for the PPD.
Lieutenant Sturtevante and her people continued to be cooperative, pleased for the most part with the FBI involvement. The case had simply ground to a frightful halt, and
for a time, it appeared that perhaps the Poet Killer had either committed suicide or left the city, or perhaps been arrested and imprisoned on some other charge.

The PPD, under Sturtevante's guidance, looked over the
suicide records and any recent arrests and incarcerations
that might point to a suspect. With thousands of people
leaving Philadelphia on any given day, there appeared little hope of locating the killer if the stepped-up pressure of
police surveillance of Second Street and its nightlife had
caused him to take flight.

Jessica again looked up from her paperwork, intuitively feeling someone staring at her from the doorway of the temporary office she sat in. A squat little man with a cane who looked like Truman Capote, down to the dark glasses, stared back at her, giving her a moment's fright.

"Sorry, I didn't mean to startle you," he said in a voice that sounded trapped in his windpipe, the gravelly sound requiring her to translate each word. "Bit of a cold," apologized Peter Flavius Vladoc. "I've come to help you on the Poet Killer case."

"That's a relief, because we do need help, sir."

"Not every professional will admit such a fact. Sturtevante told me you were a beautiful creature, but she did you no justice. I wished to tell you as much the other night at Merlin's, but I did not wish to embarrass you or put you on the spot."

"Thank you—for the compliment, I mean."

"I looked over the material you forwarded me. We should talk."

"Very good. What do you make of the killer?"

"I have looked closely at the poetry, you see, and it has meaning for me, and I have made some sense, I believe, of what he or she wants."

"You think you know what the Poet wants?"

"It is nothing he wants of us; authorities can give in to no demands, for there are none being made."

"Still the killer wants *something*," she said.

Vladoc indicated the chair with his cane. "Do you mind?"

"Please, sit down. What's happened to your leg?"

"Degenerative condition; flares up now and again. Slows me down; makes me feel damned old." He stepped slowly to the chair, banging the wooden cane against the chair legs like a blind man. As he came into the light, she suddenly realized that he was blind or partially so, but that he had hidden it well that night at the club—maybe because of the lighting, maybe because Jessica had had one too many. "Rheumatoid arthritis; can only get worse with each step I take. Eyes are going as well. Require a high-powered magnifying glass given me by Shockley to even read."

"I'm so sorry to hear it."

He waved it off as if it were nothing.

"So, what is it our killer wants, Dr. Vladoc?"

"Peace."

"Peace? World peace, peace for himself?"

"Peace for his victims."

"Peace . . ."

"And one other thing."

"And that is?"

"Validation."

The man had a fondness for enigmas, she thought. "Validation of what? His actions?"

"No, validation of myth, legend, fairy tale even, validation of a magical way of thought that he has fully given himself over to, you see."

"I see, and this is your revelation for me?"

"Your killer is seeking his own peace and purification and the validation of his magical thinking."

"And he does this by killing young people?"

"He kills in order to cleanse them and make them over as . . . well, in his or her mind, as the beings they were before being born into this world. Beings born of gods, not of tainted flesh—in other words not born into our tribe, the tribe we call *Homo sapiens*."

"Beings . . . beings born of God?"

"More superior beings, better, yes." The little man leaned forward in the chair, which was too large for him, knowing he had Jessica's attention now. "Not born of man and woman or flesh. In other words, *angels*. He's in the business of making, that is, creating angels of them, you see."

She felt incredulity fill her mind. "He kills them to turn them into angels?"

"I know it sounds like full-blown madness, but there are precedents for such behavior. People have killed others to release them from the bondage of the human coil before, and in fact poetry and literature are filled with examples of such homicides. Look, it goes back to childhood fantasies and beliefs and upbringing, and you know how weird and warped and dysfunctional that can get."

"Are we going to excuse the killer on the basis of his traumatic childhood, Dr. Vladoc?"

"I do not offer an excuse but an explanation, a reason why."

"His motivation."

"His or hers, yes. It could well be a woman."

"Let's order in some food and talk about this further, shall we? I want to hear all you have to say on the subject. But I would like Dr. Desinor to join us."

"Coffee and a sandwich would be pleasant, yes, and as for your associate joining us, I have no objections."

Jessica made the arrangements.

AFTER Kim came in to join them, Vladoc began. "The behavior exhibited by the Poet Killer—I have seen milder examples of it in my practice over the years. It is normally at its height in late adolescence when years of belief in magic are called upon to compensate for a person's having been deprived of it—"

"Deprived of it?" interrupted Jessica.

"—prematurely in childhood. Fantasy, I mean."

"Bruno Bettelheim," said Kim.

"I believe Bettelheim was right about the importance of childhood fantasy."

"You mean the importance of fantasy in understanding and coping with the world."

"Yes," replied Vladoc, who returned to his exposition. "All of your victims as well as the poisoner here, I strongly suspect, these are young people who now feel that it is their last chance to make up for a severe deficiency in their life experience. You see, without having had a period of belief in magic—as all healthy children do in interpreting the world—they are then unable to meet the rigors of adult reality."

"Are you suggesting," Jessica said, "that many young people today who seek escape in drugs and other addictions were deprived of childhood fantasies?"

"If not drugs, then they will apprentice themselves to some guru, go crazy over astrology, engage in black magic, rites, and rituals, or some other obsession, Vladoc assured them."

Kim explained further, in obvious sync with Vladoc on the subject. "Such deprived people are engaging in escape from reality into daydreams about magical experiences which they believe will change their lives for the better; drugs are an avenue for such thinking, yes, but those prematurely pressed into an adult view of reality can only sustain themselves through magical thinking and doing."

"So the cause is in the formative years," said Vladoc, "when experiences prevented early development of skills that can only be mastered later in life, in realistic as opposed to mythical ways."

"And this is how the Poet thinks?" Jessica asked.

"He is committing their souls over to the angels. What does that tell you about his worldview?" asked Vladoc, shaking his head. "And that of his victims?"

Jessica leaned back in her chair, the movement making the old wood groan. "You're sure of this, are you?"

"Quite. I'm good at reading between the lines. Each poem is about a chance encounter that ends in his cleansing them—body and soul—in preparation for their return to their true reality, a reality populated by only the pure. That is, in a nutshell, this killer's pathological mind-set."

"What did Sturtevante think of your interpretation?" Jessica took a leap, guessing that Vladoc had already shared his findings with the lead investigator on the task force.

"She agreed with it, of course. I have studied such lunacy for well over a quarter century. She has confidence in my judgment."

Words like *angelic* and *pure* did seem to apply to the victims, she thought. Vladoc stood, his head barely above hers, although she remained seated. With a Danny DeVito–like glint in his eye, he half smiled and said, "I hope this information helps to stop this poor, driven devil."

"You're not sure he's . . . that the killer is male?"

"It is impossible to say from what I saw in the writing, but you have handwriting experts who might help there, right? Don't graphologists claim to know how to differentiate a woman's handwriting from a man's?"

"Our experts have not been able to determine gender on the basis of the handwriting, no." Not even Wahlbore's program made that claim.

"Perhaps the killer is like his victims in more ways than we think; perhaps he or she is androgynous," Kim suggested. "We know that the less secure a man—or woman—is within himself, the more he cannot afford to accept an explanation of the world that says he is of minor significance in the grand scheme of the cosmos."

"True, the one you are after believes himself or herself to be at the center of the universe," said Vladoc. "Think of it. As long as a child is unsure of his immediate environment, that it will protect him, the more he must believe that superior powers, such as a guardian angel, watch over him, and that his place in the world is of supreme and paramount importance."

"It's far preferable to zero security," Jessica agreed.

"Imagine parents who make it their full-time job to denigrate protective imagery like angels and invisible friends as mere childish projections, the flotsam of immature minds," added Vladoc.

"And you rob the child of one aspect of the prolonged safety and comfort he or she requires," finished Kim.

"Precisely. To quote Bettelheim, 'The child knows that he was created by his parents, so it makes sense that, like himself, all men, and where they live, were created by a superhuman figure not so different from his parents—some male or female god.' "

"He comes to believe that something like his parents, only far more powerful, intelligent, and reliable, will care for him in the world—something like a guardian angel," added Kim.

Vladoc launched into his conclusion. "To feel secure on this planet, our killer needs to believe there is a place where the world is firmly held in place by rules and immutable laws, where *terra firma* means *terra firma,* and it's all held in place by loving, caring beings, or one superbeing who wishes to cloak and envelop him with love and an outpouring of concern, and a peace that can never be achieved in this life, not through drugs, not through preachings, not through sex or food or material wealth or fame. It is that which cannot be achieved on this plane that our killer is interested in, not unlike the desires of the great Romantics in art and literature, not unlike Byron's mad quest across the continent in search of the perfect love and the perfect peace."

"Our killer has been given the unenviable chore of sending over those who believe strongly in the world of invisible spirit?" asked Jessica. "Do you think he hears voices telling him what he's supposed to do?"

"Of that I have no doubt," said Vladoc. "Killer and victim share a faith in the angelic world, and magical thinking—taken to the extreme—is as dangerous as reality itself, or religious fanaticism, or any other *ism* you may go completely obsessive over." With that, Vladoc bid Jessica and Kim farewell and good night.

The two FBI agents sat alone in the darkened office.

The phone rang, and Jessica picked it up.

"Jessica, it's James. I want to apologize for my behavior the last time we were alone together. I had no right to say some of the things I said. Certainly no right to hurl accusations at you."

"Apology accepted, James." She spoke his name for Kim's information. Kim stood, waved, and disappeared, giving her privacy.

James said, "Think for the good of the case, we need a reconciliation? For the good of the case. We must be able to work together."

"Agreed."

"So, it appears your visit to the university was pretty much a bust, from the report you and Kim filed."

Jessica filled him in on their visit.

"Still, I think we need to follow up, talk to this Leare woman and this guy Locke. Shake some trees, see what falls out."

"Jim, Vladoc has given us some useful insights into the mind of the killer. Now we must match a person to those insights, and I don't see Burrwith fitting in here."

"Vladoc's pretty strange, Jess. Sturtevante filled me in on where he's headed with the case. You buy any of it?"

She told him about Vladoc's visit and his strange but eerily on-target conclusions about the killer, drawn from his reading of the poems. "Kim and I think he's right on with this magical-thinking business being at the bottom of the killings."

"Even more reason to follow up on our concrete leads. We need to talk to this Leare and Locke about Burrwith from my perspective, you know, one grounded in his reality."

"Tonight—now?"

"Let's stay on the university poets," replied Parry, after considering all that she'd passed along from the psychiatrist, Vladoc. "You got those addresses handy?"

Jessica hesitated a moment, wishing to go back to her hotel, call Richard, shower, and sleep. But she relented, saying, "No time like the present. All right. You're the boss."

"I'll meet you out front of the crime lab in fifteen minutes with a sack of burgers and chili."

"Sounds good. I'm starved. Bring enough for Kim, too. See you then."

"She there?"

"Yeah."

"You're on."

But when Jessica hung up, she could not find Kim; the psychic had literally disappeared, but she had left a note on her office door for Jessica.

Dear Jess,

Took all my stuff to the hotel. In view of Dr. Vladoc's findings, I'm going to retrace my steps, go back over all my notes on the psychometric readings to see what, if anything, jumps out. Need a quiet, secure, safe place to work.

Yours, Kim

"Dr. Plummer did say that Leare was out of town," Jessica told Parry. They stood outside the professor's home on the northern outskirts of the city. Several days' worth of newspapers adorned Dr. Donatella Leare's doorstep. A weak light illuminated little of the interior, but to Jessica it looked dark and grim.

On the way to Dr. Leare's place, Jessica had confided in Parry exactly what Vladoc had told her. "I suspect the dwarf is onto something," said Parry, "I just have trouble with such notions. I'm a pragmatic realistic myself. Can't believe a grown man or woman could buy into such thinking to the degree he kills—albeit benignly—over it."

"Come on, Jim, it's not so different from Lopaka Kowona's trade winds god telling him to mutilate young women in the islands, or have you forgotten his magical thinking, his god, Ku, talking through the winds. And as for the strange little Vladoc, I don't think he's actually a dwarf, Jim, merely stunted. As to his theory, it plugs into our own theories about the killer rather well, perhaps too well."

"It does fit with the known clues pretty neatly. What do you mean, *too* well?"

"I'm not sure, but Vladoc sees a lot of mentals; maybe he actually knows this guy and is bound by, you know, patient-client confidentiality."

"That old twisted ethical argument that the doctor protects his Frankenstein at all costs, despite the fact that the insane monster is on the loose and killing people? I never understood that. Talk about magical thinking."

"If it's true, we need to look at Vladoc's patient list, see who's on it. I don't know about you, but I'm generally skeptical of theories that fit too neatly."

"Agreed. All the same, I suppose we have to entertain the notion that Vladoc's information is . . . well informed. Else, if it is not true, then the killer wants us to believe that it is?"

"Perhaps to point the finger at someone else?"

"Perhaps. We'll have to keep an open mind to all possibilities."

"Yes, as we should."

Parry picked up a stone and threw it into the trees. "Don't you find it strange that both Locke and Leare are out of town at the same time?"

"You mean at the same time that the killings have stopped?" she asked.

"That, too, yes. You say the two are returning from some sort of conference in Texas?"

"College and university teachers' conference, yes."

"And have been there for what—two days and nights?"

"Something like that, yes."

"And from what you tell me, everyone in the English department is sleeping around. These two might be off screwing their intellectual brains out, mightn't they?"

"I have no idea if there's anything between them, Jim, other than a love of poetry. Any suspicions you have are all rather hypothetical, wouldn't you say?"

"Agreed."

They'd already tried Dr. Lucian Locke's residence, and had found it equally abandoned and nearly as dark.

Jessica took a deep breath. "I say we get out of here."

"Where to?" he asked.

"That bookstore, Darkest Expectations, on Second Street. I understand it's open till midnight."

"All right, I'm game if you are."

As they climbed into Parry's official car, Jessica realized only now what Jim had hinted at earlier. "You're not suggesting that we might possibly have two killers, two poets poisoning kids, are you?"

"Stranger things have happened."

"And you're betting on Locke and Leare as the bloody-minded duo?"

"Not necessarily, no, but Leanne knows Leare personally, you see."

"Oh, yeah, I do remember her mentioning Leare as a

friend at the university to whom she was talking, an expert in poetry."

Parry continued speaking as he drove toward Second Street. "And she's had discussions with her about the murders, you see, and when she spoke to Vladoc about the killings, well, she got it in her head that Donatella Leare knows something. Fact is, this Leare woman is one of Vladoc's private patients, and so is Harriet Plummer. He has a lot of female patients, according to Leanne."

"It's a reach, Jim. The whole thing is a real reach. I've seen nothing to indicate two perpetrators here. Are you thinking Leare and Plummer, two women, could be the Killer Poet?"

"Other than your tearstained evidence, Shockley had found trace elements of two sets of DNA on one of the victims, and neither set matches the victim, or any known person on the evidence-gathering team."

"Then the meeting with DeAngelos was meant to ask him to be on the lookout for two contradictory sets of information, and he was informed by Dr. Shockley of these suspicions? Suspicions I'm only now hearing about?"

"DeAngelos and Shockley have been working the case together far longer than we have, Jess. Don't go crazy over this little mix-up. The notion had life breathed back into it by Sturtevante, who, while she's looking at this poet Leare as a possible suspect, does not want to believe her friend is our killer."

"I see, and when were you and Sturtevante going to inform Kim and me of all this?"

"When we got some evidence; we have DeAngelos looking into the possibility of separating out two kinds of poisons. One of Leare's poems is about someone poisoned twice, by two separate lovers. What more can I say?"

"Nothing . . . not a word."

The interior of the car remained icily silent the rest of the way to Second Street.

When they entered the bookstore called Darkest Expectations, they weren't prepared for the amount of dust and mildew, or for the prevailing motif—Early Draconian meets the Orgone Box. Fake blood wept from the walls and clotted in the iron maiden in the corner, the same one they'd seen in Maurice Deneau's apartment.

"Got her for seventy percent off at the Louvre, a furniture place around the corner," said the young man covering the register. "Really brightens up the place, don't you think?"

Jessica stepped up to the guy, a bald, plump, earringed, postapocalyptic beatnik with a lot of facial hair and beady eyes; his nose had been buried in an Owl Goingback horror novel before the jingle of a bell hanging on the entryway door had disturbed him. When James Parry, standing beside Jessica, flashed his FBI badge, he said, "Hey, cool! Just like Mulder and Scully in *The X-Files*. Wow, wait till I tell DeWitt."

Jessica introduced herself as an ME, which only heightened the young man's sense of awe. He dropped the Goingback book on the counter, his tiny pupils enlarged, and with both of his hands propped on the counter, Jessica thought for a crazy moment that he meant to lean in to her for a kiss. "Wow . . . freaky, really, how can I help you?"

"I have a series of names and photos here," she replied. "I'd like to know if you recognize any of them."

"You mean did I know them personally, or as customers? Cops have already asked me the same—"

"Regardless, we're not the cops, and we'd like to know."

"Sure, any way I can help. This *is* about those murdered kids, right? The ones the Poet Killer poisoned, right?"

Parry, reading the man's name tag, said, "Don't concern yourself with that, just look at the photos and names and answer the questions, Marc." Parry's officious-sounding tone appeared to hit the young man like a blow, if Jessica read his reaction correctly; he seemed to lean back exaggeratedly, straighten, and take a deep breath, as if assessing the agents anew.

"Tamburino," he said to Parry, "my name's Tamburino to you."

As Jessica laid out the photos and names, she asked, "You always on the day shift, Mr. Tamburino?"

"Day, night, all the time. It's mine," he said throwing his hands skyward. "Bought out the owner, Nelson DeWitt. Took every penny I had plus a major-assed loan I'll die paying back, but it's a living, sorta."

"Do you recognize any of these young people?" she asked again.

"This one looks familiar," he said, pointing to Maurice Deneau's picture, "and I remember this guy," he added, pointing to Pierre Anton's image. "I like guys." He eyeballed Parry hard now. "Hell, they all look familiar. One time or another, I do believe they've all been in my store . . . These two for absolute certain." He again fingered the pictures of the two male victims. "And this babe, always in here—browsing and sitting on the floor and reading in-house mostly. Seldom to never purchased. Had the need but not the bread." He indicated Micellina Petryna with a jab of his left index finger.

"What about the others?"

"Not so regular, but yeah, I'd almost swear all of 'em's been in at one time or another, sure. Why? I mean anyone living around here? They're going to be a full- or part-time student somewhere, and students read, and therefore they wind up at my store. I order books for the classes at the community college and at University of Philly, undercut their on-campus stores, you see. Everybody knows it, so they come to me for textbooks and they browse and buy other kinds of books while they're here. Doesn't mean I had anything to do with their getting themselves killed."

"No one is accusing you of anything, Mr. Tamburino," Jessica soothed.

"That'd be a switch," he replied, and winked. "*You* can call me Marc."

"The victims didn't have too far to come for reading material," said Parry in her ear.

"Only decent independent bookseller in the area," said Tamburino. "Nearest Barnes and Noble is out at the merchant mall at the Trump Casino Hotel. If somebody collects books, or just has a love affair with the printed word, and he or she lives on Second Street . . . well, eventually, they come to me. That's the store motto."

"What is?" asked Parry.

"Expect Darkest Expectations to book your darkest needs," he said with a self-deprecating smile and shrug. "Made up the motto for DeWitt couple of years ago. Put it in the window. Told him he needed to get wired to the Web, that I'd put it on a Web site for him. But he's . . . he was resistant to change."

"I don't see that you've got any computers here," remarked Parry.

"Took all my cash to buy the store. Computers'll have to wait."

"How long have you owned it?"

"DeWitt's just putting the finishing touches onto the sale. He's retiring to a farm he bought in Ontario."

"Canada?" asked Parry.

"No Arizona or Florida for DeWitt. DeWitt's . . . well . . . different."

"How long did you work for him?" questioned Parry.

" 'Bout several years now."

"You think he's strange?"

"Different. I didn't say strange."

"How do you mean different?" Parry pressed.

Tamburino shook his head. "Contrary is all. Contrary as hell and with everything. You tell him Florida's warm year-round, and he counters with the body needs cold, not hot, to live a long life. Nonsense like that. You tell him that the moon's in the sky, he tells you it's a fake, created by the U.S. government to delude us into believing it's the moon. Different like that is all."

"What can you tell us about these people?" Jessica pointed to the photos on the counter.

"Not a whole lot; some were heavily into the Romantics—the poets—while others liked Lovecraft, Poe, Kafka, even Chekhov, early Koontz, vampire novels, you name it. How should I know?"

"Do you have receipts that might tell us about their purchases?"

"Does this place look like I own the latest in merchandising software? Look around. I use an adding machine."

"Did any of them, to your recollection, purchase any poems by Garrison Burrwith?"

"Who's that?"

"Donatella Leare, then?"

"Oh, sure, they were into Leare's stuff."

"And the poet Lucian Locke?"

"Yeah, pretty heavily there, too. How'd you know?"

"Wouldn't Scully on *X-Files* know?"

"Yeah, you're good." He smiled. "But you know I've had both Locke and Leare in the store to sign copies of their latest works, so a lotta people came in just for the wine, cheese, and signature, among them your victims maybe. Kinda undercuts your cool score, heh, Scully?"

"Then these two authors are big in Philly?"

"Around this area, they're the biggest. Best thing since Byron, Shelley, and Keats in my humble opinion."

"Do you have any copies of their books?"

"Right behind you, follow the poetry section to the *L*s."

As she and Parry searched for the slim volumes of poetry, Tamburino shouted, "You gotta love their dark sincerity, man. The dark sincerity of their profound words. It's like Poe and Byron all rolled into one."

Jessica returned with the books. "Highly recommended, then? Are these signed copies?"

"Yes, they are."

"I'll take them both." To Parry she whispered, "A handwriting expert like Eriq might be able to do something with the signatures. Might even find match points between the signature of one of the poets and the killer."

"Both of these authors have cult followings," said Tamburino. "Lot of word of mouth about both. The kids around here love 'em like they love Ginsberg; really can't get enough, like what Burroughs these days is to kids who read novels."

"Thanks, Mr. Tamburino, and how much?" she asked, reaching for her purse.

"I've got it, Jess," said Parry, placing a twenty on the counter.

"For the two signed copies, it's forty-nine ninety-nine," Tamburino informed them. "Signatures make the books more valuable, along with the fact they're first editions."

"Forty-nine ninety-nine for two little books of poetry? That's like a dollar a page," Parry complained. "Awfully expensive paper and ink."

"Locke and Leare keep my doors open."

Jessica snatched out thirty more dollars while Parry, digging for more bills, muttered, "We'll put it on the company tab."

While Tamburino rang up the order, Jessica started to

collect the photos of the dead young men and women when she noticed the walls. They had been done up with a gray, wrinkled wallpaper that created the appearance of leather or even stone. A sponge-painted finish picked up the light and reflected it back. Jessica looked about at the self-consciously creepy, sooty store and realized that even the soot was painted on. So real looking, she thought. The place evoked the interior of a medieval castle down to the fixtures and the frames around the artwork. Wherever one found a break in the floor-to-ceiling bookshelves, a photograph was displayed, each depicting some dense forest or ideal-ized landscape populated with mythological creatures, winged nymphs and fawns and angels. Stepping closer to one of these, she did a double take, realizing that they were not photographs at all, but paintings, meticulously rendered to resemble photographs, and displaying an ethereal use of light that bordered on uncanny. The term *magical realism* immediately sprang to her mind to describe the paradoxical mixture of "realistic" and fantastic in the pictures.

"Cool paintings, huh?" asked Tamburino, seeing her in-terest.

"Yeah, unusual."

"Maxfield Parrish–inspired, I'd say," replied the store owner. "My full name's Marc Maxfield Tamburino. Close look at the signature, and you'll see the artist's name. She's a friend of mine. I've had her in to sign prints and every-thing."

Jessica read the signature—Samtouh Raphael, it looked like. This meant nothing to her, but her eyes locked on one of the more unusual paintings, which depicted a beautiful woman lying at peace in a coffin, her lover holding on to her with one hand, lightly setting a book of poems into the coffin with the other.

"Dante Gabriel Rossetti," said Tamburino, a little shake of

the head accompanying a large sigh. He lifted himself onto a stool, perching there like a heavyset contemporary gargoyle. "One of the most romantic gestures in all of history. He wrote a book of poetry, every poem inspired by her, his deceased lover. You see, when his love died, he had the poems bound and he placed his only copy into the crypt with her."

"Big deal," said someone who suddenly stepped from the stacks, a tall, gangly woman whom Jessica for a moment took to be Leanne Sturtevante until the woman's face came into light. She was athletically thin, her cheek and jawbones protruding sharply. Her movements gave the impression of a windup toy at first, but then their oddness meshed with the rest of her and one realized that she moved like a ballerina. Gangly like a giraffe but just as graceful, Jessica thought.

Marc Tamburino instantly assailed the woman, obviously well known to him. "*Big deal?* How can you say that? It was from the heart when the man did it. It was passion beyond anything in the modern world."

She instantly showed her teeth in a curling smile, and raised her hand like a menacing claw, showing her long nails, painted green and black, each finger alternating in color. "A few years later, on second thought, Rossetti had the eternal love of his life exhumed to retrieve the poetry. That kind of romantic love is beyond contempt."

"Lucky for us the man retrieved the book," replied Tamburino. "Else the world would be deprived of those fantastic love poems."

"All the same, it tells you something about the value of grand dramatic gestures, including those of a poet smitten by love," replied the book-laden woman, who was staring a hole through Jessica, as if determining what kind of underwear she might be wearing. The sexual interest in the stare was unmistakable.

Jessica wondered how long the woman had been in the store and how much she had overheard.

"That's a grim way to think, Doctor," replied Tamburino.

"I do love a dark statement, indeed," the woman replied, placing her books onto a nearby cart. Next, she opened her arms with an extravagant flourish and curtsied to Jessica, who noticed that the woman had had the crown of her head shaved and the tattoo of a bat inked on the bare scalp. Since, standing up, she was half a head taller than Jessica, the sight of the flashing bat came as a surprise. As she curtsied, the woman said, "Detectives, this creature before you is Dr. Donatella Leare, full professor at the University of Philadelphia. A fortuitous coincidence, a kind of Jungian synchronicity, finds us all here at the same moment. I hope it leads to something . . . fruitful."

"Dr. Leare?" Jessica was surprised that this person, dressed in what appeared to be an Indian costume, with strings of beads and crucifixes snaking about her neck and wrists, could be teaching young people at a major university, but when she flashed on some of the unusual and eccentric instructors of her own youth, she put the prejudice aside. "This is indeed a fortuitous meeting. We have been wishing to discuss the spate of deaths in the area with experts such as yourself, people who have some connection with darkside poetry. In addition, we understand you may have known some of the victims. Isn't that so, Dr. Leare?"

Jessica had to pull her hand away, the professor was holding so fast to it, smiling as she did so. Jessica wondered what sort of relationship existed between Leare and Leanne Sturtevante.

"We've been anxious to meet you. Missed you at the university and at your residence," added Parry, staring.

"Yes, well, I understand you wanted to speak to me. Dr. Plummer's message made that clear, but coming back to this dreadful, awful business, and the lateness of the hour, I simply did not wish to deal with it tonight, so instead I came to see Marc and purchase some books I'd been wanting to delve into, and to clarify my thoughts, cleanse my mind of the wretchedness of existence, the human condition, all that, so to speak. Books do that for me. Intoxicating, really. Some people call me a literary junkie."

"Sounds like an escape," replied Jessica, recalling what Vladoc had said about people who had an insatiable need to run away from reality. Did Leare do this through poetry, through teaching, through sex, or a mixture of them all?"

"Yes, all the same . . . bumping into you like this . . . well, it's obviously positive karma at work—that is, I hope it's positive. The moment I began overhearing your conversation with Marc, I realized just who you were. Dr. Plummer told me I should expect a visit from you and another woman. You disappoint me, coming with a new partner in tow. Plummer told me of your visit to the school."

Parry quickly introduced himself, his eyes still unashamedly taking in the strange-looking poet, her dress, makeup, and nails. "What do you make of the dean's claims against Garrison Burrwith?"

"Silly. She's really an intelligent woman except when it comes to men and managing her emotions. Dreadful what's going on here. It's like a totalitarian state where everyone is encouraged to squeal on his neighbor. As a result of all this, I found even the wasteland of Houston a relief."

"You knew one or more of the victims?" Parry asked. He'd circled behind her, as if curious to see if there was any tattoo or lines of poetry scribbled on her back.

"You won't find what you're looking for on me, big boy. As to your questions, yes. I knew several of the victims. At one time or another, three of them were . . . had taken one or more of my classes. Aside from freshman English, I teach the Romantic poets, Women in Literature, and other classes. So now you have me cornered, what else can I answer for you? Am I upset over these awful killings? Absolutely. Do I know anything pertaining to them? Absolutely not. So, now you tell me, how can I help you? I do wish to be cooperative with you, Dr. Coran."

Jessica pointed to the photos still spread out on the counter. "Tell us what you know about these kids."

"They all loved poetry—passionately, I'd say. Not your run-of-the-mill students when it came to beauty. Ironic, isn't it?"

"What's that?" asked Parry.

"That they should all die having poetry literally branded on them."

"How did you get that information? It hasn't been publicly released."

"You forget. I know someone close to the investigation, and I think we should leave it at that. Back to my point—perhaps your killer hates poetry lovers? Maybe a geek who failed a literature class miserably and is taking his revenge out on better students. That would certainly satisfy audiences of most TV mysteries, wouldn't it?"

"We'll take that theory into consideration," said Parry—not meaning it in the least, Jessica surmised, on seeing the glint in his eye as he peeked over the professor's shoulder.

Stabbing at the photo array with her index finger, she said, "Did any one of the students you knew ever speak to you about the coffeehouse poetry fad going around Second Street?"

"Ever eat raw meat? Ever sniff glue? Ever do heroin?" Leare shot back, somewhat inappropriately. "The backside writings? Certainly. It became common talk at the university as just the latest *thing* to do. No one for a moment thought it would catch on the way it has, and certainly no one could have predicted that it might lead to . . . to murder." She paused, removing the stack of books from the cart and placing them, one by one, onto the counter. Jessica noticed they were all old paperbacks with lurid covers, mystery and suspense novels by Glenn Hale and Stephen Robertson. "Lot of jokes about the fad." She continued to talk in a casual, breathy voice. "You know, like how do you do a rewrite, anal alliteration, anal performance, do you show it on a first date, all that."

"Any of the victims ever confide in you that they were thinking of having anything like this done?" Jessica inquired.

"No . . . never. It was, I believe, something done on the spur of the moment, like getting it on, getting a tattoo, a tongue, navel, or clit piercing, typically after having consumed a good deal of alcohol or having smoked *mucho dinero* in the form of grass."

"ME's not seeing heavy concentrations of either in the victims," said Parry.

"Which means these kids went into it with eyes wide open," added Jessica. "Now, between the two of you, Mr. Tamburino, Dr. Leare, can you tell us anything about these victims in the way of character traits that might lead to such victimization?"

"Trusting souls, all of them," said Donatella Leare. "Of course, I didn't know them all, but they're of a type."

"Oh, and what type would that be?"

"Fragile, fragile as wounded birds, their hearts pumping far harder, far stronger than yours or mine, I can assure you, Doctor. No distrust gene. They open up to people immediately and deeply, which pleases most people but may well trigger your everyday sociopath, could it not?"

Tamburino elaborately shrugged, saying, "Victims. They were all perfect victims. I've read about the type. They lay down for anybody, man, except maybe this time it's for good."

"Don't you find it odd so many in so small an area would so easily take on that role?" asked Jessica.

"Mr. Tamburino's crude assessment may not be to your liking, Dr. Coran," said Leare, "but there is some truth to it. All of the ones I knew personally—that is, through my work—well . . . they saw life through rose-colored glasses, to say the least, and they are a product of a generation raised in the beliefs that, while beautiful in theory, can be deadly in practice."

"Such as?"

"Such as all mankind has a purity of soul and goodness that need only be touched into life; such as there is no such thing as evil, only the absence of good—that sort of thinking."

"Like there's no such thing as a bad kid?" asked Parry.

"Something like that, yes. No such thing as a natural-born killer, a bad seed, a killer gene," added Donatella Leare. "We artists can portray such utopias in our poems, books, paintings, but if you try to live such a life, you might easily be heading for disaster."

Jessica agreed. "You mean these kids saw life like one of these paintings there done by . . . by . . ." She could not recall the artist's name.

"Samtouh Raphael, one of our local artists. It's computer graphics, really. She's become so successful that she quit her teaching job at Penn State to devote herself full-time to her painting, moved into a loft apartment here. A local success story."

"Derivative of Maxfield Parrish," repeated Tamburino, "only the brushstroke is that of a Macintosh PC."

Tamburino's comment seemed to irritate Leare, who icily said, "Everything is derivative, Marc, if you scratch the surface; even Shakespeare stole plots from Plutarch. What's important is that the artist make his plunder his or her own. Obviously, Samtouh learned to create light in her paintings from Parrish, but regardless, she has found her own vision."

"Some of the subject matter overlaps," he argued.

"To hell with that; the woman clearly has something unique, quite her own, that has sparked a mad interest in her work, especially among the young."

"I do real photography myself," said Tamburino. "Been relegated to a hobby since I took on the store, but for a time, I was making good money, doing weddings and other tribal ceremonies."

"You mean like that *wake* you photographed?" Leare asked pointedly.

"Hey, it was an interesting gig, and the customer paid well."

She turned to Jessica. "I see you're delving into my work," said Leare. "Do enjoy it." She reached out and massaged the copy of her work entitled *The Eternal Dream of Still and the Dream of Dirth.*

"Interesting title," Jessica said. "I'm given to understand many of the victims not only took your class but read and enjoyed your poetry, along with—"

"Lucian Burke Locke's, I know." She now snatched Locke's book from Jessica, asking, "Which of his titles do you have here, his latest, ahhh, *Sex—the Melancholy Distress.* The man is obsessed with getting it right—sex, that is—glorifying it to a fever pitch that tries to reach a nirvana of absolute peace—in his poetry, I mean—a kind of death and birth through the penis. The perfect balm for mankind's ills and confusions, sex as the coiled snake, as in the Kundalini myths and religious beliefs of the East. That sort of thing."

"But like the computer artist, he appeals to the young, yes?" Jessica asked.

"Why don't you talk to him about that? He's back, too. We made the trip to Houston together. Got back late due to an accident at the airport, huge delays. Only saving grace was that the conference was better this year than last."

Jessica picked up the photos of the dead, telling Dr. Leare, "Please, you will make yourself available to us, Dr. Leare, should we have further questions."

"Absolutely."

The poet made her purchases and said her good-byes. At the door, she hesitated. "I dearly hope you catch this fiend and stop him before anyone else is harmed. It's terribly upsetting for all involved, the academic community and the young people who populate Second Street."

"Trust me," Jessica returned, "it's just as upsetting for law enforcement."

The tall, domineering Leare, her gait that of a regal if somewhat ostentatious-looking bird, disappeared through the door. Jessica retrieved her books and photo file, and she and Parry bid Tamburino and his little shop of curiosities good-bye.

SIXTEEN

To him the book of Night was open'd wide,
And voices from the deep abyss reveal'd
A marvel and a secret.

—Lord Byron, "The Dream"

A call from headquarters sent them next to the home of Lucian Burke Locke. The poet had telephoned in when he learned that he was being sought for questioning in the case of the Poet Killer. On their previous visit to his home, Parry had left his calling card. FBI dispatch informed Parry that Dr. Locke wished to cooperate in any way possible, and he'd left word that he would be home for the rest of the evening.

They drove back out to Locke's home, a pleasant, rambling two-story Victorian in need of some serious repairs to the exterior walls and the porch, but otherwise in good shape, well landscaped and the lawn well lit by light that spilled out of the huge, open windows. The place felt cozy and large at the same time, and the atmosphere felt welcoming. Lucian Locke met them at the door, urging them inside, into a spacious living room decorated in subdued grays and beiges, with blond Scandinavian furniture that starkly contrasted with oaken beams in the ceiling, and yet somehow it all worked.

To Jessica, the man appeared a strange mix. While his hands and feet were oversized, his body was dwarflike, reminding Jessica of Peter Flavius Vladoc, only Locke was shorter still, and a decade younger. In an otherwise handsome face, one eye fixed on the person he spoke to, while the other eye wandered, as if staring off into another realm. Jessica stared back curiously, then suddenly realized that what she was looking at was a glass eye.

Locke noticed her noticing and immediately said, "Had it put out by a mangy lover when I was only seventeen; wore a black patch to impress the ladies thereafter, until the piratical look grew tiresome. That's when I had the glass eye put in."

"Sorry, I didn't mean to stare."

"But of course you did. Aren't we all fascinated with the maimed, the damaged, and the twisted, if not consciously then subconsciously? It's not a character flaw, but a part of our common human nature to find the freakish of great fascination. Hence the geek shows, and their legacy, TV and film."

Jessica attempted another apology, but he shrugged it off with a wave of the hand and asked them, "May I offer you tea, coffee? Anything to drink?"

Jessica replied, "Coffee sounds good," while Parry declined.

"You live here alone?" she asked when he returned to the living room with two cups of coffee and a small pot.

"No, no! I have Evelyn, my angel of a wife, and my children, Beverly and Robert, six and seven respectively. They're off on a trip up to the country to see Evey's parents. Back soon, I expect."

Jessica now saw the photos of wife and children atop the piano. She'd hardly had time to study them in detail when Locke asked if she played.

"No, not a note, but I love to listen. Do you play?"

"That's Evey's gift, not mine. She learned as a child, growing up in her homeland."

"Oh, and where was that?"

"Austria."

After the initial shock of discovering Locke to be a short gnarled man with a glass eye, Jessica found herself fascinated by him. There was something extraordinary about the man. She wondered if he was not one of those people who, from birth, have to strive extremely hard to overcome what nature has done to them.

During the time she laid out the photos of the victims, and while Parry asked him the same questions they had asked of Dr. Leare, Jessica caught herself staring at the queer little gnome of a man. His face in the light revealed pockmarks, and he looked as if he'd had his features reshaped by a plastic surgeon after an automobile accident or a fire. His nose appeared to be the size of an onion. The look of a deformed cherub, she thought, her eyes going over the stubby, swollen hands, and yet at first sight he did not appear quite so grotesque. How could that be?

Locke caught her eye with his one good one, smiling. He knew she could not help staring at his physical shortcomings.

Embarrassed, she pulled her eyes away.

"I am somewhat familiar with these two, but the others, no. None of the others I've seen in my classes. They all have a similar emaciated look, though, don't they. Micellina Petryna, now she was a lovely, lovely young woman with a boundless spirit, although subdued. Caterina Mercedes quite the same, really. Loved poetry, everything to do with it, particularly the English Romantics."

"And were they enamored of your work, sir?" asked Jessica.

"Not so's it would go to my head, no, but they were fans. Either that or both were smart in another way. Both flattered me by coming to my recent book singing at that strange little shop on Second Street—Darkest Instinct or something."

"Expectations," said Parry. "Darkest Expectations."

"Yes, well, they came fawning for my autograph, ostensibly, but it would be more accurate to say they came hoping to improve their grade, I'm quite sure."

"Did it work?" asked Jessica.

"Flattery to a gnome like me always works, but it's never believed, my dear."

Jessica could not for the life of her fix the man's age, but his speech and manner and formality suggested he was Donatella Leare's senior by at least a decade. He led them to a screened-in pool that looked out over a lake. It was a beautiful setting. "My little slice of heaven on earth," he said, shrugging. They each found seats. Locke's backyard lights lit up an array of plants and a flower garden as well as a children's toyland. A lantern-styled fixture hung on the dock, revealing a small boat.

"Is there anything you can tell us, anything at all, that might shed some light on who might have, so to speak, 'written' these people into early graves?"

"I wish I could help you, but no. Not a thing useful comes to mind. Such a waste, I know—first these children's lives, and now you're coming all the way out here to talk to me—just as much a waste. I do wish I could be of more help."

Jessica once again collected the photographs. She and Parry stood to leave.

"You've got to do whatever you can to stop this monster, Dr. Coran, Chief Parry. It's horrible, and I can only imagine the enormity of the pain inflicted on the families of these children. I mean, if such a death came to one of my children . . . well, I would simply go mad."

Jessica's eyes fell on a photo of Locke with his two children on his lap. Neither child looked like their father, and one was clearly Oriental. Jessica guessed that Locke and his wife had adopted the children. She wanted to ask, but she felt it too prying a question, and it had nothing to do with the investigation.

On the ride back to the hotel, Parry told her, "I can't imagine such a strange little man as Locke capable of convincing a tortoise to move, much less convincing young men and women to lay down and die."

He then told her that Sturtevante's people had been all over everything they had gathered from each victim, and his own time spent on Maurice Deneau's diary had "netted nothing specific; certainly no rendezvous dates with any mysterious poets."

"Are we continuing to watch the pubs and coffeehouses along Second Street?"

"They arrested a number of perverts and mashers in and around Second Street, and we've had half a dozen so-called confessions to the murders—none of which can be given credence—so no one has been held for long."

Jessica said good night to Parry and retired to her room. She imagined that Kim had probably wondered where she had gone off to, but it was far too late to knock at the other woman's door. She went directly into her room, stripped and showered, allowing the hot spray to relax her and free her mind of all but this moment's experience. Her shrink had always said, "Live the moment." Easier said than done, she now mentally chided herself.

After showering, she wrapped herself in one of the thick terrycloth hotel robes, curled up in bed, and began reading Lucian Burke Locke's volume of poetry. She skimmed most of the selections, just getting a feel for the voice and style. Then she settled on one or two poems, slowly reading them through after being enticed by their titles. Locke's work was grim and passionate in the depth of its dark and brooding imagery, she felt. She mentally compared his work with the killer's. There was an odd sort of fit, but she refused to consider Locke a suspect just yet.

She next lifted Donatella Leare's volume. She skimmed it as she'd done Locke's, and becoming intrigued by certain titles, she read a few in their entirety, but soon her eyes could no longer focus, and her mind ceased to process the language. She didn't know when she fell asleep.

Now her experience of the moment became a dream—and a dream to run screaming from. She found herself, figuratively speaking, in bed with both Locke and Leare, finding both poets equally disturbing in appearance and actions. Each reached out at her, tearing at her with clawed hands in vulture fashion. Each poet, dwarf and lesbian, spouted words as meaningless and confused as any jabberwocky she had ever heard until the words crystallized into somber, grim, dreary, and scary. Although it was Locke who had won the more prestigious awards, Leare's haunting look and work proved to be the darker and more sensual of the two poets.

Marc Tamburino, the store-clerk-turned-owner, a fan of both "artists," as he'd called them, now stepped into Jessica's dream to say, "I find that Leare is, in the end, the stronger of the two poets. Leare's images . . . they don't go away."

Jessica felt a disturbance at her core, and images of a dark, empty world filled her mind, but the images both poets had created were not of another world—they expressed the awfulness of this world—in the past, present, and future. While horror writers and poets of horror generally depicted the supernatural as frightening, these two depicted the real world that way. The surreal horror of reality, or, as Geoffrey Caine described his work, "reality-based horror."

A small voice, rational and firm, deep within her kept denying that either of these poets could be the killer she and the task force sought. Whereas the work of both tore at the reader with a raging anger, the words of the Killer Poet joined a gentleness to the dark themes. That's what the poisoning poet had left as an indelible signature to his crimes, a most gentle touch, that lethal gentleness of hand and word, a quiet horror played out on the backs of the victims.

She awoke with a start of recognition at this notion, accepting it as a gift of the unconscious, and asked herself what specifically had so bothered her about Leare and Locke? Was it that these two and many another dark poet since Poe had caught the fevered imagination of whole generations of children and young people? Or was it the nature of the cult that followed their work? Was the killer a part of this cult, and did he choose his victims from its ranks? Or was he himself one of the lionized poets, or another poet of similar stature, who decided to exploit the adoration of his or her fans? What young, impressionable kid could say no to an accomplished, well-respected poet like Leare, or for that matter Locke?

With these thoughts swirling about her brain, Jessica again sought sleep.

The following day

Wɪᴛʜ the core members of the task force assembled, Jessica discussed her suspicions that all the victims read Locke, Leare, and other poets of this strange dark school, and while Kim and Parry considered the idea important, Sturtevante was quite vocal in her opinion of the opposite.

During her reading of Leare's volume, a few poems had struck Jessica as especially relevant to the case. " 'Archetypes of Desire and Hatred: A Verse Dialogue at the End of the Millennium,' " she read aloud, and paused, adding, "and that's just the title. Listen to this one entitled 'The End of Thought.' "

> *You're the evil that flogs*
> *my welted back,*

and I'm the one
who must overcome.
So nature made her judgment
on our vows—
when you touch my hand,
all I feel
is your blood
running down my fingers,
dripping onto the ruined street
where we were wed.
>   *"Let's kill each other.*
>   *Here's my knife; please,*
>   *I want to feel you twist inside me.*
>   *And as for you—*
>   *I'll break your neck;*
>   *quick-kiss your swollen lips.*
>   *You won't feel death,*
>   *I promise."*
Amniotic decadence
twists their faces;
an anguish life of rage
crawls from the womb.
A final sweet embrace,
surrendering to temptation
to die in the guarded
of rusty buildings.
This is the final excretion,
and you can see it coming
to the surface,
a caduceus canker,
the scepter of maleness—
suspended in the alchemy
of the prima materia.
This is the beginning
of Time.

"They never left,
and neither did we.
There is only one
person here."

"Okay, so what the hell does it mean?" asked Parry, garnering a laugh from Jessica.

"The poem is equating making love with death," Kim replied. "At least, that's what I'm hearing."

"So it's not about someone murdering the sex partner?" asked Sturtevante, her eyes wide at Kim's words.

"Not exactly," Kim answered.

"It's still damned grim," said Parry, plopping into a chair.

"It may be just this kind of so-called art that is motivating the Killer Poet to murder," Jessica suggested.

"What are you saying?" asked Sturtevante, standing and pacing. "That the killer is motivated by these poets at the university? Or . . . or that he reads into their poems a motive for killing?"

Jessica calmly answered, "Either theory is a possibility."

"So take my pick?" Sturtevante shouted, losing her temper now. "What a defense for the accused. 'I read a book of poems, Your Honor, and it sent me over the edge,'" the detective mocked, her voice rising shrilly, "and if you believe that fairy tale . . .'"

"Fiction, novels, short stories, and movies have been known to influence people," Jessica countered. "Whether we want to face it or not, an open society such as ours breeds killers and insanity, and often our literature and other cultural artifacts reflect this truth, and then the person raised on violence begins to act with violence."

"Criminals who decide to mimic what they see or read about," said Kim, her steepled fingers twitching at her chin. "Over the years, we've seen many instances of young people doing just that."

Jessica added, "We've all seen such cases in the news, after the fact, when it's too late. I'm merely suggesting—"

"Suggestions, more suggestions and guesswork," muttered Sturtevante, pacing now like a nervous cat. "Well, frankly, Dr. Coran, we in the PPD expected FBI involvement to bring great and swift results. Not a lot of speculation, and thus far all I've heard is bullshit spec—"

"Leanne's just a little on edge today," Parry began to apologize when Sturtevante glared at him and suddenly the doors burst open and in came Chief Aaron Roth with two men wearing three-piece, expensive-looking suits. It became immediately apparent to Jessica and the others why Sturtevante was on edge, as Parry had put it. Her superiors were on edge.

No one in the complex chain of command, from detective room to governor's mansion, was happy with the slow progress of the Poet Killer case.

"Deputy Mayor Alsop," Chief Roth began, introducing the man on his left. "And this is Senator Patrick Harmon, father of the late Anton Pierre."

Immediately upon being introduced, Senator Harmon placed a hand against Chief Roth's chest and said, "I'll take it from here, Aaron." The tall, imposing senator, his gray-to-white hair long and striking, making him look like a nineteenth-century patriarch, almost shouted, "I want some fucking answers, and I want some fucking results. You people have been sitting on your asses longer than Snuffy Smith has been sitting in his rocker. Now, what in God's name do you have for me on the death—murder—of my child?"

Beneath his bluster, Harmon was like any other father caught up in so horrific a circumstance. He had had to bury his own child; the natural order of his universe had been shaken to the core. He felt a rage and had nowhere to express it.

"I demand to know what's being done!"

Parry immediately took charge, standing, offering his hand and introducing first himself and the task-force leadership. Finishing with Kim, he added, "We've even put a psychic on the case. It's only a matter of time before we nail this bastard, sir. If you'd like to come with me, I can show you the mounting evidence we are assembling. Trust me, no one's resting on their rears or leaning on any walls here."

The senator looked around the room, gritted his teeth, and finally nodded. "Yes, I expect you are doing all you can."

"All that is humanly possible," added Parry.

The senator's entire body told them that he had relented. "Doing all that is humanly possible, yes, and I will take you up on your invitation—Agent Parry, is it?"

Parry's strong suit, Jessica recalled, had always been dealing with the bereaved family members, never an easy task. Now, much to everyone's comfort, the FBI agent led the distraught father away. Parry, who had handled both situation and man with great sensitivity and care, had earned back some points with Jessica.

When they were gone, Chief Roth stood aside, rather agitatedly, to hear a brief "pep talk" from the deputy mayor, whose final cliché—"I hope you all good hunting"—fell flat.

Then Chief Roth, his bulldog face turning stony, said, "Senator Harmon is not the only one ready to throw you people to the dogs. I had another father in my office late yesterday. It was Maurice Deneau's father, a local alderman and minister, who collapsed under the strain right there in my office. Paramedics rushed him to St. Stephen's; he's expected to recover, but the man's a basket case; so depressed that he's under a suicide watch. His family's going through a double hell now."

"We're getting closer every hour, every day." Kim told them what they wanted to hear. "I am seeing more details; each vision I have of the killer brings me more words and symbols to puzzle out and piece together."

Jessica helped Kim calm Chief Roth and Deputy Mayor Alsop, both fathers themselves, with assurances that the agents themselves did not wholly believe.

A telephone call came an hour later; another body had surfaced, discovered this time in the first stages of decomposition. Over the weekend both Leare and Locke had been in Houston, there had been a murder after all, but the body had gone undetected. Jessica steeled herself as she walked into the now familiar "cozy" death scene, a set of props and surroundings created between lovers, between victim and killer, or so it seemed, down to the leftover Pinot Noir, the candles, and soft music.

Time had taken its toll on the crime scene. Candles had burned out, spilling wax like small pools of lava over surfaces. This young woman's body had been discovered by her mother, who, after numerous attempts to reach her daughter by phone, had driven to her apartment and quietly let herself in; the hysterical woman now sat sobbing in a neighbor's apartment down the hall, a cluster of building residents standing about her in a protective circle.

It proved to be a carbon-copy murder scene, and it took little time to determine that the MO was that of the Poet Killer. Victim facedown on living-room floor, this time a pillow under her head, a soft down comforter pulled to her waist, a blatant message left by her killer, penned once again in angry red-to-ocher-burnished ink that made the words appear to be written in dried blood.

The only difference with this victim was the more advanced stage of decomposition; decay had caused some of the killer's penned words to sink inward, as it were, creating puckering slashlike wounds in the skin. This time, the victim's skin had to be pulled tight on either side, held by forceps, in order for the poetic lines to be completely made out. Rigor mortis had set in days before and had long since released its grip on the corpse.

"Same MO, same setup," muttered Parry, just to hear himself speak.

"It's definitely the work of the Poet," Sturtevante agreed.

"The body gently posed for all eternity, and the victim is familiar as well. She is all the others, all the others are her," added Kim Desinor.

After a cursory examination of the body, Jessica stepped aside for Kim to "read" it, but Kim's examination fell short. "Getting nothing; emptiness, save for those words again: *rampage . . . quark, preflight,* and *outing . . .* At least I . . . I think it's *outing.*"

Jessica then began collecting the minutiae of evidence left by the killer, searching in particular for the tearstained evidence. Under her magnifying glass, she found it. Using an adhesive, she collected the sample and placed it in a vial, labeling it and carefully putting it away.

Parry and Sturtevante had been searching about the room, Parry again going for the books. He held up a copy of Locke's poems. "It was on her shelf," he said, opening the volume to a marker. "She appears to have been reading a poem entitled 'The Stage Is Set.' " He began to read:

> *The Enochian world*
> *is made of gritty*
> *tectonics of mind,*
> *pressed against*
> *the choking smokestack*
> *of our lonely city,*
> *a place of diastrophic shifts:*

thought masquerading as
landmasses
that grind into
one another.
There, at the hazy altar
of ruined pavement,
vested in soot,
the twin lovers
to be wed;
purity and iniquity.
They stand in pools
of nervous devils,
clutching one another
with vows of betrothal,
caught in the tactile rush
of Thorazine bedlam.
They are the lost children
elected to host
the supraliminal.

On the marker, Jessica read the name and address of the bookstore where the victim had purchased this auto-graphed copy of the book—Darkest Expectations. Also on the marker was a scribbled note, which the victim had apparently written as a reminder to herself. *Purchase Leare's work next,* it read.

From the look of the apartment, Jessica imagined that the victim could ill afford to purchase both books at the same time, but then Kim entered from the bathroom, carrying a copy of Leare's book.

"It all keeps going back to Locke and Leare and that bookstore," said Jessica. "Somehow I believe their work is connected to the killings."

"What are you saying?" asked Sturtevante. "You have no proof of that. None whatever."

"I believe that somehow Locke, Leare, or both are connected to the killings, or at the very least, their poetry is somehow inextricably mixed with the reasoning behind the killing spree."

Kim supported Jessica. "Such phrases as *Enochian world* in Locke's poem—that refers to occultism and ancient rites and conversations with God or his agents, angels?"

"Vladoc spoke of it," said Sturtevante. "But Leare was out of the city all weekend, and Locke with her. Neither of them could possibly have had anything to do with this."

Jessica felt a sense of relief coming from Sturtevante. Had she begun to suspect her friend Donatella Leare?

"Yes, so they say," Jessica commented.

"They were both out of the city all weekend, and according to your own findings, the victim died Saturday night," countered Sturtevante. "And as for Locke's reference to Enoch, Donatella tells me that many poets are familiar with ancient religions and magical practices. Hell, that Dr. Burrwith guy, his poetry alludes to the Four Quarters all the time. Vladoc told me that that's part of the Enochian belief system, too. It's more widespread among artists and writers than you would imagine."

"Vladoc did make some brief mention of strange belief systems," said Kim. "I think I remember that."

"They both left the city on a flight for Houston, or so we are told," Jessica said, thinking aloud. "But suppose one or the other faked the flight out of here, not getting on that plane, asking the other to cover for him or her?"

Jessica stepped out and down the hallway to talk to the mother. Sturtevante followed. The woman said she was Rowena Metzger, wife of Phillip K. Metzger. Sturtevante knew what this meant, so she explained for Jessica's sake. "Only the most powerful business leader in the city."

"Cinthia, our daughter, absolutely rejected her father's

and my lifestyle and all that we offered her. This began after she started at the university."

"University of Philadelphia?" asked Jessica.

The mother nodded, still sobbing. Finally, she added, "She wanted so to become an artist and poet. Now . . . my God . . . nooooo!" The wailing moan ripped at Jessica's heart.

"Take her to St. Behan's Hospital," Sturtevante told a nearby medic as she helped Mrs. Metzger to her feet. "She will need something to calm her down until her husband can be located."

When the sobbing woman was led away, Sturtevante said to Jessica, "The Metzgers, Phillip and Rowena there, regularly appear on the society pages."

"And now they're front-page news."

Jessica and Sturtevante returned to the death room to find Kim Desinor attempting a second reading of the body. "It's teasing, something being held out of reach," Kim muttered, when suddenly Phillip Metzger, a tall, barrel-chested, white-haired man, charged in bull-like. He had become another of the walking wounded—another victim.

"Get away from her! Get away!" he cried out at them as if they were all ghouls, and as if he somehow believed the girl might be saved by his touch. He fell to his knees over his daughter, grabbed her up in his arms, and rocked and sobbed as uncontrollably as a hurt child.

Sturtevante looked shaken, Jessica thought as the PPD detective moved her toward the door. "Can we talk privately?" the detective asked. "I need to talk to you alone . . . now."

Jessica did not argue; Sturtevante's voice had become at once tremulous and conspiratorial.

SEVENTEEN

If poisonous minerals, and of that tree
whose fruit threw death on else immortal us,
If lecherous goats, if serpents envious
cannot be damned; alas, why should I be?

—John Donne (1572–1631)

THEY went to a small stairwell just down from the death room, and Leanne Sturtevante was pacing there like a caged tiger. "I don't know how to tell you this any way but straight out. Leare . . . Donatella . . . she is the Poet Killer. Leare—she has done this."

"What are you saying?"

"She killed that kid down the hall!"

"How do you know this?"

"You were right. Donatella never left for Houston."

"How do you know this?"

"I confronted her with it."

"Confronted her with it? When? Did you call her in for questioning? What?"

"No, I arranged a meeting."

"A meeting?"

"You don't understand."

"No, I don't. Enlighten me."

Leanne finally stopped pacing. "Donatella . . . she and I . . . we've known each other for several years, and she's become . . . well, obsessed of late."

Jessica finally felt the lightbulb go on in her head. Leanne and Donatella were—or had been—lovers. "Obsessed? How? In what manner?"

"She's been baiting me with these murders, playing me! Don't you get it? Ever since I broke it off with her, she's been obsessed, fixated on getting us back together. She knows I . . . I've complained volumes about how unfair the PPD is when it comes to giving women detectives a chance, and I fear . . . I believe she *created* this case for me!"

This was beginning to sound to Jessica as if Leanne Sturtevante were the delusional one in the relationship. "She is arranging to help you in the department by killing all these kids?"

"I know it sounds crazy! It *is* crazy. *She's* crazy. She fits Vladoc's profile of the killer, and—"

"Have you any proof? Has she said anything, made any kind of confession?"

"She got off that plane to Houston, like I suspected, Jessica."

"Are you sure?"

"She pleaded with Locke to keep it to himself. She has become . . . desperate . . . since, since our breakup."

"So, she is a spurned lover, but she doesn't take her anger out on you. Instead she takes it out on these young people . . . in a bid to *help* your career? Some thoughtful lover she turned out to be . . ."

"Cut it out. I broke it off a couple of months ago, and just after, the killings began . . . and I checked. She never boarded that plane. I confronted her with it, and she confessed, after she told me she had seen me somewhere in the company of a friend on a day when she was supposed to be in Houston."

"I see. So you put two and two together and—"

"She never got on the plane, and now this kid is dead, and I'm telling you all of it equates to her as the killer."

"But what *evidence* do you have that she was involved in what's happened down the hall, Leanne?"

"She's scary, always has been, and now all this. I'd been subconsciously denying that she had anything to do with it, but now . . . now I can't deny it any longer. I know the poetry is hers. I've read enough of her crap to know she's the one who has penned the death verses."

"You've got to have more than your hunches and your emotional involvement in order to make an arrest."

"She lied about her whereabouts on the night when this young woman died. She tracked you down, didn't she? Found out you were working the case from another angle? Picked you out as one to watch and learn from so she can keep a step ahead of you."

"We still need more than your suspicions to make an arrest, Leanne. So far as I can tell, your hypothesis about Leare is as uncorroborated as Dean Plummer's against her old boyfriend, Burrwith."

"This isn't the same. Donatella calls herself the reincarnated soul of the poets of the Romantic period. She believes in all that kind of crap—past lives, karma, love that transcends time, you name it. And the fake alibi, that's significant; plenty enough for an arrest."

"So someone has to bring her in for questioning?"

"But it can't be me."

"Are you asking me to arrest Dr. Leare on the basis of her feelings about the breakup of your relationship or because she lied to us about her whereabouts and was stalking you instead of attending a conference?"

"She once talked me into it."

"Into what?"

"Into sitting for a poem, writing it out on my back. I still have deep scars from it. It was as if she wanted to brand me as hers for life."

"And you've been living with this knowledge all this time?"

"No, I didn't think it was her until I learned she had not

gotten onto that plane, and I even rationalized that away until now, until you said that this one died on Saturday. It's an indication how far she will take this delusion that we still have this . . . this connection."

"It sounds like enough to warrant a surveillance, but hardly enough to haul her in."

"Fine, I'll talk to someone else. Goddammit, I know she's the Poet Killer. I know it in my bones."

Sturtevante stormed off, fuming. As she disappeared down the hallway and out of the building, Jessica returned to the crime scene to finish processing it, Donatella Leare very much on her mind.

JESSICA would have liked nothing better than to make an arrest, but a false arrest could prove embarrassing for everyone involved, not to mention the amount of wasted time and effort. Instead, she returned to Dr. Stuart Wahlbore and Rocky, taking her copies of both Leare's and Locke's book for analysis and comparison to the verses used by the killer. She asked Dr. Wahlbore if he would put his electronic language sleuth onto the case. Wahlbore was in raptures.

"Can you also examine the two poets as possible collaborators?" she asked.

"Create a composite of stylistic features of Locke and Leare's work Rocky can do; designed to do such work, he was."

"And then match this composite of their work with the killer's poetry, should you find no match with either separately?"

"The suspicion being that the killer's pen might be the work of their collaboration. Most interesting, indeed."

"How long will it take?"

"An hour, maybe two."

Again, a weekend approached, and it promised another

corpse. Jessica stayed with the linguistics professor until he made the comparisons. Dr. Wahlbore came back with his verdict.

"While similar to our killer, not so close a match is Locke as Leare."

"Then Leare's style is closer to that of the Poet Killer?"

"Yes, but a precise or exact match, I fear it is not."

"And when the two styles are combined?"

"Closer to the truth, according to Rocky."

Given his fractured syntax, Jessica imagined what kind of poetry Dr. Wahlbore would write. The news provided corroboration of Leanne Sturtevante's worst fears. At least on the evidence of her poetic style and linguistic mannerisms, Donatella Leare was looking more and more like a suspect. Still, it was not enough to rush in and make an arrest. Jessica certainly could not arrest a person on the basis of a computer program, even though Dr. Wahlbore assured her that Rocky was also programmed as a lie detector, should she get Leare to agree to a test.

"Rocky is far more accurate than any lie detector, even," Dr. Wahlbore added.

"Still, it's inadmissible in a court of law," she reminded him.

"Well, we'll see about that, I suppose."

"What do you mean, Doctor?"

"Any findings over to local FBI and PPD I must send."

"What? I didn't ask for you to do any such thing."

"Requested of me it was, after your first visit, that apprised I keep them."

"By whom?"

"Agent Parry and a Lieutenant Sturtevante."

"Sonovabitch," she muttered. "Don't send these findings."

"Already done so, electronically. For any offense to you, I am sorry."

I'll just bet you are, she thought, realizing that Dr. Wahlbore only wanted someone, anyone in power, to lend credibility to his program, and now that the renowned Dr. Jessica Coran of the FBI had asked for his assistance, he'd no doubt do anything to keep the ball rolling.

Jessica immediately dug out her cell phone and called Parry, locating him in the field. "We're moving on Sturtevante's girlfriend, Jessica," he informed her.

"Don't do this, Jim. It's a mistake."

"We don't think so."

"You can't go forward on the basis of Dr. Wahlbore's work. It's no more reliable than—"

"It's just another piece of the puzzle, Jess, added to what Sturtevante knows about her, and the lie about being in Houston last Saturday when the last victim was killed. It's enough for us to move on; we get her into the sweatbox, get a confession, and the mayor and the governor and the senator'll all be happy."

"You've fallen pretty far, haven't you, Jim?"

"What's that supposed to mean?"

"You, James Parry, caving in to political pressure on a case. I remember a fellow in Hawaii who would have told the politicians where they could stuff it."

"That was Hawaii, Jess, and a long time ago. This is now and this is Philly, and I've changed. I make no apologies for moving on Leare. I like her for the crimes, and you will, too, when she confesses."

"That isn't going to happen, Jim."

"How can you be so sure? Your famous instinct?"

"Yeah, intuition tells me it isn't her."

"Well, Jess, it's largely been because of your findings that the finger points to her and her colleague Locke. You'll be happy to know that in the meantime, we will be watching Locke for his every reaction," Parry added. "At the moment, whether we like it or not, Leare's our best shot; hell, she's our only shot. If you hadn't noticed, the Poet hasn't left us much to go on. Still, I think I know a judge that will issue a warrant for her arrest on what we do have."

He hung up. She felt deflated. Some voice in her head, whether of reason or intuition, told her the others were chasing the wrong person.

The next day's newspapers would carry the story: DONATELLA LEARE, RESPECTED TEACHER AND POET, ARRESTED IN CONNECTION WITH THE SECOND STREET KILLINGS.

Jessica imagined the fallout. Tensions would ease all across the city as a result of the headline that Leare, local professor and celebrated poet, had been taken into custody as a suspect in the killings. Meanwhile, everyone in law enforcement, with the exception of Leanne Sturtevante, would withhold judgment, and many would be closely watching Lucian Burke Locke's every move, as Parry had indicated.

Jessica telephoned Kim, bringing her up to date; Kim agreed with her that the Philadelphia authorities were acting prematurely. "They have a twenty-four-hour surveillance on Locke, and this action the team has agreed upon, Jess," Kim informed her.

"The team agreed on all this? In my absence?"

"They knew you were checking up on Professor Leare's handwriting, and they added it to the mix. I tried to be the voice of reason, but they weren't interested. Trust me, there was nothing you could've done at this end."

"Meanwhile, we sit and wait to see if, in the next two days, another poor soul will be sent across the River Styx by the gentle killer who pens poems on his victims' backs?"

"With Leare in custody, eating well on the taxpayers' money and the notoriety and publicity this arrest affords her poetry, book sales are likely to skyrocket."

"So much that Locke will no doubt want to join her in the slammer, realizing only too late the marketing power of being arrested on suspicion of murder?"

"It's worked for others—actors as well as authors."

"Then the expected happens. The killer comes and goes again, undetected, leaving yet another murder victim and another bit of verse. This while Leare remains in lockup, and while Locke remains under surveillance."

"Should that turn out to be the case, it would effectively exonerate both poets."

"I keep feeling that somehow both are connected to the case, Kim. I just don't know how."

"Yes, I've been getting that from you."

"If in no other way than that their grim poetry has filled the imagination of the killer, whoever he or she is."

"We'll have to look closely into the lives of every student that both professors have ever had," suggested Kim.

"No, we save time by getting you to hypnotize the two, and we hope something relevant shakes out," Jessica countered.

"You can't use hypnosis in a Pennsylvania courtroom."

"We'll use it, not the courts."

"You'll have to get their approval, and once Leare's arrested, I imagine she will be pissed off, and as long as Locke is a free man, what possible motivation would he have to submit to hypnosis?"

"Leave that to me."

JESSICA knew she had to work fast. Enlisting Kim's help, they contacted both Locke and Leare, asking if they might all meet. It took some powers of persuasion, but with Jessica appealing to the poets' vanity, and the possibility of "major" publicity for their works, she managed to gain their assent to do a hypnosis session with Dr. Kim Desinor in order to jog their memories about the victims they'd had as students.

When Jessica and Kim arrived at Locke's home, they found Dr. Harriet Plummer in the company of her two colleagues. "Here," she said, "to lend moral support. I think it wretched and disgusting that you people have badgered Donatella and Lucian in the manner you have," the dean declared. "Now you've flashed their pictures about and talked to students hanging out at the local pubs, again and again, first creating a sense of guilt where there is no reason for guilt, and then perpetuating it. Meanwhile, you do nothing about looking into Garrison Burrwith. I can't understand you people."

They were interrupted by Locke's wholesome, plump wife, who suddenly appeared in the doorway, asking, "Dear, what is this all about?"

"Never mind, sweetheart. Just a bit of a problem with finals coming up; you know how that is. You know Dr. Plummer; Donatella," he said.

Mrs. Locke icily acknowledged both women with a simple nod before turning her attention to Jessica and Kim.

"More playmates, I see," she muttered, and disappeared.

"See to the children, dear," he called after her. "Wonderful person, really, and the children are my perfect little people."

He saw that Jessica was staring at the photos of the children, as she had done on her first visit. He asked, "Do you have children, Dr. Coran?"

"No; no, I do not."

"Why not adopt, as we have? It was a wonderful decision."

"Yes, I can well imagine."

"Children are the pearls of this universe, really, far more so than any jeweled poem, wouldn't you agree, Harriet, Donatella? They're so magical."

The women agreed with nods and mutterings, but Harriet Plummer wanted again to know, "How can you badger these two wonderful poets so, Dr. Coran?"

"Both Dr. Locke and Dr. Leare's names keep coming up in our investigation, Dr. Plummer," countered Jessica.

Kim tried to soothe the woman, calmly adding, "We believe that perhaps Dr. Locke and/or Dr. Leare may know something, may have seen something, may have some special, inside information on the counterculture of this area and the college, as all the victims held, at one time or another, some ties—even if tenuous—to the university."

"That's a lot of *may haves,*" Plummer grumbled.

"One or both must know something, even if they do not consciously know that they know," Kim continued.

"So reason the detectives," said Plummer, fuming, "when I've told you repeatedly that if anyone, anyone at the university is involved in these heinous crimes, it can only be Garrison Burrwith."

"We've found nothing to link Dr. Burrwith to the crimes, Dr. Plummer. In fact, no one has ever seen him in any of the pubs or coffeehouses save you."

"Are you calling me a liar? Tell them, Lucian. Tell them how he insulted us."

"I had Burrwith's poetry compared stylistically with what we've taken from the crime scenes. It in no way resembles the killer's work," said Jessica.

"He masks himself well, this man," countered Plummer, still fuming. Locke took her aside to calm her down.

"By comparison, both Locke's and Leare's poems are far, far closer in imagery and the nuances of tone to what we find in the killer's poetry, and their styles are far closer," continued Jessica. "I picked up one of Dr. Locke's books, a collection of dark, brooding poems—as are all his books, I'm given to understand."

"Three in total," interjected Locke, a smug look on his face.

Jessica recalled how each title said little about the contents of the volume, yet each title was turgid, abstruse, and not a little pompous. The titles, all listed inside the book she had in her possession, were: *Oration of the Gifts of Those Angels Who Rule the Four Quarters, Lurkers in the Stillness of the Forest Soul,* and *Various Jottings—Collectively Known As Folly and Light.*

Jessica had had every piece of information on Locke duplicated and forwarded to her, and she studied it all before coming to see him a second time. She was stuck by the memory of another killer who had wrapped himself in the cloak of civility and science, and she feared making the same mistake with Dr. Locke, who cloaked himself in genteel intellectual pursuits. Should he be hiding a dark and evil secret, perhaps doing her homework might help her illuminate the depths of this man.

She and Kim exchanged a look now, as Jessica had shared her suspicions of Locke and the possibility that Locke and Leare were in some sort of twisted collaboration.

Apparently sensing the suspicion in the room, Locke suddenly burst out, "And just why am I suspect at all? Because I sat on a stool at a number of coffeehouses and bars in the old Warehouse District and on Second Street? What nerve, what gall, what desperate grasping at straws on the part of an inept police department!" He finished with a dramatic wave of the hand.

Kim assured him, "We're just following leads, Dr. Locke. We suspect that somewhere in your memory banks, some key to this nightmare may reside. If not in your memory, then perhaps in Dr. Leare's."

"This is bound to make the newspapers," said Plummer. "The university can't sustain such bad publicity."

"Are you sure of that, Harriet?" asked Leare, smiling. "Think of it: 'Two Noted Philly U Poets Hypnotized to Determine Guilt or Innocence in Series of Murders.' "

"I'm sure you'll put the best spin on it," Jessica predicted. "Fact is, it could be good for book sales, Dr. Plummer."

Locke managed a wry smile as well. "You see, I'm up for tenure and promotion here. At least, since you are talking to Donatella as well as to me, and you have had Burrwith under suspicion, it doesn't appear as if I am the exclusive target of your probe. That much is good."

A nice guy with an ulterior motive for ratting out his colleagues, Jessica thought.

"Good gal Leare is, and a fine poet, though something of a Jekyll and Hyde type; I doubt her capable of killing anyone, despite the method," Locke said, with forced jocularity.

"Exactly what do you mean by 'Jekyll and Hyde type,' Dr. Locke?" Leare replied archly, playing the game.

Harriet Plummer quickly interceded. "He means, Dr. Leare, that you are sometimes moody, that's all. Right, Lucian?"

"Oh, yes, that's precisely what I meant. The woman has, of course, read all my work, and she's won accolades and one of the more important poetry prizes, all on the basis of her last volume, which I gave advice on. Still, that hardly makes it derivative of my own work, although writers do work on the backs of those who came before them."

The sexual innuendo could not be missed, nor the reference to the murders.

"Dr. Leare is working her way up the literary ladder, and her recent success has mitigated her moodiness, wouldn't you say, Lucian? I believe she is working new ground now, aren't you, dear?"

Jessica could not help but note the sexual tension among

the colleagues. Had they all slept with each other at one time or another? Leare obviously swung both ways.

"New poems?" asked Jessica.

"Free verse."

"Is that 'new ground'?"

Donatella Leare replied for herself. "Oh, definitely! Aside from no forced rhyming, it changes the pitch, tone, and hue of a work of poetry to cast it in free verse. Frees the mind from petty constraints, you see."

"I see I have some studying to do," Jessica responded.

Lock interjected. "I would offer you a lesson, but the well's run dry. A bookstore in the Second Street area, quite quaint and out of the way, called Darkest Expectations, carries my book on how to read poetry. Be prepared for a great deal of dust, which I suspect is all you will gain from a hypnosis session, but then, you are the experts."

"Shall we begin with you, Dr. Leare?" asked Kim, who had quietly prepared herself for the hypnosis session, which involved holding the hands of the person being hypnotized. This would allow her to do a full psychometric reading of both the poets as well.

After ten minutes, Donatella Leare revealed little knowledge of the victims who had been her students; she managed only to repeat the cursory information she had already given them. Lucian Locke, by comparison, detailed the study habits of each in cogent specifics, down to what sort of writing tool each preferred. Still, little came of the hypnotic net Kim cast out—certainly nothing revealing enough to uncover the killer.

"I had thought that between you two, you might have some knowledge of the killer, perhaps not consciously but subconsciously," Kim apologetically said once the session with Lock had come to a close.

"You don't mean to say you're giving credence to Dr. Plummer's batty notion that Professor Burrwith is the Poet

Killer, are you?" Leare fairly screamed. "Burrwith hasn't got it in him to kick your ass, Locke, for stealing his woman; he hasn't even got the guts to call your wife on it."

"It may be worth pursuing, Donatella," countered Locke. "I told you how he's been stalking Plummer, how he made a scene at the café, and you know very well that Plummer and I have a purely platonic re—"

"That hardly makes him a poisoner, any more than it makes me a killer," she replied, pacing Locke's living room.

"Why do you suspect that we might know this killer?" asked Locke.

Jessica took a deep breath before replying. "I believe you may know who the killer is on a subconscious level, since his writing has obviously been influenced by both of your works."

"Are you quite sure of this?"

In response, Jessica went to a table and unrolled a computer graphic display she'd held back until now. "This is what the artificial intelligence computer program that examined your work alongside that of the killer's came up with. It's not really close; not a match. Where Locke is bleak, Leare is dark, and the combination is a dark bleakness of style that parallels the style of the killer."

Locke and Leare studied the many connections the computer program had found between their poems and those of the Poet Killer. Leare protested, saying, "This is crazy. No computer program can precisely read style and nuance and innuendo and a hundred other tools of the skillful poet. This is so entirely bogus, Lucian."

"Remarkable nonetheless, but Leare and I have never collaborated, and to ask a machine to collaborate for us, well, I should think that's some sort of infringement of copyright protection. It is absurd to have machines pointing fingers at us on the flimsy basis of similarities between our styles and that of some amateur who also happens to be a murderer."

"You must admit that there appears to be a close tie," said Jessica.

Locke's good eye seemed to double in size, and his glass eye looked to be in danger of rolling out of its socket. "Are you suggesting that we two, together, somehow compose the Poet Killer?" he asked, his dwarfed body shaking with laughter and a gleeful sort of astonishment. "Leare, imagine what such nonsense will do for our reputations and book sales! This is remarkable, wouldn't you say, Donatella?"

"Most assuredly so. In fact, it may be remarkable enough to send us to prison, Lucian."

Just then a pounding on the door and shouting from outside indicated that Leare's arrest was now imminent. "Damn," muttered Jessica.

"What the devil is all this?" asked Locke.

"I think I know, Lucian," said Leare. "I believe they have come for me, not you. Sturtevante's behind this, isn't she?" she asked Jessica.

"I . . . I couldn't say."

"Couldn't or won't?"

"Just know that I was against it."

"Shall I thank you now?"

Locke answered the door, protesting, but the uniformed police, followed by Parry and a pair of his agents, rushed in with a warrant for Leare's arrest. On seeing Jessica and Kim, Parry said, "I thought you had more sense than to get in the way, Jessica."

She pulled him aside, whispering, "And I thought you had more sense period, Jim. You know this arrest is not warranted. You haven't enough to hold her."

"She's a photographer as well as a poet, Jess, and Quantico just came back with our killer poison, something used in photo processing and filmmaking."

"They isolated it?"

"Selenium."

"Selenium." Jessica repeated the word.

"Highly toxic concentration of it in the ink, and it's used by photographers in developing film. It's one more nail in the proverbial coffin."

Parry stepped away from her and walked toward the uniformed men, one of whom had just finished reciting Lear's Miranda rights to her. "Take her to PPD headquarters for interrogation," he barked.

"This is pure, unadulterated madness!" Locke shouted after them as his home emptied of police and FBI agents.

Distraught, Harriet Plummer swooned and fell into an overstuffed chair. Jessica and Kim took their leave.

"I want to see the lab report Quantico came up with on the poison," Jessica told Parry as he rushed away from her.

"Copy will be in your mailbox." He climbed into his car and sped away.

TRUE to his word, James Parry had the report waiting for Jessica the following morning. "Happy reading," he told her on his way out, "and quite revealing of our killer."

"Oh, and how's that?"

"Like I told you yesterday, she is into photography as well as poetry; the poison derives from a chemical used quite heavily in photography work."

"That still doesn't make Leare the Poet Killer, Jim."

"It will suffice until a better choice comes along, Jess."

She gritted her teeth and watched him waltz off, smug and secure in his and Sturtevante's action. She turned her attention to the folder he'd dropped on her desk. "Time to read up on selenium," she told herself.

The toxicology report from Quantico read:

H/2SeO/3—Selenius acid—colorless crystalline poisonous acid, formed by oxidation of selenium to easily yield the element by reduction. Selenite is a salt or ester of selenius acid. A brick-red, water-soluble powder in one form, a brownish, thick glossy mass in another, a metallic crystalline mass in a third form; mixing with ink for the purpose of "writing" into a victim's epidermis requires liquid form, a form readily available for a number of industrial jobs as well as a staple in any photographic darkroom.

The substance burns with a bluish flame, and in its metallic form, it conducts electricity much more readily in light than in the dark. In fact, the higher the intensity of light, the faster it burns. It is used in photoelectric devices such as movies, photometry, and in coloring glass and enamels red.

As to symptoms when ingested/injected: a reddish rash is caused, tingling at the extremities, dizziness, a sulfuric smell, and a metallic taste in the mouth, followed by stomach cramps. Eventually leads to delirium and heart failure, as well as a shutdown of electrical impulses from the brain. Harmless in small doses, lethal in large doses. Some might mistake its actions for those of sodium cyanide, as it appears extremely similar both in chemical makeup and the physical symptoms it induces.

"So, we can infer, the longer the poem, the deadlier the dose," Jessica mused aloud, recalling how the poems snaked along the backs of each victim, from neck and shoulders to pelvis.

She knew the toxicologist Anderson Turner back at Quantico well enough to guess that he had more thoughts on the poison than was described in his official report.

She dialed the number and got him on the line, asking him to tell her everything he had failed to put into the report. "All the good stuff, Anderson. Out with it. I need your input here."

"Well, to begin with, selenium is an element of a type we call an 'inhabitant of the seasons.' "

"Meaning what, precisely?"

"As in, it waxes and wanes with the moon."

"The moon? It's somehow cued into the moon?"

"Its movements at least, like many minerals."

"I see. Anything else?"

He sighed. "You might find it interesting to hear what it was named for . . . *from,* that is."

"And it derives its name from?"

"Selina, goddess of the Moon, who sprang full-blown from the head of Hecate or Artemis, depending on whether you're an ancient Greek or Roman. Each culture had its own version."

"I see . . . I think."

"You do?"

"May tie in with our killer's thinking."

"Yeah, I heard you guys have someone in custody already. Way to go."

"Hold your accolades, Anderson. I'm not so sure we have the right person in custody."

"Bummer."

"Yeah, I think so, but we're not interested in locking up the wrong man—person—for the crime."

"She's a she-killer, is she? I might've known. Why're you all sitting on that information?"

"We're not on solid ground with the arrest. You know how that goes."

"Yeah, guess I do know about spongy cases; hope this one doesn't turn all mushy on you. Good luck, same to the others for me."

"Will do, and thanks, Dr. Turner, for this. We've been working blind too long here."

Jessica put the phone down, stared again at the toxicology report, and her mind played over the victims once more, and the poems inked onto their backs, all linked by identical lines and a unifying theme . . . but exactly what that theme was remained a mystery.

Still, armed with the new information about the poison used by the killer, Jessica felt somewhat fortified. Now, if they could get a fix on the DNA makeup of the tearstains, the noose would tighten about the neck of the real Poet Killer.

EIGHTEEN

The greatest poetry does not exist in a physical world, but inside desire and despair.

—Donatella Leare, Live Poet

THE information on selenium pointed to someone with a background in photography, as the chemical was heavily used in film processing. However, a little more research, and Jessica learned that selenium was also found in battery casings, and the report out of Quantico added that shavings from batteries could have been pounded down and liquefied before being mixed into ink, but it seemed much easier to obtain the substance in liquid form, the form found in vats in darkrooms.

Jessica recalled the beautiful "photopaintings" on the walls at Darkest Expectations that had turned out to be computer-generated, and realized that their production would not require normal photo processing, and, therefore, would not involve the element selenium. However, she also recalled that Marc Tamburino, the current owner of the bookstore, had bragged about being a photographer; making money at weddings and wakes, he'd put it. Leare had joked about his doing a wake, she seemed to remember. Perhaps Tamburino processed photos on the premises, in which case he would have a supply of selenium.

She confided her thoughts to Kim, who thought them sound. "Perhaps you and I maybe ought to have another chat with this fellow Tamburino," she suggested.

"Yeah, if nothing else, he could shed some light on just how readily available our poison is."

Kim nodded. "Hanging around here isn't getting us anywhere, and you're entirely right about Leare. She's not our killer."

"The others would like to believe that it's a woman killer; given the condition of the scenes, it's comforting for them to think the perp belongs to the so-called gentler sex."

Jessica and Kim commandeered a car from the pool in the underground lot and were soon on their way to Darkest Expectations in search of more and better answers.

BOOKSTORE owner and sometime photographer Marc Tamburino, somewhat beguiled by Jessica's return to his store, and thrilled by her interest in his photography, was proudly displaying his work. Jessica at once saw the hopelessness of thinking Tamburino their killer; his wedding photos displayed little talent. She could tell that Kim agreed.

"Do you have any special ones, photos I mean?" asked Kim.

"Ones you show only to your closest friends?" Jessica coaxed.

"I keep my best work in my apartment over the store. You're welcome to come up and have a look. About to close up; the three of us could call it a ménage à trois," he joked, but his attempt at flirtatious banter fell flat. Jessica realized only now what a geek Tamburino was.

"Just show us your photographs, Mr. Tamburino," she said, "and tell me what you know about the use of selenium in photography."

"Selenium?" he asked as he led them up to his apartment. Jessica immediately noticed that the place needed a thorough cleaning.

His private collection revealed him to be a competent, avid amateur with aspirations to becoming a professional who had sold a few of his photos for advertising purposes. The portfolio he showed them contained much better work than the wedding photos. He sensed that the two FBI agents were reconsidering their earlier assessment of his craftsmanship, and said, "It's easier to do good work if you're interested in the subject."

As they perused his framed photos, Jessica saw a door marked by a red bulb and a sign proclaiming it as a darkroom.

"Do all of my own processing. A hell of a lot cheaper that way," he said in her ear, noticing what she had been staring at.

Jessica asked him about processing, and he walked her back to the rear and the darkroom. "Have a look. Showin's better'n tellin', as they say."

Jessica stepped through the door he held open. She saw no evidence of anything amiss here, no photos of the victims lying about or hung up and drying. For that much, she felt grateful, when her glance fell on a tall, cylindrical container marked SELENIUM. Three skulls-and-crossbones indicated the level of toxicity in the liquid they contained.

Jessica again casually asked about the selenium.

"Oh, it's a staple in every darkroom."

"How do you use it?"

"With every precaution. It's highly toxic, and deadly if absorbed through the skin. Highly toxic stuff."

She felt for a moment that she was in the lair of the killer, but then realized that she had not seen a single photo of any of the victims anywhere in the establishment. Perhaps Marc Tamburino kept such shots hidden, only taking them out when driven to do so by his other, more deadly persona. All sheer speculation, she silently reminded herself. Still, mightn't he have a secret collection? Perhaps a thorough search of his home was in order, but she found nothing to justify such a search. She had no probable cause, save the selenium drum in the darkroom, and to request a search warrant on this basis alone would be a waste of time. As she asked her questions rapid-fire now, Jessica saw that the young man's eyes were averted; suddenly he looked crestfallen. She realized that she'd burst his bubble, whatever that bubble might have been, and now he was on the defensive.

"I know what's going on here," he said.

"Oh, really?" she asked. "Tell us about it, Marc."

"I know that you . . . that the authorities are 'desperate' for a whachamacallit, an escapegoat—"

"It's *scapegoat,* and don't be foolish. We already *have* a scapegoat in custody, Marc."

"I could remark on the official stupidity that has caused Donatella Leare to be arrested for all those killings. Leare's not capable of this kind of crap."

"What makes you so sure?" she pressed.

"It'd take a calculating bastard with a strong stomach to talk those kids into suicide."

"You discussed this very scenario with Dr. Leare, didn't you?"

"Do you mean did she know your kind would arrest her and charge her with . . . with all this?"

"She did, didn't she?"

"Yeah, but that's because she'd been sleeping with a Philly cop."

This information came as no revelation to Jessica, but she faked surprise, wondering just how many people knew of Leare's involvement with Leanne Sturtevante.

Tamburino winked conspiratorially, as if he and the agents shared some dirty little secret. He looks like a malicious snowman, Jessica suddenly thought as she watched him walk back to the main room.

"Myself, I could never, ever take a life, despite my own grim outlook and dark poetry."

"Oh, you write poetry?" She practically had to run in order to keep pace with him as he rushed about the room, picking up dirty clothing, discarded magazines and books, replacing them on shelves and tabletops. In a corner stood an opened box marked INGRAM. Realizing the word was not an anagram of *rampage,* Jessica decided she was a little desperate for evidence herself.

"Matter of fact, I do."

"Will you turn some of your poetry over to me?"

"What, for analysis? Against the killer's handwriting?"

"Exactly."

"Not exactly like asking for a fingerprint or DNA. And who knows, word leaks out, and maybe—"

"Maybe your poetry is printed on 'page one'?" she asked, smiling. "Couldn't hurt your career as a poet, now could it? You think that's what the Poet Killer is after, page-one publicity?"

"Amazingly enough, that's what I thought all along, that the killer wanted to publicize himself. I've thought that from the beginning, but the papers haven't printed his poetry. Why?"

She shrugged. "Just another mystery, I guess."

"News guys are cooperating with the cops, right? Cops cut a deal with the press, right, to keep it out?"

"Can't say. So you really think that's what the killer has wanted all along? Publicity for his work?"

"That's really sick, man, I know, but it's got to be the reason. What other reason could he have?"

"You'll let me take a look then at your poems, to compare?"

"They don't come anywhere near Locke or Leare. You'll be disappointed, Dr. Coran."

"Let me be the judge of that."

"All right." He walked them back downstairs, and there he produced a volume from behind the counter.

"You've sold some of your work? Who's the publisher?" she asked.

"No publisher. Just had the one copy bound. Gave up on publication years ago, but figured, what the hey, I'll make a single copy, call it my rare first edition, and put it on my shelf. So, you see, I'm over that black depression time when you first realize no one's ever going to buy a single word from you. So I wouldn't make a good rejected Poet Killer, so forget about it."

"I see you managed to get hold of a computer," she said, tapping his monitor. "What about the Internet? You put anything out on the 'Net these days?" she asked.

"Some, just in the chats. No big deal."

"Can I get a copy of your more . . . recent work?"

He breathed deeply, then sighed and shrugged. "Sure, I'll run you a disk copy."

The moment she delved into the book of poetry, entitled *Brain Lizards,* Jessica knew that Marc Tamburino could not be the Poet Killer. His work, compared with the killer's, was immature and maudlin, filled with awkward constructions and forced, often ridiculous rhymes.

She asked if he knew any other people who hung about his store, liked Locke and Leare, and were also into photography.

"Whaddaya mean? Like you want a list of names?"

"Yes, that could be helpful."

"You want me to be some sort of whaddayacall'ems? A snitch?"

"Snitches get paid."

"Exactly what I was thinking."

She located a twenty in her purse and handed it to him. When he balked, she asked him to name a price. He took a moment to consider. "A hundred?"

She brought forth two fifties and added it to the twenty. He in turn jotted down a list of names. There were several characters who fit the bill. One of these was Dr. Harriet Plummer, Dean Plummer of the University of Philadelphia.

The sight of this name hit Jessica like a freight train. She knew now that she must look a great deal closer at Dr. Harriet Plummer.

JAMES Parry produced a janitor in the last building where a victim had died; the superintendent's assistant, as he called himself, had been persuaded to come forward to ID someone leaving the crime scene. The description was of a young man, not a woman—a young man perhaps in his mid to early twenties, ordinary looking, the sort no one would pay the least attention to. The artist sketch that was ordered resulted in a likeness so generic as to be useless. This did not strengthen the case against either Locke or Leare, who, whatever one might say about them, were not ordinary looking.

Meanwhile, Jessica pursued information about Harriet Plummer, all to a dead end, but she did learn that Plummer held Locke in great esteem, and that the poet had not, until recently, produced any significant new work in years. Plummer and Locke had an ongoing affair, much of which was devoted to her efforts to bolster his ego. Lock and his wife were estranged, although he continued to live with her and the children. He and Plummer maintained an apartment on Second Street.

Again the PPD brass sent undercover teams into every pub and coffeehouse in the area, flooded already by people who'd read about the murders and wanted a glimpse of the grisly "scene" from which so many had "disappeared." Jessica found this morbid curiosity ironic and yet typical of human beings.

Open-mike night brought everyone out, and it brought on as well a party atmosphere as one by one the young performers stood up, pranced to the stage, and raised their arms in the gesture of a winner even before they began to read their poems. Some used well-placed mirrors to read the poems on their bodies, while others relied on their sponsor poet. Often the performer was the actual poet.

To the last, every poem depicted a dismal future for mankind, and their utter grimness and grayness felt disturbing. None of them were as good as those on the backs of the murder victims; none were so well conceived or executed as the killer's, and none so hopeful. For the killer's words spoke of a new beginning for the deceased. In the coffeehouse poems, many of the lines were bursting with violent words. Some sounded like rip-offs of Clive Barker and Stephen King themes, what with devils roaming the earth in search of just the right woman to spawn a son, while others, far more personal, were geared to push all the right buttons on a listener who was undergoing teen angst at age twenty-seven.

Most of the night's poets had used erasable Magic Marker on their backs, but some had had the words cut into their flesh. These, Jessica had been told by those in the know, were the true artists.

Jessica had informed everyone to be on the lookout for anyone with a camera, anyone overly interested in photographing the poets on display or the other patrons. "Detain for questioning anyone doing so," came the order. Meanwhile, they looked high and low for George Gordonn, the photographer they'd met the last time they'd come down to the Second Street coffeehouses and bars, the young man who'd been hired to film the night's activities, but he was nowhere to be found.

While the other investigators listened, trying to distinguish the truly disturbed from the merely troubled, Jessica kept vigilant for any photographer/poet matching the general description given them by their lone, admittedly weak witness.

Jessica realized now that their killer could be someone behind the counter at the Brick Teacup, where she and Kim had wound up this night. Kim agreed, saying, "Someone in a position to see these poetry shows each night, and to learn the likes and dislikes of the poets, down to finding out where they lived, down to weaseling into their homes, seeing the layout, and continuing to weasel into their lives until the young people felt at ease with the wolf at the threshold."

"They paid in the end with their lives." Jessica sipped at her coffee, trying to stay awake.

After an hour of listening to what amounted to, in her estimation, drivel and brain snot purporting to be art, Jessica wanted to run out screaming; she felt absolutely certain that she could easily kill a few so-called poets herself.

To add insult to injury, the few people detained by the police tonight, from bars up and down the Second Street area, netted them nothing new. In fact, now that Leare was in custody, the police presence had slackened considerably, and the reasons for arrests were far more mundane than seeking out a serial killer.

THE following day, Jessica and Kim again canvassed the pubs and coffeehouses along Second Street, and Jessica, knowing now of Locke's apartment in the vicinity, felt an eerie sensation of being watched from the many windows that looked down on the strip.

In each closed business establishment they badgered their way into, the women asked after anyone coming in to do photo shoots of patrons, or attempting to lure people away with promises of a professional photo shoot. Most of the leads turned out to be "photo-shoot Casanovas," but not a one of them could be linked to the killings. The day's work then led to several weak leads and zero arrests, and Jessica knew that the longer Leare remained in lockup, and the longer the killer remained silent, the stronger Leanne Sturtevante's conviction that her former live-in lover—as Leare turned out to be—was guilty of premeditated murder by poisoning.

"Whoever the guy is, he must blend into the walls. No one knows anything; no one has seen anything," Jessica told Kim as they once again pored over the files on each victim. "Frustrated at every turn," she added from her seat at the desk they shared. "I'm at my wit's end."

Kim didn't answer. In her hands, she held a crystal wrapped in tight brilliant wire, the wire twisted into knots about the blue stone and attached to a keychain, a possession of one of the victims. Kim had gone into a trance while holding on to the item that had come out of a box taken from the evidence room, a box labeled VICTIM #3321—MICELLINA PETRYNA. Jessica watched as Kim writhed in something other than agony, something that appeared more than pleasant; indeed, the sounds coming out of her mouth were those of a person at the peak of ecstasy.

Then in a blink, it was over, and Kim looked as if she'd been shocked into consciousness, her color returning, her eyes no longer glazed or shadowed. "I think I got something, a hit that may mean something, Jess."

"What is it?"

"Earlier, in the earliest reading, I kept seeing the crime scene, but in a blindingly bright light that eventually coalesced into letters, spelling out the single word *rampage*. This alongside the number nineteen, sometimes transposed as ninety-one. I just saw another flashing, blinding light that not only spelled out *rampage,* but the other words I've been getting, too. Remember I saw the word *quark* and *preflight*?"

"Yes, of course."

"Add to them the word *output*. It wasn't *outing,* but *output* coming through."

"Is that it? Any additional words that cropped up around your reading?"

"None . . . that's it."

"Could these words have something to do with poetry?"

"More likely quantum mechanics," Kim replied, her shoulders heaving.

"What about photography?" Jessica considered this possibility and balling up her fists, she added, "Imagine . . . if they have something to do with photography?" She grabbed the phone and dialed Marc Tamburino at Darkest Expectations.

"Who're you calling?" asked Kim.

Jessica put up a hand to her and said into the phone, "Mr. Tamburino? This is Dr. Coran. I have a quick question for you; do you mind?"

Kim heard a raspy, static-charged reply from the phone, the bookstore owner saying, "Sure thing, but whatever it is, it'll cost you more."

"Whatever you like, but can you tell me if the numbers nineteen and/or ninety-one have any special significance in photography?"

"No, none that I know of."

"In the world of words, poetry?"

"Again, doesn't ring any bells, not like you know, sixty-nine or nine-nine-nine or six-six-six."

"What about the word *rampage*?"

"Rampage?"

"Has it anything to do with photography?"

"Yeah, sorta . . . it has to do with photo finishing; it's a machine."

"And what about *quark* and *preflight* and *output*?"

"Yeah, all terms in the business, but some of that . . . well, that's pretty high-quality, resolution-specialty programming shit in film developing. I don't know a whole hell of a lot about that particular specialty, but I'm sure some of the photog profs at the university could tell you. They have classes on everything to do with photography over there."

"Just tell me what you know about these terms."

"I'd be blowing smoke up your . . . skirt. Look, I suggest you speak to the geniuses over to the colleges about these things."

"Who, Marc? Who do I call?"

"The university has a specialist in film and photography, I'm sure. Why don't you talk to him or her? And by the way, when's my poetry going to appear in the *Philly Inquirer*? And when do I get it back?"

Jessica hung up to Tamburino's chorus of, "When do I see the bread? When, when?"

NINETEEN

He then believed the world to be governed by a Malignant Spirit, and at one time conceived himself . . . a fallen angel, though he was half-ashamed of the idea, and grew cunning and mysterious about it after I seemed to detect it . . .

—Lady Byron's statement to a doctor on the supposed insanity of her husband

PROFESSOR Leonard Throckmorton greeted Jessica and Kim in a stern, cool manner. A small man, he looked dwarfed by his desk, but his manners were impeccable. Hadn't their only witness said something about the politeness of the young man he'd seen leaving the crime scene? Throckmorton appeared to be in his late twenties, but in a dark corridor he could easily pass for a younger man. Something diffident in his manner made him seem feminine. Jessica realized that since he was chairman of the department at such a young age, his rise must have been nothing short of meteoric, but some probing told her and Kim that the man answered to Dr. Harriet Plummer, who appeared to like her department heads and colleagues on the youthful side.

"When I called Dr. Plummer to ask whom to speak to in the photography department, she instantly told me that you, sir, were the man to see if I wanted an expert in all facets of photography."

"She does flatter me."

"I told her I needed to know some details about film processing."

Kim added, "And she instantly recommended you, Professor Throckmorton."

He remained seated behind the desk, using it as a kind of barrier. "So, how can I help you, ladies . . . ah, Doctors?"

Kim told him of her psychometric hits. She finished with the list of words that had insinuated themselves into her mind, adding, "Each word gets more forceful as time goes on, as if each has a life of its own."

Throckmorton chewed on his lower lip.

Jessica asked, "Do these words have any significance for you, sir?"

"They carry great meaning, yes." Throckmorton informed them, "The list of words Detective Desinor is referring to all have to do with the job of a specialist in film."

"And that specialty would be?"

"Film output, a film output specialist."

"And this specialist . . . he does what, exactly?"

"Processes on a Quark system. You preflight film, trap the image you want, then you print it—that would be output—on a Rampage."

"Rampage?"

"That is an NT system."

"A computer photoshop processor?"

"Not unlike the sort you have yourself used at your local Kmart, but this is with film, video equivalents, and the job is done by a technician, a specialist, not a machine."

"I see . . . I think."

Kim asked, "Would this involve photo-processing toxins, say like selenium?"

"Indeed it would."

"How many such specialists work in the city, Dr. Throckmorton?"

"Oh, I'd say you're looking at between twenty and thirty people. It's a highly skilled task when done the old-fashioned way. In a self-contained computerized system like you find at Wal-Mart, all the ingredients for processing are never touched by the operator. The specialist, on the other hand, gets his hands dirty— chemically speaking, of course—as he is required to do all the mixing and processing work by hand."

The detectives stared at one another and Jessica said, "Then we have a poet and a photography specialist who is something of a chemist as well."

"That does narrow the field," Kim agreed, a slight smile of satisfaction curling her lips.

Jessica again turned to Throckmorton, who worked to light a pipe he'd pulled from a rack. She asked, "What sort of companies use such specialists?"

"Oh, production companies."

"As in movies?"

"Movies, ads, business tapes, anything to do with video production. The key word for the film output specialist is *video*. He works with video."

"Most major companies, including ad agencies, hire their work out, right?" Jessica wanted Throckmorton to give her every shred of information she could get. The man seemed to play the role of expert only reluctantly.

"You got it. The number of such companies is on the decline, and the call for a specialist in this area is rare nowadays, but I saw an ad in the paper just the other day for one."

"Really?"

"Yes, which likely means—"

"That some poor slob lost his job not long ago?"

"Could be our man," suggested Kim. "Serial killing is often triggered by a dramatic or traumatic event."

"As in locating a lost memory?" asked Throckmorton. "I've read a number of true-crime books, and I follow *The Edge* series on TV," he explained in an apologetic voice.

"Say as in a threat to one's life, and losing a job for most ranks right up there with the biggies in the trauma department," Jessica replied.

"Look, do you recall the ad and the paper you saw it in?" Kim tapped her knuckles on the desk.

"Wrapped some tools in it at home. But it was two days ago, deep in the *Philadelphia Inquirer* want ads, so . . . no promises."

"How was it listed?"

"Under 'Film Output Specialist.' "

"We'll find it, and thanks."

A check of the Philadelphia Yellow Pages turned up eighteen local production companies, and after phone calls, Kim and Jessica narrowed these down to eleven that did their own Rampage/NT work on the premises via computer-driven machinery, which meant they would have no need of a film output specialist.

The detectives narrowed the field further by learning of the three companies that had had recent openings in this field. Only two of these had recently fired someone from the position, a man named Stuart David Andrews from McReel Industries, and another named George Linden Gordonn from Record-Time Custom Photo & Video.

"George Gordonn," said Jessica, "the name rings a bell . . ."

"I requested and finally received a patient list from Dr. Vladoc. He sent two lists, the cop list and the civilian list," said Kim.

"He maintains a civilian practice as well?"

"Yes, out of his apartment on Second Street. Anyway, our boy George was on that list. Along with another surprise. Let me find it. Here . . . here is his name. He has been Vladoc's patient for the past year."

"You don't suppose he's . . . yes, he's got to be our George from the Teacup, or was it another joint—you remember . . . the night we talked to the guy who was doing the video work."

"Has to be one and the same. He said his name was George Gordonn, didn't he?" Jessica was pacing now as she thought. "It's too much of a coincidence to ignore. He was filming the poet performers, in a place Vladoc no doubt frequents."

"What do you mean, Jess?"

"Remember the bartender, the one who said he'd had to throw out an older guy who was extremely short?"

"Are you saying that Vladoc was bounced, or that Vladoc might be in on the hunt and possibly the kill? That he's a predator?"

"I don't know, but I think we have to be cautious. Look further down the list."

"Jesus—I see Garrison Burrwith's name."

"The one Dean Plummer is convinced is the killer. Maybe she knew he was seeing a shrink, fueling her fears? And look. Locke is on the list as well."

Kim asked, "Do you think it's significant that Vladoc is treating Gordonn, Locke, and Burrwith?"

"I can't say, but why didn't Vladoc come forward with these facts early in the investigation?"

"He didn't know we ever considered Burrwith a viable suspect. Because we didn't. And as for Gordonn, it's quite likely that no one asked Vladoc about him."

Jessica felt a wave of incredulity wash over her. "So Vladoc had said nothing about working with Locke. He doesn't think that relevant to the case?"

"You are making it sound like Vladoc's part of the killings, or at the very least that he closed his eyes to it. Don't forget, Jessica, that he must work under a strict code of confidentiality."

"Yeah, yeah, I know."

"You asked him for a patient list, and he complied, but he still cannot give up patient secrets, their absolute right to privacy."

"He ought to've found a way to . . . to leak this information to us."

"No."

"No?"

"Only in the event that a patient confesses to a crime or displays incriminating evidence is the doctor required by law to turn over his notes. Only then does the privilege issue take a backseat. Vladoc has likely done what any self-respecting psychiatrist would have done."

"He might have saved a life had he spoken up."

"If he held suspicions that one of his patients had taken a life, he could only attempt to convince the criminal to step forward and accept punishment. Until the dangerous patient confesses and becomes a menace to others, the shrink's hands remain bound by client privilege. Vladoc can't give up his notes or make any comment on what passed between himself and a patient."

"We have to share our findings and suspicions with Parry and Sturtevante, and while the evidence against Locke or Gordonn appears strong, despite its circumstantial nature, the case against 'Weird Al' Vladoc is not firm at all."

"Neither Parry nor Sturtevante will be able to deny the strange coincidence that ties George Gordonn with both the Second Street scene in a big way—taking live-action video." Kim believed this all tied in to her visions neatly, almost too neatly.

"Get on the horn to the others. We're going to bust this asshole Gordonn," Jessica declared.

"Are you quite sure?"

"Quite. Given what we know, there's no telling what a thorough search of the man's place will turn up."

THE FBI and PPD investigators organized into two teams, which stormed the production companies simultaneously for personnel records on each suspect. They learned that Stuart Andrews had caused some difficulty for his employers by excessive absence due to alcoholism, and that while he had not been fired, he was encouraged to take his gold watch and pension a little earlier than planned, whereas Gordonn, a young man, had indeed been dismissed for repeatedly missing days and showing up late and hungover.

They closely scrutinized the background of George Linden Gordonn, aware that with the weekend looming, the killer would probably be selecting a new victim. The personnel file showed that he had been let go as recently as the week before the first Killer Poet victim had surfaced.

When the file came up empty of photos of the suspect, one of the personnel secretaries assured James Parry that, "You really don't want to see a photo of that man. He's repulsive." She had shivered on saying his name. "Warned them against hiring him in the first place."

"How long did he work here?"

"Two years, three months, and eleven days. I know 'cause I do payroll, and I had to count every one of those days." She burst into laughter at her own remarks.

Parry and Sturtevante radioed their concern to everyone else, Parry saying over the wire, "We're reluctant to let the news spread about Gordonn, fearful of interviewing his working buddies, since one or more of them could tip him off to our interest. We're not exactly in Oz anymore, and so no one expects anyone outside of law enforcement to be cooperative. That would be asking too much."

"We've got to obtain a federal warrant to stake out his home, and to get a photo surveillance under way," said Sturtevante. "And I know you feds will have a lot more influence on a federal judge than I could ever hope to have, so it's up to you."

"And you're a lot easier on an old judge's eyes than I am by a hefty margin, Jess," added Parry.

"All right . . . I get the picture, but I think Dr. Desinor here can handle obtaining the warrant. She's got a lot more patience with local federal judges than I do, believe me."

Kim nodded. "And besides, Jessica doesn't want to let this guy out of her sight for a moment."

Jessica glared at her. "You reading my mind again?"

WITH Gordonn on her mind, Jessica hummed and half sang the words to an old favorite Gordon Lightfoot tune, "If You Could Read My Mind."

"Just like an old-time novel, the kind the drugstores sell," piped in Parry, equally bored with staring through binoculars at Gordonn, who was nervously pacing behind the curtains. Jessica watched now as Gordonn's dark silhouette suddenly disappeared. Had he stepped into another room? Had he sat down on a couch, into an armchair, prone on the floor? Had he gone out the back?

"He's on the move!" Jessica suddenly called out.

Parry looked out to see Gordonn burst through the front door, moving directly for the street. Jessica said, "He appears as harmless as a puppy dog; slight of build, thinning hair, undistinguished face, pale skin tone, small and unassuming in every way. Yet he somehow held sway over people's minds, convinced them to go wherever he wanted, to step softly right into their own deaths. He literally talked them out of their lives once he talked them into becoming the 'canvases' for his seemingly benign art form."

"Yeah, how'd this weasel do that?" asked Parry.

Kim still hadn't gotten back with the search-and-seizure warrants, and Jessica had heard from her only once, something about a hard-nosed, liberal-assed judge who worried about "vi-o-lating Gordonn's guar-an-teed rights for reasonable expectation of privacy." Kim wanted to kill the man. Instead, she took her request to another judge during a break in the session, something to do with the original judge having the runs. "In the meantime, I had a psychic episode since last I saw you, Jess."

"Having to do with the case?"

"Yes, well . . . I believe so, yes."

"Tell me about it."

"Further visions of the crimes, picking up images which lead me to images of . . . the victims posed for photos."

"Posed?"

"The killer wanted and got photos of the poems, the killer's handiwork on their backs, before leaving each crime scene."

"Souvenirs to treasure," said Jessica, knowing serial killers' penchant for retaining mementos of their victims and the moment they had shared, souvenirs to help them relive the moment.

"This memorabilia of his work," said Kim, "the killer must keep close at hand."

"Gordonn just left the premises, Kim. I'll search for the nasty mementos in his home, if you can get me inside."

"I'm working on it."

ASAC FBI Agent James Parry and PPD Detective Leanne Sturtevante could feel the tension wringing out of their every pore. Each killing had raised the pressure on them, but with the arrest of Sturtevante's former girlfriend on suspicion of being the Poet Killer, the level became all but unbearable.

Jim Parry, to his credit, did not know of Sturtevante's personal involvement with Donatella Leare until well after the arrest, learning of it only during interrogation sessions with the suspect.

Since then, Leare had posted bond and was released easily and quickly. From all accounts, she had made a great adjustment to her newfound notoriety. Her books were selling like hotcakes, according to Marc Tamburino, who was heard to exclaim, "Man, you can't buy that kind of publicity. Not even Donald Trump can buy that kind of publicity. The news media can't even manufacture that kind of story, I tell you."

Jessica had passed word along to Sturtevante that she—Leanne—had, however unwittingly, given Leare's career the proverbial shot in the arm, that people all over Philadelphia were vying for copies of her poems, and that Leare was being asked to speak publicly at functions all across the state. The detective had taken the news badly, as a slight, a lousy joke. She had pointed the finger at Leare, had arranged for her arrest, and now she felt like a fool. She had taken the action against Leare in spite of Jessica's better judgment, and Parry had sided with her; now both had come to the realization that Leare was not the Poet Killer after all. All three of them—Jessica, Sturtevante, and Parry—knew that Sturtevante's personal involvement with Leare had impaired her judgment. This fact, unspoken among them, colored every word now of their discussions of the case, and made them all intensely uncomfortable.

Parked alongside Gordonn's rambling, aged house, atop a cracked and weed-choked driveway, a battered beige late-model Oldsmobile had been waiting. Once the suspect had gotten into the car, and once he sped off, disappearing around the corner, an unmarked police vehicle took off after him.

Inside the surveillance van, Parry told Jessica, "We can't wait any longer. We go in now while he's out." He started for the door, stooped and cramped in the small interior with Jessica, Leanne Sturtevante, and a technician named Jake Towne.

"Go in without paper?" protested Sturtevante.

"If we miss this chance, we may not have another to bug the place before he decides to scratch his itch again," Towne warned the others, taking Parry and Jessica's side.

"We need the warrant, Jim," Sturtevante cautioned. "We've already made one mistake. Let's not compound it with another."

Parry protested. "*You* made the mistake, Leanne; you were so convinced of Leare's guilt that you convinced me, and now that we have a viable suspect, it's time you owned up to your error. But I have to agree with Towne, this guy could return at any time."

Leanne checked with the team that now followed Gordonn. She spoke to them on a closed line. Then she told Parry and Jessica, "According to the team that's on him, Gordonn appears to be driving aimlessly about the city."

"In the vicinity of Second Street?" Jessica asked.

"No, he's wandering around the warehouse district."

"Looking for new prowling grounds, perhaps?"

"Perhaps."

"All right, then. I say we go in and hope the warrant arrives before we leave the premises," Parry said, his hand on the door.

Jessica readily agreed. "I'm with you, Jim."

Sturtevante warned, "Any word of this gets out, no matter what you collect from bugging the place, Jim, it'll be tossed. I know the system in Philly, and that kind of thing will get you nothing but a reprimand. The prosecutor's office won't touch tainted evidence or evidence gathered by criminal means, and that's what you two are talking about."

Parry looked Jessica in the eye. "Are you sure you want in on this?"

"I am." Jessica took it as a challenge.

"It could backfire, Jess."

"I'll take that risk."

"Like you did in Hawaii?"

"Yeah, guess so."

He turned to Sturtevante. "Stay on Dr. Desinor to get the paperwork to us ASAP."

"I just want it noted that your action is—"

"So noted, Lieutenant Sturtevante, so noted. In the meantime, why aren't you on the phone to your contacts, getting a local warrant?"

"We're doing the best we can. I've gotten the mayor out of bed."

"Good, he wanted results, right? Where're all those clowns in their three-piece suits when you need them? Where's your boss, Roth?"

"Hospital. Family emergency. Wife's been fighting cancer."

"Shhheeesh, sorry to hear that."

Parry threw open the surveillance van doors. "You with me, Jess?" he asked, extending a hand.

"I want inside," she replied, following him out.

"No radio contact," said Sturtevante, who remained inside the van, bent up like a yogi on a bad day. "Towne, you got that?"

"Got it," replied the technician.

The three exchanged glances, all of them knowing that radio contact meant that the exact timing on this would be recorded. No radio contact meant an ambiguous time line later if anyone should ask. Don't ask, don't tell would be the rule of the day. "It'll keep us all a little more . . . honest," said Sturtevante. "Just a little."

"Good thinking," Parry told her.

"Good hunting," Sturtevante said. "I'll watch your backs. If Gordonn makes a move anywhere near here, I'll break radio silence with a single word."

"And what would that be?"

"Rampage."

The other task-force members, watching Gordonn's movements, kept in constant radio contact with Detective Sturtevante while Jessica and Parry entered Gordonn's home. Parry had brought along his lock-picking tools, and it took him only a few minutes to gain entry. He broke in like a pro, disturbing nothing.

Once inside, Parry expertly wired the place, setting taps on Gordonn's phones and placing bugs in his walls.

Meanwhile, Jessica wandered about freely until she came upon a collection of photo albums. She opened one after another in search of the incriminating evidence—Exhibit A.

"Even if you found something, without that warrant we can't produce if for a jury; no prosecutor would touch it." Parry was telling her what she already knew, but he also knew that she, like himself, felt an insatiable need to learn if they were or were not on the right trail.

"I just want to find out if it *is* him, if we're really onto the right man here," she confessed, now telling him what he already knew. She continued to thumb through Gordonn's photos and books, private papers and file boxes in an attempt to at last discover the truth.

Then Jessica came across a photo of Gordonn as a child with his mother and father. She noticed that his father was separated from his wife and son, who huddled together as if in a shared cocoon, as if they were protecting each other. Perhaps for good reason? she silently asked, her eyes searching every detail, every nuance of the snapshot.

In another photo, mother and child were captured in the nude, and their obvious delight at playing whatever game they were playing again suggested how terribly close they were, maybe a bit too close, Jessica caught herself thinking.

Jessica wondered who had taken the photo—Gordonn's

father, perhaps? Flipping to yet another photo, she gasped. "My God, Jim, he's got to be the Poet Killer. Look at this photo."

Parry came to her side and looked at the strange photograph. What he saw caused him to gasp as well. The words *Happy 6th Birthday* in an angry, burnt-orange color seemed to scream at him from little George's back, where they had apparently been scrawled. Evidence or sheer coincidence? the detectives wondered, their eyes meeting.

"God bless me," said Parry, swallowing his own words. The message written across the child's back looked like a banner; these words were followed by the lines of a poem: *Spirit child of my spirit/Soar to the estate/Of star and moon/To return to us soon . . .* On his sixth birthday, either Gordonn's mother, Lydia Byron Gordonn, or his father had written lines of poetry on the child's back, as if to carve them into his flesh.

This single photo spoke volumes in and of itself, Jessica believed, but photos of Gordonn's victims would prove absolutely damning. It all gave her pause, and her thoughts fluttered like so many nervous pigeons now as she considered the mother's maiden name of Byron and her married name, Gordonn. It was yet another damning apparent coincidence, for the Romantic Poet Lord Byron, Jessica knew, had been born George Gordon, the same name minus an *n*.

She wondered if the mother had perhaps been a failed poet, and a failed person as well, and if she meant more by these words on her son's back than anyone knew, if she had been the one who penned them. She wondered about the relationship between mother and son, and between father, Harold Gordonn, and son. She wondered just how balled up and twisted up with Byron's dark and somber personality the relationship between father and mother had become. Myths and legends had grown up around Lord

Byron, both during his scandalous lifetime and after; Jessica even remembered hearing it said that he had become a vampire, or simply a person who lived the life of a vampire in some ways. Yet his poetry was as beautiful as it was disturbing. Some considered him a fallen angel, and there was evidence in his reported conversations and poetry to suggest that he himself had started this particular bit of folklore.

Parry cursed first under his breath, and then aloud. "Fucking A—these shots of little George ought to come in handy at trial, once we can get our hands on them again, but for now, darlin', they have to stay put. Place them back exactly as you found them. We don't want Gordonn to have the slightest inkling we've been here or that we're onto him."

"I need to search for photos of his victims. These won't convince a jury that he's guilty of murder. It's far too circumstantial and could be presented as mere coincidence, chance, by a good defense lawyer." She began a frantic search through the remaining albums on the shelf but stopped when several clippings from the *Philadelphia Inquirer* fell onto the dirty carpet.

Jessica now knelt, dirtying her skirt and knees, to reclaim the clippings, ecstatic, certain they had located more incriminating evidence. But her bubble burst when her eyes lit on the date of the clippings: May 4, 5, 6, and 10, 1969. Another clipping was dated a year later, 1970. The clippings dealt with the suicide pact of Gordonn's mother and father, and with the surviving child, who had been turned over to Child Protective Services, a child with a strange poem emblazoned on his back. Jessica only had time to scan the clippings when Parry shouted, "We've got to get out of here—now!"

"Just a minute."

"We're out of time. Leanne's calling 'rampage.' " Jessica could hear the word like a mantra over the police band. "Get moving, Jess. It's the warning we agreed upon earlier. Gordonn's returning home."

"Then we take these with us," she said, pointing to the photos and clippings.

"No, we can't take a thing; we've already disturbed too much here. If he knows we've been inside, he'll know the place is bugged, and all our efforts will have been for nothing. No, you can't leave the premises with a thing. As for the clippings, they're public record. We can duplicate them at the *Inquirer*'s microfiche library."

"But, Jim, the photos, these could disappear; he could burn them at any time."

"He hasn't burned them in all these years. Why would he do it now?"

"If he feels threatened, he might."

"We'll just have to take that chance."

"And I still want to locate victim photos."

"You don't even know if they exist. It's just something Kim Desinor thinks she knows, another trance image."

Jessica and Parry were still arguing when Sturtevante pushed through the door and shouted, "He's only a block away. Get out of here—now!"

"Put everything back the way you found it, Agent Coran. That's an order!" shouted Parry.

"Going to pull rank on me now, Jim?" Jessica bit her lip but did as he ordered, tucking the loose photos back into the album from which they had spilled, her hands steady but her nerves pulled taut.

Parry said, "Sorry, Jess, but we haven't enough evidence on the guy to get a warrant, obviously, so how're we going to justify taking stuff out of his home?"

Jessica replaced the albums on the shelf where they had sat gathering dust, dust that she had disturbed. She had wanted to find a stash of victim shots, a diary perhaps, a running tally of his victims, maybe some newspaper clippings that referred to the ongoing investigation, but none of these had surfaced, only the telltale shots of the child with the writing on his back.

Parry continued his tirade. "And to prematurely abscond with anything from the house will open up a legal hole in a later trial that any defense lawyer could run a tractor trailer through."

"Allow the creep time to incriminate himself fully," Sturtevante said, putting her hand on Jessica's shoulder to emphasize her words. "It's time you took your own advice, Jessica. I wish I had heeded it earlier."

Parry tugged at her now, losing patience. "We've already broken the law by being here and bugging his place. Let's not compound that. This gets out and my next assignment will be in Podunk."

"It's the first break we've had, and you're asking me to just walk away from it?" Jessica demanded. "Suppose he burns all the stuff tonight?"

"We all want to nail this bastard, Jessica," soothed Sturtevante, "but we need to do it by the book to make it stick. Desinor has the warrant in hand, but she isn't here, and it isn't kosher until she gets here with it. Besides, we've bugged the place. Jim's right. Let's do the rest of this by the book."

Jessica knew they were right, yet she found it difficult to let go of the only incriminating evidence in the case anyone had seen. On their way out of Gordonn's bungalow residence, she told Sturtevante, who hadn't taken the time to look, what she had shown to Parry.

"Then at least we know we have the right suspect this time," the detective replied. "We won't let him out of our sight."

"Or hearing," Parry added.

They climbed into the surveillance van and closed the doors just as Gordonn pulled into sight.

"It sure was hard to leave those photos behind," Jessica said in frustration.

"You didn't leave much behind, Jessica," Parry said, one eye on the returning Gordonn. Carrying a small plastic grocery bag, he stepped casually up to his door, unlocked it, took a moment to glance about to see if anyone was watching his comings and goings, and then disappeared through the door.

Parry continued to soothe Jessica. "What those photos represent is . . . well, it's just too nebulous, and a strong defense-team shrink could paint it as a healthy sign that Gordonn was strong enough, despite the trauma he suffered, to go back to research how his parents died."

"And the part he played in their deaths?"

"He had no part in it. He was a child."

"The dysfunctional family on overdrive involves every member."

Parry shook his head. "The child was an innocent victim in a suicide pact made by his parents."

"I am talking about the sordid, twisted family matrix of these three people. No, the child did not have any conscious part in it, but the parents were motivated by the child's being . . . just being, in every sense of the word. Existing in innocence, his angelic nature. They did it for him, seeing themselves as heroically saving the boy. His very innocence set his parents on the deadly path. And by now he knows this."

"Sounds like a candidate for some serious psychoanalysis," said Sturtevante.

"According to the story, each of them, including the child, had a poem incised on their back."

"We'll have to get copies of the articles from the newspaper library."

"Said that the mother wrote the poem into the back of her husband, and the husband into the back of the mother."

"And the child?"

"No way to tell for certain which of the parents wrote on the child's back, but whichever parent it was, he or she intentionally withheld the poison, allowing the son to survive the suicide pact."

"And the poems are similar to the ones the killer is using today," added Parry.

"Whoever did the writing had not given the child the poison. Therefore, one of the parents must have balked at ending the child's life. Possibly as the partner lay dying, making the decision to allow the child to live at the last moment, possibly while feeling the first effects of the poisoned ink himself or herself."

"Mother or father?" wondered Sturtevante, echoing Jessica's theory.

"And what difference does this make to Gordonn?" Parry asked.

"Possibly the answer to the question, the answer he is so desperately searching for. But for us, the more important question to our case, now that we're seeing victims all being poisoned in exactly the same manner, is why Gordonn sees a need to reenact such killings. I say there's enough evidence to involve the DA's office, maybe get an indictment," Jessica told Parry.

"No, not necessarily," Sturtevante said. "This story is public knowledge. Likely can be accessed through on-line sources—hell, *likely* isn't the word, *absolutely* can be accessed via the *Inquirer*'s dot-com."

Parry scratched his chin. "If Gordonn has shared this tale of the suicide pact of his parents and his own near death at their hands with people around him, any one of them could have taken the idea and run with it, including our friends at the college, Locke and Leare, or for that matter someone in the photography department, or Harriet Plummer, Professor Burrwith, anyone with whom George Gordonn may have had any dealings."

"Or it could be Gordonn himself, acting out, repeating the twisted logic of his parents, who set him on this path as an infant," Jessica insisted.

Parry calmed her, placing a gentle hand on each shoulder. "Remember your profiler training, Jess."

"Of course I remember it. What about it?"

"It taught you that a killer will have a circle of attachments, acquaintances, friends or people he thinks are friends, relatives. Any one of these people could be using Gordonn, or Gordonn's story, for his own twisted ends."

"According to records, Gordonn took photography courses at one of the local colleges. The University of Philadelphia—coincidentally."

"It occurs to me he had to learn his specialty somewhere, yes. What are you getting at?"

"It's pretty obvious, Jim. All roads seem to lead us back to the university."

Before Parry could respond to her words, Sturtevante interrupted. "Message coming through from Dr. Desinor. She has the warrant and is a block off. We have a go on bugging the place but a no-go on search and seizure. Best she could do. It would've been a serious mistake to have taken anything out of the home."

Jessica nodded. "Got it."

TWENTY

We are ne'er like angels till our passions die.

—Thomas Dekker (1572–1632)

LEAVING George Gordonn to a fresh surveillance team, Jessica, Sturtevante, Parry, and Kim regrouped at PPD headquarters. There Jessica called in Peter Vladoc to look at the latest findings and make an assessment of George Gordonn, openly and honestly.

"My dear, Lord Byron's given name was George Gordon. Gordonn's mother's maiden name was Byron. Byron marries Harold Gordonn and the two would-be artists romantically concoct a quick exit from this world. As a photographic artist, Gordonn senior would have known the properties of selenium. The killings are based on this incident, but the story had been told in and around Philadelphia for so long that everyone considers it just another urban legend. Only thing is, young Gordonn researched his parents' death, and he learned that they intended for him to go out with them."

"And you didn't think it relevant to tell us about this?"

"He's never threatened anyone in my presence; he's never admitted to being the Poet Killer, and he comes off as extremely well grounded, mentally speaking, for someone who began life as he did. Harmless, searching . . . these are words to describe George. Patient-doctor privilege forbids me to discuss our sessions in any but the most general of terms."

"Ironic," said Sturtevante.

"More like Byronic," Vladoc countered. "Someone too

fine, too delicate, too good for this world, too heroic in the sense of having the most exquisite of human sensibilities, an angelic nature too sublime to withstand the slings and arrows of this existence. That's what your killer thinks of his victims. Gordonn, on the other hand, detests what his parents did to him, leaving him alone in the world, and he hates them for attempting to kill him as well. A Byronic personality would be the last thing he would emulate."

"But one of the parents actually saved him," Jessica said.

"Exactly, and he is wrestling with his ambivalence, and has from the outset of our talks attempted to learn which one showed him more mercy. You see, he has a right to be angry with his parents for deserting him as they did, leaving him to grow up alone."

"Was he given to foster care?" asked Kim.

"His foster parents have since passed on; natural causes."

"You're speaking as if you are certain Gordonn is not our killer," said Sturtevante.

Jessica added, "As if the killer is a heroic person by mere virtue of being . . . sensitive to the supposed needs of his victims, Dr. Vladoc, and you don't believe Gordonn sensitive enough to be this killer?"

"Your killer is a worshiper of the angelic," Vladoc countered. He nodded, his eyes going from Parry to each of the women investigators. "He sees himself this way, and sees each of his victims the same way." His pause allowed them time to digest this.

Sturtevante found a seat and fell into it. Clearing her throat, her eyes glassy, she said, "Maybe it's in their nature—the poets; the real ones, I mean—to feel only resentment for this world and all the sorrow it brings down around them."

"The ideals of beauty and spiritual wholeness subjected

to ugliness and fragmentation," said Jessica, "are the same that are expressed in Leare's poetry."

"As well as Locke's," added Sturtevante. "And doubtless countless others'."

"We still need to catch George Gordonn in the act or speaking about the act, Jess," said Parry. "We need someone to get him to open up."

Vladoc quickly agreed. "While you have some impressive patterns emerging here, the dots have yet to be connected, and I sincerely believe, from all my time spent with Gordonn, that he is incapable of such heinous acts."

"Perhaps you can locate some of the dots," suggested Jessica, an edge to her voice.

"In point of fact, I have one major dot for you. I know this George Gordonn and have known him as a patient for almost a year now."

"You've treated him?" asked Sturtevante, this news being new to her.

"That's certainly a strange coincidence, Dr. Vladoc," Parry observed dryly. He then asked, "Why didn't you tell us about him sooner?"

"I have never known him to be violent; it never occurred to me that he could be a killer. I am still having trouble grasping the idea. He just doesn't fit the profile, despite all the business with his ruined family life."

Parry nearly shouted, "You didn't think it relevant to tell us about the man whose parents started the urban legend that began this back-writing fad among the young?"

"I had and still have patient privilege to consider. But I tell you, Gordonn never gave me the least concern. I can't see him perpetrating the very act which took his parents' lives and nearly took his."

"He doesn't appear to have enough money to pay the normal household bills, Dr. Vladoc," said Jessica. "How does he afford your sessions?"

"He pays with cash, always. I've never seen him use a check or credit card. He always insists on cash."

"Isn't that a bit strange?" asked Parry.

"What isn't strange about this entire business?" Sturtevante put in.

"Perhaps, since Dr. Desinor is also a psychiatrist," began Jessica, a fist balled up and held against her teeth, "sharing information on Gordonn's case would only amount to consultation with a . . . a consultant, a colleague. That may not be a violation of the young man's civil rights or a breaking of your code of conduct."

"Yes, perhaps with Dr. Desinor's help, I'm sure you two can and will help this case along," agreed Parry.

"Then, after, we can do more research in the archives at the *Inquirer.*"

"I'll be glad to help you in any way possible, Dr. Vladoc," said Kim, striking a match and lighting the elderly psychiatrist's pipe.

"And you have no idea where he's getting the money to pay your bills?" pressed Sturtevante.

Jessica stood, nodding. "All right, while Dr. Vladoc and Kim make their determinations, we will pursue a line of questioning with Dr. Throckmorton at the university."

"It appears Gordonn took some classes in the photography department at the University of Philadelphia," Sturtevante informed the others, and Vladoc knowingly nodded.

"We'll rendezvous back here at five P.M.," said Jessica, "if everyone is in agreement."

"Five it is," said Vladoc. "We must get past this wrong direction you have all taken so that we can get back to the real madman, checkmate *him* before his next move."

By now, Jessica had become a familiar face on campus, but Parry and Sturtevante drew a few stares from students passing them in the hallways. They had returned to the photography department, where they spoke with Leonard Throckmorton, who informed them that Gordonn had indeed taken classes in the department with Professor Zachary Goldfarb, and that he had begun but not finished an ambitious film project on the life of Lord Byron.

"What kind of film do you mean?"

"Why, a documentary about the poet's greatest accomplishments. Do you know that it is impossible to find a bust of Lord Byron anywhere? You can get Beethoven, Mozart, but try to find Shelley, Keats, Byron, or any of the major poets—except for Shakespeare, of course. Not a large enough market, I suppose. Meanwhile, you can't throw a stone without hitting the bust of a composer."

"What can you tell us about Gordonn?"

"Very little, I'm afraid."

"Start by telling us how much you knew of this Byron film he was intending to make."

"He was nearly finished with the project when he suddenly disappeared, dropped out, and as far as I know, the project went with him. But then, Dr. Goldfarb can tell you more about that than I can."

"Where is Goldfarb now?"

"Presumably in class."

"We need to see him. When's class out?"

"Twenty minutes. If you care to wait, I'll have him sent for."

"That would be helpful."

"There's a lounge just down the hallway if you care to wait there."

"No, I'm quite sure the twenty minutes will be filled up right here, Dr. Throckmorton, because I have more questions." Jessica sat down in a chair opposite the man's desk. "Since you know little about George Gordonn, then perhaps you can tell us about another suspect."

"Another suspect?"

"The original George Gordon—Lord Byron."

"What do you now wish to know about Byron?" he asked, confused. "And how is a dead poet—one dead for well over a hundred and fifty years, I believe, a suspect in a murder investigation today?"

"I was hoping you could tell us that."

Parry plopped down in the plush leather chair beside Jessica. He explained the connection they'd made between the Byron volume found at one of the victim's homes, George Gordonn, and Gordon's "twisted, deceased" parents. Finally, after explaining about the suicide-pact death that was meant to take little George out as well, Parry told the other man about the poem on the six-year-old's back.

"And now he's been making a film homage to Byron," said Throckmorton. "I see why you are interested in Gordonn." The department chairman then said, "Actually, Byron has become a kind of cult hero for many of America's youth, particularly those given over to the goth lifestyle, those black-trench-coated legions whose preoccupation with romanticism, heroism, and death have catapulted the Byron type and the Byronic hero into a kind of . . . well, I guess you'd call it godhead."

"Byronic hero?" asked Sturtevante, who'd remained standing. "Now I need a cup of coffee."

"Well, the Byronic hero . . . he occurs in many guises, taking on different characteristics in Byron's poetry, you know, the extremes of passion, the fervent and moody antihero, solitary, doomed, the one who stands outside or above ordinary criteria and jurisdictions or notions of right and wrong, good and evil."

"Yeah, I know what Byronism is if I search my memory banks from college lit. courses," said Sturtevante, sounding more frustrated than skeptical. "I just didn't expect this."

"Nor I," the professor replied. "Are you detectives sure

you weren't simply influenced by the volume of Byron's work you saw placed alongside the body?"

"The Byron book was found with pages marked and lying on the nightstand," Parry returned. "We think it's a strong, unifying element in George's twisted logic."

"What're you saying, Dr. Throckmorton?" put in Sturtevante. "That we have a killer with a Byron complex?" She turned to the others. "By the way, is there any such thing as a Byron complex?"

"Why, yes," Throckmorton explained. "A person with a Byron complex sees himself as a doomed and tragic figure, a kind of Prometheus who is pecked to death not by an eagle but by the smug, indifferent, and uncomprehending world to which, like the Prometheus of myth, he has brought light. Perhaps you ought to talk to a shrink about this, not a photography professor," he finished.

"We are, as we speak, getting support from that quarter," Jessica informed him.

"How amazing. I had no idea that Lord Byron had any connection whatsoever to . . . to these deaths."

The twenty-minute wait for Dr. Goldfarb was up, and so Dr. Throckmorton, fearing he'd miss Zach, as he called the other man, rushed out himself to fetch him.

"Not a very forthcoming fellow at first but once he gets to know you . . ." Jessica observed with a smile to lighten Parry's mood.

"Rather uptight, I agree."

Leanne said nothing, pacing instead.

"Why don't you sit down somewhere, Detective?" asked Parry.

In a moment, Dr. Goldfarb stepped in, saying, "Dr. Throckmorton has informed me of your interest in a former student of mine, a George Gordonn, and his film project." He held up a black record book, scanning it for Gordonn's grades. "He accumulated a series of D's and low C's before dropping out, withdrawing from the class. What more can I tell you?"

"Is there anything you can tell us about him of a more personal nature? What was he like?"

"I had no discipline problems with him; he displayed no odd behavior, if that's what you mean. Somewhat subdued, sullen as I recall, a bit withdrawn."

"I see."

"I fear I can tell you very little, but I will be happy to assist in any way that I can. Outside of classwork, I know next to nothing about any of my students, and Gordonn wasn't an especially notable student, to be frank, save for his interest in Byron, his proposed project. I remember being surprised that he selected the poet for his term project. Most admirable. I usually get projects about the effects of concussions on NFL quarterbacks."

"So George Gordonn challenged himself and that surprises you?"

"By term's end, I only knew him as a grade. Over a hundred students in my Literature in Film class, so sorry, but he really made little impact on me, and as for his film and aspirations to do definitive work on Byron, it was a joke. He couldn't do it. He simply hadn't the intellect for it; it's as simple as that. What little of the film I saw in its early stages was merely . . . pitiable."

"But he works as a specialist, or has worked as a specialist with film development."

"Workhorse stuff in this arena. He was no photographer, and certainly no writer/director."

"So he failed to complete your course?"

"Dropped out, at my urging, you see. He and I both knew he was heading straight for an F. I do remember one strange thing he told me once, but I thought it a mere affectation, so I paid it little attention."

"Until now?" asked Parry. "What strange thing did he tell you?"

"Said he had been the first young person ever to disrobe and show a poem emblazoned on his back as so many do now in the pubs on Second Street; said he started the trend in a South Street pub and coffeehouse called Charlie's or Charles's Manse or something of the sort."

"That clinches it," said Sturtevante. "He's got to be our man."

Goldfarb looked stricken. "Do you actually think him capable of murdering people?"

"Did you believe him? About his starting this fad in the coffeehouses and pubs?" asked Jessica, startled at this news.

"I chalked it up to bravado, talk, you know."

"And that's the last you saw of him?" asked Sturtevante, her eyes locked onto the professor.

"Well, yes, we had no further reason for contact."

"Thanks for your help, Professor Goldfarb. I think we've got all we came for."

"I'm sorry I could be of no more help," finished the pompous little man before disappearing through the door.

"Little weasel," said Sturtevante in his wake.

A quick check in the phone book showed no Charlie's or Charles's Manse, but there was a listing for Charlemagne's. The trio of detectives headed directly for the coffeehouse, the oldest in the area, according to its sign. Tucked away on a dead-end street off Second, it was out of the way of the normal flow past such places as Starbucks.

It had not been overlooked in the police sweep of the coffeehouses, but it had produced no leads, and so, like the others, it had ceased to be of interest, until now. When they got to the door, Sturtevante begged off, telling the others to work the place. "Two detectives are unwanted company," she said, "three's a police action."

"But I was going to suggest a bite to eat, Leanne, at Sitale's," Parry said.

"Not for me."

Parry protested. "A late-afternoon lunch/dinner before rendezvousing with Desinor and Vladoc back at headquarters. Come on, you haven't eaten all day."

She didn't go into any details but claimed she had an urgent private matter to deal with. "Something I must take care of."

Jessica imagined it had something to do with her broken relationship with Donatella Leare.

At Charlemagne's they learned very little. No one working the day shift had any recollection of Gordonn, and when they flashed his photo, hastily taken by the detectives who'd been watching the man and forwarded to them, everyone in the establishment drew a blank. Either that or they were good actors. They weren't particularly interested in cooperating with authorities. This much was clear.

Jessica and Parry left feeling unhappy with the continued lack of results, cheering each other with the fact that Goldfarb could be called in to testify to what Gordonn had said to him about starting the back-poetry fad. "Another nail in his coffin," Parry, using his favorite figure of speech, commented.

Parry located a small Italian restaurant in the heart of Philadelphia, a place that had become his favorite among the downtown eateries.

The restaurant turned out to be splendid, the dishes authentic old-world cuisine. Over wine and food, James Parry opened up to Jessica, telling her how he had lost his post in Hawaii, and how much it had devastated him. "It was all a lot of hogwash, but hogwash that had been accumulating since . . . well, before I met you."

"Hogwash in the FBI has a way of accumulating to the point where you find yourself drowning in it," she replied, commiserating with his situation. "If I had a dime for every time some BS-stuffed official in the ranks came into my lab and made demands, well . . . go on, Jim."

"It was based on my not following proper procedure during just such a case as we have today."

"Really?"

"A murder conviction on a mobster had been thrown out of court, and the resulting fallout rained down on me. It had been a case the Bureau had been building for years."

"So they needed a scapegoat."

"In the islands it's known as a sacrificial pig. You know how they like to roast pigs in Hawaii."

"Funny, Jim, but I'm sorry for what happened to you."

"I'll be a damned sight more careful in the future, and that's got to be the case with Gordonn."

"Are you suggesting that we can only arrest him with the deadly pen in his hand?"

"Something like that, yes. If we want an airtight case against the freak."

"God, I wish we'd had more time at his place to locate his stash of photos of the victims, assuming he had any— something beyond his collection of news clips of his parents' deaths."

"Even if we'd found such evidence, if you'd walked out of there with them, they would have been inadmissible in a court of law. Besides, we couldn't disturb the place. Like I said before, if Gordonn caught on . . . I mean if he somehow figured out that we were in his pad, he'd know it's bugged. We've got to get him to incriminate himself in one fashion or another."

"All right," she said, relenting, "but I still wonder if we won't both regret the decisions we made back there at his place."

"Are you referring to Sturtevante? Has she a hidden agenda?"

"Something like that. She's kinda closed off, or hadn't you noticed?"

"Holds her cards close to her chest, yeah," he agreed.

"Do you trust her, Jim?"

"I do, and you can as well."

"Fine . . . good to hear it."

"Does that mean you trust me, too?"

"I trust that you're at my back."

"Yeah . . . you can bank on that, Jess."

"I haven't forgotten how you saved my life in the Cayman Islands," she told him.

He stabbed at his fettuccini. "We'd best get out of here and to that meeting with Vladoc and Desinor. See if they've come up with anything useful on Gordonn."

STURTEVANTE was late for the meeting. "Gordonn is on the prowl, heading down Second Street as we speak," she told them as she entered the meeting room. "Surveillance is on him, but I think we ought to get out in the field."

"I want to know what Dr. Vladoc and Dr. Desinor have to say first," Parry told her.

Jessica remained silent. Vladoc, who had been speaking when Leanne arrived, picked up where he had left off.

"Further investigation into Gordonn's past and parents reveals much to us," he declared, twirling his glasses as he spoke. "Dr. Desinor has unearthed all the local newspaper articles from the various papers, including those she found at the *Philadelphia Inquirer*'s microfiche library."

"There's sufficient detail in the stories," said Kim, "to link what happened to Gordonn as a child with what is going on today."

Jessica stared at the array of articles Kim had collected, squinting in order to follow the fuzzy microfiche copies. In the days before computers, microfiche had seemed a miracle of an invention, but today it seemed about as advanced as chiseling on stone tablets. The images and words on the poor-quality copy she held in her hand were hard to see, but the headline was easy enough to read: FAMILY SUICIDE PACT ENDS LIFE OF POET LYDIA BYRON AND ARTIST HUSBAND HAROLD GORDONN—CHILD SURVIVES.

The story summarized the macabre little family suicide pact that became as powerful an urban legend as any in Philadelphia artistic circles, in addition to being the great motivating force of George Gordonn's life, the origin of the living-poem fad and the reason he was on the prowl that very night.

The phone rang, breaking everyone's intense concentration. Jessica picked it up and heard Marc Tamburino's voice, sounding loud and shaken. "Dr. Coran, I have some information you might like to know about."

"Pay for, you mean? You're suddenly getting very good at digging up stuff, Marc. I think we've discovered a hidden talent in—"

"I located information about how the Philadelphia fad of writing poetry into the skin began."

"Is that right? Go ahead," she told him, curious now.

"There've been several explanations over the years that have attached themselves to the fad, but one in particular I found in my research . . . well, it's weird enough for *The X-Files,* and I wanted to share it with you."

She took *share* to mean *sell.*

"Does it have anything to do with a bizarre suicide pact in George Gordonn's past?"

Tamburino's silence clearly meant yes.

"Do you know this guy Gordonn?" she asked.

"Are you kidding? He's the leader of the Locke and Leare groupies. He never misses a signing, and he's taken a lot of pictures at them. Hey, just remember, without me, you'd be nowhere on this case."

"So why wasn't he on the list of names you gave me earlier."

"It never occurred to me to list him. I thought you wanted pros! He's an amateur, a goofball, a weirdo, but not the kind you'd notice particularly, and certainly not the kind who you imagine could kill somebody."

"Your information is a little late, Marc and frankly it sucks. No deals this time. In other words, thanks but no thanks." She hung up on his protests. While plainly useless at this point, Tamburino's phone call at least added to their conviction that they were on the right path.

"We're wasting time here," said Sturtevante.

"I want to see if Gordon shows up on anyone else's class list, say like Garrison Burrwith's, Leare's, or Locke's," Jessica protested. "It won't take long."

"Grab the lists; bring them along," Parry suggested.

"They're in lockup," Jessica told him, "along with all the other evidence we have. It'll take a while to get my hands on them. Go ahead. I'll catch up."

"Let's hit the streets, people," said Parry. "Get on the track of this creep. Tonight I feel lucky."

With that, everyone but Vladoc and Jessica hurried out of the office. When they were gone, Vladoc muttered, as if to himself, "I still can't believe it of George. He's so mild-mannered and pleasant."

"So was Ted Bundy, Doctor."

Jessica left the police psychiatrist and went to the evidence room, where she signed out the class lists they'd acquired from the university and quickly scanned for George Gordonn's name. It appeared three times. He'd taken poetry classes with Locke, Leare, and Burrwith.

She ran into Kim on her way toward a waiting car. "Thought I'd ride with you," said her psychic friend. "What did the class lists reveal about George's career as a student?"

"He took classes with the whole triumvirate—Locke, Leare, and Burrwith."

"Why didn't we see this before?"

"It's not unusual for the same students to be showing up in a series of lit. courses, especially when one is a prerequisite for the other. A lot of the names on the lists were repeated."

"Including those of the victims. George Gordonn knew the victims."

"He took Burrwith first, a year ago, followed by Locke last summer, and then Leare most recently, fall term. After that he signed up for Goldfarb's film class. He's been busy."

"It would seem so . . . researching the life of Byron perhaps?"

"It would seem so . . ."

As the car pulled out of the underground lot, Jessica at the wheel, Kim said what both of them were thinking. "It would appear that we are finally on the trail of the Poet Killer, Jess."

GEORGE Linden Gordonn, it seemed, having somehow learned of the police's interest in him, most likely from noticing that he was being followed and watched, had fled. At first, this presented no problem to the surveillance team, as they had him in their sights, driving his sedan. It was only when he slipped out of sight, veering into an underground lot and speeding out at an exit around the block, that it became a problem. But when they went to round him up—they figured he'd shot himself in the head or something—they found an empty car.

"How the hell did he just vanish?" the police chief, Roth, asked, having joined them at the car with a warrant in hand to search the vehicle, "and exactly how did Gordonn know that we were onto him?" He'd been kept apprised of events by Sturtevante. Angry, he shouted, "The surveillance team was never compromised, and yet he knew he was being watched. How?"

"Perhaps he simply *felt* the police presence everywhere, picked it up in, I don't know, some supersensory way," Jessica wondered aloud. "Perhaps that's how he's stayed a step ahead of us."

"You saying he's psychic?" asked Kim.

"That or very 'blue-sensed.' "

Roth and the others knew she was referring to police jargon for a cop's instincts. Sturtevante offered another possibility. "Maybe someone's keeping him informed."

"What do you mean?"

"Maybe someone close to the case is in some way close to him. I'd thought that was the case when . . . when I suspected Leare, that she was getting the information from me."

"Pillow talk?" asked Parry. "You think Gordonn is sleeping with someone close to the investigation? Who?"

"I don't know. Someone on the task force, maybe, someone in the ME's office. I'm just grasping at straws here, Jim."

"Like everyone else," Kim commented.

Jessica said, "If so, then he knew when we were on, when we were off." She wondered if some more mundane answer was closer to the truth. "At any rate, it's as if the city has swallowed our boy up. He won't easily be located."

While Jessica and Parry cruised in Parry's car, FBI dispatch alerted them to an urgent call from Dr. Coran's "snitch," Marc Tamburino.

"I've got more than you bargained for this time, Dr. Coran."

"No games, Marc. I've got no time for nonsense. What is it?"

"Gordonn is being helped out of the city by well-meaning friends, friends who have already had their asses in a sling thanks to the police, if you get my drift."

"Are you telling me that Leare is protecting Gordonn? That she knows him well enough to help him escape?"

"All I know is what I hear, and what I hear is that the poets of this city are fed up with your gestapo tactics, and they've banded together to help Gordonn out. How do you think he so thoroughly disappeared while under surveillance?"

"Some poets did this? I've never known poets to be so militant, Marc. What exactly are you telling me? No riddles, okay? Tell me, how did Gordonn learn that he was under suspicion?"

"I haven't a clue, but I do know that what I've heard is accurate information. I'll expect a healthy check for this piece, love."

"So, a group of right-thinking, well-meaning artists have banded together to protect Gordonn."

"He's like a cult figure to some of them, like a symbol or something. The founder of the fad, don't you see? It's earned him a measure of respect."

"And his poisoning people to death?"

"That, too, with some in this crowd, believe me."

"All right, Marc. Thanks for the lead. You'll be hearing from us."

Jessica conveyed Tamburino's information, and while Parry admitted to being skeptical, he could not argue with following up on it. "We go back to Leare, Locke, possibly Burrwith, Plummer, and the photography people."

"Well-meaning friends who cannot conceive of his guilt in this bizarre business are hiding and abetting him?" Kim asked when she heard the news. She had a sudden flash of how they all looked from afar, a flock of buzzards standing around Gordonn's vehicle as it was searched from top to bottom before being towed to the police lot.

Aaron Roth put an APB out for Gordonn, and he arranged to have all highway entrances from the city closed off and roadblocks put up. Photos of George Linden Gordonn were circulated. All this, and still George did not surface.

The search brought them back to Donatella Leare's home, the suspicion being that she had picked up loose bits of information about Gordonn from Sturtevante or notes Sturtevante may have left about. They found the place dark, but could just make out some music, soft and melodious, playing in one of the rear rooms. Jessica rang repeatedly, but there was no answer. Peeking through the curtained door, she saw the flickering light of candles, and she caught a whiff of incense.

"Could be lounging in a bath and can't hear the bell with that music turned up so loud," Parry suggested.

Kim had joined Leanne in her cruiser, and they arrived behind Jessica and Parry. Leanne now rushed toward the house, a look of dread etched on her features. Jessica apprised them of the situation.

"God, she's taken that creep in, and he's killed her!" Leanne cried. "I just know it!"

"Break down the door," Jessica told Parry.

"No," said Sturtevante. "I still have a key. I'll go in."

"She's likely in the shower, but you tell her if she's aiding and abetting Gordonn, she's in trouble," said Parry. "Make it clear to her that she has to tell us where he is."

The detective nodded. "Will do." She then entered the premises, calling out to her former girlfriend, while the others waited outside. In the time it took for Leanne Sturtevante to walk from the front room to the master bedroom and bath, all they could hear was the soft music and an occasional shout of "Donatella! Donatella!" Then a sudden scream sent a horrid ice pick into Jessica's spine. Sturtevante shouted hysterically that her friend Leare was dead.

The others raced in to find Donatella Leare lying face-down on her bed, rather haphazardly so. On the poet's back were the now familiar blood-orange words of the Poet Killer, carved into her skin with the selenium-laced ink. The poem on Leare's back stared back at them like a laughing skull, Jessica thought.

She wondered now if Gordonn or Tamburino or both of them together were not having fun with them all, PPD and FBI alike.

"Bastard! Bastard's killed Dona!" wailed Sturtevante, distraught and on her knees, her gun beside her.

"Locke—Locke and Burrwith!" shouted Jessica. "We've got to get to Lucian Locke's place, and to Garrison Burrwith's, and now! If the Poet Killer has targeted Leare for death, then he'll try to kill his other instructors as well."

"Come on, Jessica. We'll let Kim take care of Leanne, and the crime scene will take care of itself," said Parry. "Let's go. We've got to get a radio car dispatched to both locations. Someone close at hand."

"Someone close to the investigation," she muttered. "Who . . . who close to the investigation has given up our every move to the killer?"

"Vladoc," shouted Sturtevante.

"Vladoc? But why?"

"He drinks, he talks. Someone knows this, uses him. Gordonn is shrewd. Doubled back on us all and escaped, didn't he? And we thought him a pitiful slob who had a miserable beginning and would have a miserable end, and left it at that. Meantime, he's busy killing . . . killed Donatella."

Parry's cell phone went off. He lifted it and barked, "What is it?"

"Dispatch, sir. Another urgent for Dr. Coran, sir. Patch him through, now!"

"It's for you," he told Jessica, his eyes bulging. "Says it's Lucian Burke Locke."

Strange coincidence, she thought, taking the phone in hand. She repeated the garbled words she heard coming through for the benefit of the others. "Says he knows where we can find George Linden Gordonn."

The strange little man, Locke, said clearly into the phone, "I have information as to where George can be found, or rather where what remains of him can be found."

Parry snapped the button to place the cell phone on speaker so that the others could hear the conversation. "What do you mean, the remains of him?"

"He's dead."

"Dead?"

"Ready for burial, yes."

"Can't you be a little more descriptive? How did he die? Where are you?"

"He's lying dead alongside another of his victims," Locke shouted into the phone, making Parry jump back.

"Where are the bodies, Dr. Locke?"

"My house."

"We'll be right over. Don't touch a thing, do you understand?"

"Yes, yes, of course."

He hung up and said, "We should still send a cruiser to Burrwith's place, have them look in on him. Meantime, we'd best get over to Locke's."

Kim had been holding Sturtevante's hand as the other woman continued to cry over the loss of her friend. "I'll stay here with Leanne. You two go."

"Be certain to maintain the integrity of the scene," Jessica told her. "Call for Shockley to get over here and walk the grid."

"Will do."

With that, Parry and Jessica rushed to the home of Lucian Burke Locke in search of George Gordonn . . . or what remained of him.

TWENTY-ONE

I saw the pale student of unhallowed arts kneeling beside the thing that he had put together.

—Mary Shelley, introduction to *Frankenstein*

"I knew young Gordonn only through a class I taught nearly a year ago; didn't hear from him or about him again until he began working on his Byron project in the film department, you see. He took my course to learn more about Byron and the Romantics; he loved the notions of romantic love, enduring, undying love, but he remained primarily focused on Lord Byron. I took him under my wing, so to speak, and just recently, he began to brag about how he was party to the killings."

"That's how he would put it?" asked Jessica.

"Precisely, but I blew it off, as they say. Of course, knowing him, even for a short time, I knew this was all a lie, bravado, all that. I never for a moment believed George to be guilty, and so when I learned he was under suspicion, I gave him safe haven until the young man should feel secure enough to leave."

"That's a felony, Dr. Locke," said Parry, "one which you could be tried for."

"I realized that at the time, but I felt an overwhelming need to help George. He had that effect on people; people wanted to 'fix' him."

"And precisely how did you know he was under suspicion, Dr. Locke?"

"That's right," added Parry. "It wasn't public knowledge."

"Information I gleaned from Leare, who had it from her lover, Sturtevante. Seems Sturtevante went to apologize to Donatella about all the misunderstanding, the mishandling of the case, all that, and she let it slip that you were zeroing in on George. Leare knew of George through me, and she had had him as a student once as well. I was trying to help George to stay . . . stable, you know. I knew what he had gone through. But of late, George had begun to seriously worry me."

"How's that?"

"Even in the face of being arrested for these crimes he professed to have committed, well . . . not believing him, I paid little attention until recently. I tell you, he went out last evening and returned to my house with a young woman, although Leare and I had told him specifically that he must remain in hiding."

"He came back with a woman, a stranger to you?"

"A young woman. She looks to be another coed, I fear, but I didn't know her. I immediately protested when he entered the room I'd turned over to George, only to find him and the girl writing out poetry on each other's nude back.

"I was assured by George that it was a mere dalliance on his part, and his interest in body poetry had nothing whatsoever to do with the murders, and then he confessed to having lied about his involvement in the killings, telling me his shrink had said he had an insatiable need for attention.

"When I first met him, in my class, he told me about his parents, that he was in fact the living proof of the urban legend that had started the back-writing poetry fad, and now, that is a few hours ago, he told me how angry he was at this killer, whoever he was, to have turned his poetic 'invention,' as he called it, into a horror of death.

"He then lamented the deaths of all those young people; he said he felt great guilt since the killer had obviously

been inspired by his invention, but again he insisted that he
had killed no one, and that his earlier confessions to me
were simply to gain attention."

"And you believed him?" asked Jessica.

"I wasn't hearing his cry. I know, I was a fool, and I
could have prevented so much death."

"What happened next?" Parry asked.

"Something made me look in on him around midnight. I
found the girl and George both dead in my home, victims
of the poisoned pen that each had used on the other, just as
George's parents had done. I was horrified, so I called
you."

"You did the right thing," Jessica assured him, Parry
agreeing.

"Poor lamentable George," Lock proclaimed. "And this
other creature he duped into his final trap."

"Forensics is going to have a long night of it," said Jessica. "Let's get a team of evidence techs over here. I'll
need all the help I can get with the two corpses."

Parry got on his cell phone and made the call.

It appeared to all involved to be over. All the evidence
pointed to one perpetrator, to George Linden Gordonn. All
the information collected at Locke's house and later at
Gordonn's also bore this out. Finally, the city of Philadel-
phia could breathe again and would hear no more from the
Lord Poet of Misspent Time, George Gordonn, the Killer
Poet who, bizarrely, professed his kinship with Lord
Byron.

At Gordonn's home, a stash of poetry in George's hand
was taken into custody and remanded to evidence lockup.
Jessica heard about the poems, which had been scrawled
longhand into a notebook. Along with this, Gordonn had
kept a diary in which he fantasized about helping people to

commit suicide in order to leave this world of "putrid flesh," as he called it.

Still, something nagged at Jessica. The number of his victims, including himself, amounted to far fewer than the number nineteen, which Kim had seen again and again. But it was more than this. Something wasn't right about the timing and the circumstances surrounding Gordonn's death in the home of the famous dark poet Lucian Burke Locke, whose wife and children were conveniently away at the time.

After all the protocol work on Gordonn's remains and those of Ariana Dupree, his final victim, Jessica found a moment to confer with Kim Desinor. Kim had taken time to read through Gordonn's diary and poems, and she'd shown copies to Dr. Wahlbore, who fed them into Rocky. Kim's gut reaction to Gordonn's poetry told her the poems didn't match with those of the killer, and Rocky bore her out. Kim had telephoned with this information, saying she was coming right over to discuss what this meant.

Kim showed up at Jessica's office, slipped into a chair, and exasperatedly asked, "How did the quality of Gordonn's poetry go from the junk I found in the notebooks to what he supposedly wrote on the backs of his victims? Did he somehow sprout poetic wings when he had a back to compose on?"

"From what you and Wahlbore say, I would have to assume, as Vladoc suggests, that Gordonn killed under another personality altogether, obviously one who could write a sight better than his regular self."

"Sounds ludicrous; sounds like Vladoc's interested in covering his ass, Jess. A dual personality explains away how the good doctor could be treating a man and not know a goddamn thing about him."

"What're you talking about, Kim?"

"I've seen what was collected at the Gordonn home, and

I'm telling you, it doesn't cut the mustard. It's not . . . it didn't come out of the same mind."

"I see. Doesn't compare well with the killer's verse. You think Parry and Sturtevante and Roth and the city are going to want to hear that?"

"I'm only telling you what you already know in your heart to be true."

"That we've tagged the wrong man for the killings?"

"I fear so."

"But what about all those psychic hits that had to do with his profession?" Jessica countered.

"They may well have been pointing to this, that one day we'd have the wrong man, a technical film specialist, in custody for murder, only he isn't here to tell us so or to refute it."

"Have you ever known cases of dual personality—both being writers—but who write in totally different ways?"

"I just don't buy it. Vladoc says Gordonn may have been a dual personality, in which case perhaps one of the personalities was a poet, the other not. I just think it's too pat, too easy a way out." Kim was adamant about this. "His poetry was not up to the standard of the killer's. Was he then inspired when he wrote on the back of his victims but not before?" she repeated her earlier question.

"Everyone has laid the case to rest. Parry, Roth, and Sturtevante are happy to turn it over to the DA's office."

"While you and I, dear, remain skeptical," said Kim. "I just have a gut feeling about it. Call it—"

"Instinct? Combine your gut feeling with mine, and we have one hell of a big gut feeling between us," finished Jessica.

"I hate to think that our killer is slipping through legal hands, and that Gordonn was set up by the obvious candidate, Lucian Burke Locke."

"We need more to go on than a gut feeling," Jessica countered.

"What about warming up your cold hypothesis with this?" a male voice interrupted.

Both Jessica and Kim swung around to see Dr. Leonard Shockley, holding a manila folder overhead and slapping it against the doorjamb where he stood.

"And what's *this*?" Jessica asked the ME.

His hands slightly shaking, Shockley spread the contents of the folder before her where she sat. "Take a look." He gave Jessica time to read the information from his work on the final corpse, Ariana Dupree.

Jessica stood, came around the desk, and kissed Dr. Shockley, while Kim asked, "What? What is it?"

Jessica announced, "DNA . . . the killer's DNA from the tears . . . doesn't match up with Gordonn's DNA."

"Then the last two victims were killed to cover the real killer's tracks."

Jessica kissed Shockley again and started out on the first step in a long journey, one that now had a specific goal: to nail Lucian Burke Locke, the strange little man with the picture-perfect home and the picture-perfect—but only in appearance—family.

"A closer look at Locke is in order," she announced.

The closer look into the life of Lucian Burke Locke revealed that he was the product of a home dominated by an alcoholic father who had made life a nightmare for Lucian and his mother. It was Dr. Harriet Plummer who provided this information, all the while defending Lucian to the detectives when they suggested that he was not telling the entire truth the night of Gordonn's death. The police also talked about Locke with Garrison Burrwith, who was only too happy to inform them that he had learned from campus rumors and word of mouth that Locke had always been fascinated with the urban legend that turned out to have originated with Gordonn's family. There were even students who swore that Locke referred to the story of the Gordonn family deaths in his lectures as an example of the power and influence of the Byronic image nearly two centuries after the poet's death.

"But no one knew at the time that George Gordonn was part of the ill-fated family," Burrwith explained, "no one except Professor Locke, I suspect. I suspect the boy informed his revered instructor when Locke spoke of the story as an urban legend. George was extremely shy, you know. He would never have announced such a thing in public, no more than he would tell a classroom full of people that he had been the first to disrobe and display a poem etched on his back."

"Strange that someone you call shy could do that."

"Some say he did it at the urging of a psychiatrist, who was helping him to face his fears."

"Vladoc," muttered Kim.

Burrwith continued, his bow tie bobbing as he spoke. "I suspect the boy told Locke every detail, down to the fact that he was seeing a shrink."

"If so, Locke would have to know not only Gordonn's secret, but what was going on in his mind—now," said Kim.

"The diary entries," Jessica said, thinking aloud. "Gordonn wrote about his fantasy to kill and be killed in the manner of his parents. Said he had recurring dreams about it."

Kim nodded. "The diary entries alone would likely have ensured life imprisonment, but Locke didn't count on the chips falling as they have."

"I hope you nail that brash, arrogant SOB," said Garrison Burrwith, which brought Jessica sharply back from her thoughts. She thanked Burrwith for his time and help."

"You're going to put him away for life, aren't you?"

"We will if he is our killer, yes."

"Then you don't believe Gordonn did those horrible things."

"At the moment, we are not a hundred percent certain of it, no, but we must ask you to keep this to yourself. Word of our suspicions gets out, and, as we said to Dr. Plummer, anything could happen. We don't want to damage a man's reputation without airtight evidence, you see."

"Of course, like you people did with poor Donatella."

They left abruptly then.

"Vladoc isn't telling us everything he knows, Jessica," Kim said as they located the car in the lot outside the building, a bright Philadelphia sun momentarily blinding Jessica before she slipped on her dark glasses.

"What do you think Vladoc is hiding?"

"I don't know exactly. But something's not right. For one thing, how could Gordonn afford Vladoc's rates for therapy?"

"You think the shrink was using the boy? How and for what?"

"I don't know. I just know that on Gordonn's salary, he could ill afford a downtown shrink like Vladoc, unless they had cut some other deal."

"Like access free and clear to the kid's story?"

"You mean for a book or something? Who knows?"

"That night at the club, when I spoke to Gordonn, before I knew who he was, when he was videotaping the nude poets . . ."

"Yes . . ." Kim leaned over the hood of the car so as to hear over traffic.

"He said he had been hired by the owners of the club, and that he got free copies of the tapes for his own use."

"Go on."

"Suppose Vladoc had cut a deal with the owners in order to put George to work doing what George wanted to do, and making money in the bargain. Each video sold to the clubs to create a kind of library, which they could use to create their ads."

"Yeah, I've seen a few while flipping through channels in the hotel room. They're enticing in a crude way. And their makers must get well paid."

"George does the work, George obtains free psychiatric help, Vladoc gets paid—the old barter system at work."

"I hope that's all Vladoc is hiding."

"Yeah, me, too."

They drove to Locke's place, Jessica telling Kim, "We need to get a sample of his DNA any way we can, from a beer glass to a cigarette, anything he has recently touched."

"You distract him, and I'll filch something."

"It has to be in plain sight, and preferably something he hands over, to please the court."

"Sheeeeesh."

"Obviously he knew of the urban legend long before the night George Gordonn supposedly killed himself and his supposed final victim."

"Are you going to confront him with it? Tell him we know he shared the particulars of the so-called legend with his students, discussing it as yet another example of Lord Byron's mythic legacy, further evidence of a poetic voice and legend that defy death and the passage of time?"

"Burrwith hinted at a bond between Locke and George Gordonn, after Gordonn had become his student. The bond may well have been the poet Byron."

"A poet out of time," said Kim.

"I'm going to tell him that we know that Gordonn had approached him—his professor at the time—that Gordon told him that the story Locke had repeatedly used over the years in his lectures was in fact a true story and not merely an urban legend, as Locke had thought. That Locke became extremely interested in Gordonn as a result. Learning that the legend was in fact true, seeing Gordonn's clippings, and learning that Gordonn had been the forlorn child who survived his parents' suicide, Locke became obsessed with the why of it all, delving into the depths of Gordonn's mind for answers."

"I'd certainly like to get my hands on Vladoc's records on Gordonn, see what shakes out there. Suppose out of the goodness of his heart, Locke began to pay Gordonn's psychiatric bills?"

"You're really hung up on the cost of therapy, aren't you?"

As they passed a row of small antique stores while searching for the Interstate, Kim replied, "At one-fifty an hour, I'm telling you, Gordonn could not afford Vladoc. Perhaps the video thing paid for a portion of his bill, but it couldn't have covered all of it."

Jessica picked up the radio and asked dispatch to put her through to Dr. Vladoc. When he came on the line, she held nothing back, telling him they were onto Locke, and then she asked, "How did Gordonn pay you rates on his salary and go to classes at the same time? Did Locke have anything whatever to do with George's therapy?"

"I can only tell you that when . . . after his bill became too high and I cut him off from any further sessions, he came to me with the full amount and then some, asking to continue his therapy."

"Did he empty his bank account, cash in annuities, what?"

"He never said. He would have the money in an envelope, white and unmarked, but all the money ready and up front after that."

"You never questioned him further about his newfound income?"

"He once said that he'd gotten the money from the Lord Poet of Misspent Time."

"Who was . . . ?"

"I swear to you, he never said."

"Did you have any suspicions?"

"About Locke giving him the money? No, not until now. They knew each other, passed one another in my office when I would take a breather. One going out, one coming in."

"What were sessions with Locke like?"

"A pain, a real headache. A man with an ego the size of Pennsylvania. He liked to hear the sound of his own voice, and he liked taking over the sessions, in a sense doing all the work he paid me to do. As to his subsidizing or floating George a loan, I can't be sure, but I was sure that Locke had a special—how would you put it?—attraction for the boy, yes, he acted hopelessly attracted to George and George's story."

"His family history?"

"That and how George had so heroically pulled himself out of the state of depression which for years had engulfed him."

"And the videotaping for the club owners, Dr. Vladoc; was that your idea or Gordonn's?"

"Ah, well, it was Gordonn's."

"Was it Gordonn's idea or *Locke's*? If we dig a bit more, will we learn that Locke owns a half interest in one of the clubs? Or will we learn that you, sir, do?"

There was a long pause filled with a bit of static over the police radio. Then Vladoc said, "Silent partner; it was an exciting investment. That's all."

"And Locke?"

"Also a co-owner."

"He had a special reason to be at the clubs, just as you and George had a reason, so much so that you all became fixtures, and no one took much notice of you after a while. Why didn't you inform us of this sooner? Why have we had to pry it from you?"

"He . . . Lucian is . . . well, my brother."

Jessica was silent for a moment, taking in the revelation. "Your spiritual brother?"

"No, my actual brother. He changed his name the day he

turned eighteen. Parry's doorman saw a short man, and he assumed him a boy."

Jessica recalled the bartender at one of the coffeehouses telling him of a man of extremely short stature, an older man, who had left with a young woman on his arm. Jessica had figured it was Vladoc, when, in fact, it might well have been Lucian Locke.

Kim, hearing all this, yanked the receiver from Jessica's hand and shouted at Vladoc, "Are you blinded by the fact that he's your brother? Go over your records for Gordonn's psychiatric care, and compare them to what you know of your brother's problems, why he comes to you. There will be innumerable correlations between Gordonn's fantasy life and your brother's real life. Your brother has been acting out Gordonn's fantasies, and both men at some point knew this, and in the end—"

It was as if Kim's outburst suddenly startled her into silence, and Jessica completed her thought. "Gordonn so trusted Locke that he believed Locke knew what was best for him, and so he allowed Locke to take him from this life without argument, as did most of the other victims. They so trusted him that it did not matter what the ultimate result might be."

"I . . . I had thought George was doing remarkably well. It came as a shock to me when I began to suspect that he could be doing the killings, but I confronted him with my suspicions, and he laughed in my face, said he only wished he were capable of taking such action, but that he could not, that it wasn't in him to take another life. Years of therapy had brought George around to a level of acceptance of what had happened to him as a child, and to this day I believe that the boy's progress toward mental health simply admirable."

Kim said, "You mean he was a challenge to you as a therapist?"

"And your brother?" asked Jessica. "What kind of patient was he?"

"I pleaded with him to get another, more objective and distanced person to work with; I told him that I could not be both his brother and his shrink, but week after week, he kept coming."

"And he showed an interest in how Gordonn's therapy was going?"

"An inordinate interest, yes."

"I ask you again, Dr. Vladoc, did it ever occur to you that Gordonn's bill was being paid by your brother?"

"Well, frankly, yes, I gave that a lot of thought, and I asked Gordonn about it, but he denied it. After that, I never questioned him about it again, and I am still of the opinion that you two must be wrong."

"Will you prepare a full report about the two patients' therapy, Doctor?"

"I can only reveal such detail on the dead man, not my living brother. Ethics prevent it."

"Then do it for yourself, Doctor. Heal thyself," Kim fairly sneered, and hung up.

THEY sped toward Lucian Locke's house with the intent of somehow gathering a DNA sample from the man. To date, he had played the role of a man desperate to help out in the investigation, but now, with the supposed murderer dead and the case supposedly closed, they could not be certain how he would react to their request, and Jessica doubted that he would voluntarily give them a sample of his bodily fluids for analysis.

"Suppose . . . just suppose," she told Kim, "that Locke had become infatuated with the romantic details of the suicide pact, and he learned that the mother believed herself to be the reincarnation of Lord Byron trying on a woman's body. 'Lady' Byron found modern life too wretched for his/her sensibilities, and so s/he had decided first to marry, to conceive a child, and then to convince her husband, Gordonn, to join her in a pact to affirm themselves as progeny of Byron through their art."

"Weird theory, yet according to Vladoc, Gordonn believed that his mother thought this possible through her poetry, and that Gordonn's father believed it possible through his painting and photography. With them joining forces, they expected to shake the world. When this failed to occur, and all life became a miserable spiral of financial ruin and frustration, coupled with the agony of life in this dimension, and after they had had the child which Lydia now hated herself for having brought into this world, they hit upon the suicide pact."

Jessica came in sight of the Locke home. "I see," she said. "Sounds strange enough to be true."

"Gordonn believed that it had been his father who had spared him, his reasoning being that his mother loved him too much to leave him behind, while his father loved him too much to take his life."

"Then Locke becomes his spiritual father; a kid like that is all too easy a mark for the likes of Lucian Locke."

Gordonn's revelations to Vladoc during his therapy sessions must have certainly fascinated Locke. Probably he met with Gordonn to hear what Gordonn had learned about himself in therapy. Footing the bill, he likely stipulated that he be privy to the details of Gordonn's progress."

Jessica stepped on the accelerator. Outside, the orange glow of sodium vapor lights flooded across the hood and windshield at regular intervals. "Since we're dealing in hypotheses here, I suspect that Locke was particularly fascinated by the genesis of the skin poetry and by the kind of poison on the pen. He could have learned about the use of selenium from the story of Gordonn's father and mother."

"And he would have been interested in the reasoning of the mother. Locke began to think in a way similar to Lydia."

Outside the cocoon of the car, the world sped by faster and faster.

Jessica gripped the steering wheel, trying to control the rage growing within her. "He may well have come to believe that the world held a magical secret, that there was some rare race of angelic people, hidden within our race, people so close to ethereality that being born into this existence was a kind of imprisonment."

"What if Locke had begun to hear voices that corroborated his gestating beliefs, the voices of angels, encouraging him in his beliefs, imploring him to send their brothers and sisters back to them? What then?"

Jessica pulled to a stop before Locke's home. "Is that how he embarked on this deadly odyssey? Is this how the Lord Byron Poet Killer was born?"

THE answers were housed somewhere deep within the recesses of Lucian Locke's mind and possibly hidden someplace in this house as well. The answer, for example, to the question of why he had chosen to kill Leare. Was it something beyond his control, an order he could not refuse, or had she gotten too close to the truth, threatening to expose him? If it were the latter, he had to have rationalized her death by seeing her as one of his chosen, despite everything against such a view, from her appearance to the profanity that she liberally used in speaking. Leare hardly matched the victim choice, although a case could be made for Gordonn and the young woman he had died alongside.

Jessica and Kim had stepped halfway out of the cruiser, their eyes pinned to the professor's car, which was parked in front of the house, telling them that he was home, when radio dispatch called with an urgent message from Leanne Sturtevante. It was obvious that Locke wasn't going anywhere, so Jessica sighed, dropped back into the unmarked cruiser, and took the call. Kim sat beside her.

"What's up, Leanne?"

"There've been two Poet Killer murders tonight—two!"

"My God, when, who?"

"At the bookstore, Darkest Expectations, Marc Tamburino, dead in his upstairs apartment. Same MO as Gordonn's. Someone's decided to take up where he left off."

So Tamburino wouldn't be collecting that snitch money after all, Jessica thought. She tried to put this new information together with Locke, who was now their primary suspect.

Sturtevante, her voice shaky, added, "He was alive when I found him, but before he could be gotten to a hospital, the poison did its work. I had gone to check out a few details with him; when I found the place locked, I tried his apartment. He didn't answer, so I got the super of the building to open it up. I heard music inside, and when I saw him, I thought he might have overdosed, until I saw the poem cut into his back. Began with the same three lines as the others."

"You said there was a second victim?"

"Yes . . . Dr. Harriet Plummer."

Jessica and Kim exchanged a shocked look. "Plummer?" Jessica exclaimed. "We just spoke to her earlier today."

"Garrison Burrwith found her at her place; her back was cut with a poem. Same MO."

"The man's on a rampage," Jessica said. "Now he's murdering anyone his fevered mind perceives as a threat."

"He needs nineteen angels, Jessica," Kim reminded her.

"What is your location?" Parry asked suddenly over the police radio. Jessica assumed that Leanne had called him to the crime scene at Plummer's residence.

"We're sitting outside Lucian Locke's house; we have good reason to believe him the Poet Killer. We were wrong about Gordonn, dead wrong."

"Wait for backup. This guy's flipped out, and he's extremely dangerous. Hold on until we get there."

"We were just about to call for backup, Jim."

"You've got it. I'll radio the nearest cruiser to join you, and we're on our way. And remember, you don't need a warrant if you at all *suspect* his children to be in danger from him . . . if you know what I mean."

"His angels, he called them," Jessica replied, realizing only now what a target this made of the two children, and possibly of their mother, Locke's wife, if the three had returned to the house from wherever it was that they had gone.

"We've got to get in there, Jess. If the children have been poisoned, and if we're not too late, perhaps we can do for them what Sturtevante was unable to do for Tamburino— get them to a poison center for treatment."

"Agreed."

"We can't sit idly waiting for backup knowing what we know."

Jessica agreed, lifting her .38 automatic from her ankle holster below her slacks. Kim, too, found her weapon. They advanced on the house quickly but cautiously, and as they did so, the dim lighting became dimmer and dimmer until only a great darkness awaited them inside.

When they got to the front porch, Jessica put a hand on Kim's shoulder. "I'm going to need you to direct traffic when backup arrives. We have to get medics in here, immediately, so hold this position."

"Oh no you don't. If you go in, it isn't alone."

Jessica tried reasoning with her friend, but Kim remained adamant. As they argued, the lights inside flickered and died again, leaving the place as black and still as a mausoleum.

"It's so quiet here my ears are ringing," Jessica commented.

"Far too quiet."

"Where's the requisite music, the obligatory candle-light? His vat of selenium? All of the rest?"

"I think he's spotted us out here."

"What's he going to do? Kill us with a pen?"

Jessica's joke notwithstanding, they approached with extreme caution, guns held at the ready. The door was not locked, and within they now heard the faint sound of music coming from somewhere upstairs. Faint sounds other than music could also be heard—rustling, the pitter-patter of someone in slippers moving casually about, ghostlike sounds that mixed with the shadows and played pranks on the ear, making Jessica wheel and bring up her gun only to realize that what she heard was only the faint meowing of a cat.

In the living room, she saw the piano and the pictures of Locke and his adopted children, cute urchins at play, she could see, even in the darkened room, one as adorable as the other. Jessica and Kim could also see a pair of large adult eyes, the penetrating eyes of Evey, Locke's wife, but this image staring back at them, Jessica suddenly realized, was propped up in a chair, and it was no photograph.

The corpse of Evey Locke sat upright in the chair across the room. From her pose, she seemed to have been tied there, but closer inspection revealed that this was not so. She was dead, but she was sitting up. From the impressions on the deep-piled rug, picked up by a flashlight Kim had grabbed from the glove compartment of the car, it appeared that she had crawled to this, her last resting place in this life.

No blood trail, only a dead body, naked and stiff. Jessica stood over Mrs. Locke now, and placing a hand on her cold form, pronounced her dead.

Kim, standing next to Jessica, flashed the light on the woman's back and said, "Look at this. More proof that we're right about Locke."

Jessica looked, and seeing the familiar cuts, nodded. "He did her, all right."

"The children've got to be upstairs."

Jessica turned and headed for the stairwell, Kim directly behind her. Fearing the worst, they made their way up the stairs, cautious and not very hopeful about the children.

The master bedroom was empty, so they made their way down the hall toward the children's rooms. Passing a large guest room, again they saw nothing. The first child's room was empty of all but stuffed animals. In the second child's room, they located the children, huddled together, their backs covered with the words of the Poet Killer.

Apparently, after both children died, killed by the powerful poison selenium, their mother had somehow found the strength to get downstairs. The impression on the bed where she had been lying clearly indicated this to be the case.

But where was Papa Locke? The mastermind of this mayhem?

As if in answer to their thoughts, a creaking, groaning sound, followed by a thwacking sound rose up from downstairs. Jessica and Kim rushed out of the chamber of death that the children's room had become, hearing police sirens and the squeal of tires outside. They moved toward the apparent source of the strange noises that welled up from somewhere in the bowels of the large house.

The sound of spurting, gurgling water led them to the kitchen. There they located a door that led to the basement, and the moment they opened this door, they knew they'd found the source of the gurgling. It was a busted pipe.

Going cautiously down the steps, their guns extended along with the flashlight, they were stopped when the light hit the prone figure of a man with a noose around his neck. It was Locke, small and misshapen, lying below the busted pipe, which spewed water over him. His pitiful suicide attempt had apparently failed not once but twice. His back was etched with a poem, and his throat was raw and swollen from his attempted hanging, but he was still alive. Somehow the selenium had not killed him and the pipe he hanged himself from had torn loose, sending him falling to the concrete floor and saving his miserable life.

"Kill me . . . kill me," he pleaded, lying over a gutter and holding his hands over his eyes.

"We'll let the state decide whether or not you live, Locke. Not our job," replied Jessica.

"Put me out of my misery. Send me over."

Sturtevante and Parry rushed into the now cramped basement, bringing with them a floodlight. The light made the little man on the floor look all the more disgusting and ugly and pitiable.

"The children?" asked Parry.

"Dead, along with their mother."

"Angels one and all," muttered Locke.

At that moment, Parry lost control, kicking out at the lump of tortured flesh on the cold floor, sending him reeling over. "You lousy *sonovabitchingmotherfucking* child killer!" Again Parry kicked him, this time in the teeth. Jessica and Sturtevante pulled and shoved Parry into a corner, shouting for him to cool down, when suddenly an explosion filled the small room, and they all saw Kim Desinor standing over Lucian Locke, a bullet hole through his head and a shocked look in his eyes.

"He . . . he grabbed out at my gun!" Kim shouted. "He took hold of the barrel. I didn't mean for it to go off, but it did. It all happened in the blink of an eye. It was an accident."

"Good riddance," Parry said in a raspy whisper, patting Kim on the back, as if to congratulate her. "Imagine what the literati of this country would turn him into if he lived to a ripe old age in prison, writing poems from his cell, given his own Web site like Charlie Manson. He'd probably become the most celebrated poet of his generation." Parry then turned and rushed up the noisy, wooden stairwell to the kitchen, where backup cops had turned on lights.

Kim kept repeating, "It was an accident. The gun went off when he grabbed the barrel. He yanked at it with my finger on the trigger. I was distracted by you guys and Parry, all the fighting, and then the explosion."

"We believe you," said Sturtevante. "No one will dispute your need to kill that piece of shit."

Jessica put her arm around Kim, telling her that it would be all right. "It will be investigated and there will be no charges of wrongful death. You did what you had to do."

"It wasn't like that, Jess. Truly, he grabbed the gun and pulled it straight at himself, but I had a strong grip on it, and it went off, all quite unintentionally."

"Perhaps not on your part, but what about his? He asked us to put him down, and when we didn't respond in the manner he wanted, he created the circumstance in which you had to end his life. Simple as that."

"It's such a horror for me, taking a life. I feel less of a human being for it."

"He left you with no choice; he wanted you to act instinctively, intuitively, and you did. You did for him what the rope over the pipe couldn't do . . . and I'm getting wetter'n than the proverbial drenched rat in here, so let's vacate this place for now. Come on upstairs with me into the light."

Kim nodded weakly and allowed Jessica to lead her away from the body and this place. "And for the sake of protocol," Jessica added as they turned to go, "since I was on hand when the perpetrator of this bloodless slaughter was shot to death, I'd best call Shockley and his ETs in to collect evidence and to deal with the bodies."

Jessica led her friend and colleague out of the death grid, neatly defined here in the basement to await Shockley. "It's always difficult to take a life, but if he'd gotten firm hold on that gun and turned it on all of us, well . . . suffice to say, we wouldn't be having this conversation."

"He didn't want to fire the gun on any of us; he wanted it for himself, and he managed to use me to that end, didn't he? Clever SOB, I'd say, very clever indeed."

THE core task-force team felt a great weight lifted off their collective shoulders, knowing now for certain that the serial killer called the Poet had finally been identified and his career ended.

Jessica remained close to Kim while both the PPD's Internal Affairs cops and the FBI's own Internal Affairs people asked questions about the death of the suspect, Lucian Locke.

Everyone found the scene gruesome, and emotionally painful to process, especially the room where the two children lay in bed, faces down, their backs revealing the final verses of the poem Locke had written. By now all the verses had come together to make a whole.

Jessica felt little pleasure in having been proven right, that each of the poems was a section of one large, ambitious work. She supported Kim's version of the shooting one hundred percent, telling the IAD guys that she had seen the shooting go down exactly as Dr. Desinor described it.

Meanwhile, Sturtevante and Parry, their services no longer being required, had gotten a federal warrant for search and seizure at Dr. Lucian Locke's office, club locker, Second Street apartment, and home. Parry meant to go by the book, to create an airtight, hermetically sealed case against the now dead poet.

The news of the Lockes' deaths following so quickly on the heels of Leare's, and the even more lurid news that Locke had murdered Leare—everyone agreed that such news was tailor-made to increase dramatically the appeal of their poetry to young people fascinated with death and the trappings of death.

Parry, Sturtevante, and a small army of white-gloved detectives combed the house for incriminating evidence that might explain Locke's behavior, explain why he had killed his wife and children, and the series of people who had come before them. Nothing came of the search, not a shred of useful information, not even from his locked desk drawer in the spacious den.

A team of evidence techs were sent to his university office, and they, too, came up empty. But a third team, sent to his Second Street apartment, hit the mother lode. Pinned on the walls were the photos Jessica had been looking for, shots of each of the victims who had preceded his final rampage. These, combined with the photographic record of the poems etched in poisoned ink, proved irrefutable.

Vladoc showed up at the scene of the crime now, and as he walked among the living scurrying about doing their work, he looked like a dead man. "Poor Evey, and those children, I loved them as if they were my own," he repeatedly told anyone who would listen, as if saying the words over and over would make them sound more true.

How could Vladoc not have known that his brother was so deeply disturbed?

"I had no idea, I swear to you all," he finally said. "I was as much in the dark as you. He . . . Lucian always appeared happy, pleased with his life. He only spoke on occasion of minor problems in his marriage, his desire to be free of all the responsibilities of work and fatherhood and being a husband, but nothing serious, you see. He always worked things out in his head, I was certain. Obviously, I never heard his cry. He never allowed me to."

"He may well have thought you blind to the reality he lived," Jessica suggested in an attempt to ease Vladoc's obvious pain.

"Such a waste of human life and potential . . ." Vladoc, unable to stand another moment in the house, tearfully made his way out into the night. Jessica feared he would blame himself for the rest of his life, not only for what had happened here, but for all the victims of his brother's quiet madness.

Jessica had to fight off the recurring image of the children upstairs. Locke's two children, aged six and seven, along with his beautiful wife, had returned early from a trip to the Florida Keys, all suntanned and healthy-looking, but now all were quite dead, each with a poem scrawled across his or her back.

From the basement, Shockley shouted for Dr. Coran to come downstairs. She reluctantly complied, taking the steps down to the blinding field of lights that had been set up in the basement. Water sloshed around her ankles as the drains fought a losing battle with the leaking pipes. "We were in the process of moving the body out of this damned deluge when this floated by." He extended a handwritten note.

"What is it?" she asked.

"Read it. It's his last remarks. Quite incriminating."

Jessica read the note scrawled in the killer's shaky hand.

I loved them all. Even poor George. I loved each and every one of them. They were all broken-winged fairy angels, not of this world, certainly not needing to endure life on this plane a moment longer. I love all of those whom I have sent over. There was no other choice.

The note ended with Lucian Locke's familiar signature. Jessica looked up to see Kim and a retinue of uniformed police standing nearby, everyone watching as Locke's body was hoisted onto a stretcher. Only now did she see the words written in blood orange along his arms and chest.

"He tried to write himself to death," Shockley lamely joked. "Get it? But he appears to have run out of ink. Used it all up on everyone else."

"We found leather straps around the wife's legs and wrists," commented one of the evidence techs who'd taken charge of the scene in the room where Evey Locke had been found. Apparently she had not willingly complied with her husband's plan to send her to a better world. According to the ETs who worked the upstairs room, the children had been drugged into a stupor before the quill pen dug into their flesh.

"In the end, he pulled out all the stops," said Jessica. "He didn't have time for the niceties, like convincing his victims that to have a Lucian Locke poem emblazoned on their backs was their ticket to paradise."

Locke, his body misshapen and his hair matted and disheveled, was carried up the stairs and to one of the two waiting emergency vans, their strobe lights having wakened the entire neighborhood. As one of the ETs plunked out a rendition of "Chopsticks" on the piano next to Evey Locke, the old ME, Shockley, made his way upstairs to the children. "I want a firsthand look at the boy and girl," he said sadly.

"Angels he had called them." Jessica shook her head. "I'll go with you."

"Thanks. I'll need your help."

"We know now how he kept abreast of the investigation."

"Yes, I heard. Through his brother, Vladoc. Don't you find it strange, though, that Vladoc didn't recognize his own brother's handwriting and poetry? After all, he was studying it, he made pronouncements on it, told us all about that Enochian thing, and yet he had no idea his brother was so deeply into this warped philosophy?"

"I've wondered the same, yes," said Kim, who had come into the room and overheard them. "But while subconsciously he may have known, consciously I'm not so sure. I just spent time with him outside, and he's a broken man. He could not have taken part in his brother's actions. His brother's DNA will tell the story, and I don't believe he was involved from afar, like some master puppeteer."

"Locke was the only puppeteer here," Jessica returned. "Still, now that he's dead, we should confiscate all of Vladoc's records on his patient."

"Just to be sure," Shockley agreed.

"He could not have accepted such a truth; only now has he been able to, now that the evidence is irrefutable," Kim assured them. "I held his hand, and I tell you he is horrified at what has happened to the only family he has."

With the final evidence gathered and the last photograph of the death scenes at the Locke house taken, Jessica rushed outside to the predawn air, breathing it in deeply several times, attempting to clear her head. Nothing so affected the death investigator as the unnecessary death of a

child, and here were two innocents taken. Leanne Sturtevante and James Parry had returned to the scene, and Parry
asked her how she was holding up.

"I've been better. It's horrible what's happened here."

Parry and Sturtevante confessed to having had the same
discussion as the others regarding Vladoc. They all agreed
that his brother had used him, duped him.

Sturtevante remained with Jessica while Parry
stepped back inside for a final look around the
murder/suicide house. Locke's death had been ruled as
suicide in that he had caused it knowingly and willingly,
when he realized the poison he'd used on himself had
not been a toxic enough dosage and his attempt to hang
himself also failed. Jessica now learned from Sturtevante how she had discovered Marc Tamburino in the
final throes of death.

"Before he died he told me it was Locke. It was the only
word he managed to speak before he choked and expired.
From the mouth of a dying man. I knew it couldn't be ignored. Tamburino's back had been turned into a grid of
death by Locke's letters."

"What's amazing to me," Jessica said, "is that he would
go off like this after so carefully constructing a scapegoat
in the person of George Gordonn. I suppose we can only
infer that after he manipulated things so that no suspicion
could fall on him, the irrational powers and forces driving
Locke proved stronger than his logical mind."

"Marc Tamburino didn't know Locke was the killer until
it was too late. He figured it out as he lay dying, about the
time I found him in his apartment this evening. Locke
rushed out before I got there, leaving Marc still alive. I
must have frightened Locke as I approached."

Kim, who had been standing nearby listening to Sturtevante describe the path that had led her to Locke, offered
her thoughts. "Tamburino no doubt thought it a great honor

to be wearing an original Lucian Locke poem emblazoned across his body to the clubs last night, I suppose."

"Who wouldn't?" Sturtevante said. "Even Donatella thought it'd be cool to display an original Locke on her back. It's what's gotten all of them killed."

Jessica asked for more of the details surrounding Tamburino's death.

"I carried him down to my car rather than wait for any ambulance, and I rushed him to Cellmark, the closest hospital with a poison center, but we were simply too late. An attempt to save him from the selenium, even though I could identify the poison coursing through his body, fell short. Time was not on Marc's side."

"Didn't he die en route to the hospital?" Jessica asked.

"No, no, we had him almost stabilized when his heart stopped and no amount of effort on the part of the medical team could bring him back."

"You did all you could for him," said Jessica.

"I realized immediately that Dr. Harriet Plummer, who'd been seeing Locke, might well be another target, guessing that Marc was killed as much for his nosing around and asking one too many questions as anything else. He hardly fit the victim profile, and neither did Plummer, but on a hunch, I telephoned Dr. Plummer to warn her."

"But it was too late for her as well?"

" 'Fraid so. She was alive but just barely. Somehow she lifted the phone, and I identified myself and she simply babbled, 'I . . . could never . . . not love . . . Lucian. Could never say no . . . to him. Never could not love him.' She sounded drugged."

"What did you do next?"

"I shouted for her to stay on the phone, to keep talking to me, and at the same time, I got someone on the line so that I could dial 911 and get a cruiser over there immediately with instructions to treat her for selenium poisoning.

Plummer dropped the phone before I could get help. I made the calls and raced to her location from the hospital.

"I figured that Locke had killed her, too. The man was on a rampage, just as you said, Jessica. As I drove to the Plummer location, I contacted Jim, and he met me there. The result was another corpse filled with Locke's poison and poetry. The two of us realized that the man was on a kill spree now, probably fearing that he'd be identified as the Poet Killer—that he had framed George Gordonn. At least that's my guess."

"It sounds about right to me," Jessica told her.

"So Jim and I asked ourselves who else might he harm? And Jim remembered the children and his wife. That's when we heard from you, and we raced to this location direct from Plummer's."

"And Burrwith? Was he killed, too?"

"No, just disturbed to be awakened in the middle of the night, or so the officers who rushed to his home said."

"Thanks for filling us in, Leanne, and again, my sincerest regrets over your loss of Donatella."

"Dona was never one to play it safe; imagine, allowing Lucian Locke to write across her back."

"Likely with the promise that he'd let her do him. A pact of sorts, to prove to each other that neither was the killer."

"She so admired Locke's work. She knew the killer's hand was inspired by her and Locke's poetry. She confessed that much to me once."

Jessica and Kim went toward their waiting vehicle, tired and exhausted, talking about hot baths, body oils, warm candlelight, and distancing themselves from the horror of this time and place. Jessica had left the formalities of the crime-scene investigation and the chain-of-evidence duties to Shockley, who appeared to be basking in his supervisory role in the mop-up effort. All that remained now was to make a DNA match between Lucian Locke and the

teardrops left on the earlier victims. That kind of scientifi-
cally irrefutable evidence would put to rest any and all
speculation about Vladoc or anyone else's having taken
part in the killings.

EPILOGUE

Predicting human behavior is really about recognizing the play from just a few lines of dialogue.

—Gavin De Becker

No one doubted the innocence of Dr. Peter Flavius Vladoc in the murders committed by his brother, but his gullibility in the matter and his total failure to recognize that a man he was treating was so seriously disturbed resulted in his ruined reputation as a psychiatrist. Finally, he had no choice but to pack his things and vacate his office at the PPD. He told Jessica that henceforth he'd concentrate on private practice, but he would have to do so elsewhere, somewhere far from Philadelphia, the city he loved.

"It's the price I must pay for being blind, but in the end, I fear that it will be Philadelphia that will pay a far greater price," he declared, not a little pompously.

The DNA match on Vladoc's brother, Locke, was made, and there was no longer any doubt as to who the killer had been.

"What price is that, sir?" Jessica couldn't help asking.

"The final act in this morbid play of good and evil, Dr. Coran, I fear, has yet to be performed."

"Whatever do you mean, Dr. Vladoc?"

"You've been too busy with your lab work and your crucifying my brother to notice that others are in the business of doing just the opposite—deifying him."

"Really? And who are these fools?"

"The youth of this city. While you have been busily working behind these walls, tying up all the usual loose ends—and I include myself in the category of loose end—making it unequivocally clear that my brother was a vicious serial killer, the youth of Philadelphia have also been talking about Lucian Locke. They have, in fact, apotheosized the man as their light and savior."

Jessica was horrified. "I had no idea."

"And they continue to pen poems on the bodies of friends and on themselves, carrying on the tradition born of the suicide pact of 'Lady Byron' and Harold Gordonn, continued by their spiritual son, Lucian Burke Locke. I fear nothing good can come of it."

"We can't dictate lifestyles or faiths, beliefs in fetish objects or cults, Dr. Vladoc. All we can do is make sure that anyone turning such things into crime and murder is stopped."

"Meanwhile, Jessica, I have felt it an honor to have worked closely with you and Dr. Desinor. Please give her my regards. I understand she is taking some R&R in Baltimore? Of all places to vacation . . . well, to each his own."

"Where will you go now, Dr. Vladoc?"

"China perhaps . . ." He chuckled at his own joke. "At least as far away as China. I'm thinking perhaps people in Anchorage or Seattle might have me."

"You've done nothing to deserve what has befallen you, sir, and without your help, we would still be stumbling about in the dark."

"Yes, well, stumbling about in the dark is sort of the way the PPD brass put it to me. Not to worry. They offer a generous retirement package."

Jessica saw a kindness in him she hadn't glimpsed before, his eyes as he smiled suddenly causing her to think of the actor/director/writer Peter Ustinov.

As they shook hands and said their final good-byes, she

said, "If ever I'm involved in a case in the Pacific North-west, I'll call on you."

"Please do, by all means."

Jessica turned her attention back to the labs where Shockley and DeAngelos and others were busy finishing work on the Poet Killer case. Through the glass partitions she saw that James Parry was on his way to bid her good-bye, knowing she was scheduled to return to Quantico that night.

"Jessica," he said. "Couldn't let you go without saying so long."

"This time face-to-face."

"I thought we had hashed that out?"

"Yeah . . . yeah, we did. Sorry for the cattiness."

"Without the cattiness gene, what kind of woman would you make?" he joked.

"How are you doing—I mean with your new digs and Philadelphia post, Jim?"

"It's not going to be so bad after all. We've come out of this shining, Jess, and it's largely due to your being here."

"Don't be foolish. It was a team effort, all—almost all the way."

"Give my regards and thanks to Kim when you see her. She was right on with her psychic hits all along. We've got to learn how to better read *her*!"

"And tell Leanne thanks from us. It was a rocky start, but we did get the job done after all."

"She's taken some time off, reassessing her life. Losing her lover, Donatella, has been an incredibly debilitating blow to her. She's not even sure she wants to come back to the force, but a lot of us are urging her to do so. She's too good to lose."

"If you think that highly of her, why don't you send her to Quantico for basic training and put her on in your shop?"

"Hey, not a bad idea at that." He paused, thinking. "I'll give her a call. See what she thinks of the offer. I'm sure it can be arranged. We've lost a couple of people to retirement."

"Go for it, Jim." Jessica smiled warmly at him.

When they shook hands, Jim held on to hers, squeezing it with obvious feeling, and smiling. "I sometimes so miss what we had together, Jess. I really, really do."

"I know, Jim, Believe me."

"I wish the best for you, you know, even if it's with that Englishman."

"Richard is his name."

"Yes, well . . . settled our differences, then . . . I'll be off. Don't be a stranger when—if you're ever back this way."

"You, too, whenever you're in D.C. or anywhere near Quantico, Jim. I mean that."

Parry leaned forward to give her a peck on the cheek, but she pulled back.

"Bye now, Jim, and good luck here."